"*My Brilliant Friend* is a sweeping family-centered epic that encompasses issues of loyalty, love, and a transforming Europe. This gorgeous novel should bring a host of new readers to one of Italy's most acclaimed authors."—The *Barnes and Noble Review*

"Elena Ferrante is the author of several remarkable, lucid, austerely honest novels . . . [*My Brilliant Friend*] is a large, captivating, amiably peopled bildungsroman."—James Wood, *The New Yorker*

"Both *The Days of Abandonment* and *Troubling Love* are tour de forces, and harrowing tours of a feminine psyche under siege. They both confirm Ferrante's reputation as one of Italy's best contemporary novelists."—*The Seattle Times*

"Halfway through my second reading of Elena Ferrante's *Troubling Love*—70 more pages to go in steamy Naples—I tore the book down the middle. It's the first time a novel ever made me get physical, and it was the first good mood I'd been in for weeks. Then I gave a friend an unimpaired copy; she called the next morning: 'Ferrante is fantastic. I hope you say something nice.' Ferrante will recognize my compliment since she's clearly an idolizer of the unchecked urge, the gut response."—David Lipsky, *The New York Times*

"[*The Lost Daughter*] is so refined, almost translucent, that it seems about to float away, in the end this piercing novel is not so easily dislodged from the memory."—*The Boston Globe*

"*My Brilliant Friend*, translated by Ann Goldstein, is stunning: an intense, forensic exploration of the friendship between Lila and the story's narrator, Elena. Ferrante's evocation of the working-class district of Naples where Elena and Lila first meet as two wiry eight-year-olds is cinematic in the density of its detail."—*The Times Literary Supplement*

ALSO BY

ELENA FERRANTE

The Days of Abandonment
Troubling Love
The Lost Daughter
My Brilliant Friend
Those Who Leave and Those Who Stay

THE STORY
OF A NEW NAME

Elena Ferrante

THE STORY
OF A NEW NAME

Book Two, The Neapolitan Novels
Youth

*Translated from the Italian
by Ann Goldstein*

Europa
editions

Europa Editions
214 West 29th Street
New York, N.Y. 10001
www.europaeditions.com
info@europaeditions.com

Tenth printing, 2015

Translation by Ann Goldstein
Original title: *Storia del nuovo cognome*
Translation copyright © 2013 by Europa Editions

Library of Congress Cataloging in Publication Data is available
ISBN 978-1-60945-134-9

Ferrante, Elena
The Story of a New Name

Book design by Emanuele Ragnisco
www.mekkanografici.com

Cover photo © Ismo Holtto/Getty Images

Prepress by Grafica Punto Print – Rome

Printed in Italy

INDEX OF CHARACTERS AND NOTES ON THE EVENTS OF VOLUME I.

The Cerullo family (the shoemaker's family):

Fernando Cerullo, shoemaker, Lila's father.

Nunzia Cerullo, Lila's mother. She is close to her daughter, but doesn't have the authority to support her against her father.

Raffaella Cerullo, called Lina, or Lila. She was born in August, 1944, and is sixty-six when she disappears from Naples without leaving a trace. A brilliant student, at the age of ten she writes a story titled *The Blue Fairy.* She leaves school after getting her elementary-school diploma and learns to be a shoemaker.

Rino Cerullo, Lila's older brother, also a shoemaker. With his father, Fernando, and thanks to Lila and to Stefano Carracci's money, he sets up the Cerullo shoe factory. He becomes engaged to Stefano's sister, Pinuccia Carracci. Lila's first son bears his name, Rino.

Other children.

The Greco family (the porter's family):

Elena Greco, called Lenuccia or Lenù. Born in August, 1944, she is the author of the long story we are reading. Elena begins to write it when she learns that her childhood friend Lina Cerullo, called Lila only by her, has disappeared. After elementary school, Elena continues to study, with increasing success. Since childhood she has been secretly in love with Nino Sarratore.

Peppe, Gianni, and *Elisa,* Elena's younger siblings.

The *father* is a porter at the city hall.
The *mother* is a housewife. Her limping gait haunts Elena.

The Carracci family (Don Achille's family):
Don Achille Carracci, the ogre of fairy tales, dealer in the black market, loan shark. He was murdered.
Maria Carracci, wife of Don Achille, mother of Stefano, Pinuccia, and Alfonso. She works in the family grocery store.
Stefano Carracci, son of the deceased Don Achille, husband of Lila. He manages the property accumulated by his father and is the proprietor, along with his sister Pinuccia, Alfonso, and his mother, Maria, of a profitable grocery store.
Pinuccia, the daughter of Don Achille. She works in the grocery store. She is engaged to Rino, Lila's brother.
Alfonso, son of Don Achille. He is the schoolmate of Elena. He is the boyfriend of Marisa Sarratore.

The Peluso family (the carpenter's family):
Alfredo Peluso, carpenter. Communist. Accused of killing Don Achille, he has been convicted and is in prison.
Giuseppina Peluso, wife of Alfredo. A former worker in the tobacco factory, she is devoted to her children and her imprisoned husband.
Pasquale Peluso, older son of Alfredo and Giuseppina, construction worker, militant Communist. He was the first to become aware of Lila's beauty and to declare his love for her. He detests the Solaras. He is engaged to Ada Cappuccio.
Carmela Peluso, also called *Carmen,* sister of Pasquale. She is a sales clerk in a notions store. She is engaged to Enzo Scanno.
Other children.

The Cappuccio family (the mad widow's family):
Melina, a relative of Nunzia Cerullo, a widow. She washes the stairs of the apartment buildings in the old neighborhood.

She was the lover of Donato Sarratore, Nino's father. The Sarratores left the neighborhood precisely because of that relationship, and Melina has nearly lost her reason.

Melina's husband, who unloaded crates in the fruit and vegetable market, and died in mysterious circumstances.

Ada Cappuccio, Melina's daughter. As a girl she helped her mother wash the stairs. Thanks to Lila, she will be hired as salesclerk in the Carracci's grocery. She is engaged to Pasquale Peluso.

Antonio Cappuccio, her brother, a mechanic. He is Elena's boyfriend and is very jealous of Nino Sarratore.

Other children.

The Sarratore family (the railway-worker poet's family):

Donato Sarratore, conductor, poet, journalist. A great womanizer, he was the lover of Melina Cappuccio. When Elena went on vacation to Ischia, she is compelled to leave in a hurry to escape Donato's sexual molestations.

Lidia Sarratore, wife of Donato.

Nino Sarratore, the oldest of the five children of Donato and Lidia. He hates his father. He is a brilliant student.

Marisa Sarratore, sister of Nino. She is studying, with mediocre success, to be a secretary.

Pino, Clelia, and *Ciro Sarratore*, younger children of Donato and Lidia.

The Scanno family (the fruit-and-vegetable seller's family):

Nicola Scanno, fruit-and-vegetable seller.

Assunta Scanno, wife of Nicola.

Enzo Scanno, son of Nicola and Assunta, also a fruit-and-vegetable seller. Lila has felt a liking for him since childhood. Their friendship begins when Enzo, during a school competition, shows an unsuspected ability in mathematics. Enzo is engaged to Carmen Peluso.

Other children.

The Solara family (the family of the owner of the Solara bar-pastry shop):

Silvio Solara, owner of the bar-pastry shop, a Camorrist tied to the illegal trafficking of the neighborhood. He was opposed to the Cerullo shoe factory.

Manuela Solara, wife of Silvio, moneylender: her red book is much feared in the neighborhood.

Marcello and Michele Solara, sons of Silvio and Manuela. Braggarts, arrogant, they are nevertheless loved by the neighborhood girls, except Lila, of course. Marcello is in love with Lila but she rejects him. Michele, a little younger than Marcello, is colder, more intelligent, more violent. He is engaged to Gigliola, the daughter of the pastry maker.

The Spagnuolo family (the baker's family):

Signor Spagnuolo, pastry maker at the Solaras' bar-pastry shop.

Rosa Spagnuolo, wife of the pastry maker.

Gigliola Spagnuolo, daughter of the pastry maker, engaged to Michele Solara.

Other children.

The Airota family:

Airota, professor of Greek literature.

Adele, his wife.

Mariarosa Airota, the older daughter, professor of art history in Milan.

Pietro Airota, student.

The teachers:

Maestro Ferraro, teacher and librarian.

Maestra Oliviero, teacher. She is the first to notice the potential of Lila and Elena. When Lila writes *The Blue Fairy*, Elena, who likes the story a lot, and gives it to Maestra Oliviero to read. But the teacher, angry because Lila's parents decided not to send their daughter to middle school, never says anything about the story. In fact, she stops concerning herself with Lila and concentrates only on the success of Elena.

Professor Gerace, high-school teacher.

Professor Galiani, high-school teacher. She is a very cultured woman and a Communist. She is immediately charmed by Elena's intelligence. She lends her books, protects her in the clash with the religion teacher.

Other characters:

Gino, son of the pharmacist.

Nella Incardo, the cousin of Maestra Oliviero. She lives in Barano, on Ischia, and Elena stayed with her for a vacation at the beach.

Armando, medical student, son of Professor Galiani.

Nadia, student, daughter of Professor Galiani.

Bruno Soccavo, friend of Nino Sarratore and son of a rich industrialist in San Giovanni a Teduccio, near Naples.

Franco Mari, student.

YOUTH

1.

In the spring of 1966, Lila, in a state of great agitation, entrusted to me a metal box that contained eight notebooks. She said that she could no longer keep them at home, she was afraid her husband might read them. I carried off the box without comment, apart from some ironic allusions to the excessive amount of string she had tied around it. At that time our relationship was terrible, but it seemed that only I considered it that way. The rare times we saw each other, she showed no embarrassment, only affection; a hostile word never slipped out.

When she asked me to swear that I wouldn't open the box for any reason, I swore. But as soon as I was on the train I untied the string, took out the notebooks, began to read. It wasn't a diary, although there were detailed accounts of the events of her life, starting with the end of elementary school. Rather, it seemed evidence of a stubborn self-discipline in writing. The pages were full of descriptions: the branch of a tree, the ponds, a stone, a leaf with its white veinings, the pots in the kitchen, the various parts of a coffeemaker, the brazier, the coal and bits of coal, a highly detailed map of the courtyard, the broad avenue of *stradone*, the rusting iron structure beyond the ponds, the gardens and the church, the cut of the vegetation alongside the railway, the new buildings, her parents' house, the tools her father and her brother used to repair shoes, their gestures when they worked, and above all colors, the colors of every object at different times of the day. But there were not only pages of description. Isolated words appeared, in dialect and in Italian, sometimes circled, without comment. And Latin and Greek translation exercises. And entire passages in English on the neighborhood shops and their wares, on the cart loaded with fruit and vegetables that Enzo Scanno took through the streets every day, leading the mule by the halter. And many observations on the books she read, the films she saw in the church hall. And many of the ideas that she had asserted in the discussions with Pasquale, in the talks she and I used to have. Of course, the progress was sporadic, but whatever Lila captured in writing assumed importance, so that even in the pages written when she was eleven or twelve there was not a single line that sounded childish.

Usually the sentences were extremely precise, the punctuation meticulous, the handwriting elegant, just as Maestra Oliviero had taught us. But at times, as if a drug had flooded her veins, Lila seemed unable to bear the order she had imposed on herself. Everything then became breathless, the sentences took on an overexcited rhythm, the punctuation disappeared. In general it didn't take long for her to return to a clear, easy pace. But it might also happen that she broke off abruptly and filled the rest of the page with little drawings of twisted trees, humped, smoking mountains, grim faces. I was entranced by both the order and the disorder, and the more I read, the more deceived I felt. How much practice there was behind the letter she had sent me on Ischia years earlier: that was why it was so well written. I put everything back in the box, promising myself not to become inquisitive again.

But I soon gave in—the notebooks exuded the force of seduction that Lila had given off since she was a child. She had treated the neighborhood, her family, the Solaras, Stefano, every person or thing with ruthless accuracy. And what to say of the liberty she had taken with me, with what I said, with what I thought, with the people I loved, with my very physical appearance. She had fixed moments that were decisive for her without worrying about anything or anyone. Here vividly was the pleasure she had felt when at ten she wrote her story, *The Blue Fairy*. Here just as vivid was what she had suffered when our teacher Maestra Oliviero hadn't deigned to say a single word about that story, in fact had ignored it. Here was the suffering and the fury because I had gone to middle school, neglecting her, abandoning her. Here the excitement with which she had learned to repair shoes, the desire to prove herself that had induced her to design new shoes, and the pleasure of completing the first pair with her brother Rino. Here the pain when Fernando, her father, had said that the shoes weren't well made. There was everything, in those pages, but especially hatred for the Solara brothers, the fierce determination with which she had rejected the love of the older, Marcello, and the moment when she had decided, instead, to marry the gentle Stefano Carracci, the grocer, who out of love had wanted to buy the first pair of shoes she had made, vowing that he would keep them forever. Ah, the wonderful moment when, at fifteen, she had felt herself a rich and elegant lady, on the arm of her fiancé, who, all because he loved her, had invested a lot of money in her father and brother's shoe business: Cerullo shoes. And how much satisfaction she had felt: the shoes of her imagination in large part realized, a house in the new neighborhood, marriage at sixteen. And what a lavish wedding, how happy she was. Then Marcello Solara, with his brother Michele, had appeared in the middle of the festivities, wearing on his feet the very shoes that her husband had said were so dear to him. Her husband. What sort of man had she married? Now, when it was all over, would the false face be torn off, revealing the horribly true one underneath? Questions, and the facts, without embellishment, of our poverty. I devoted myself to those pages, for days, for weeks. I studied them. I ended up learning by heart the passages I liked, the ones that thrilled me, the ones that hypnotized me, the ones that humiliated me. Behind their naturalness was surely some artifice, but I couldn't discover what it was.

Finally, one evening in November, exasperated, I went out carrying the box. I couldn't stand feeling Lila on me and in me, even now that I was esteemed myself, even now that I had a life outside of Naples. I stopped on the Solferino bridge to look at the lights filtered through a cold mist. I placed the box on the parapet, and pushed it slowly, a little at a time, until it fell into the river, as if it were her, Lila in person, plummeting, with her thoughts, words, the malice with which she struck back at anyone, the way she appropriated me, as she did every person or thing or event or thought that touched her: books and shoes, sweetness and violence, the marriage and the wedding night, the return to the neighborhood in the new role of Signora Raffaella Carracci.

2.

I couldn't believe that Stefano, so kind, so in love, had given Marcello Solara the vestige of the child Lila, the evidence of her work on the shoes she had designed.

I forgot about Alfonso and Marisa, who, sitting at the table, were talking to each other, eyes shining. I paid no more attention to my mother's drunken laughter. The music faded, along with the voice of the singer, the dancing couples, and Antonio, who had gone out to the terrace and, overwhelmed by jealousy, was standing outside the glass door staring at the violet city, the sea. Even the image of Nino, who had just left the room like an archangel without annunciations, grew faint. Now I saw only Lila, speaking animatedly into Stefano's ear, she very pale in her wedding dress, he unsmiling, a white patch of unease running over his flushed face from his forehead to his eyes like a Carnival mask. What was happening, what would happen? My friend tugged her husband's arm with both hands. She used all her strength, and I who knew her thoroughly felt that if she could she would have wrenched it from his body, crossed the room holding it high above her head, blood dripping in her train, and she would have used it as a club or a donkey's jawbone to crush Marcello's face with a solid blow. Ah yes, she would have done it, and at the idea my heart pounded furiously, my throat became dry. Then she would have dug out the eyes of both men, she would have torn the flesh from the bones of their faces, she would have bitten them. Yes, yes, I felt that I wanted that, I wanted it to happen. An end of love and of that intolerable celebration, no embraces in a bed in Amalfi. Immediately shatter everything and every person in the neighborhood, tear them to pieces, Lila and I, go and live far away, lightheartedly descending together all the steps of humiliation, alone, in unknown cities. It seemed to me the just conclusion to that day. If nothing could save us, not money, not a male body, and not even studying, we might as well destroy everything immediately. Her rage expanded in my breast, a force that was mine and not mine, filling me with the pleasure of losing myself. I wished that that force would overflow. But I realized that I was also afraid of it. I understood only later that I can be quietly unhappy, because I'm incapable of violent reactions, I fear them, I prefer to be still, cultivating resentment. Not Lila. When she left her seat, she got up so decisively that the table shook, along with the silverware on the dirty plates; a glass was overturned. As Stefano hurried mechanically to cut off the tongue of wine that was heading toward Signora Solara's dress, Lila went out quickly through a side door, jerking her dress away whenever it got caught.

I thought of running after her, grabbing her hand, whispering to her let's get out, out of here. But I didn't move. Stefano moved, after a moment of uncertainty, and, making his way among the dancing couples, joined her.

I looked around. Everyone realized that something had upset the bride. But Marcello continued to chat in a conspiratorial way with Rino, as if it were normal for him to have those shoes on his feet. The increasingly lewd toasts of the metal merchant continued. Those who felt at the bottom of the hierarchy of tables and guests went on struggling to put a good face on things. In other words, no one except me seemed to realize that the marriage that had just been celebrated—and that would probably last until the death of the spouses, among the births of many children, many more grandchildren, joys and sorrows, silver and gold wedding anniversaries—that for Lila, no matter what her husband did in his attempt to be forgiven, that marriage was already over.

3.

At first the events disappointed me. I sat with Alfonso and Marisa, paying no attention to their conversation. I waited for signs of revolt, but nothing happened. To be inside Lila's head was, as usual, difficult: I didn't hear her shouting, I didn't hear her threatening. Stefano reappeared half an hour later, very friendly. He had changed his clothes; the white patch on his forehead and around his eyes had vanished. He strolled about among friends and relatives waiting for his wife to arrive, and when she returned to the hall not in her wedding dress but in her traveling outfit, a pastel-blue suit, with very pale buttons, and a blue hat, he joined her immediately. Lila distributed sugared almonds to the children, taking them from a crystal bowl with a silver spoon, then she moved among the tables handing out the wedding favors, first to her relatives, then to Stefano's. She ignored the entire Solara family and even her brother

Rino, who asked her with an anxious half-smile: Don't you love me anymore? She didn't answer, but gave the wedding favor to Pinuccia. She had an absent gaze, her cheekbones appeared more prominent than usual. When she got to me, she distractedly handed me, without even a smile of complicity, the white tulle-wrapped ceramic basket full of sugared almonds.

The Solaras were irritated by that discourtesy, but Stefano made up for it, embracing them one by one, with a pleasant, soothing expression, and murmuring, "She's tired, be patient."

He kissed Rino, too, on the cheeks, but his brother-in-law gave a sign of displeasure, and I heard him say, "It's not tiredness, Ste', she was born twisted and I'm sorry for you."

Stefano answered seriously, "Twisted things get straightened out."

Afterward I saw him hurry after his wife, who was already at the door, while the orchestra spewed drunken sounds and people crowded around for the final goodbyes.

No rupture, then, we would not run away together through the streets of the world. I imagined the newlyweds, handsome, elegant, getting into the convertible. Soon they would be on the Amalfi coast, in a luxurious hotel, and every bloodcurdling insult would have changed into a bad mood that was easily erased. No second thoughts. Lila had detached herself from me definitively and—it suddenly seemed to me—the distance was in fact greater than I had imagined. She wasn't *only* married, her submission to conjugal rites would not be limited merely to sleeping with a man every night. There was something I hadn't understood, which at that moment seemed to me obvious. Lila—bowing to the fact that some business arrangement or other between her husband and Marcello had been sealed by her girlish labors—had admitted that she cared about him more than any other person or thing. If she had *already* yielded, if she had *already* swallowed that insult, her bond with Stefano must truly be strong. She loved him, she loved him like the girls in the photonovels. For her whole life she would sacrifice to him every quality of her own, and he wouldn't even be aware of the sacrifice, he would be surrounded by the wealth of feeling, intelligence, imagination that were hers, without knowing what to do with them, he would ruin them. I, I thought, am not capable of loving anyone like that, not even Nino, all I know is how to get along with books. And for a fraction of a second I saw myself identical to a dented bowl in which my sister Elisa used to feed a stray cat, until he disappeared, and the bowl stood empty, gathering dust on the landing. At that point, with a sharp sense of anguish, I felt sure that I had ventured too far. I must go back, I said to myself, I should be like Carmela, Ada, Gigliola, Lila herself. Accept the neighborhood, expel pride, punish presumption, stop humiliating the people who love me. When Alfonso and Marisa went off to meet Nino, I, making a large detour to avoid my mother, joined my boyfriend on the terrace.

My dress was too light: the sun had gone, it was beginning to get cold. As soon as he saw me, Antonio lit a cigarette and pretended to look at the sea again.

"Let's go," I said.

"Go yourself, with Sarratore's son."

"I want to go with you."

"You're a liar."

"Why?"

"Because if he wanted you, you would leave me here without so much as a goodbye."

It was true, but it enraged me that he said it so openly, heedless of the words. I hissed, "If you don't understand that I'm here running the risk that at any moment my mother might show up and start hitting me because of you, then it means that you're thinking only of yourself, that I don't matter to you at all."

He heard scarcely any dialect in my voice, he noted the long sentence, the subjunctives, and he lost his temper. He threw

away the cigarette, grabbed me by the wrist with a barely controlled force and cried—a cry locked in his throat—that he
was there for me, only for me, that it was I who had told him
to stay near me in the church and at the celebration, yes, I,
and you made me swear, he gasped, swear, you said, that you
won't ever leave me alone, and so I had a suit made, and I'm
deep in debt to Signora Solara, and to please you, to do as you
asked, I didn't spend even a minute with my mother or my sisters and brothers: and what is my reward, my reward is that
you treat me like shit, you talk the whole time to the poet's son
and humiliate me in front of my friends, you make me look
ridiculous, because to you I'm no one, because you're so educated and I'm not, because I don't understand the things you
say, and it's true, it's very true that I don't understand you, but
God damn it, Lenù, look at me, look me in the face: you think
you can order me around, you think I'm not capable of saying
That's enough, and yet you're wrong, you know everything,
but you don't know that if you go out of that door with me
now, if now I tell you O.K. and we go out, but then I discover
that you see that jerk Nino Sarratore at school, and who knows
where else, I'll kill you, Lenù, so think about it, leave me here
this minute, he said in despair, leave me, because it's better for
you, and meanwhile he looked at me, his eyes red and very
large, and uttered the words with his mouth wide open, shouting at me without shouting, his nostrils flaring, black, and in
his face such suffering that I thought Maybe he's hurting himself inside, because the words, shouted in his throat like that,
in his chest, but without exploding in the air, are like bits of
sharp iron piercing his lungs and his pharynx.

I had a confused need for that aggression. The vise on my
wrist, the fear that he would hit me, that river of painful
words ended by consoling me: it seemed to me that at least he
valued me.

"You're hurting me," I muttered.

He slowly relaxed his grip, but remained staring at me with his mouth open. The skin of my wrist was turning purple, giving him weight and authority, anchoring me to him.

"What do you choose?" he asked.

"I want to stay with you," I said, but sullenly.

He closed his mouth, his eyes filled with tears, he looked at the sea to give himself time to suppress them.

Soon afterward we were in the street. We didn't wait for Pasquale, Enzo, the girls, we didn't say goodbye to anyone. The most important thing was not to be seen by my mother, so we slipped away on foot; by now it was dark. For a while we walked beside each other without touching, then Antonio hesitantly put an arm around my shoulders. He wanted me to understand that he expected to be forgiven, as if he were the guilty one. Because he loved me, he had decided to consider the hours that, right before his eyes, I had spent with Nino, seducing and seduced, a time of hallucinations.

"Did I leave a bruise?" he asked, trying to take my wrist.

I didn't answer. He grasped my shoulder with his broad hand, I made a movement of annoyance that immediately caused him to relax his grip. He waited, I waited. When he tried again to send out that signal of surrender, I put an arm around his waist.

4.

We kissed without stopping, behind a tree, in the doorway of a building, along dark alleys. We took a bus, then another, and reached the station. We went toward the ponds on foot, still kissing each other on the nearly deserted street that skirted the railroad tracks.

I was hot, even though my dress was light and the cold of the evening pierced the heat of my skin with sudden shivers.

Every so often Antonio clung to me in the shadows, embracing me with such ardor that it hurt. His lips were burning, and the heat of his mouth kindled my thoughts and my imagination. Maybe Lila and Stefano, I said to myself, are already in the hotel. Maybe they're having dinner. Maybe they're getting ready for the night. Ah, to sleep next to a man, not to be cold. I felt Antonio's tongue moving around my mouth and while he pressed my breasts through the material of my dress, I touched his sex through the pocket of his pants.

The black sky was stained with pale clouds of stars. The ponds' odor of moss and putrid earth was yielding to the sweeter scents of spring. The grass was wet, the water abruptly hiccupped, as if an acorn had fallen in it, a rock, a frog. We took a path we knew well, which led to a stand of dead trees, with slender trunks and broken branches. A little farther on was the old canning factory, with its caved-in roof, all iron beams and fragments of metal. I felt an urgency of pleasure, something that drew me from inside like a smooth strip of velvet. I wanted desire to find a violent satisfaction, capable of shattering that whole day. I felt it rubbing, caressing and pricking at the base of my stomach, stronger than it had ever been. Antonio spoke words of love in dialect, he spoke them in my mouth, on my neck, insisting. I was silent, I was always silent during those encounters, I only sighed.

"Tell me you love me," he begged.

"Yes."

"Tell me."

"Yes."

I said nothing else. I embraced him, I clasped him to me with all my strength. I would have liked to be caressed and kissed over every inch of my body, I felt the need to be rubbed, bitten, I wanted my breath to fail. He pushed me a little away from him and slid a hand into my bra as he continued to kiss me. But it wasn't enough for me, that night it was too little. All the contact that we had had up to that minute, that he had imposed on me with caution and that I had accepted with equal caution, now seemed to me inadequate, uncomfortable, too quick. Yet I didn't know how to tell him that I wanted more, I didn't have the words. In each of our secret meetings we celebrated a silent rite, stage by stage. He caressed my breasts, he lifted my skirt, he touched me between the legs, and meanwhile he pushed against me, like a signal, the convulsion of tender flesh and cartilage and veins and blood that vibrated in his pants. But that night I delayed pulling out his sex; I knew that as soon as I did he would forget about me, he would stop touching me. Breasts, hips, bottom, pubis would no longer occupy him, he would be concentrated only on my hand, in fact he would tighten his around it to encourage me to move it with the right rhythm. Then he would get out his handkerchief and keep it ready for the moment when a light rattling sound would come from his mouth and from his penis his dangerous liquid. Finally he would draw back, slightly dazed, perhaps embarrassed, and we would go home. A habitual conclusion, which I now felt a confused need to change: I didn't care about being pregnant without being married, I didn't care about the sin, the divine overseers nesting in the cosmos above us, the Holy Spirit or any of his stand-ins, and Antonio felt this and was disoriented. While he kissed me, with growing agitation, he tried repeatedly to bring my hand down, but I pulled it away, I pushed my pubis against his fingers, I pushed hard and repeatedly, with drawn-out sighs. Then he withdrew his hand, he tried to unbutton his pants.

"Wait," I said.

I drew him toward the skeleton of the canning factory. It was darker there, more sheltered, but I could hear the wary rustling of scampering mice. My heart began to beat hard, I was afraid of the place, of myself, of the craving that possessed me to obliterate from my manners and from my voice the sense

of alienation that I had discovered a few hours earlier. I wanted
to return, and sink into that neighborhood, to be as I had been.
I wanted to throw away studying, the notebooks full of exercises. Exercising for what, after all. What I could become outside of Lila's shadow counted for nothing. What was I compared with her in her wedding dress, with her in the
convertible, the blue hat and the pastel suit? What was I, here
with Antonio, secretly, in this rusting ruin, with the scurrying
rats, my skirt raised over my hips, my underpants lowered,
yearning and anguished and guilty, while she lay naked, with
languid detachment, on linen sheets, in a hotel that looked out
on the sea, and let Stefano violate her, enter her completely,
give her his seed, impregnate her legitimately and without
fear? What was I as Antonio fumbled with his pants and
placed his gross male flesh between my legs, against my naked
sex, and clutching my buttocks rubbed against me, moving
back and forth, panting? I didn't know. I knew only that I was
not what I wanted at that moment. It wasn't enough for him to
rub against me. I wanted to be penetrated, I wanted to tell Lila
when she returned: I'm not a virgin, either, what you do I do,
you can't leave me behind. So I held Antonio tight around his
neck and kissed him, I stood on tiptoe, I sought his sex with
mine, I sought it wordlessly, by trial and error. He realized it
and helped me with his hand, I felt him entering just a little, I
trembled with curiosity and fear. But I also felt the effort he
was making to stop, to keep from pushing with all the violence
that had been smoldering for an entire afternoon and surely
was still. He was about to stop, I realized, and I pressed against
him to persuade him to continue.

But with a deep breath Antonio pushed me away and said
in dialect, "No, Lenù, I want to do it the way it's done with a
wife, not like this."

He grabbed my right hand, brought it to his sex with a kind
of repressed sob, and I resigned myself to masturbating him.

Afterward, as we were leaving the ponds, he said uneasily that he respected me and didn't want to make me do something that I would later regret, not in that place, not in that dirty and careless way. He spoke as if it were he who had gone too far, and maybe he believed that. I didn't utter a single word the whole way, and said goodbye with relief. When I knocked on the door, my mother opened it and, in vain restrained by my brothers and sister, without yelling, without a word of reproach, began hitting me. My glasses flew to the floor and immediately I shouted with bitter joy, and not a hint of dialect, "See what you've done? You've broken my glasses and now because of you I can't study, I'm not going to school anymore."

My mother froze, even the hand she had struck me with remained still in the air, like the blade of an axe.

Elisa, my little sister, picked up the glasses and said softly, "Here, Lenù, they're not broken."

5.

I was overcome by an exhaustion that, no matter how much I rested, wouldn't go away. For the first time, I skipped school. I was absent, I think, for some two weeks, and not even to Antonio did I say that I couldn't stand it anymore, I wanted to stop. I left home at the usual time, and wandered all morning through the city. I learned a lot about Naples in that period. I rummaged among the used books in the stalls of Port'Alba, unwillingly absorbing titles and authors' names, and continued toward Toledo and the sea. Or I climbed the Vomero on Via Salvator Rosa, went up to San Martino, came back down by the Petraio. Or I explored the Doganella, went to the cemetery, wandered on the silent paths, read the names of the dead. Sometimes idle young men, stupid old men, even respectable middle-aged men pursued me with obscene offers. I quickened my pace, eyes lowered, I escaped, sensing danger, but didn't stop. In fact the more I skipped school the bigger the hole that those long mornings of wandering made in the net of scholastic obligations that had imprisoned me since I was six years old. At the proper time I went home and no one suspected that I, *I*, had not gone to school. I spent the afternoon reading novels, then I hurried to the ponds, to Antonio, who was very happy that I was so available. He would have liked to ask if I had seen Sarratore's son. I read the question in his eyes, but he didn't dare ask, he was afraid of a quarrel, he was afraid that I would get angry and deny him those few minutes of pleasure. He embraced me, to feel me compliant against his body, to chase away any doubt. At those moments he dismissed the possibility that I could insult him by also seeing that other.

He was wrong: in reality, although I felt guilty, I thought only of Nino. I wanted to see him, talk to him, and on the other hand I was afraid to. I was afraid that he would humiliate me with his superiority. I was afraid that one way or another he would return to the reasons that the article about my quarrel with the religion teacher hadn't been published. I was afraid that he would report to me the cruel judgments of the editors. I couldn't have borne it. While I drifted through the city, and at night, in bed, when I couldn't sleep and felt my inadequacy with utter clarity, I preferred to believe that my text had been rejected for pure and simple lack of space. Let it diminish, fade. But it was hard. I hadn't been equal to Nino's brilliance, and so I couldn't stay with him, be listened to, tell him my thoughts. What thoughts, after all? I didn't have any. Better to eliminate myself—no more books, grades, praise. I hoped to forget everything, slowly: the notions that crowded my head, the languages living and dead, Italian itself that rose now to my lips even with my sister and brothers. It's Lila's fault, I thought, if I started down this path, I have to forget her, too: Lila always knew what she wanted and got it; I don't want anything, I'm made of nothing. I hoped to wake in the morning without desires. Once I was emptied—I imagined—the affection of Antonio, my affection for him will be enough.

Then one day, on the way home, I met Pinuccia, Stefano's sister. I learned from her that Lila had returned from her honeymoon and had had a big lunch to celebrate the engagement of her sister-in-law and her brother.

"You and Rino are engaged?" I asked, feigning surprise.

"Yes," she said, radiant, and showed me the ring he had given her.

I remember that while Pinuccia was talking I had a single, twisted thought: Lila had a party at her new house and didn't invite me, but it's better that way, I'm glad, stop comparing myself to her, I don't want to see her anymore. Only when every detail of the engagement had been examined did I ask, hesitantly, about my friend. With a treacherous half smile, Pinuccia offered a formula in dialect: *she's learning*. I didn't ask what. When I got home I slept for the whole afternoon.

The next morning I went out at seven as usual to go to school, or, rather, to pretend to go to school. I had just crossed the *stradone*, when I saw Lila get out of the convertible and enter our courtyard without even turning to say goodbye to Stefano, who was at the wheel. She had dressed with care, and wore large dark glasses, even though there was no sun. I was struck by a scarf of blue voile that she had knotted in such a way that it covered her lips, too. I thought resentfully that this was her new style—not Jackie Kennedy but, rather, the mysterious lady we had imagined we would become ever since we were children. I kept going without calling to her.

After a few steps, however, I turned back, not with a clear intention but because I couldn't help it. My heart was pounding, my feelings were confused. Maybe I wanted to ask her to tell me to my face that our friendship was over. Maybe I wanted to cry out that I, too, had decided to stop studying and get married—to go and live at Antonio's house with his mother and his brothers and sisters, wash the stairs like Melina the madwoman. I crossed the courtyard quickly, I saw her go in the entranceway that led to her mother-in-law's apartment. I started up the stairs, the same ones we had climbed together as children when we went to ask Don Achille to give us our dolls. I called her, she turned.

"You're back," I said.

"Yes."

"Why didn't you tell me?"

"I didn't want you to see me."

"Others can see you and not me?"

"I don't care about others, I do care about you."

I looked at her uncertainly. What was I not supposed to see? I climbed the stairs that separated us and delicately pulled aside the scarf, raised the sunglasses.

6.

I do it again now, in my imagination, as I begin to tell the story of her honeymoon, not only as she told it to me there on the landing but as I read it later, in her notebooks. I had been unjust to her, I had wished to believe in an easy surrender on her part to be able to humiliate her as I felt humiliated when Nino left the reception; I had wished to diminish her in order not to feel her loss. There she is, instead, the reception now over, shut up in the convertible, the blue hat, the pastel suit. Her eyes were burning with rage and as soon as the car started she blasted Stefano with the most intolerable words and phrases of our neighborhood.

He swallowed the insults in his usual way, with a faint smile, not saying a word, and finally she was silent. But the silence didn't last. Lila started again calmly, but panting slightly. She told him that she wouldn't stay in that car a minute longer, that it disgusted her to breathe the air that he breathed, that she wanted to get out, immediately. Stefano saw the disgust in her face, yet he continued to drive, without saying anything, so she raised her voice again to make him stop. Then he pulled over, but when Lila tried to open the door he grabbed her firmly by the wrist.

"Now listen to me," he said softly. "There are serious reasons for what happened."

He explained to her in placid tones how it went. To keep the shoe factory from closing down before it even opened its doors, he had found it necessary to enter into a partnership with Silvio Solara and his sons, who alone could insure not only that the shoes were placed in the best shops in the city but that in the fall a shop selling Cerullo shoes exclusively would open in Piazza dei Martiri.

"What do I care about your necessities," Lila interrupted him, struggling to get free.

"My necessities are yours, you're my wife."

"I? I'm nothing to you, nor are you to me. Let go of my arm."

Stefano let go of her arm.

"Your father and brother are nothing, either?"

"Wash your mouth out when you talk about them, you're not fit to even mention their names."

But Stefano did mention their names. He said that it was Francesco himself who had wanted to make the agreement with Silvio Solara. He said that the biggest obstacle had been Marcello, who was extremely angry at Lila, at the whole Cerullo family, and, especially, at Pasquale, Antonio, and Enzo, who had smashed his car and beaten him up. He said that Rino had calmed him down, that it had taken a lot of patience, and so when Marcello had said, then I want the shoes that Lina made, Rino had said O.K., take the shoes.

It was a bad moment, Lila felt as if she'd been stabbed in the chest. But just the same she cried, "And you, what did you do?"

Stefano had a moment of embarrassment.

"What was I supposed to do? Fight with your brother, ruin your family, start a war against your friends, lose all the money I invested?"

To Lila, every word, in both tone and content, seemed a hypocritical admission of guilt. She didn't even let him finish, but began hitting him on the shoulder with her fists, yelling, "So even you, you said O.K., you went and got the shoes, you gave them to him?"

Stefano let her go on, but when she tried again to open the door and escape he said to her coldly, Calm down. Lila turned suddenly: calm down after he had thrown the blame on her father and brother, calm down when all three had treated her like an old rag, a rag for wiping up the floor. I don't want to calm down, she shouted, you piece of shit, take me home right now, repeat what you just said in front of those two other shit men. And only when she uttered that expression in dialect, shit men, *uommen'e mmerd*, did she notice that she had broken the barrier of her husband's measured tones. A second afterward Stefano struck her in the face with his strong hand, a violent slap that seemed to her an explosion of truth. She winced, startled by the painful burning of her cheek. She looked at him, incredulous, while he started the car and said, in a voice that for the first time since he had begun to court her was not calm, that in fact trembled, "See what you've made me do? See how you go too far?"

"We've been wrong about everything," she murmured.

But Stefano denied it decisively, as if he refused even to consider that possibility, and he made a long speech, part threatening, part didactic, part pathetic.

He said, more or less, "We haven't been wrong about anything, Lina, we just have to get a few things straight. Your name is no longer Cerullo. You are Signora Carracci and you must do as I say. I know, you're not practical, you don't know what business is, you think I find money lying on the ground. But it's not like that. I have to make money every day, I have to put it where it can grow. You designed the shoes, your father and brother are good workers, but the three of you together aren't capable of making money grow. The Solaras are, and so—please listen to me—I don't give a damn if you don't like those people. Marcello is repulsive to me, too, and when he looks at you, even so much as out of the corner of his eye, when I think of the things he said about you, I feel like sticking a knife in his stomach. But if he is useful for making money, then he becomes my best friend. And you know why? Because if we don't make money we don't have this car, I can't buy you that dress, we lose the house with everything in it, in the end you can't act the lady, and our children grow up like the children of beggars. So just try saying again what you said tonight and I will ruin that beautiful face of yours so that you can't go out of the house. You understand? Answer me."

Lila's eyes narrowed to cracks. Her cheek had turned purple, but otherwise she was very pale. She didn't answer him.

7.

They reached Amalfi in the evening. Neither had ever been to a hotel, and they were embarrassed and ill at ease. Stefano was especially intimidated by the vaguely mocking tones of the receptionist and, without meaning to, assumed a subservient attitude. When he realized it, he covered his discomfiture with brusque manners, and his ears flushed merely at the request to show his documents. Meanwhile the porter appeared, a man in his fifties with a thin mustache, but Stefano refused his help, as if he were a thief, then, thinking better of it, disdainfully gave him a large tip, even though he didn't take advantage of his services. Lila followed her husband as he carried the suitcases up the stairs and—she told me—for the first time had the impression that somewhere along the way she had lost the youth she had married that morning, and was in the company of a stranger. Was Stefano really so broad, his legs short and fat, his arms long, his knuckles white? To whom had she bound herself forever? The rage that had overwhelmed her during the journey gave way to anxiety.

Once they were in the room he made an effort to be affectionate again, but he was tired and still unnerved by the slap he had had to give her. He assumed an artificial tone. He praised the room, it was very spacious, opened the French window, went out on the balcony, said to her, Come and smell the fragrant air, look how the sea sparkles. But she was seeking a way out of that trap, and, distracted, shook her head no, she was cold. Stefano immediately closed the window, and remarked that if they wanted to take a walk and eat outside they'd better put on something warmer, saying, Just in case get me a vest, as if they had already been living together for many years and she knew how to dig expertly in the suitcases, to pull out a vest for him exactly as she would have found a sweater for herself. Lila seemed to agree, but in fact she didn't open the suitcases, she took out neither sweater nor vest. She immediately went out into the corridor, she didn't want to stay in the room a minute longer. He followed her muttering: I'm also fine like this, but I'm worried about you, you'll catch cold.

They wandered around Amalfi, to the cathedral, up the steps and back down again, to the fountain. Stefano now tried to amuse her, but being amusing had never been his strong point, sentimental tones suited him better, or the sententious phrases of the mature man who knows what he wants. Lila barely responded, and in the end her husband confined himself to pointing out this and that, exclaiming, Look. But she, who in other times would have appreciated every stone, wasn't interested in the beauty of the narrow streets or the scents of the gardens or the art and history of Amalfi, or, especially, the voice of her husband, who kept saying, tiresomely, Beautiful, isn't it?

Soon Lila began to tremble, but not because she was particularly cold; it was nerves. He realized it and proposed that they return to the hotel, even venturing a remark like: Then we can hug each other and get warm. But she wanted to keep walking, on and on, until, overcome by weariness, and though she wasn't at all hungry, she entered a restaurant, without consulting him. Stefano followed her patiently.

They ordered all kinds of things, ate almost nothing, drank a lot of wine. At a certain point he could no longer hold back, and asked if she was still angry. Lila shook her head no, and it was true. At that question, she herself was amazed not to feel the least rancor toward the Solaras, or her father and brother, or Stefano. Everything had rapidly changed in her mind. Suddenly, she didn't care at all about the shoes; in fact she couldn't understand why she had been so enraged at seeing them on Marcello's feet. Now, instead, the broad wedding band that gleamed on her ring finger frightened and distressed her. In disbelief, she retraced the day: the church, the ceremony, the celebration. What have I done, she thought, dazed by wine, and what is this gold circle, this glittering zero I've stuck my finger in. Stefano had one, too, and it shone amid the black hairs, hairy fingers, as the books said. She remembered him in his bathing suit, as she had seen him at the beach. The broad chest, the large kneecaps, like overturned pots. There was not the smallest detail that, once recalled, revealed to her any charm. He was a being, now, with whom she felt she could share nothing and yet there he was, in his jacket and tie, he moved his fat lips and scratched the fleshy lobe of an ear and kept sticking his fork in something on her plate to taste it. He had little or nothing to do with the seller of cured meats who had attracted her, with the ambitious, self-confident, but well-mannered youth, with the bridegroom of that morning in church. He revealed white jaws, a red tongue in the dark hole of his mouth: something in and around him had broken. At that table, amid the coming and going of the waiters, everything that had brought her here to Amalfi seemed without any logical coherence and yet unbearably real. Thus, while the face of that unrecognizable being lighted up at the idea that the storm had passed, that she had understood his reasons, that she had accepted them, that he could finally talk to her about his big plans, she suddenly had the idea of stealing a knife from the table to stick in his throat when, in the room, he tried to deflower her.

In the end she didn't do it. Since in that restaurant, at that table, to her wine-fogged mind, her entire marriage, from the wedding dress to the ring, had turned out to make no sense, it also seemed to her that any possible sexual demand on Stefano's part would make no sense, above all to him. So at first she contemplated how to get the knife (she took the napkin off her lap, covered the knife with it, placed both back on her lap, prepared to drop the knife in her purse, and put the napkin back on the table), then she gave it up. The screws holding together her new condition of wife, the restaurant, Amalfi, seemed to her so loose that at the end of dinner Stefano's voice no longer reached her, in her ears there was only a clamor of objects, living beings, and thoughts, without definition.

On the street, he started talking again about the good side of the Solaras. They knew, he told her, important people in the city government, they had ties to the parties, the monarchists, the Fascists. He liked to speak as if he really understood something about the Solaras' dealings, he took a knowing tone, he said emphatically: Politics is ugly but it's important for making money. Lila remembered the discussions she had had with Pasquale in earlier times, and even the ones she'd had with Stefano during their engagement, the plan to separate themselves completely from their parents, from the abuses and hypocrisies and cruelties of the past. He said yes, she thought, he said he agreed, but he wasn't listening to me. Who did I talk to. I don't know this person, I don't know who he is.

And yet when he took her hand and whispered that he loved her, she didn't pull away. Maybe she planned to make him think that everything was in order, that they really were bride and groom on their honeymoon, in order to wound him more profoundly when she told him, with all the disgust she felt in her stomach: to get into bed with the hotel porter or with you—you both have smoke-yellowed fingers—it's the same revolting thing to me. Or maybe—and this I think is more likely—she was too frightened and by now was striving to delay every reaction.

As soon as they were in the room, he tried to kiss her, and she recoiled. Gravely, she opened the suitcase, took out her nightgown, gave her husband his pajamas. That attention made him smile happily at her, and he tried again to grab her. But she shut herself in the bathroom.

Alone, she washed her face for a long time to get rid of the stupor from the wine, the impression of a world that had lost its contours. She didn't succeed; rather, the feeling that her very gestures lacked coordination intensified. What can I do, she thought. Stay locked in here all night. And then.

She was sorry that she hadn't taken the knife: for a moment, in fact, she believed that she had, then was forced to admit she hadn't. Sitting on the edge of the bathtub, she compared it appreciatively with the one in the new house, thinking that hers was nicer. Her towels, too, were of a higher quality. Hers? To whom, in fact, did the towels, the tub—everything—

belong? She was bothered by the idea that the ownership of the nice new things was guaranteed by the last name of that particular individual who was waiting for her out there. Carracci's possession, she, too, was Carracci's possession. Stefano knocked on the door.

"What are you doing, do you feel all right?"

She didn't answer.

Her husband waited a little and knocked again. When nothing happened, he twisted the handle nervously and said in a tone of feigned amusement, "Do I have to break down the door?"

Lila didn't doubt that he would have been capable of it— the stranger who waited for her outside was capable of anything. I, too, she thought, am capable of anything. She undressed, she washed, she put on the nightgown, despising herself for the care with which she had chosen it months earlier. Stefano—purely a name that no longer coincided with the habits and affections of a few hours earlier—was sitting on the edge of the bed in his pajamas and he jumped to his feet as soon as she appeared.

"You took your time."

"The time needed."

"You look beautiful."

"I'm very tired, I want to sleep."

"We'll sleep later."

"Now. You on your side, I on mine."

"O.K., come here."

"I'm serious."

"I am, too."

Stefano uttered a little laugh, tried to take her by the hand. She drew back, he darkened.

"What's wrong with you?"

Lila hesitated. She sought the right expression, said softly, "I don't want you."

Stefano shook his head uncertainly, as if the three words were in a foreign language. He murmured that he had been waiting so long for that moment, day and night. Please, he said, in a pleading tone, and, with an expression almost of dejection, he pointed to his wine-colored pajama pants, and mumbled with a crooked smile: See what happens to me just when I look at you. She looked without wanting to and, with a spasm of disgust, averted her gaze.

At that point Stefano realized that she was about to lock herself in the bathroom again and with an animal leap he grabbed her by the waist, picked her up, and threw her on the bed. What was happening. It was clear that he didn't want to understand. He thought they had made peace at the restaurant, now he was wondering: Why is Lina behaving like this, she's too young. In fact he was laughing, on top of her, trying to soothe her.

"It's a beautiful thing," he said, "you mustn't be afraid. I love you more than my mother and my sister."

But no, she was already pulling herself up to get away from him. How difficult it is to keep up with this girl: she says yes and means no, she says no and means yes. Stefano muttered: No more of these whims, and he stopped her again, sat astride her, pinned her wrists against the bedspread.

"You said that we should wait and we waited," he said, "even though being near you without touching you was terrible and I suffered. But we're married now—behave yourself, don't worry."

He leaned over to kiss her on the mouth, but she avoided him, turning her face forcefully to right and left, struggling, twisting, as she repeated, "Leave me alone, I don't want you, I don't want you, I don't want you."

At that point, almost against his will, the tone of Stefano's voice rose: "Now you're really pissing me off, Lina."

He repeated that remark two or three times, each time

louder, as if to assimilate fully an order that was coming to him from very far away, perhaps even from before he was born. The order was: be a man, Ste'; either you subdue her now or you'll never subdue her; your wife has to learn right away that she is the female and you're the male and therefore she has to obey. And Lila hearing him—you're pissing me off, you're pissing me off, you're pissing me off—and seeing him, broad, heavy above her narrow pelvis, his sex erect, holding up the material of his pajamas like a tent support, remembered when, years before, he had wanted to grab her tongue with his fingers and prick it with a pin because she had dared to humiliate Alfonso in a school competition. He was never Stefano, she seemed to discover suddenly, he was always the oldest son of Don Achille. And that thought, immediately, brought to the young face of her husband, like a revival, features that until that moment had remained prudently hidden in his blood but that had always been there, waiting for their moment. Oh yes, to please the neighborhood, to please her, Stefano had striven to be someone else, softening his features with courteousness, adapting his gaze to meekness, modeling his voice on the tones of conciliation; his fingers, his hands, his whole body had learned to restrain their force. But now the limits that he had imposed for so long were about to give way, and Lila was seized by a childish terror, greater than when we had gone down into the cellar to get our dolls. Don Achille was rising from the muck of the neighborhood, feeding on the living matter of his son. The father was cracking his skin, changing his gaze, exploding out of his body. And in fact look at him, he tore the nightgown off her chest, bared her breasts, clasped her fiercely, leaned over to bite her nipples. And when she, as she had always been able to do, repressed her horror and tried to tear him off her by pulling his hair, groping with her mouth as she sought to bite him until he bled, he drew back, seized her arms, pinned them under his huge bent legs, said to her contemptuously: What are you doing, be quiet, you're just a twig, if I want to break you I'll break you. But Lila wouldn't calm down, she bit the air, she arched to get his weight off of her. In vain. He now had his hands free and leaning over her he slapped her lightly with the tips of his fingers and kept telling her, pressing her: see how big it is, eh, say yes, say yes, say yes, until he took out of his pajamas his stubby sex that, extended over her, seemed like a puppet without arms or legs, congested by mute stirrings, in a frenzy to uproot itself from that other, bigger puppet that was saying, hoarsely, Now I'll make you feel it, Lina, look how nice it is, nobody's got one like this. And since she was still writhing, he hit her twice, first with the palm of his hand, then with the back, and so hard that she understood that if she continued to resist he would certainly kill her—or at least Don Achille would: who frightened the neighborhood because you knew that with his strength he could hurl you against a wall or a tree—and she emptied herself of all rebellion, yielding to a soundless terror, while he drew back, pulled up her nightgown, whispered in her ear: you don't realize how much I love you, but you will know, and tomorrow it will be you asking me to love you as I am now, and more, in fact you will go down on your knees and beg me, and I will say yes but only if you are obedient, and you will be obedient.

When, after some awkward attempts, he tore her flesh with passionate brutality, Lila was absent. The night, the room, the bed, his kisses, his hands on her body, every sensation was absorbed by a single feeling: she hated Stefano Carracci, she hated his strength, she hated his weight on her, she hated his name and his surname.

8.

They returned to the neighborhood four days later. That

same evening Stefano invited his parents-in-law and his brother-in-law to the new house. With a humbler expression than usual, he asked Fernando to tell Lila what had happened with Silvio Solara. Fernando confirmed to his daughter, in unhappy, disjointed sentences, Stefano's version. As for Rino, Carracci asked him, right afterward, to tell why, in the end, they had made the mutual but painful decision to give Marcello the shoes he insisted on. Rino, in the manner of a man who knows what's what, declared pompously: There are situations in which certain choices are obligatory, then he started in with the serious trouble Pasquale, Antonio, and Enzo had got into when they beat up the Solara brothers and wrecked their car.

"You know who was more at risk?" he said, leaning toward his sister and raising his voice. "Them, your friends, those knights in shining armor. Marcello recognized them and was convinced that you had sent them. Stefano and I—what were we supposed to do? You wanted those three idiots to get a beating a lot worse than the one they gave? You wanted to ruin them? And for what, anyway? For a pair of size 43 shoes that your husband can't wear because they're too narrow for him and when it rains the water gets in? We made peace, and, since those shoes were so important to Marcello, we gave them to him."

Words: with them you can do and undo as you please. Lila had always been good with words, but on that occasion, contrary to expectations, she didn't open her mouth. Relieved, Rino reminded her spitefully that it was she who, ever since she was a child, had been harassing him, telling him they had to get rich. Then, she said, laughing, make us rich without complicating our life, which is already too complicated.

At that point—a surprise for the mistress of the house, though certainly not for the others—the doorbell rang, and Pinuccia, Alfonso, and their mother, Maria, appeared, with a tray of pastries freshly made by Spagnuolo himself, the Solaras' pastry maker.

At first it seemed that they had come to celebrate the newlyweds' return from their honeymoon, since Stefano passed around the wedding pictures, which he had just picked up from the photographer (for the movie, he explained, it would take a little longer). But it soon became clear that the wedding of Stefano and Lila was already old news, the pastries were intended to mark a new happy event: the engagement of Rino and Pinuccia. All the tension was set aside. Rino replaced the violent tones of a few minutes earlier with tender modulations in dialect, exaggerated pronouncements of love, the wonderful idea of having the engagement party right away, in his sister's lovely house. Then, with a theatrical gesture, he took a package out of his pocket; the package, when it was unwrapped, revealed a dark rounded case; and the case, when it was opened, revealed a diamond ring.

Lila noted that it wasn't that different from the one she wore on her finger, next to the wedding ring, and wondered where her brother had got the money. There were hugs and kisses. There was a lot of talk of the future, speculation about who would manage the Cerullo shoe store in Piazza dei Martiri when the Solaras opened it, in the fall. Rino supposed that Pinuccia would manage it, maybe by herself, maybe with Gigliola Spagnuolo, who was officially engaged to Michele and so was making claims. The family reunion became livelier and full of hope.

Lila remained standing most of the time, it hurt to sit down. No one, not even her mother, who was silent during the entire visit, seemed to notice her swollen, black right eye, the cut on her lower lip, the bruises on her arms.

9.

She was still in that state when, there on the stairs that led to the house of her mother-in-law, I took off her glasses, unwound her scarf. The skin around her eye had a yellowish color, and her lower lip was a purple stain with fiery red stripes.

To her friends and relatives she said that she had fallen on the rocks in Amalfi on a beautiful sunny morning, when she and her husband had taken a boat to a beach just at the foot of a yellow wall. During the engagement lunch for her brother and Pinuccia she had used, in telling that lie, a sarcastic tone and they had all sarcastically believed her, especially the women, who knew what had to be said when the men who loved them and whom they loved beat them severely. Besides, there was no one in the neighborhood, especially of the female sex, who did not think that she had needed a good thrashing for a long time. So the beatings did not cause outrage, and in fact sympathy and respect for Stefano increased—there was someone who knew how to be a man.

But when I saw her so battered, my heart leaped to my throat, I embraced her. And when she said she hadn't come to visit because she didn't want me to see her in that state, tears came to my eyes. The story of her honeymoon, as the photonovels put it, although stripped down, almost cold, made me angry, pained me. And yet, I have to admit, I also felt a tenuous pleasure. I was content to discover that Lila now needed help, maybe protection, and that admission of fragility not toward the neighborhood but toward me moved me. I felt that the distances had unexpectedly gotten shorter again and I was tempted to tell her right away that I had decided to quit school, that school was useless, that I didn't have the right qualities. It seemed to me that the news would comfort her.

But her mother-in-law looked out over the banister on the top floor and called her. Lila ended her story with a few hurried sentences, she said that Stefano had tricked her, that he was just like his father.

"You remember that Don Achille gave us money instead of the dolls?" she asked.

"Yes."

"We shouldn't have taken it."

"We bought *Little Women*."

"We were wrong: ever since that moment I've been wrong about everything."

She wasn't upset, she was sad. She put her dark glasses back on, she reknotted the scarf. I was pleased about that *we* (*we* shouldn't have taken it, *we* were wrong), but the abrupt transition to the *I* annoyed me: *I* have been wrong about everything. *We*, I would have liked to correct her, *always we*, but I didn't. It seemed to me that she was trying to comprehend her new condition, and that she urgently needed to know what she could hold on to in order to confront it. Before starting up the flight of stairs she asked, "Would you like to come and study at my house?"

"When?"

"This afternoon, tomorrow, every day."

"Stefano will be annoyed."

"If he is the master, I am the master's wife."

"I don't know, Lila."

"I'll give you a room, I'll shut you in."

"What's the point?"

She shrugged.

"To know that you're there."

I didn't say yes or no. I went off, and wandered through the city as usual. Lila was sure that I would never quit school. She had assigned me the role of the friend with glasses and pimples, always bent over her books, smart in school, and she couldn't even imagine that I might change. But I didn't want that role anymore. It seemed to me that, thanks to the humiliation of the unpublished article, I had thoroughly understood my inadequacy. Even though Nino was born and had grown up like Lila and me in that wretched outlying neighborhood, he was able to use school with intelligence, I was not. So stop deluding myself, stop striving. Accept your lot, as Carmela, Ada, Gigliola, and, in her way, Lila herself have long since done. I didn't go to her house that afternoon or the following ones, and I continued to skip school, tormenting myself.

One morning I went wandering not far from the school, along Via Veterinaria, behind the Botanic Garden. I thought of the conversations I had had recently with Antonio: he was hoping to avoid military service, as the son of a widowed mother and the sole support of the family; he wanted to ask for a raise in the shop, and also save so that he could take over the management of a gas pump along the *stradone*; we would get married, I would help out at the pump. The choice of a simple life, my mother would approve. I can't always please Lila, I said to myself. But how hard it was to erase from my mind the ambitions inspired by school. At the time when classes were over, I went, almost without intending it, to the neighborhood of the school, and walked around there. I was afraid of being seen by the teachers, and yet, I realized, I wished them to see me. I wanted to be either branded irremediably as a no longer model student or recaptured by the rhythms of school and submit to the obligation to go back.

The first groups of students appeared. I heard someone calling me, it was Alfonso. He was waiting for Marisa, but she was late.

"Are you going together?" I asked, teasing.

"No, she's the one who's got a crush."

"Liar."

"You're the liar, telling me you were sick, and look at you, you're fine. Professor Galiani is always asking about you, I told her you had a bad fever."

"I did, in fact."

"Obviously."

He was carrying his books, tied up with elastic, under his arm, his face was strained by the tension of the hours of school.

Did Alfonso also conceal Don Achille, his father, in his breast, despite his delicate appearance? Is it possible that our parents never die, that every child inevitably conceals them in himself? Would my mother truly emerge from me, with her limping gait, as my destiny?

I asked him, "Did you see what your brother did to Lina?"

Alfonso was embarrassed. "Yes."

"And you didn't say anything to him?"

"You have to see what Lina did to him."

"Would you be able to act the same way with Marisa?"

He laughed timidly. "No."

"You're sure?"

"Yes."

"Why?"

"Because I know you, because we talk, because we go to school together."

At the moment, I didn't understand: what did "I know you" mean, what did "we talk" and "we go to school together" mean? I saw Marisa at the end of the street, she was running because she was late.

"Your girlfriend's coming," I said.

He didn't turn, he shrugged, he mumbled, "Come back to school, please."

"I'm sick," I repeated, and left.

I didn't want to exchange even a hello with Nino's sister, any sign that evoked him made me anxious. But Alfonso's obscure words did me good, I turned them over in my mind as I walked. He had said that because he knew me, we talked to each other, we sat at the same desk, he would never impose his authority on a possible wife by beating her. He had expressed himself with a frank sincerity, he wasn't afraid of attributing to me, even if in a confused way, the capacity to influence him, a male, to change his behavior. I was grateful to him for that tangled message, which consoled me and set in motion a reconciliation between me and myself. It doesn't take much for a conviction that has become fragile to weaken to the point of giving way. The next day I forged my mother's signature and returned to school. That evening, at the ponds, clinging to Antonio to escape the cold, I promised him: I'll finish the school year and we'll get married.

10.

But I had a hard time making up the ground I had lost, especially in science, and I tried to reduce my meetings with Antonio so that I could concentrate on my books. When I missed a date because I had to study, he became gloomy, he asked me, in alarm, "Is something wrong?"

"I've got a lot of homework."

"How is it that all of a sudden you've got more homework?"

"I've always had a lot."

"Before you didn't have any."

"It was a coincidence."

"What are you hiding from me, Lenù?"

"Nothing."

"Do you still love me?"

I reassured him, but meanwhile the time moved quickly by us and I went home angry at myself because I still had so much studying to do.

Antonio's fixation was always the same: Sarratore's son. He was afraid that I would talk to him, even that I would see him. Naturally, to prevent him from suffering, I concealed the fact that I ran into Nino entering school, coming out, in the corridors. Nothing particular happened, at most we exchanged a nod of greeting and went on our way: I could have talked to my boyfriend about it without any problems if he had been a reasonable person. But Antonio was not reasonable and in truth I wasn't, either. Although Nino gave me no encouragement, a mere glimpse of him left me distracted during class. His presence a few classrooms away—real, alive, better educated than the professors, and courageous, and disobedient—drained meaning from the teachers' lectures, the pages of books, the plans for marriage, the gas pump on the *stradone*.

Even at home I couldn't study. Added to my confusing thoughts about Antonio, about Nino, about the future was my mother's irritability, as she yelled at me to do this or that, and my siblings, who came one by one to have me look at their homework. That permanent turmoil wasn't new, I had always studied in disorder. But the old determination that had allowed me to do my best even in those conditions seemed to be used up, I couldn't or didn't want to reconcile school with everyone's needs anymore. So I would let the afternoon go by helping my mother, correcting my sister's and brothers' exercises, and studying little or not at all for myself. And if once I had sacrificed sleep to books, now, since I was still exhausted and sleep seemed to me a respite, at night I forgot about homework and went to bed.

And so I began to show up in class not only inattentive but unprepared, and I lived in fear that the teachers would call on me. Which soon happened. Once, in the same day, I got low marks in chemistry, art history, and philosophy, and my nerves were so frayed that right after the last bad grade I burst into tears in front of everyone. It was a terrible moment: I felt the horror and the pleasure of losing myself, the fear and the pride in going off the rails.

As we were leaving school Alfonso told me that his sister-in-law had asked him to tell me to go and see her. Go on, he urged me anxiously, surely you'll study better there than at your house. So that afternoon I made up my mind and walked to the new neighborhood. But I didn't go to Lila's house to find a solution to my problems with school, I took it for granted that we would talk the whole time and that my situation as a former model student would get even worse. I said to myself, rather: better to go off the rails talking to Lila than in the midst of my mother's yelling, the petulant demands of my siblings, the yearnings for Nino, Antonio's recriminations; at least I would learn something about married life, a life that soon—I now assumed—would be mine.

Lila greeted me with obvious pleasure. Her eye was no longer swollen, her lip was healing. She was nicely dressed, her hair was carefully combed, she wore lipstick, yet she moved through the apartment as if her house were alien to her and she herself felt like a visitor. The wedding presents were still piled up near the door, the rooms had a smell of plaster and fresh paint mixed with the vaguely alcoholic scent that emanated from the new furniture in the dining room, the table, the sideboard with a mirror framed by dark-wood foliage, the silver chest full of silver, the plates, glasses, and bottles of colored liquors.

Lila made coffee: it was pleasant to sit with her in the spacious kitchen and play at being ladies, as we had done as children in front of the cellar air vent. It's relaxing, I thought, I was wrong not to come sooner. I had a friend of my age with her own house, full of opulent, orderly things. That friend, who had nothing to do all day, seemed happy for my company. Although we had changed and the changes were still occurring, the warmth between us endured intact. Why, then, not give in to it? For the first time since her wedding day I felt at ease.

"How's it going with Stefano?" I asked.

"Fine."

"You've cleared things up?"

She smiled in amusement.

"Yes, it's all clear."

"And so?"

"Disgusting."

"The same as Amalfi?"

"Yes."

"Did he beat you again?"

She touched her face.

"No, this is old stuff."

"Then?"

"It's the humiliation."

"And you?"

"I do what he wants."

I thought for a moment, I asked her, suggestively, "But at least when you sleep together, isn't it nice?"

She made a grimace of discomfort, became serious. She began to speak of her husband with a sort of loathing acceptance. It wasn't hostility, it wasn't a need for retaliation, it wasn't even disgust, but a placid disdain, a contempt that invested Stefano's entire person like polluted water in the ground.

I listened, I understood and I didn't understand. Long ago she had threatened Marcello with the shoemaker's knife simply because he had dared to grab my wrist and break the bracelet. From that point on, I was sure that if Marcello had just brushed against her she would have killed him. But toward Stefano, now, she showed no explicit aggression. Of course, the explanation was simple: we had seen our fathers beat our mothers from childhood. We had grown up thinking that a stranger must not even touch us, but that our father, our boyfriend, and our husband could hit us when they liked, out of love, to educate us, to reeducate us. As a result, since Stefano was not the hateful Marcello but the young man to whom she had declared her love, whom she had married, and with whom she had decided to live forever, she assumed complete responsibility for her choice. And yet it didn't add up. In my eyes Lila was Lila, not an ordinary girl of the neighborhood. Our mothers, after they were slapped by their husbands, did not have that expression of calm disdain. They despaired, they wept, they confronted their man sullenly, they criticized him behind his back, and yet, more and less, they continued to respect him (my mother, for example, plainly admired my father's devious deals). Lila instead displayed an acquiescence without respect.

I said, "I feel comfortable with Antonio, even though I don't love him."

And I hoped that, in accord with our old habits, she would be able to grasp in that statement a series of hidden questions. Although I love Nino—I was saying without saying it—I feel pleasantly excited just thinking of Antonio, of our kisses, of holding and touching each other at the ponds. Love in my case is not indispensable to pleasure, nor is respect. Is it possible, therefore, that *the disgust, the humiliation* begin *afterward,* when a man subdues you and violates you at his pleasure solely because now you belong to him, love or not, respect or not? What happens when you're in a bed, crushed by a man? She had experienced that and I would have liked her to talk about it. Instead she confined herself to saying, sarcastically, Better for you if you're comfortable, and she led me to a small room that looked out onto the railroad tracks. It was a bare space, there was only a desk, a chair, a cot, nothing on the walls.

"Do you like it here?"

"Yes."

"Then study."

She left, closing the door behind her.

The room smelled of damp plaster more than the rest of the house. I looked out the window, I would have preferred to go on talking. But it was immediately clear to me that Alfonso had told her about my absence from school, maybe even about my bad grades, and that she wanted to restore to me the wisdom she had always attributed to me, even at the cost of imposing it on me. Better that way. I heard her moving through the house, making a phone call. It struck me that she didn't say *Hello, it's Lina*, or, I don't know, *It's Lina Cerullo*, but *Hello, this is Signora Carracci*. I sat down at the desk, opened my history book, and forced myself to study.

11.

The close of the school year was inauspicious. The building that housed the high school was crumbling, rain leaked into the classrooms, after one violent storm a street nearby caved in. There followed a period when we went to school on alternate days, homework began to count more than the normal lessons, the teachers loaded it on to the point where it was unbearable. Despite my mother's protests, I got in the habit of going to Lila's right after school.

I arrived at two in the afternoon, I dropped my books somewhere. She made me a sandwich with prosciutto, cheese, salami—anything I wanted. Such abundance was never seen at my parents' house: how good the smell of the fresh bread was, and the taste of the fillings, especially the prosciutto, bright red edged with white. I ate greedily and Lila made me coffee. After we'd had some intense conversation, she closed me in the little room and seldom looked in, except to bring me a snack and to eat or drink with me. Since I had no wish to run into Stefano, who generally returned from the grocery around eight at night, I always left right at seven.

I became familiar with the apartment, with its light, with the sounds that came from the railroad. Every space, every thing was new and clean, but especially the bathroom, which had a sink, a bidet, a bathtub. One afternoon when I felt particularly lazy I asked Lila if I could have a bath, I who still washed under the tap or in a copper tub. She said I could do what I wanted and went to bring me towels. The water came out hot from the tap and I let it run. I undressed, I sank in up to my neck.

That warmth was an unexpected pleasure. After a while I tried out the numerous little bottles that crowded the corners of the tub: a steamy foam arose, as if from my body, and almost overflowed. Ah, how many wonderful things Lila possessed. It was no longer just a matter of a clean body, it was play, it was abandon. I discovered the lipsticks, the makeup, the wide mirror that reflected an image without deformities, the hair dryer. Afterward, my skin was smoother than I had ever felt it, and my hair was full, luminous, blonder. Maybe the wealth we wanted as children is this, I thought: not strongboxes full of diamonds and gold coins but a bathtub, to immerse yourself like this every day, to eat bread, salami, prosciutto, to have a lot of space even in the bathroom, to have a telephone, a pantry and icebox full of food, a photograph in a silver frame on the sideboard that shows you in your wedding dress—to have *this entire* house, with the kitchen, the bedroom, the dining room, the two balconies, and the little room where I am studying, and where, even though Lila hasn't said so, soon, when it comes, a baby will sleep.

That evening I hurried to the ponds, I couldn't wait for Antonio to caress me, smell me, marvel, enjoy that luxurious cleanliness that highlighted beauty. It was a gift that I wanted to give him. But he had his anxieties: he said, I'll never be able to offer you these things, and I answered, Who says that I want them, and he replied, You always want to do what Lila does. I was offended, we quarreled. I was independent. I did only what I liked, I did what he and Lila didn't and couldn't do, I went to school, I studied hard, was going blind over my books. I cried that he didn't understand me, that all he did was disparage and insult me, and I ran away.

But Antonio understood me too well. Day by day my friend's

house charmed me more, it became a magical place where I could have everything, far from the wretched gray of the old buildings where we had grown up, the flaking walls, the scratched doors, the same objects always, dented and chipped. Lila was careful not to disturb me, I would call out: I'm thirsty, I'm kind of hungry, let's turn on the television, can I see this, can I see that. I was bored by studying, I struggled. Sometimes I asked her to listen to me while I repeated the lessons aloud. She sat on the cot, I at the desk. I showed her the pages I had to repeat, I recited, Lila checked me line for line.

It was on those occasions that I realized how her relationship with books had changed. Now she was intimidated by them. She no longer wanted to impose on me an order, her own rhythm, as if just a few sentences were enough to get a picture of the whole and master it so that she could tell me: This is the important concept, start here. When, following me in the textbook, she had the impression that I was mistaken, she corrected me with a thousand apologies, such as: Maybe I didn't understand it, maybe you should check. She seemed not to realize that her capacity to learn effortlessly remained intact. But I knew. I saw, for example, that chemistry, so boring for me, provoked in her that narrow look, and her few observations awakened me from my apathy, excited me. I saw that after half a page of the philosophy textbook she was able to find surprising connections between Anaxagoras, the order that the intellect imposes on the chaos of things, and Mendeleev's tables. But more often I had the impression that she was aware of the inadequacy of her tools, of the naïveté of her observations, and she restrained herself on purpose. As soon as she realized that she had let herself get too involved, she retreated as if before a trap, and mumbled: Lucky you who understand, I don't know what you're talking about.

Once, she closed the book abruptly and said with annoyance, "That's enough."

"Why?"

"Because I've had it, it's always the same story: inside something small there's something even smaller that wants to leap out, and outside something large there's always something larger that wants to keep it a prisoner. I'm going to cook."

And yet I wasn't studying anything that had to do in an obvious way with the small and the large. Her own capacity to learn had irritated her, or perhaps frightened her, and she had retreated.

Where?

To make dinner, to clean the house, to watch television with the volume low in order not to disturb me, to look at the tracks, the train traffic, the fleeting outline of Vesuvius, the streets of the new neighborhood, still without trees and without shops, the rare car traffic, the women with their shopping bags, small children attached to their skirts. Occasionally, and only on Stefano's orders, or because he asked her to go with him, she went out to the place—it was less than five hundred meters from the house; once I went with her—where the new grocery was to be built. There she took measurements with a carpenter's measuring tape to plan shelves and furnishings.

That was it, she had nothing else to do. I soon realized that, being married, she was more alone than before. I sometimes went out with Carmela, with Ada, even with Gigliola, and at school I had made friends with girls in my class and other classes, so that sometimes I met them for ice cream on Via Foria. But she saw only Pinuccia, her sister-in-law. As for the boys, if during the period of her engagement they still stopped to exchange a few words, now, after her marriage, they gave a nod of greeting, at most, when they met on the street. And yet she was beautiful and she dressed like the pictures in the women's magazines that she bought in great numbers. But the condition of wife had enclosed her in a sort of glass container, like a sailboat sailing with sails unfurled in an inaccessible place, without the sea. Pasquale, Enzo, Antonio himself would never have ventured onto the unshaded white streets of newly built houses, to her doorway, to her apartment, to talk a little or invite her to take a walk. And even the telephone, a black object attached to the kitchen wall, seemed a useless ornament. The whole time I studied at her house, it seldom rang and when it did it was usually Stefano, who had put one in the grocery as well, to take orders from customers. Their conversations as newlyweds were brief, she answered listlessly, yes, no.

She used the telephone mainly for making purchases. In that period she hardly ever went out of the house, as she waited for the signs of the beating to completely disappear from her face, but she bought things just the same. For example, after my joyous bath, after my enthusiasm about the way my hair had turned out, I heard her order a new hair dryer, and when it was delivered she wanted to give it to me. She uttered that sort of magic formula (*Hello, this is Signora Carracci*) and then she negotiated, discussed, gave up, bought. She didn't pay, the shopkeepers were all from the neighborhood, they knew Stefano well. She merely signed, *Lina Carracci*, name and last name, as Maestra Oliviero had taught us, and she wrote the signature as if it were an assignment, with an intent half-smile, never even checking the merchandise, as if those marks on paper mattered more to her than the objects that were being delivered.

She also bought some big albums with green covers decorated with floral motifs, in which she arranged the wedding photographs. She had printed just for me copies of I don't know how many of them, all the ones in which I, my parents, my sister and brothers, even Antonio appeared. She telephoned and ordered the photographs. I found one in which Nino could be seen: there was Alfonso, there was Marisa, and he was at the right, cut off by the edge of the frame, only his hair, his nose, his mouth.

"Can I have this, too?" I asked without much enthusiasm.

"You're not in it."

"I'm here, from the back."

"All right, if you want it I'll have it printed for you."

I abruptly changed my mind.

"No, forget it."

"Really, go ahead."

"No."

But the acquisition that most impressed me was the projector. The movie of the wedding had finally been developed; the photographer came one night to show it to the newlyweds and their relatives. Lila found out how much the machine cost, she had one delivered to her house and invited me to watch the film. She put the projector on the dining-room table, took a painting of a stormy sea off the wall, expertly inserted the film, lowered the blinds, and the images began to flow over the white wall. It was a marvel: the movie was in color, just a few minutes long. I was astonished. Again I saw her enter the church on Fernando's arm, come out into the church square with Stefano, their happy walk through the Parco delle Rimembranze, ending with a long kiss, the entrance into the restaurant, the dance that followed, the relatives eating or dancing, the cutting of the cake, the handing out of the favors, the goodbyes addressed to the lens, Stefano happy, she grim, both in their traveling clothes.

The first time I saw it I was struck most of all by myself. I appeared twice. First in the church square, beside Antonio: I looked awkward, nervous, my face taken up by my glasses. The second time, I was sitting at the table with Nino, and was barely recognizable: I was laughing, hands and arms moved with casual elegance, I adjusted my hair, toyed with my mother's bracelet—I seemed to myself refined and beautiful.

Lila in fact exclaimed, "Look how well you came out."

"Not really," I lied.

"You look the way you do when you're happy."

The second time we watched (I said to her, Play it again, she didn't have to be asked twice), what struck me instead was the Solaras' entrance into the restaurant. The cameraman had caught the moment that had registered most profoundly in me: the moment Nino left the room and Marcello and Michele burst in. The two brothers entered side by side, in their dress clothes; they were tall and muscular, thanks to the time they spent in the gym lifting weights; meanwhile Nino, slipping out, head lowered, just bumped Marcello's arm, and as Marcello abruptly turned, with a mean, bullying look, he vanished, indifferent, without looking back.

The contrast seemed violent. It wasn't so much the poverty of Nino's clothes, which clashed with the opulence of the Solaras', with the gold they wore on their necks and their wrists and their fingers. It wasn't even his extreme thinness, which was accentuated by his height—he was at least three inches taller than the brothers, who were tall, too—and which suggested a fragility opposed to the virile strength that Marcello and Michele displayed with smug satisfaction. Rather, it was the indifference. While the Solaras' arrogance could be considered normal, the haughty carelessness with which Nino had bumped into Marcello and kept going was not at all normal. Even those who detested the Solaras, like Pasquale, Enzo, or Antonio, had, one way or another, to reckon with them. Nino, on the other hand, not only didn't apologize but didn't so much as glance at Marcello.

The scene provided documentary proof of what I had intuited as I was experiencing it in reality. In that sequence Sarratore's son—who had grown up in the run-down buildings of the old neighborhood just like us, and who had seemed so frightened when it came to defeating Alfonso in the school competitions—now appeared completely outside the scale of values at whose peak stood the Solaras. It was a hierarchy that visibly did not interest him, that perhaps he no longer understood.

Looking at him, I was seduced. He seemed to me an ascetic prince who could intimidate Michele and Marcello merely by means of a gaze that didn't see them. And for an instant I hoped that now, in the image, he would do what he had not done in reality: take me away.

Lila noticed Nino only then, and said, curious, "Is that the same person you sat with at the table with Alfonso?"

"Yes. Didn't you recognize him? It's Nino, the oldest son of Sarratore."

"He's the one who kissed you when you were on Ischia?"

"It was nothing."

"Just as well."

"Why just as well?"

"He's a person who thinks he's somebody."

As if to excuse that impression I said, "This year he graduates and he's the best in the whole school."

"You like him because of that?"

"No."

"Forget him, Lenù, Antonio is better."

"You think?"

"Yes. He's skinny, ugly, and most of all really arrogant."

I heard the three adjectives like an insult and was on the point of saying: it's not true, he's handsome, his eyes sparkle, and I'm sorry you don't realize it, because a boy like that doesn't exist in the movies or on television or even in novels, and I'm happy that I've loved him since I was little, and even if he's out of my reach, even if I'm going to marry Antonio and spend my life pumping gas, I will love him more than myself, I'll love him forever.

Instead, unhappy again, I said, "I used to like him, in elementary school: I don't anymore."

12.

The months that followed were packed with small events that tormented me a great deal, and even today I find it difficult to put them in order. Although I imposed on myself an appearance of self-assurance and an iron discipline, I gave in continuously, with painful pleasure, to waves of unhappiness. Everything seemed to be against me. At school I couldn't get the grades I used to, even though I had begun to study again. The days passed without even a moment during which I felt alive. The road to school, the one to Lila's house, the one to the ponds were colorless backdrops. Tense, discouraged, I ended up, almost without realizing it, blaming Antonio for a good part of my troubles.

He, too, was very upset. He wanted to see me continuously, sometimes he left work and I found him waiting for me, self-conscious, on the sidewalk across from the school entrance. He was worried about the crazy behavior of his mother, Melina, and was frightened by the possibility that he wouldn't be exempted from military service. He had submitted, in time, application after application to the recruiting office documenting the death of his father, the condition of his mother's health, his role as the sole support of his family, and it seemed that the Army, overwhelmed by the papers, had decided to forget about him. But now he had learned that Enzo Scanno was to leave in the autumn and he was afraid that his turn would come, too. "I can't leave my mother and Ada and the other children with no money and no protection," he said in despair.

One day he appeared at school out of breath: he had learned that the carabinieri had come to get information about him.

"Ask Lina," he said anxiously, "ask her if Stefano had an exemption because his mother is widowed or for some other reason."

I soothed him, tried to distract him. I organized an evening for him at the pizzeria with Pasquale and Enzo and their girl-friends, Ada and Carmela. I hoped that, seeing his friends, he would calm down, but it didn't help. Enzo, as usual, showed not the least emotion about his departure, he was sorry only because, while he was in the Army, his father would have to go back to walking the streets with the cart, and his health wasn't good. As for Pasquale, he revealed somewhat morosely that he had been rejected for military service because of an old tuber-cular infection. But he said that he regretted it, one ought to be a soldier, though not to serve the country. People like us, he muttered, have a duty to learn to use weapons, because soon the time will come when those who should pay will pay. From there we went on to discuss politics, or, to be exact, Pasquale did, and in a very intolerant way. He said that the Fascists wanted to return to power with the help of the Christian Democrats. He said that the police and the Army were on their side. He said that we had to be prepared, and he spoke in par-ticular to Enzo, who nodded assent and, though he was gener-ally silent, said, with a little laugh, don't worry, when I get back I'll show you how to shoot.

Ada and Carmela appeared very impressed by that conver-sation, and pleased to be the girlfriends of such dangerous men. I would have liked to speak, but I knew little or nothing of alliances between Fascists, Christian Democrats, and police, in my head I had not even a thought. Every so often I looked at Antonio, hoping that he would get excited about the subject, but he didn't, he just kept trying to go back to what was tor-turing him. He asked over and over what it was like in the Army, and Pasquale, even though he hadn't been there, answered: a real shithole, if you don't knuckle under they break you. Enzo was silent, as if the question didn't concern him. Antonio, on the other hand, stopped eating, and, playing with the pizza on his plate, kept saying things like: They don't know who they're dealing with, let them just try, I'll break them.

When we were alone he said to me, all of a sudden, in a depressed tone of voice, "I know if I leave you won't wait for me, you'll go with someone else."

. At that point I understood. The problem wasn't Melina, wasn't Ada, wasn't his other brothers and sisters, who would be left without a means of support, and it wasn't even the harassments of Army life. The problem was me. He didn't want to leave me, even for a minute, and it seemed that no matter what I said or did to reassure him he wouldn't believe me. I decided to take the offensive. I told him to follow the example of Enzo: He's confident, I whispered, if he has to go he goes, he doesn't whine, even if he's just gotten engaged to Carmela. Whereas you're complaining for no reason, yes, for no reason, Antò, especially since you won't go, because if Stefano Carracci got an exemption as the son of a widowed mother, certainly you will, too.

That slightly aggressive, slightly affectionate tone eased him. But before saying goodbye he repeated, in embarrassment, "Ask your friend."

"She's your friend, too."

"Yes, but you ask."

The next day I talked to Lila about it, but she didn't know anything about her husband's military service; reluctantly she promised that she would find out.

She didn't do it immediately, as I'd hoped. There were constant tensions with Stefano and with Stefano's family. Maria had told her son that his wife spent too much money. Pinuccia made trouble about the new grocery, she said that she wasn't going to be involved, if anyone it should be her sister-in-law. Stefano silenced his mother and sister, but in the end he reproached his wife for her excessive spending, and tried to find out whether she might if necessary be willing to work in the new store.

Lila in that period became, even in my eyes, particularly evasive. She said that she would spend less, she readily agreed to work in the grocery, but meanwhile she spent more than before and if previously she had stopped in at the new shop out of curiosity or duty she no longer did even that. Now that the bruises on her face were gone, she had an urgent desire to go out, especially in the morning, when I was at school.

She would go for a walk with Pinuccia, and they vied to see who was better dressed, who could buy more useless things. Usually Pina won, mainly because, with a lot of coyly childish looks, she managed to get money from Rino, who felt obliged to prove that he was more generous than his brother-in-law.

"I work all day," said the fiancé to the fiancée. "Have fun for me, too."

And proudly casual, in front of the workers and his father, he pulled out of his pants pocket a crumpled fistful of money, offered it to Pina, and immediately afterward made a teasing gesture of giving some to his sister, too.

His behavior irritated Lila, like a gust of wind that causes a door to slam and knocks objects off a shelf. But she also saw signs that the shoe factory was finally taking off, and all in all she was pleased that Cerullo shoes were now displayed in many shops in the city, the spring models were selling well, the reorders were increasing. As a result Stefano had taken over the basement under the factory and had transformed it into a warehouse and workshop, while Fernando and Rino had had to hire another assistant in a hurry and sometimes even worked at night.

Naturally there were disputes. The shoe store that the Solaras had undertaken to open in Piazza dei Martiri had to be furnished at Stefano's expense, and he, alarmed by the fact that no written contract had ever been drawn up, squabbled a lot with Marcello and Michele. But now it seemed that they were arriving at a private agreement that would set out in black and white the figure (slightly inflated) that Carracci intended to invest in the furnishings. And Rino was very satisfied with the result: while his brother-in-law put down the money, he acted like the boss, as if he had done it himself.

"If things continue like this, next year we'll get married," he promised his fiancée, and one morning Pina decided to go to the same dressmaker who had made Lila's dress, just to look.

The dressmaker welcomed them cordially, then, since she was crazy about Lila, asked her to describe the wedding in detail, and insisted on having a large photograph of her in the wedding dress. Lila had one printed for her and she and Pina went to give it to her.

As they were walking on the Rettifilo, Lila asked her sister-in-law how it happened that Stefano hadn't done his military service: if the carabinieri had come to verify his status as the son of a widowed mother, if the exemption had been communicated by mail from the recruiting office or if he had had to find out in person.

Pinuccia looked at her ironically.

"Son of a widowed mother?"

"Yes, Antonio says that if you're in that situation they don't make you go."

"I know that the only certain way not to go is to pay."

"Pay whom?"

"The people in the recruiting office."

"Stefano paid?"

"Yes, but you mustn't tell anyone."

"And how much did he pay?"

"I don't know. The Solaras took care of everything."

Lila froze.

"Meaning?"

"You know, don't you, that neither Marcello nor Michele served in the Army. They got out of it owing to thoracic insufficiency."

"Them? How is that possible?"

"Contacts."

"And Stefano?"

"He went to the same contacts as Marcello and Michele. You pay and the contacts do you a favor."

That afternoon my friend reported everything to me, but it was as if she didn't grasp how bad the information was for Antonio. She was electrified—yes, electrified—by the discovery that the alliance between her husband and the Solaras did not originate in the obligations imposed by business but were of long standing, preceding even their engagement.

"He deceived me from the start," she repeated, with a kind of satisfaction, as if the story of military service were the definitive proof of Stefano's true nature and now she felt somehow liberated. It took time before I was able to ask her, "Do you think that if the recruiting office doesn't give Antonio an exemption the Solaras would do a favor for him, too?"

She gave me her mean look, as if I had said something hostile, and cut me off: "Antonio would never go to the Solaras."

13.

I did not report a single word of that conversation to my boyfriend. I avoided meeting him, I told him I had too much homework and a lot of class oral exams coming up.

It wasn't an excuse, school was really hell. The local authority harassed the principal, the principal harassed the teachers, the teachers harassed the students, the students tormented each other. A large number of us couldn't stand the load of homework, but we were glad that there was class on alternate days. There was a minority, however, who were angry about the decrepit state of the school building and the loss of class time, and who wanted an immediate return to the normal schedule. At the head of this faction was Nino Sarratore, and this was to further complicate my life.

I saw him whispering in the hall with Professor Galiani; I passed by hoping that the professor would call me over. She didn't. So then I hoped that he would speak to me, but he didn't, either. I felt disgraced. I'm not able to get the grades I used to, I thought, and so in no time I've lost the little respect I had. On the other hand—I thought bitterly—what do I expect? If Nino or Professor Galiani asked my opinion on this business of the unused classrooms and too much homework, what would I say? I didn't have opinions, in fact, and I realized it when Nino appeared one morning with a typewritten sheet of paper and asked abruptly, "Will you read it?"

My heart was beating so hard that I said only, "Now?"

"No, give it back to me after school."

I was overwhelmed by my emotions. I ran to the bathroom and read in great agitation. The page was full of figures and discussed things I knew nothing of: plan for the city, school construction, the Italian constitution, certain fundamental articles. I understood only what I already knew, which was that Nino was demanding an immediate return to the normal schedule of classes.

In class I showed the paper to Alfonso.

"Forget it," he advised me, without even reading it. "We're at the end of the year, we've got final examinations, that would get you in trouble."

But it was as if I had gone mad, my temples were pounding, my throat was tight. No one else, in the school, exposed himself the way Nino did, without fear of the teachers or the principal. Not only was he the best in every subject but he knew things that were not taught, that no student, even a good one, knew. And he had character. And he was handsome. I counted the hours, the minutes, the seconds. I was in a hurry to give him back his page, to praise it, to tell him that I agreed with everything, that I wanted to help him.

I didn't see him on the stairs, in the crush of students, and in the street I couldn't find him. He was among the last to come out, and his expression was more morose than usual. I went to meet him, cheerfully waving the paper, and I poured out a profusion of words, all exaggerated. He listened to me frowning, then he took the piece of paper, angrily crumpled it up, and threw it away.

"Galiani said it's no good," he mumbled.

I was confused.

"What's no good about it?"

He scowled unhappily and made a gesture that meant forget about it, it's not worth talking about.

"Anyway, thank you," he said in a somewhat forced manner, and suddenly he leaned over and kissed me on the cheek.

Since the kiss on Ischia we had had no contact, not even a handshake, and that way of parting, utterly unusual at the time, paralyzed me. He didn't ask me to walk a little distance with him, he didn't say goodbye: everything ended there. Without energy, without voice, I watched him walk away.

At that point two terrible things happened, one after the other. First, a girl came out of a narrow street, a girl certainly younger than me, at most fifteen, whose pure beauty was striking: she had a nice figure, and smooth black hair that hung down her back; every gesture or movement had a gracefulness, every item of her spring outfit had a deliberate restraint. She met Nino, he put an arm around her shoulders, she lifted her face, offering him her mouth, and they kissed: a kiss very different from the one he had given me. Right afterward I realized that Antonio was at the corner. He was supposed to be at work and instead he had come to get me. Who knew how long he had been there.

14.

It was hard to convince him that what he had seen with his

own eyes was not what he had for a long time imagined but only a friendly gesture, with no other purpose. "He's already got a girlfriend," I said, "you saw it yourself." But he must have caught a trace of suffering in those words, and he threatened me, his lower lip and his hands began to tremble. Then I muttered that I was tired of this, I wanted to leave him. He gave in, and we made up. But from that moment on he trusted me even less, and the anxiety of departure for military service was welded conclusively to the fear of leaving me to Nino. More and more often he abandoned his job to be in time, he said, to meet me. In reality his aim was to catch me in the act and prove, to himself above all, that I really was unfaithful. What he would do then not even he knew.

One afternoon his sister Ada saw me passing the grocery, where she now worked, to her great satisfaction and to Stefano's. She ran out to see me. She wore a greasy white smock that covered her to below the knees, but she was still very pretty and it was clear from her lipstick, her made-up eyes, the pins in her hair that, under the smock, she was dressed as if for a party. She said she wanted to talk to me, and we agreed to meet in the courtyard before dinner. She arrived breathless from the grocery, along with Pasquale, who had picked her up.

They spoke to me together, an embarrassed phrase from one, an embarrassed phrase from the other. I understood that they were worried: Antonio lost his temper for no reason, he no longer had patience with Melina, he was absent without warning from work. And even Gallese, the owner of the shop, was upset, because he had known him since he was a boy and had never seen him like this.

"He's afraid of military service," I said.

"So if they call him, of course he has to go," Pasquale said, "otherwise he becomes a deserter."

"When you're around, it all goes away," said Ada.

"I don't have much time," I said.

"People are more important than school," said Pasquale.

"Spend less time with Lina, and you'll see, you'll find the time," said Ada.

"I do what I can," I said, offended.

"His nerves are fragile," Pasquale said.

Ada concluded abruptly, "I've been taking care of a crazy person since I was a child—two would really be too much, Lenù."

I was annoyed, and scared. Filled with a sense of guilt, I went back to seeing Antonio often, even though I didn't want to, even though I had to study. It wasn't enough. One night at the ponds he began to cry, he showed me a card. He hadn't received an exemption, he was to leave with Enzo, in the fall. And at a certain point he did something extremely upsetting. He fell on the ground and in a frenzy began sticking handfuls of dirt in his mouth. I had to hold him tight, say that I loved him, wipe the dirt out of his mouth with my fingers.

What kind of mess am I getting myself into, I thought later, in bed, unable to sleep, and I discovered that suddenly the wish to leave school—to accept myself for what I was, to marry him, to live at his mother's house with his siblings, pumping gas—had faded. I decided that I had to do something to help him and, when he recovered, get myself out of that relationship.

The next day I went to Lila's, really frightened. I found her overly cheerful; during that period we were both unsettled. I told her about Antonio, and the card, and I told her that I had made a decision: in secret from him, because he would never give me permission, I intended to go to Marcello or even Michele to ask if they could get him out of his predicament.

I was exaggerating my determination. In reality I was confused: on the one hand it seemed to me that I was obliged to try, since I was the cause of Antonio's suffering; on the other, I was consulting Lila precisely because I took it for granted that she would tell me not to. But I was so absorbed by my own emotional chaos that I hadn't taken into account hers.

Her reaction was equivocal. First she teased me, she said I was a liar, she said I must really love my boyfriend if I was willing to go in person and humble myself with the Solaras, even though I knew that, given all that had happened, they would not lift a finger for him. Immediately afterward, however, she began nervously going in circles, she laughed, became serious, laughed again. Finally she said: all right, go, let's see what happens. And then she added:

"After all, Lenù, where's the difference between my brother and Michele Solara or, let's say, between Stefano and Marcello?"

"What do you mean?"

"I mean that maybe I should have married Marcello."

"I don't understand you."

"At least Marcello isn't dependent on anyone, he does as he likes."

"Are you serious?"

She quickly denied that she was, laughing, but she didn't convince me. She can't possibly be reconsidering Marcello, I thought: all that laughter isn't real, it's just a sign of ugly thoughts, of suffering because things aren't going well with her husband.

I had proof of that immediately. She became thoughtful, she narrowed her eyes to cracks, she said, "I'm going with you."

"Where."

"To the Solaras."

"To do what?"

"To see if they can help Antonio."

"No."

"Why?"

"You'll make Stefano angry."

"Who gives a damn. If he goes to them, I can, too, I'm his wife."

15.

I couldn't stop her. One Sunday—on Sundays Stefano slept until noon—we were going out for a walk and she pressed me to go to the Bar Solara. When she appeared on the new street, still white with lime, I was astonished. She was extravagantly dressed and made up: she was neither the shabby Lila of long ago nor the Jackie Kennedy of the glossy magazines but, based on the films we liked, maybe Jennifer Jones in *Duel in the Sun*, maybe Ava Gardner in *The Sun Also Rises*.

Walking next to her I felt embarrassment and also a sense of danger. It seemed to me that she was risking not only gossip but ridicule, and that both reflected on me, a sort of colorless but loyal puppy who served as her escort. Everything about her—the hair, the earrings, the close-fitting blouse, the tight skirt, the way she walked—was unsuitable for the gray streets of the neighborhood. Male gazes, at the sight of her, seemed to start, as if offended. The women, especially the old ones, didn't limit themselves to bewildered expressions: some stopped on the edge of the sidewalk and stood watching her, with a laugh that was both amused and uneasy, as when Melina did odd things on the street.

And yet when we entered the Bar Solara, which was crowded with men buying the Sunday pastries, there was only a respectful ogling, some polite nods of greeting, the truly admiring gaze of Gigliola Spagnuolo behind the counter, and a greeting from Michele, at the cash register—an exaggerated hello that was like an exclamation of joy. The verbal exchanges that followed were all in dialect, as if tension prevented any engagement with the laborious filters of Italian pronunciation, vocabulary, syntax.

"What would you like?"

"A dozen pastries."

Michele shouted at Gigliola, this time with a slight hint of sarcasm:

"Twelve pastries for Signora Carracci."

At that name, the curtain that opened onto the bakery was pushed aside and Marcello looked out. At the sight of Lila right there, in his bar and pastry shop, he grew pale and retreated. But a few seconds later he came out again and greeted her. He mumbled, to my friend, "It's a shock to hear you called Signora Carracci."

"To me, too," Lila said, and her amused half-smile, her total absence of hostility, surprised not only me but the two brothers as well.

Michele examined her carefully, his head inclined to one side, as if he were looking at a painting.

"We saw you," he said, and called to Gigliola. "Right, Gigliò, didn't we see her yesterday afternoon?"

Gigliola nodded yes, unenthusiastically. And Marcello agreed—*saw, yes saw*—but without Michele's sarcasm, rather as if he had been hypnotized at a magic show.

"Yesterday afternoon?" Lila asked.

"Yesterday afternoon," Michele confirmed, "on the Rettifilo."

Marcello came to the point, irritated by his brother's tone of voice. "You were on display in the dressmaker's window—there's a photograph of you in your wedding dress."

They talked a little about the photograph, Marcello with devotion, Michele with irony, both asserting in different ways how perfectly it captured Lila's beauty on her wedding day. She seemed annoyed, but playfully: the dressmaker hadn't told her she would put the picture in the window, otherwise she would never have given it to her.

"I want *my* picture in the window," Gigliola cried from behind the counter, imitating the petulant voice of a child.

"If someone marries you," said Michele.

"You're marrying me," she replied darkly, and went on like that until Lila said seriously:

"Lenuccia wants to get married, too."

The attention of the Solara brothers shifted reluctantly to me; until then I had felt invisible, and hadn't said a word.

"No." I blushed.

"Why not, I'd marry you, even if you are four-eyed," said Michele, catching another black look from Gigliola.

"Too late, she's already engaged," said Lila. And slowly she managed to lead the two brothers around to Antonio, evoking his family situation, including a vivid picture of how much worse it would be if he had to go into the Army. It wasn't just her skill with words that struck me, that I knew. What struck me was a new tone, a shrewd dose of impudence and assurance. There she was, her mouth flaming with lipstick. She made Marcello believe that she had put a seal on the past, made Michele believe that his sly arrogance amused her. And, to my great amazement, toward both she behaved like a woman who knows what men are, who has nothing more to learn on the subject and in fact would have much to teach: and she wasn't playing a part, the way we had as girls, imitating novels in which fallen ladies appeared; rather, it was clear that her knowledge was true, and this did not embarrass her. Then abruptly she became aloof, she sent out signals of refusal, I know you want me but I don't want you. Thus she retreated, throwing them off balance, so that Marcello became self-conscious and Michele darkened, irresolute, with a hard gaze that meant: Watch it, because, Signora Carracci or not, I'm ready to slap you in the face, you whore. At that point she changed her tone again, again drew them toward her, appeared to be amused and amused them. The result? Michele didn't commit himself, but Marcello said: "Antonio doesn't deserve it, but Lenuccia's a good girl, so to make her happy I can ask a friend and find out if something can be done."

I felt satisfied, I thanked him.

Lila chose the pastries, was friendly toward Gigliola and also toward her father, the pastry maker, who poked his head out of the bakery to say: Hello to Stefano. When she tried to pay, Marcello made a clear gesture of refusal, and his brother, if less decisively, seconded him. We were about to leave when Michele said to her seriously, in the slow tone he assumed when he wanted something and ruled out any disagreement:

"You look great in that photograph."

"Thank you."

"The shoes are very conspicuous."

"I don't remember."

"I remember and I want to ask you something."

"You want a photo, too, you want to put it up here in the bar?"

Michele shook his head with a cold little laugh.

"No. But you know that we're getting the shop ready in Piazza dei Martiri."

"I don't know anything about your affairs."

"Well, you should find out, because our affairs are important and we all know that you're not stupid. I think that if that photograph is useful to the dressmaker as an advertisement for a wedding dress, we can make much better use of it as an advertisement for Cerullo shoes."

Lila burst out laughing, she said, "You want to put that photograph in the window in Piazza dei Martiri?"

"No, I want it enlarged, huge, in the shop."

She thought about it for a moment, then made a gesture of indifference.

"Don't ask me, ask Stefano, he's the one who decides."

I saw the brothers exchange a puzzled glance, and I understood that they had already discussed the idea and had assumed that Lila would never agree, so they couldn't believe that she hadn't been indignant, that she hadn't immediately said no, but had surrendered without argument to the authority of her husband. They didn't recognize her, and, right then, even I didn't know who she was.

Marcello went to the door with us. Outside, he became solemn, and said, "This is the first time in a long while that we've spoken, Lina, and it's disturbing. You and I didn't go with each other—all right, that's the way it is. But I don't want anything between us to remain unclear. And especially I don't want blame that I don't deserve. I know that your husband goes around saying that as an insult I claimed those shoes. But I swear to you in front of Lenuccia: he and your brother gave me the shoes to demonstrate that there was no more bad feeling. I had nothing to do with it."

Lila listened without interrupting, a sympathetic expression on her face. Then, as soon as he had finished, she became herself again. She said with contempt, "You're like children, accusing each other."

"You don't believe me?"

"No, Marcè, I believe you. But what you say, what they say, I don't give a damn about it anymore."

16.

I dragged Lila into our old courtyard, I couldn't wait to tell Antonio what I had done for him. I confided to her, trembling with excitement: as soon as he calms down a little, I'll leave him, but she had no comment, she seemed distracted.

I called. Antonio looked out, came down, serious. He said hello to Lila, apparently without noticing how she was dressed, how she was made up, in fact trying to look at her as little as possible, maybe because he was afraid that I would read in his face some male agitation. I told him that I couldn't stay, I had only time to give him some good news. He listened, but as I was speaking I realized that he was pulling back as if before the point of a knife. He promised he'll help you, I said anyway, emphatically, enthusiastically, and asked Lila to confirm it.

"Marcello said so, right?"

Lila confined herself to assenting. But Antonio had turned very pale, he lowered his eyes. He muttered, in a strangled voice:

"I never asked you to talk to the Solaras."

Lila said right away, lying, "It was my idea."

Antonio answered without looking at her. "Thank you, it wasn't necessary."

He said goodbye to her—said goodbye to her, not to me—turned his back, and vanished into the doorway.

I felt sick to my stomach. Where was my mistake, why had he gotten angry like that? On the street I exploded, saying to Lila that Antonio was worse than his mother, Melina, the same unstable blood, I couldn't take it anymore. She let me speak and meanwhile wanted me go to her house with her. When we got there, she asked me to come in.

"Stefano's there," I objected, but that wasn't the reason. I was upset by Antonio's reaction and wanted to be alone, to figure out where I had made the mistake.

"Five minutes and you can go."

I went up. Stefano was in his pajamas, disheveled, unshaved. He greeted me politely, glanced at his wife, at the package of pastries.

"You were at the Bar Solara?"

"Yes."

"Dressed like that?"

"I don't look nice?"

Stefano shook his head ill-humoredly, opened the package.

"Would you like a pastry, Lenù?"

"No, thank you, I have to go and eat."

He bit into a pastry, turned to his wife. "Who did you see at the bar?"

"Your friends," said Lila. "They paid me a lot of compliments. Isn't that true, Lenù?"

She recounted every word the Solaras had said to her, except the matter of Antonio, that is to say the real reason we had gone to the bar, the reason that, I thought, she had decided to go with me. Then she concluded, in a tone of deliberate satisfaction, "Michele wants to put an enlargement of the photograph in the store in Piazza dei Martiri."

"And you told him it was all right?"

"I told him they had to speak to you."

Stefano finished the pastry in a single bite, then licked his fingers. He said, as if this were what had upset him most, "See what you force me to do? Tomorrow, because of you, I have to go and waste time with the dressmaker on the Rettifilo." He sighed, he turned to me: "Lenù, you who are a respectable girl, try to explain to your friend that I have to work in this neighborhood, that she shouldn't make me look like a jerk. Have a good Sunday, and say hello to Papa and Mamma for me."

He went into the bathroom.

Lila behind his back made a teasing grimace, then went with me to the door.

"I'll stay if you want," I said.

"He's a son of a bitch, don't worry."

She repeated, in a heavy male voice, words like *try to explain to your friend, she shouldn't make me look like a jerk*, and the caricature made her eyes light up.

"If he beats you?"

"What can beatings do to me? A little time goes by and I'm better than before."

On the landing she said again, again in a masculine voice:

Lenù, I have to work in this neighborhood, and then I felt obliged to do Antonio, I whispered, *Thank you, but there was no need,* and suddenly it was as if we saw ourselves from the outside, both of us in trouble with our men, standing there on the threshold, actors in a recital of women, and we started laughing. I said: The minute we move we've done something wrong, who can understand men, ah, how much trouble they are. I hugged her warmly, and left. But I hadn't even reached the bottom of the stairs when I heard Stefano shouting odious curses. Now he had the voice of an ogre, like his father's.

17.

Already on the way home I began to worry both about her and about me. If Stefano killed her? If Antonio killed me? I was racked by anxiety, I walked quickly, in the dusty heat, along Sunday streets that were beginning to empty as lunchtime approached. How difficult it was to find one's way, how difficult it was not to violate any of the incredibly detailed male regulations. Lila, perhaps based on secret calculations of her own, perhaps only out of spite, had humiliated her husband by going to flirt in front of everyone—she, Signora Carracci—with her former wooer Marcello Solara. I, without intending to, in fact convinced that I was doing good, had gone to argue the case of Antonio with those who years before had insulted his sister, who had beaten him up, whom he in turn had beaten up. When I entered the courtyard, I heard someone calling me, I started. It was him, he was at the window waiting for me to return.

He came down and I was afraid. I thought: he must have a knife. Instead, the whole time he spoke with his hands sunk in his pockets as if to keep them prisoner, calmly, his gaze distant. He said that I had humiliated him in front of the people he despised most in the world. He said I had made him look like someone who sends his woman to ask a favor. He said that he would not go down on his knees to anyone and that he would be a soldier not once but a hundred times, that in fact he would die in the Army rather than go and kiss the hand of Marcello Solara. He said that if Pasquale and Enzo should find out, they would spit in his face. He said that he was leaving me, because he had had the proof, finally, that I cared nothing about him and his feelings. He said that I could say and do with the son of Sarratore what I liked, he never wanted to see me again.

I couldn't reply. Suddenly he took his hands out of his pockets, pulled me inside the doorway and kissed me, pressing his lips hard against mine, searching my mouth desperately with his tongue. Then he pulled away, turned his back, and left.

I went up the stairs in confusion. I thought that I was more fortunate than Lila, Antonio wasn't like Stefano. He would never hurt me, the only person he could hurt was himself.

18.

I didn't see Lila the next day, but, surprisingly, I was compelled to see her husband.

That morning I had gone to school depressed: it was hot, I hadn't studied, I had scarcely slept. The school day had been a disaster. I had looked for Nino outside, I would have liked to talk just a little, but I didn't see him, maybe he was wandering through the city with his girlfriend, maybe he was in one of the movie theaters that were open in the morning, kissing her in the dark, maybe he was in the woods at Capodimonte having her do to him the things I had done to Antonio for months. In the first class I had been interrogated in chemistry and had given muddled or inadequate answers; who knows what grade I had received, and there wasn't time to make it up, I was in danger of having to retake the exam in September. I had met Professor Galiani in the hall and she had given me a gentle speech whose meaning was: What is happening to you, Greco, why aren't you studying anymore? And I had been unable to say anything but: Professor, I am studying, I'm studying all the time, I swear; she listened to me for a bit and then walked away and went into the teachers' lounge. I had had a long cry in the bathroom, a cry of self-pity for how wretched my life was. I had lost everything: success in school; Antonio, whom I had always wanted to leave, and who in the end had left me, and already I missed him; Lila, who since she had become Signora Carracci was more removed every day. Worn out by a headache, I had walked home thinking of her, of how she had used me—yes, used—to provoke the Solaras, to get revenge on her husband, to show him to me in his misery as a wounded male, and the whole way I wondered: Is it possible that a person can change like that, that now there's nothing to distinguish her from someone like Gigliola?

But at home there was a surprise. My mother didn't attack me the way she usually did because I was late and she suspected I had been seeing Antonio, or because I had neglected one of the thousands of household tasks. She said to me instead, with a sort of gentle annoyance, "Stefano asked me if you could go with him this afternoon to the dressmaker's on the Rettifilo."

Befuddled by tiredness and discouragement, I thought I hadn't understood. Stefano? Stefano Carracci? He wanted me to go with him to the Rettifilo?

"Why doesn't he go with his wife?" my father joked from the other room. Formally he was taking a sick day but in reality he had to keep an eye on some of his indecipherable deals. "How do those two pass the time? Do they play cards?"

My mother made a gesture of annoyance. She said maybe Lila was busy, she said we ought to be nice to the Carraccis, she said some people were never satisfied with anything. In reality my father was more than satisfied: to have good relations with the grocer meant that one could buy food on credit and put off paying indefinitely. But he liked to be witty. Lately, whenever the occasion arose, he had found it amusing to make allusions to Stefano's presumed sexual laziness. At the table every so often he would ask: What's Carracci doing, he only likes television? And he laughed and it didn't take much to guess the meaning of his question: how is it that the two of them don't have any children, does Stefano function or not? My mother, who in those matters understood him immediately, answered seriously: It's early, leave them alone, what do you expect? But in fact she enjoyed as much as or more than he the idea that the grocer Carracci, in spite of the money he had, didn't function.

The table was already set; they were waiting for me. My father continued to joke, with a half-sly expression, saying to my mother: "Have I ever said to you, I'm sorry, tonight I'm tired, let's play cards?"

"No, because you are not a respectable person."

"And would you like me to become a respectable person?"

"A little, but don't exaggerate."

"So starting tonight I'll be a respectable person like Stefano."

"I said don't exaggerate."

How I hated those duets. They talked as if they were sure that my brothers and sister and I couldn't understand; or maybe they took it for granted that we caught every nuance, but they considered that it was the proper way to teach us how to be males and how to be females. Exhausted by my problems, I felt like screaming—throw away the plate, run out, never see my family again, the dampness in the corners of the ceiling, the flaking walls, the odor of food, any of it. Antonio:

how foolish I had been to lose him, I was already sorry, I wished he would forgive me. If they make me retake the exams in September, I said to myself, I won't show up, I'll fail, I'll marry him right away. Then I thought of Lila, how she had dressed, the tone she had taken with the Solaras, what she had in mind, how spiteful humiliation and suffering were making her. My mind wandered like that all afternoon, with disconnected thoughts. A bath in the tub of the new house, anxiety about that request of Stefano's, how to tell my friend, what her husband wanted from me. And chemistry. And Empedocles. And school. And quitting school. And finally a cold sadness. There was no escape. No, neither Lila nor I would ever become like the girl who had waited for Nino after school. We both lacked something intangible but fundamental, which was obvious in her even if you simply saw her from a distance, and which one possessed or did not, because to have that thing it was not enough to learn Latin or Greek or philosophy, nor was the money from groceries or shoes of any use.

Stefano called from the courtyard. I hurried down and immediately saw in his face an expression of despair. He said he wanted me to go with him to retrieve the photograph that the dressmaker had displayed in her window without permission. Do me this kindness, he muttered, in a sentimental tone of voice. Then without a word he opened the door of the convertible, and we drove off, assailed by the hot wind.

As soon as we were out of the neighborhood he started talking and he didn't stop until we got to the dressmaker's. He spoke in a mild dialect, without cursing or joking. He began by saying that I must do him a favor, but he didn't immediately explain what the favor was, he said only, stumbling over his words, that if I did it for him, it would be as if I were doing it for my friend. Then he went on to talk to me about Lila, how intelligent, how beautiful she was. But she is rebellious by nature, he added, and either you do things the way she says or she torments you. Lenù, you don't know what I'm suffering, or maybe you do know, but all you know is what she tells you. Now, listen to me, too. Lina has a fixed idea that all I think about is money, and maybe it's true, but I'm doing it for the family, for her brother, for her father, for all her relatives. Am I wrong? You are very educated, tell me if I'm wrong. What does she want from me—the poverty she comes from? Should only the Solaras make money? Do we want to leave the neighborhood in their hands? If you tell me I'm wrong, I won't argue with you, I will immediately admit that I'm wrong. But with her I have to argue whether I want to or not. She doesn't want me, she told me, she repeats it to me. Making her understand that I'm her husband is a battle, and ever since I got married life has been unbearable. To see her in the morning, in the evening, to sleep next to her and not be able to make her feel how much I love her, with the strength I'm capable of, is a terrible thing.

I looked at his broad hands gripping the steering wheel, his face. With tears in his eyes, he admitted that on their wedding night he had had to beat her, that he had been forced to do it, that every morning, every evening she drew slaps from his hands on purpose to humiliate him, forcing him to act in a way that he never, ever, ever would have wanted. Here he assumed an almost frightened tone: I had to beat her again, she shouldn't have gone to the Solaras' dressed like that. But she has a force inside that I can't subdue. It's an evil force that makes good manners—everything—useless. A poison. You see she's not pregnant? Months pass and nothing happens. Relatives, friends, customers ask, and you can see the mockery on their faces: any news? And I have to say, what news, pretending not to understand. Because if I understood I would have to answer. And what can I answer? There are things you know that can't be said. With that force she has, she murders the children inside, Lenù, and she does it on purpose to make people think

I don't know how to be a man, to show me up in front of everyone. What do you think? Am I exaggerating? You don't know
what a favor you're doing to listen to me.

I didn't know what to say. I was stunned, I had never heard
a man talk about himself like that. The whole time, even when
he spoke of his own brutality, he used a dialect full of feeling,
defenseless, like the language of certain songs. I still don't
know why he behaved that way. Of course, afterward he
revealed what he wanted. He wanted me to ally myself with
him for the good of Lila. He said that she had to be helped to
understand how necessary it was to behave like a wife and not
like an enemy. He asked me to persuade her to help out in the
second grocery and with the accounts. But for that purpose he
didn't have to confess to me in that way. Probably he thought
that Lila had kept me minutely informed and therefore he had
to give me his version of the facts. Or maybe he hadn't counted
on opening himself up so frankly to his wife's best friend, and
had done so only on the wave of emotion. Or he hypothesized
that, if he moved me, I would then move Lila by reporting
everything to her. Certainly I listened to him with increasing
sympathy. I was pleased by that free flow of intimate confidences. But above all, I have to admit, what pleased me was the
importance he attached to me. When in his own words he
articulated a suspicion that I myself had always had, that is,
that Lila harbored a force that made her capable of anything,
even of keeping her body from conceiving children, it seemed
that he was attributing to me a beneficent power, one that
could win over Lila's maleficent one, and this flattered me. We
got out of the car, and arrived at the dressmaker's shop. I felt
consoled by that acknowledgment. I went so far as to say
pompously, in Italian, that I would do everything possible to
help them to be happy.

But as soon as we were in front of the dressmaker's window
I became nervous again. We both stopped to look at the

framed photograph of Lila amid fabrics of many colors. She was seated, her legs crossed, her wedding dress pulled up a little to reveal her shoes, an ankle. She rested her chin on the palm of one hand, her gaze was solemn, intense, turned boldly toward the lens, and in her hair shone a crown of orange blossoms. The photographer had been fortunate. I felt that he had caught the force Stefano had talked about; it was a force—I seemed to grasp—against which not even Lila could prevail. I turned as if to say to him, in admiration and at the same time dismay, here's what we were talking about, but he pushed open the door and let me go in first.

The tones he had used with me disappeared, and he was harsh with the dressmaker. He said that he was Lina's husband, he used that precise construction. He explained that he, too, was in business, but that it would never occur to him to get publicity in that way. He went so far as to say: You are a good-looking woman, what would your husband say if I took a photograph of you and stuck it in amid the provolone and the salami? He asked for the photograph back.

The dressmaker was bewildered; she tried to defend herself, and finally she gave in. But she appeared very unhappy, and to demonstrate the effectiveness of her initiative and the basis of her regret, she told three or four anecdotes that later, over the years, became a small legend in the neighborhood. Among those who had stopped in to ask for information about the young woman in the wedding dress during the period in which the photograph was in the window were the famous singer Renato Carosone, an Egyptian prince, Vittorio De Sica, and a journalist from the paper *Roma*, who wanted to talk to Lila and send a photographer to do a story on bathing suits like the ones worn at beauty contests. The dressmaker swore that she had refused to give Lila's address to anyone, even though, especially in the case of Carosone and of De Sica, the refusal had seemed to her very rude, given the status of those persons.

I noticed that the more the dressmaker talked the more Stefano softened again. He became sociable, he wanted the woman to tell him in more detail about those episodes. When we left, taking with us the photograph, his mood had changed, and the monologue of the return did not have the anguished tone of the earlier one. Stefano was cheerful, he began to speak of Lila with the pride of someone possessing a rare object whose ownership confers great prestige. Of course, he asked again for my help. And before leaving me at my house he made me swear over and over that I would try to make Lila understand what was the right path and what was wrong. Yet Lila, in his words, was no longer a person who couldn't be controlled but a sort of precious fluid stored in a container that belonged to him. In the following days Stefano told everyone, even in the grocery, about Carosone and De Sica, so that the story spread and Lila's mother, Nunzia, as long as she lived, went around repeating to everyone that her daughter would have had the opportunity of becoming a singer and actress, appearing in the film *Marriage Italian Style*, going on television, even becoming an Egyptian princess, if the dressmaker of the Rettifilo had not been so reticent and if fate had not let her marry, at the age of sixteen, Stefano Carracci.

19.

The chemistry teacher was generous with me (or maybe it was Professor Galiani who went to the trouble to get her to be generous), and gave me a pass. I was promoted with average grades in literary subjects, low passing grades in scientific ones, a narrow pass in religion and, for the first time, a less than perfect grade in behavior, a sign that the priest and a great many of the teachers had never really forgiven me. I was sorry about it; I felt that my old dispute with the religion teacher on the role of the Holy Spirit had been presumptuous, and I regretted not having listened to Alfonso, who at the time had tried to restrain me. Naturally I did not get a scholarship, and my mother was enraged, saying that it was all because of the time I had wasted with Antonio. Her words infuriated me. I said I didn't want to go to school anymore. She raised her hand to slap me, feared for my glasses, and hurried to get the carpet beater. Terrible days, in other words, and they got worse. The only thing that seemed positive was that, the morning I went to see the grades, the janitor came up and handed me a package left by Professor Galiani. It was books, but not novels: books full of arguments, a subtle sign of trust that still was not enough to bring me relief.

I had too many worries and, whatever I did, the feeling of always being in the wrong. I looked for my old boyfriend at home and at his job, but he always managed to avoid me. I stuck my head in the grocery to ask Ada for help. She treated me coldly, said that her brother didn't want to see me anymore, and from then on, if we met, she looked the other way. Now that there was no school, waking up in the morning became traumatic, a kind of painful blow to the head. At first I tried to read Professor Galiani's books, but I was bored, I could scarcely understand them. I started to borrow novels from the circulating library, and read one after the other. But in the long run they didn't help. They presented intense lives, profound conversations, a phantom reality more appealing than my real life. So, in order to feel as if I were not real, I sometimes went all the way to school in the hope of seeing Nino, who was taking the graduation exams. The day of the written Greek test I waited for hours, patiently. But just as the first candidates began to emerge, with Rocci under their arms, the pretty, pure girl I had seen raising her lips to him appeared. She settled herself to wait not far from me, and in a second I was imagining the two of us—models displayed in a catalogue—as we would appear to the eyes of Sarratore's son the moment he came out the door. I felt ugly, shabby, and I left.

I went to Lila's house in search of comfort. But I knew I had made a mistake with her, too. I had done something stupid: I hadn't told her about going with Stefano to get the photograph. Why had I been silent? Was I pleased with the role of peacemaker that her husband had proposed and did I think I could exercise it better by being silent about the visit to the Rettifilo? Had I been afraid of betraying Stefano's confidence and as a result, without realizing it, betrayed her? I didn't know. Certainly it hadn't been a real decision: rather, an uncertainty that first became a feigned carelessness, then the conviction that not having said right away what had happened made remedying the situation complicated and perhaps vain. How easy it was to do wrong. I sought excuses that might seem convincing to her, but I wasn't able to make them even to myself. I sensed that the foundations of my behavior were flawed, I was silent.

On the other hand, she had never indicated that she knew the encounter had taken place. She always welcomed me kindly, let me take a bath in her bathtub, use her makeup. But she made few comments on the plots of the novels that I recounted to her, preferring to give me frivolous information about the lives of actors and singers she read about in the magazines. And she no longer told me any of her thoughts or secret plans. If I saw a bruise, if I took that as a starting point to get her to examine the reasons for Stefano's ugly reaction, if I said that maybe he had been cruel because he would like her to help him, support him in his difficulties, she looked at me ironically, she shrugged, she was evasive. In a short time I understood that although she didn't want to break off her relationship with me, she had decided not to confide in me anymore. Did she in fact know, and no longer considered me a trustworthy friend? I even went so far as to make my visits less frequent, hoping that she would feel my absence, ask the reason for it, and we would explain things to each other. But she didn't seem to notice. Then I couldn't stand it and went back to visiting constantly, which seemed to make her neither happy nor unhappy.

That very hot day in July I was especially depressed when I arrived at her house and yet I said nothing about Nino, about Nino's girlfriend, because without intending to—it's the way these things go—I had ended up reducing the play of confidences almost to nothing myself. She was welcoming as usual. She made an orzata. I curled up on the couch in the dining room to drink the cold almond syrup, irritated by the clatter of the trains, by the sweat, by everything.

I observed her silently as she moved through the house; I was enraged by her capacity to travel through the most depressing labyrinths, holding on to the thread of her declaration of war without showing it. I thought of what her husband had told me, his words about the power that Lila held back like the spring of a dangerous device. I looked at her stomach and imagined that truly inside it, every day, every night, she was fighting a battle to destroy the life that Stefano wanted to insert there by force. How long will she resist, I wondered, but I didn't dare to ask explicit questions, I knew she would consider them disagreeable.

A little later Pinuccia arrived, apparently to visit her sister-in-law. But in fact ten minutes afterward Rino showed up, and he and Pina began kissing, practically right in front of us, in a way so excessive that Lila and I exchanged looks. When Pina said she wanted to see the view, he followed her, and they shut themselves in a room for a good half hour.

This happened often. Lila talked about it with a mixture of irritation and sarcasm, and I was envious of the couple's ease: no fear, no misery, when they reappeared they were more contented than before. Rino went to the kitchen to get something to eat;

returning, he talked about shoes with his sister, he said that things were constantly improving, and tried to get suggestions from her that he could later take credit for with the Solaras.

"You know that Marcello and Michele want to put your picture in the store in Piazza dei Martiri?" he asked suddenly, in an appealing tone.

"It doesn't seem appropriate," Pinuccia immediately interrupted.

"Why not?" Rino asked.

"What sort of question is that? If she wants, Lina can put the picture in the new grocery: she's going to run it, no? If I'm getting the shop in Piazza dei Martiri, will you let me decide what goes in it?"

She spoke as if she were defending Lila's rights against her brother's intrusiveness. In fact, we all knew that she was defending herself and her own future. She was tired of depending on Stefano, she wanted to quit the grocery store, and she liked the idea of being the proprietor of a store in the center of the city. So a small war had been going on for some time between Rino and Michele, whose object was the management of the shoe store, a war inflamed by pressure from their respective fiancées: Rino insisted that Pinuccia should do it, Michele that Gigliola should. But Pinuccia was the more aggressive and had no doubt that she would get the best of it; she knew that she could add the authority of her brother to that of her fiancé. And so at every opportunity she put on airs, like someone who has already made the leap, has left behind the old neighborhood and now decrees what is suitable and what is not for the sophisticated customers in the center.

I realized that Rino was afraid his sister would take the offensive, but Lila displayed complete indifference. Then he checked his watch to let us all know that he was very busy, and said in the tone of one who sees into the future, "In my opinion that photograph has great commercial possibilities." Then he kissed Pina, who immediately drew back, to signal disapproval, and left.

We girls remained. Pinuccia, hoping to use my authority to settle the question, asked me, sulkily, "Lenù, what do you think? Do you think the photo of Lina should stay in Piazza dei Martiri?"

I said, in Italian, "It's Stefano who should decide, and since he went to the dressmaker purposely to get it removed from her window, I consider it out of the question that he'll give permission."

Pinuccia glowed with satisfaction, and almost shouted, "My goodness, how smart you are, Lenù."

I waited for Lila to have her say. There was a long silence, then she spoke just to me: "How much do you want to bet you're wrong? Stefano will give his permission."

"No."

"Yes."

"What do you want to bet?"

"If you lose, you must never again pass with anything less than the best grades."

I looked at her in embarrassment. We hadn't spoken about my difficulties, I didn't even think she knew, but she was well informed and now was reproaching me. You weren't up to it, she was saying, your grades fell. She expected from me what she would have done in my place. She really wanted me fixed in the role of someone who spends her life with books, while she had money, nice clothes, a house, television, a car, took everything, granted everything.

"And if you lose?" I asked, with a shade of bitterness.

That look of hers returned instantly, shot through dark slits.

"I'll enroll in a private school, start studying again, and I swear I'll get my diploma along with you and do better than you."

Along with you and do better than you. Was that what she had in mind? I felt as if everything that was roiling inside me in that terrible time—Antonio, Nino, the unhappiness with the nothing that was my life—had been sucked up by a broad sigh.

"Are you serious?"

"When is a bet ever made as a joke?"

Pinuccia interrupted, aggressively.

"Lina, don't start acting crazy the way you always do: you have the new grocery store, Stefano can't manage it alone." Immediately, however, she controlled herself, adding with false sweetness, "Besides, I'd like to know when you and Stefano are going to make me an aunt."

She used that sweet-sounding formula but her tone seemed resentful to me, and I felt the reasons for that resentment irritatingly mixed with mine. Pinuccia meant: you're married, my brother gives you everything, now do what you're supposed to do. And in fact what's the sense of being Signora Carracci if you're going to shut all the doors, barricade yourself, obstruct, guard a poisoned fury in your stomach? Is it possible that you must always do harm, Lila? When will you stop? Will your energy diminish, will you be distracted, will you finally collapse, like a sleepy sentinel? When will you grow wide and sit at the cash register in the new neighborhood, with your stomach swelling, and make Pinuccia an aunt, and me, me, leave me to go my own way?

"Who knows," Lila answered, and her eyes grew large and deep again.

"Am I going to become a mamma first?" said her sister-in-law, smiling.

"If you're always pasted to Rino like that, it's possible."

They had a little skirmish; I didn't stay to listen.

20.

To placate my mother, I had to find a summer job. Naturally

I went to the stationer. She welcomed me the way you'd welcome a schoolteacher or the doctor, she called her daughters, who were playing in the back of the shop, and they embraced me, kissed me, wanted me to play with them. When I mentioned that I was looking for a job, she said that she was ready to send her daughters to the Sea Garden right away, without waiting for August, just so that they could spend their days with a good, intelligent girl like me.

"Right away when?" I asked.

"Next week?"

"Wonderful."

"I'll give you a little more money than last year."

That, finally, seemed to be good news. I went home satisfied, and my mood didn't change even when my mother said that as usual I was lucky, going swimming and sitting in the sun wasn't a job.

Encouraged, the next day I went to see Maestra Oliviero. I was upset about having to tell her that I hadn't particularly distinguished myself in school that year, but I needed to see her; I had to tactfully remind her to get me the books for the next school year. And then I thought it would please her to know that Lila, now that she had made a good marriage and had so much free time, might start studying again. Reading in her eyes the reaction to that would help soothe the unease it had provoked in me.

I knocked and knocked, the teacher didn't come to the door. I asked the neighbors, and around the neighborhood, and returned an hour later, but still she didn't answer. And yet no one had seen her go out, nor had I met her on the streets or in the shops. Since she was a woman alone, old, and not well, I went back to the neighbors. The woman who lived next door decided to ask her son for help. The young man got into the apartment by climbing from the balcony of his mother's apartment into one of the teacher's windows. He found her on the kitchen floor, in her nightgown—she had fainted. The doctor was called and he thought that she should be admitted to the hospital immediately. They carried her downstairs. I saw her as she emerged from the entrance, in disarray, her face swollen, she who always came to school carefully groomed. Her eyes were frightened. I gave her a nod of greeting, and she lowered her gaze. They settled her in a car that took off blasting its horn.

The heat that year must have had a cruel effect on frailer bodies. In the afternoon Melina's children could be heard in the courtyard calling their mother in increasingly worried voices. When the cries didn't stop, I went to see what was happening and ran into Ada. She said anxiously, her eyes shiny with tears, that Melina couldn't be found. Right afterward Antonio arrived, out of breath and pale; he didn't even look at me but hurried off. Soon half the neighborhood was looking for Melina, even Stefano, who, still in his grocer's smock, got in the convertible, with Ada beside him, and drove slowly along the streets. I followed Antonio, and we ran here and there, without saying a word. We ended up near the ponds, and made our way through the tall grass, calling his mother. His cheeks were hollow, he had dark circles under his eyes. I took his hand, wanting to be of comfort, but he repulsed me, with an odious phrase, he said: Leave me alone, you're no woman. I felt a sharp pain in my chest, but just then we saw Melina. She was sitting in the water, cooling off. Her face and neck were sticking out from the greenish surface, her hair was soaked, her eyes red, her lips matted with leaves and mud. She was silent: she whose attacks of madness had for ten years taken the form of shouting or singing.

We brought her home, Antonio supporting her on one side, I on the other. People seemed relieved, called to her, she waved weakly. I saw Lila next to the gate; isolated in her house in the new neighborhood, she must have heard the news late, and hadn't taken part in the search. I knew that she felt a strong bond with Melina, but it struck me that, while everyone was showing signs of sympathy, and here was Ada running toward her, crying mamma, followed by Stefano—who had left the car in the middle of the *stradone* with the doors open, and had the happy expression of someone who has had ugly thoughts but now discovers that all is well—she stood apart with an expression that was hard to describe. She seemed to be moved by the pitiful sight of the widow: dirty, smiling faintly, her light clothes soaked and muddy, the outline of her wasted body visible under the material, the feeble wave of greeting to friends and acquaintances. But Lila also seemed to be wounded by it, and frightened, as if she felt inside the same disruption. I nodded to her, but she didn't respond. I gave up Melina to her daughter, then, and tried to join Lila, I also wanted to tell her about Maestra Oliviero, about the terrible thing Antonio had said to me. But I couldn't find her; she was gone.

21.

When I saw Lila again, I realized immediately that she felt bad and tended to make me feel bad, too. We spent a morning at her house in an atmosphere that seemed to be playful. In fact she insisted, with growing spitefulness, that I try on all her clothes, even though they didn't fit me. The game became torture. She was taller and thinner; everything of hers that I put on made me look ridiculous. But she wouldn't admit it, she said all you need is an adjustment here or there, and yet her mood darkened as she gazed at me, as if my appearance offended her.

At a certain point she exclaimed that's enough: she looked as if she had seen a ghost. Then she pulled herself together, and, assuming a frivolous tone, told me that a couple of nights earlier she had gone to have ice cream with Pasquale and Ada.

I was in my slip, helping her put the clothes back on the hangers.

"With Pasquale and Ada?"

"Yes."

"And Stefano, too?"

"Just me."

"Did they invite you?"

"No, I asked them."

And, as though she wanted to surprise me, she added that she hadn't confined herself to that brief visit to the old world of her girlhood: the next day she had gone to have a pizza with Enzo and Carmela.

"Also by yourself?"

"Yes."

"And what does Stefano say?"

She made a grimace of indifference. "Being married doesn't mean leading the life of an old lady. If he wants to come with me, fine; if he's too tired in the evening, I go out by myself."

"How was it?"

"I had fun."

I hoped she couldn't read the disappointment in my face. We saw each other frequently, she could have said: Tonight I'm going out with Ada, Pasquale, Enzo, Carmela, do you want to come? Instead she had said nothing, she had arranged and managed those outings by herself, in secret, as if they had been not *our* friends forever but only hers. And now she was telling me in detail, with an air of satisfaction, everything they had said: Ada was worried, Melina ate almost nothing and threw up whatever she did eat, Pasquale was anxious about his mother, Giuseppina, who couldn't sleep, felt a heaviness in her legs, had palpitations, and when she returned from visiting her husband in prison wept inconsolably. I listened. I noticed that, more than usual, she had an involved way of talking. She chose emotionally charged words, she described Melina Cappuccio and Giuseppina Peluso as if their bodies had seized hers, imposing on it the same contracted or inflated forms, the same bad feelings. As she spoke, she touched her face, her breast, her stomach, her hips as if they were no longer hers, and showed that she knew everything about those women, down to the tiniest details, in order to prove that no one told me anything but told her everything, or, worse, in order to make me feel that I was wrapped in a fog, unable to see the suffering of the people around me. She spoke of Giuseppina as if she had kept up with her, despite the vortex of her engagement and marriage; she spoke of Melina as if the mother of Ada and Antonio had always been in her mind and she were thoroughly familiar with her madness. Then she went on to enumerate many other people in the neighborhood, people whom I hardly knew but whose histories she seemed to know, as if she had a sort of long-distance involvement in their lives. Finally she announced:

"I also had ice cream with Antonio."

That name was a punch in the stomach.

"How is he?"

"Fine."

"Did he say anything about me?"

"No, nothing."

"When does he leave?"

"In September."

"Marcello did nothing to help him."

"It was predictable."

Predictable? If it was predictable, I thought, that the Solaras would do nothing, why did you take me there? And why do you, who are married, now want to see your friends again, like that, by yourself? And why did you have ice cream with Antonio without telling me, knowing that he is my old boyfriend and that though he doesn't want to see me anymore I would like to see him? Do you want revenge because I went

driving with your husband and didn't report to you a word of
what we said to each other? I dressed nervously, mumbled that
I had things to do, had to go.

"I have something else to tell you."

In a serious voice she said that Rino, Marcello, and Michele
had wanted Stefano to go to Piazza dei Martiri to see how well
the shop was coming along, and that the three of them, amid
sacks of cement and cans of paint and brushes, had pointed
out the wall opposite the entrance and told him they were
thinking of putting the enlargement of the photograph of her
in her wedding dress there. Stefano had listened, then he had
answered that certainly it would be a good advertisement for
the shoes, but that it didn't seem to him suitable. The three
had insisted, he had said no to Marcello, no to Michele, and no
to Rino as well. In other words I had won the bet: her husband
had not given in to the Solaras.

I said, making an effort to appear enthusiastic, "See?
Always saying mean things about poor Stefano. And instead I
was right. Now you have to start studying."

"Wait."

"Wait for what? A bet is a bet and you lost."

"Wait," Lila repeated.

My bad mood got worse. She doesn't know what she wants,
I thought. She's unhappy that she was wrong about her husband. Or, I don't know, maybe I'm exaggerating, maybe she
appreciated Stefano's refusal, but she expects a more ferocious
clash of men around her image, and she's disappointed
because the Solaras weren't insistent enough. I saw that she
was lazily running a hand over her hip and along one leg, like
a caress of farewell, and in her eyes appeared for a moment
that mixture of suffering, fear, and disgust that I had noticed
the night of Melina's disappearance. I thought: and if, instead,
she secretly wants her picture to be on display, enlarged, in the
center of the city, and is sorry that Michele didn't succeed in

forcing it on Stefano? Why not, she wants to be first in every-thing, she's made like that: the most beautiful, the most elegant, the wealthiest. Then I said to myself: above all, the most intelli-gent. And at the idea that Lila would really start studying again I felt a regret that discouraged me. Of course she would make up for all the years of school she had missed. Of course I would find her beside me, elbow to elbow, taking the high-school graduation exam. And I realized that the prospect was intoler-able. But it was even more intolerable to discover that feeling in myself. I was ashamed and immediately started telling her how wonderful it would be if we studied together again, and insisting that she should find out how to proceed. She shrugged, so I said, "Now I really have to go."

This time she didn't stop me.

22.

As usual, once I was on the stairs I began to sympathize with her reasons, or so it seemed to me: she was isolated in the new neighborhood, shut up in her modern house, beaten by Stefano, engaged in some mysterious struggle with her own body in order not to conceive children, envious of my success in school to the point of indicating to me with that crazy bet that she would like to study again. Besides, it was likely that she saw me as much freer than she was. The breakup with Antonio, my troubles with school seemed like nonsense com-pared to hers. Step by step, without realizing it, I felt driven to a grudging support, then renewed admiration. Yes, it would be wonderful if she started studying again. To return to the time of elementary school, when she was always first and I second. To give meaning back to studying because she knew how to give it meaning. To stay in her shadow and therefore feel strong and secure. Yes, yes, yes. Start again.

At some point, on the way home, the mixture of suffering, fear, and disgust I had seen in her face returned to my mind. Why. I thought back to the teacher's body in disarray, to Melina's uncontrolled body. For no obvious reason, I began to look closely at the women on the *stradone*. Suddenly it seemed to me that I had lived with a sort of limited gaze: as if my focus had been only on us girls, Ada, Gigliola, Carmela, Marisa, Pinuccia, Lila, me, my schoolmates, and I had never really paid attention to Melina's body, Giuseppina Pelusi's, Nunzia Cerullo's, Maria Carracci's. The only woman's body I had studied, with ever-increasing apprehension, was the lame body of my mother, and I had felt pressed, threatened by that image, and still feared that it would suddenly impose itself on mine. That day, instead, I saw clearly the mothers of the old neighborhood. They were nervous, they were acquiescent. They were silent, with tight lips and stooping shoulders, or they yelled terrible insults at the children who harassed them. Extremely thin, with hollow eyes and cheeks, or with broad behinds, swollen ankles, heavy chests, they lugged shopping bags and small children who clung to their skirts and wanted to be picked up. And, good God, they were ten, at most twenty years older than me. Yet they appeared to have lost those feminine qualities that were so important to us girls and that we accentuated with clothes, with makeup. They had been consumed by the bodies of husbands, fathers, brothers, whom they ultimately came to resemble, because of their labors or the arrival of old age, of illness. When did that transformation begin? With housework? With pregnancies? With beatings? Would Lila be misshapen like Nunzia? Would Fernando leap from her delicate face, would her elegant walk become Rino's, legs wide, arms pushed out by his chest? And would my body, too, one day be ruined by the emergence of not only my mother's body but my father's? And would all that I was learning at school dissolve, would the neighborhood prevail again, the cadences, the manners, everything be confounded in a black mire, Anaximander and my father, Folgóre and Don Achille, valences and the ponds, aorists, Hesiod, and the insolent vulgar language of the Solaras, as, over the millenniums, had happened to the chaotic, debased city itself?

I was suddenly sure that, without being aware of it, I had intercepted Lila's feelings and was adding them to mine. Why did she have that expression, that ill humor? Had she caressed her leg, her hip, as a sort of farewell? Had she touched herself, speaking, as if she felt the edges of her body besieged by Melina, by Giuseppina, and was frightened, disgusted by it? Had she turned to our friends out of a need to react?

I remembered how, as a child, she had looked at Maestra Oliviero when she fell off the platform like a broken puppet. I remembered how she had looked at Melina on the *stradone,* eating the soft soap she had just bought. I remembered when she told the rest of us about the murder, and the blood on the copper pot, and claimed that the killer of Don Achille was not a man but a woman, as if, in the story she was telling us, she had heard and seen the form of a female body break, from the need for hatred, the urgency for revenge or justice, and lose its substance.

23.

Starting in the last week of July, I went with the stationer's daughters to the Sea Garden every day, including Sunday. Along with the thousand things that the children might need, I brought in a canvas bag the books that Professor Galiani had lent me. They were small volumes that examined the past, the present, the world as it was and as it ought to become. The writing resembled that of textbooks, but was more difficult and more interesting. I wasn't used to that sort of reading, and got tired quickly. Besides, the girls required a lot of attention. And then there was the lazy sea, the leaden sun that bore down on the gulf and the city, stray fantasies, desires, the ever-present wish to undo the order of the lines—and, with it, every order that required an effort, a wait for fulfillment yet to come—and yield, instead, to what was within reach, immediately gained, the crude life of the creatures of the sky, the earth, and the sea. I approached my seventeenth birthday with one eye on the daughters of the stationer and one on *Discourse on the Origins of Inequality*.

One Sunday I felt someone putting fingers over my eyes and a female voice asked, "Guess who?"

I recognized Marisa's voice and hoped that she was with Nino. How I would have liked him to see me made beautiful by the sun, the salt water, and intent on reading a difficult book. I exclaimed happily, "Marisa!" and immediately turned around. But Nino wasn't there; it was Alfonso, with a blue towel over his shoulder, cigarette, wallet, and lighter in his hand, a black bathing suit with a white stripe, he himself pale as one who has never had a ray of sun in his entire life.

I marveled at seeing them together. Alfonso had to retake exams in two subjects in October, and, since he was busy in the grocery, I imagined that on Sundays he studied. As for Marisa, I was sure that she would be at Barano with her family. Instead she told me that her parents had quarreled with Nella the year before and, with some friends from *Roma*, had taken a small villa at Castelvolturno. She had returned to Naples just for a few days: she needed some school books—three subjects to do again—and, then, she had to see a person. She smiled flirtatiously at Alfonso. The person was him.

I couldn't contain myself, I asked right away how Nino had done on his graduation exams. She made a face of disgust.

"All A's and A-minuses. As soon as he found out the results

he went off on his own to England, without a lira. He says he'll find a job there and stay until he learns English."

"Then?"

"Then I don't know, maybe he'll enroll in economy and business."

I had a thousand other questions, I even looked for a way to ask who the girl was who waited outside school, and if he had really gone alone or in fact with her, when Alfonso said, embarrassed, "Lina's here, too." Then he added, "Antonio brought us in the car."

Antonio?

Alfonso must have noticed how my expression changed, the flush that was spreading over my face, the jealous amazement in my eyes. He smiled, and said quickly, "Stefano had some work to do about the counters in the new grocery and couldn't come. But Lina was extremely eager to see you, she has something to tell you, and so she asked Antonio if he would take us."

"Yes, she has something urgent to tell you," Marisa said emphatically, clapping her hands gleefully to let me know that she already knew the thing.

What thing? Judging from Marisa, it seemed good. Maybe Lila had soothed Antonio and he wanted to be with me again. Maybe the Solaras had finally roused their acquaintances at the recruiting office and Antonio didn't have to go. These hypotheses came to mind immediately. But when the two appeared I eliminated both right away. Clearly Antonio was there only because obeying Lila gave meaning to his empty Sunday, only because to be her friend seemed to him a piece of luck and a necessity. But his expression was still unhappy, his eyes frightened, and he greeted me coldly. I asked about his mother, but he gave me scarcely any news. He looked around uneasily and immediately dived into the water with the girls, who welcomed him warmly. As for Lila, she was pale, without lipstick, her gaze hostile. She didn't seem to have anything urgent to tell me. She sat on the concrete, picked up the book I was reading, leafed through it without a word.

Marisa, in the face of those silences, became ill at ease; she tried to make a show of enthusiasm for everything in the world, then she got flustered and she, too, went to swim. Alfonso chose a place as far from us as possible and, sitting motionless in the sun, concentrated on the bathers, as if the sight of naked people going in and out of the water were utterly absorbing.

"Who gave you this book?" Lila asked.

"My professor of Latin and Greek."

"Why didn't you tell me?"

"I didn't think it would interest you."

"Do you know what is of interest to me and what isn't?"

I immediately resorted to a conciliatory tone, but I also felt a need to brag.

"As soon as I finish I'll lend it to you. These are books that the professor gives the good students to read. Nino reads them, too."

"Who is Nino?"

Did she do it on purpose? Did she pretend not even to remember his name in order to diminish him in my eyes?

"The one in the wedding film, Marisa's brother, Sarratore's oldest son."

"The ugly guy you like?"

"I told you that I don't like him anymore. But he does great things."

"What?"

"Now, for instance, he's in England. He's working, traveling, learning to speak English."

I was excited merely by summarizing Marisa's words. I said to Lila, "Imagine if you and I could do things like that. Travel. Work as waiters to support ourselves. Learn to speak English better than the English. Why can he be free to do that and we can't?"

"Did he finish school?"

"Yes, he got his diploma. Afterward, though, he's going to do a difficult course at the university."

"Is he smart?"

"As smart as you."

"I don't go to school."

"Yes, but: you lost the bet and now you have to go back to books."

"Stop it, Lenù."

"Stefano won't let you?"

"There's the new grocery, I'm supposed to manage it."

"You'll study in the grocery."

"No."

"You promised. You said we'd get our diploma together."

"No."

"Why?"

Lila ran her hand back and forth over the cover of the book, ironing it.

"I'm pregnant," she said. And without waiting for me to react she muttered, "It's so hot," left the book, went to the edge of the concrete, hurled herself without hesitation into the water, yelling at Antonio, who was playing and splashing with Marisa and the children, "Tonì, save me!"

She flew for a few seconds, arms wide, then clumsily hit the surface of the water. She didn't know how to swim.

24.

In the days that followed, Lila started on a period of feverish activity. She began with the new grocery, involving herself as if it were the most important thing in the world. She woke up early, before Stefano. She threw up, made coffee, threw up again. He had become very solicitous, he wanted to drive her, but Lila refused, she said she wanted to walk, and she went out in the cool air of the morning, before the heat exploded, along the deserted streets, past the newly constructed buildings, most of them still empty, to the store that was being fitted out. She pulled up the shutter, washed the paint-splattered floor, waited for the workers and suppliers who were delivering scales, slicers, and furnishings, gave orders on where to place them, moved things around herself, trying out new, more efficient arrangements. Large threatening men, rough-mannered boys were ordered about and submitted to her whims without protesting. Since she had barely finished giving an order when she undertook some other heavy job, they cried in apprehension: Signora Carracci, and did all they could to help her.

Lila, in spite of the heat, which sapped her energy, did not confine herself to the shop in the new neighborhood. Sometimes she went with her sister-in-law to the small work site in Piazza dei Martiri, where Michele generally presided, but often Rino, too, was there, feeling he had the right to monitor the work both as the maker of Cerullo shoes and as the brother-in-law of Stefano, who was the Solaras' partner. Lila would not stay still in that space, either. She inspected it, she climbed the workmen's ladders, she observed the place from high up, she came down, she began to move things. At first she hurt everybody's feelings, but soon, one after the other, they reluctantly gave in. Michele, although the most sarcastically hostile, seemed to grasp most readily the advantages of Lila's suggestions.

"*Signó*," he said teasing, "come and rearrange the bar, too, I'll pay you."

Naturally she wouldn't think of laying a hand on the Bar Solara, but when she had brought enough disorder to Piazza dei Martiri she moved on to the kingdom of the Carracci family, the old grocery, and installed herself there. She made Stefano keep Alfonso at home because he had to study for his makeup exams, and urged Pinuccia to go out more and more often, with her mother, to poke into the shop in Piazza dei Martiri. So, little by little, she reorganized the two adjacent spaces in the old neighborhood to make the work easier and more efficient. In a short time she demonstrated that both Maria and Pinuccia were substantially superfluous; she gave Ada a bigger job, and got Stefano to increase her pay.

When, in the late afternoon, I returned from the Sea Garden and delivered the girls to the stationer, I almost always stopped at the grocery to see how Lila was doing, if her stomach had started to swell. She was nervous, and her complexion wasn't good. To cautious questions about her pregnancy she either didn't respond or dragged me outside the store and said nonsensical things like: "I don't want to talk about it, it's a disease, I have an emptiness inside me that weighs me down." Then she started to tell me about the new grocery and the old one, and Piazza dei Martiri, with her usual exhilarating delivery, just to make me believe that these were places where marvelous things were happening and I, poor me, was missing them.

But by now I knew her tricks, I listened but didn't believe her, although I always ended up hypnotized by the energy with which she played both servant and mistress. Lila was able to talk to me, talk to the customers, talk to Ada, all at the same time, while continuing to unwrap, cut, weigh, take money, and give change. She erased herself in the words and gestures, she became exhausted, she seemed truly engaged in an unrelenting struggle to forget the weight of what she still described, incongruously, as "an emptiness inside."

What impressed me most, though, was her casual behavior with money. She went to the cash register and took what she wanted. Money for her was that drawer, the treasure chest of childhood that opened and offered its wealth. In the (rare) case that the money in the drawer wasn't enough, she had only to glance at Stefano. He, who seemed to have reacquired the generous solicitude of their engagement, pulled up his smock, dug in the back pocket of his pants, took out a fat wallet, and asked, "How much do you need?" Lila made a sign with her fingers, her husband reached out his right arm with the fist closed, she extended her long, thin hand.

Ada, behind the counter, looked at her the way she looked at the movie stars in the pages of magazines. I imagine that in that period Antonio's sister felt as if she were living in a fairy tale. Her eyes sparkled when Lila opened the drawer and gave her money. She handed it out freely, as soon as her husband turned his back. She gave Ada money for Antonio, who was going into the Army, she gave money to Pasquale, who urgently needed three teeth extracted. In early September she took me aside, too, and asked if I needed money for books.

"What books?"

"The ones for school but also the ones not for school."

I told her that Maestra Oliviero was still not out of the hospital, that I didn't know if she would help me get the textbooks, as usual, and here already Lila wanted to stick the money in my pocket. I withdrew, I refused, I didn't want to seem a kind of poor relative forced to ask for money. I told her I had to wait till school started, I told her that the stationer had extended the Sea Garden job until mid-September, I told her that I would therefore earn more than expected and would manage by myself. She was sorry, she insisted that I come to her if the teacher couldn't help me out.

It wasn't just me; certainly all of us, faced with that generosity of hers, had some difficulties. Pasquale, for example, didn't want to accept the money for the dentist, he felt humiliated, and finally took it only because his face was disfigured, his eye was inflamed, and the lettuce compresses were of no use. Antonio, too, was offended, to the point where to take money that our friend gave Ada in addition to her regular pay

he had to be persuaded that it was making up for the disgraceful pay that Stefano had given her before. We had never
had a lot of money, and we attached great importance even to
ten lire; if we found a coin on the street it was a celebration.
So it seemed to us a mortal sin that Lila handed out money as
if it were a worthless metal, waste paper. She did it silently,
with an imperious gesture resembling those with which as a
child she had organized games, assigned parts. Afterward, she
talked about other things, as if that moment hadn't existed.
On the other hand—Pasquale said to me one evening, in his
obscure way—mortadella sells, so do shoes, and Lina has
always been our friend, she's on our side, our ally, our companion. She's rich now, but by her own merit: yes, by her own
merit, because the money didn't come to her from the fact
that she is Signora Carracci, the future mother of the grocer's
child, but because it's she who invented Cerullo shoes, and
even if no one seemed to remember that now, we, her friends,
remembered.

All true. How many things Lila had made happen in the
space of a few years. And yet now that we were seventeen the
substance of time no longer seemed fluid but had assumed a
gluelike consistency and churned around us like a yellow
cream in a confectioner's machine. Lila herself confirmed this
bitterly when, one Sunday when the sea was smooth and the
sky white, she appeared, to my surprise, at the Sea Garden
around three in the afternoon, by herself: a truly unusual
event. She had taken the subway, a couple of buses, and now
was here, in a bathing suit, with a greenish complexion and an
outbreak of pimples on her forehead. "Seventeen years of
shit," she said in dialect, with apparent cheer, her eyes full of
sarcasm.

She had quarreled with Stefano. In the daily exchanges
with the Solaras the truth came out about the management of
the store in Piazza dei Martiri. Michele had tried to insist on

Gigliola, had harshly threatened Rino, who supported Pinuccia, had finally launched into a tense negotiation with Stefano, in which they had come close to blows. And in the end what happened? Neither winners nor losers, it seemed. Gigliola and Pinuccia would manage the store *together*. Provided that Stefano reconsider an old decision.

"What?" I asked.

"See if you can guess."

I couldn't guess. Michele had asked Stefano, in his teasing tone of voice, to concede on the photograph of Lila in her wedding dress. And this time her husband had done so.

"Really?"

"Really. I told you you just had to wait. They're going to display me in the shop. In the end I've won the bet, not you. Start studying—this year you'll have to get top marks."

Here she changed her tone, became serious. She said that she hadn't come because of the photograph, since she had known for a long time that as far as that shit was concerned she was merchandise to barter. She had come because of the pregnancy. She talked about it for a long time, nervously, as if it were something to be crushed in a mortar, and she did it with cold firmness. It has no meaning, she said, not concealing her anguish. Men insert their thingy in you and you become a box of flesh with a living doll inside. I've got it, it's here, and it's repulsive to me. I throw up continuously, it's my very stomach that can't bear it. I know I'm supposed to think beautiful things, I know I have to resign myself, but I can't do it, I see no reason for resignation and no beauty. Besides the fact, she added, that I feel incapable of dealing with children. You, yes, you are, just look how you take care of the stationer's children. Not me, I wasn't born with that gift.

These words hurt me, what could I say?

"You don't know if you have a gift or not, you have to try," I sought to reassure her, and pointed to the daughters of the stationer who were playing a little distance away. "Sit with them for a while, talk to them."

She laughed. She said maliciously that I had learned to use the sentimental voice of our mothers. But then, uneasily, she ventured to say a few words to the girls, retreated, began talking to me again. I equivocated, pressed her, urged her to take care of Linda, the smallest of the stationer's daughters. I said to her, "Go on, let her play her favorite game, drinking from the fountain next to the bar or spraying the water by putting your thumb over it."

She led Linda away unwillingly, holding her hand. Time passed and they didn't come back. I called the other two girls and went to see what was happening. Everything was fine, Lila had been happily made a prisoner by Linda. She held the child suspended over the jet, letting her drink or spray water. They were both laughing, and their laughter sounded like cries of joy.

I was relieved. I left Linda's sisters with her, too, and went to sit at the bar, in a place where I could keep an eye on all four and also read. She'll become that, I thought, looking at her. What seemed insupportable before is cheering her up now. Maybe I should tell her that things without meaning are the most beautiful ones. It's a good sentence, she'll like it. Lucky her, she's got everything that counts.

For a while I tried to follow, line by line, the arguments of Rousseau. Then I looked up, I saw that something was wrong. Shouts. Maybe Linda had leaned over too far, maybe one of her sisters had given her a shove, certainly she had escaped Lila's grasp and had hit her chin on the edge of the basin. I ran over in fear. Lila, as soon as she saw me, cried immediately, in a childish voice that I had never heard from her, not even when she was a child:

"It was her sister who made her fall, not me."

She was holding Linda, who was bleeding, screaming, crying, as her sisters looked elsewhere with small nervous movements and tight smiles, as if the thing had nothing to do with them, as if they couldn't hear, couldn't see.

I tore the child from Lila's arms and tilted her toward the jet of water, washing her face with resentful hands. There was a horizontal cut under her chin. I'll lose the money from the stationer, I thought, my mother will be angry. Meanwhile I ran for the attendant, who somehow cajoled Linda into calming down, surprised her with an inundation of rubbing alcohol, making her shriek again, then stuck a gauze bandage on her chin and went back to soothing her. Nothing serious, in other words. I bought ice cream for the three girls and went back to the concrete platform.

Lila had left.

25.

The stationer didn't seem especially upset by Linda's wound, but when I asked if I should come the next day at the usual time to pick up the girls, she said that her daughters had had too much swimming that summer and there was no need for me anymore.

I didn't tell Lila that I had lost my job. She on the other hand never asked me how things had turned out, she didn't even ask about Linda and her cut. When I saw her again she was extremely busy with the opening of the new grocery store and gave me the impression of an athlete in training, jumping rope more and more frantically.

She dragged me to the printer, from whom she had ordered a large number of flyers announcing the opening of the new store. She wanted me to go to the priest to set a time to come by for the blessing of the place and the stock. She announced that she had hired Carmela Peluso, at a salary a lot higher than what she was making at the notions store, but first of all she told me that in everything, truly everything, she was waging a serious war against her husband, Pinuccia, her mother-in-law, her brother Rino. She didn't seem especially aggressive, however. She spoke in a low voice, in dialect, doing a thousand other things that seemed more important than what she was saying. She enumerated the wrongs that her relatives, by marriage and by birth, had done and were doing to her. "They have placated Michele," she said, "just as they placated Marcello. They used me—to them I'm not a person but a thing. Let's give him Lina, let's stick her on a wall, since she's a zero, an absolute zero." As she spoke her eyes shone, full of movement, within dark circles, her skin was stretched over the cheekbones, her teeth flashed white, in quick nervous smiles. But she didn't convince me. It seemed to me that behind that raucous activity was a person who was exhausted and looking for a way out.

"What do you intend to do?" I asked.

"Nothing. All I know is they'll have to kill me to do what they want with my photograph."

"Forget it, Lila. Ultimately it's a nice thing, think about it: they only put actresses on billboards."

"And am I an actress?"

"No."

"So? If my husband has decided to sell himself to the Solaras, do you think he can sell me as well?"

I tried to soothe her, I was afraid that Stefano would lose patience and hit her. I said so, she started laughing: since she'd been pregnant her husband hadn't dared to give her even a slap. But now, just as she uttered that remark, the suspicion dawned on me that the photograph was an excuse, that really she wanted to infuriate all of them, to be massacred by Stefano, by the Solaras, by Rino, provoke them to the point where their blows would help her to crush the impatience, the pain, the living thing she had in her belly.

My hypothesis found support the night the grocery opened.

She seemed to be wearing her shabbiest clothes. In front of everyone she treated her husband like a servant. She sent away the priest she had had me call on before he could bless the store, contemptuously sticking some money in his hand. She went on to slice prosciutto and stuff sandwiches, handing them out free to anyone, along with a glass of wine. And this last move was so successful that the store had scarcely opened when it was jammed with customers; she and Carmela were besieged, and Stefano, who was elegantly dressed, had to help them deal with the situation as he was, without an apron, so that his good clothes got all greasy.

When they came home, exhausted, her husband made a scene and Lila did her best to provoke his fury. She shouted that if he wanted someone who obeyed, and that's all, he was out of luck; she was not his mother or his sister, she would always make life difficult for him. And she started with the Solaras, with the business of the photograph, insulting him grossly. First he let her have her say, then he responded with even worse insults. But he didn't beat her. When, the next day, she told me what had happened, I said that although Stefano had his faults, certainly he loved her. She denied it. "He understands only this," she replied, rubbing together thumb and index finger. And in fact the grocery was already popular throughout the new neighborhood, and was crowded from the moment it opened. "The cash drawer is already full. Thanks to me. I bring him wealth, a son, what more does he want?"

"What more do you want?" I asked, with a stab of rage that surprised me, and immediately I smiled, hoping she hadn't noticed.

I remember that she looked bewildered; she touched her forehead with her fingers. Maybe she didn't even know what she wanted, she felt only that she couldn't find peace.

As the other opening, that of the shop on Piazza dei Martiri, approached, she became unbearable. But maybe that adjective is excessive. Let's say that she poured out onto all of us, even me, the confusion that she felt inside. On the one hand, she made Stefano's life hell, she squabbled with her mother-in-law and her sister-in-law, she went to Rino and quarreled with him in front of the workers and Fernando, who, more hunched than usual, labored over his bench, pretending not to hear; on the other, she herself perceived that she was spinning around in her unhappiness, unresigned, and at times I caught her in the new grocery store, in a rare moment when it was empty or she wasn't dealing with suppliers, with a vacant look, one hand on her forehead, in her hair, as if to stanch a wound, and the expression of someone who is trying to catch her breath.

One afternoon I was at home; it was still very hot, although it was the end of September. School was about to begin, I felt at the mercy of the days. My mother reproached me for wasting time. Nino—who knows where he was, in England or in that mysterious space that was the university. I no longer had Antonio, or even the hope of getting back together with him; he had left, along with Enzo Scanno, for his military service, saying goodbye to everyone except me. I heard someone calling me from the street. It was Lila. Her eyes were shining, as if she had a fever, and she said she had found a solution.

"Solution to what?"

"The photograph. If they want to display it, they have to do it the way I say."

"And what do you say?"

She didn't tell me, maybe at that moment it wasn't clear to her. But I knew what sort of person she was, and I recognized in her face the expression she got when, from the dark depths of herself, a signal arrived that fired her brain. She asked me to go with her that evening to Piazza dei Martiri. There we would find the Solaras, Gigliola, Pinuccia, her brother. She wanted me to help her, support her, and I realized that what she had in mind would ferry her beyond her permanent war: a violent but conclusive outlet for the accumulated tensions; or a way of freeing her head, her body, from pent-up energies.

"All right," I said, "but promise not to be crazy."

"Yes."

After the stores closed she and Stefano came to get me in the car. From the few words they exchanged I understood that not even her husband knew what she had in mind and that this time my presence, rather than reassuring him, alarmed him. Lila had finally appeared to be accommodating. She had told him that, if there was no possibility of abandoning the photograph, she wanted at least to have her say on how it was displayed.

"A question of frame, wall, lighting?" he had asked.

"I have to see."

"But then that's it, Lina."

"Yes, that's it."

It was a beautiful warm evening; the brilliant lights of the shop's interior spread their glow into the square. The gigantic image of Lila in her wedding dress could be seen at a distance, leaning against the center wall. Stefano parked, we went in, making our way among the boxes of shoes, piled up haphazardly, cans of paint, ladders. Marcello, Rino, Gigliola, and Pinuccia were visibly irritated: for varying reasons they had no wish to submit yet again to Lila's caprices. The only one who greeted us cordially was Michele, who turned to my friend with a mocking laugh.

"Lovely signora, will you let us know, at last, what you have in mind or do you just want to ruin the evening?"

Lila looked at the panel leaning against the wall, asked them to lay it on the floor. Marcello said cautiously, with the dark timidity that he always showed toward Lila, "What for?"

"I'll show you."

Rino interrupted: "Don't be an idiot, Lina. You know how much this thing cost? If you ruin it, you're in trouble."

The Solaras laid the image on the floor. Lila looked around, with her brow furrowed, her eyes narrowed. She was looking for something that she knew was there, that perhaps she had bought herself. In a corner she spied a roll of black paper, and she took a pair of big scissors and a box of drawing pins from a shelf. Then, with that expression of extreme concentration which enabled her to isolate herself from everything around her, she went back to the panel. Before our astonished and, in the cases of some, openly hostile eyes, she cut strips of black paper, with the manual precision she had always possessed, and pinned them here and there to the photograph, asking for my help with slight gestures or quick glances.

I joined in with the devotion that I had felt ever since we were children. Those moments were thrilling, it was a pleasure to be beside her, slipping inside her intentions, to the point of anticipating her. I felt that she was seeing something that wasn't there, and that she was struggling to make us see it, too. I was suddenly happy, feeling the intensity that invested her, that flowed through her fingers as they grasped the scissors, as they pinned the black paper.

Finally, she tried to lift the canvas, as if she were alone in that space, but she couldn't. Marcello readily intervened, I intervened, we leaned it against the wall. Then we all backed up toward the door, some sneering, some grim, some appalled. The body of the bride Lila appeared cruelly shredded. Much of the head had disappeared, as had the stomach. There remained an eye, the hand on which the chin rested, the brilliant stain of the mouth, the diagonal stripe of the bust, the line of the crossed legs, the shoes.

Gigliola began, scarcely containing her rage: "I cannot put a thing like that in *my* shop."

"I agree," Pinuccia exploded. "We have to sell here, and with that grotesque thing people will run away. Rino, say something to your sister, please."

Rino pretended to ignore her, but he turned to Stefano as if his brother-in-law were to blame for what was happening. "I told you, you can't reason with her. You have to say yes, no, and that's it, or you see what happens? It's a waste of time."

Stefano didn't answer, he stared at the panel leaning against the wall and it was evident that he was looking for a way out. He asked me, "What do you think, Lenù?"

I said in Italian, "To me it seems very beautiful. Of course, I wouldn't want it in the neighborhood, that's not the right place for it. But here it's something else, it will attract attention, it will please. In *Confidenze* just last week I saw that in Rossano Brazzi's house there is a painting like this."

Hearing that, Gigliola got even angrier. "What do you mean? That Rossano Brazzi knows what's what, that you two know everything, and Pinuccia and I don't?"

At that point I felt the danger. I had only to glance at Lila to realize that, if when we arrived at the shop she had really felt willing to give in should the attempt prove fruitless, now that the attempt had been made and had produced that image of disfigurement she wouldn't yield an inch. Those minutes of work on the picture had broken ties: at that moment she was overwhelmed by an exaggerated sense of herself, and it would take time for her to retreat into the dimension of the grocer's wife, she wouldn't accept a sigh of dissent. In fact, while Gigliola was speaking, she was already muttering: Like this or not at all. And she wanted to quarrel, she wanted to break, shatter, she would have happily hurled herself at Gigliola with the scissors.

I hoped for a word of support from Marcello. But Marcello remained silent, head down: I understood that his residual feelings for Lila were vanishing at that moment, his old depressed passion couldn't carry them forward any longer. It was his brother who broke in, lashing Gigliola, his fiancée, in his most aggressive voice. "Shut up," he told her. And as soon as she tried to protest he became threatening, without even looking at her, staring, rather, at the panel: "Shut up, Gigliò." Then he turned to Lila.

"I like it, *signò*. You've erased yourself deliberately and I see why: to show the thigh, to show how well a woman's thigh goes with those shoes. Excellent. You're a pain in the ass, but when you do a thing you do it right."

Silence.

With her fingertips Gigliola dried silent tears that she couldn't hold back. Pinuccia stared at Rino, she stared at her brother, as if she wanted to say to them: Speak, defend me, don't let that bitch walk all over me.

Stefano instead murmured softly, "Yes, it convinces me, too."

And Lila said suddenly, "It's not finished."

"What do you still have to do?" Pinuccia shot back.

"I have to add a little color."

"Color?" Marcello mumbled, even more disoriented. "We're supposed to open in three days."

Michele laughed: "If we have to wait another little bit, we'll wait. Get to work, *signò*, do what you like."

That masterful tone, of one who makes and unmakes as he wishes, Stefano didn't like.

"There's the new grocery," he said, to let it be understood that he needed his wife there.

"Figure it out," Michele answered. "We have more interesting things to do here."

26.

We spent the last days of September shut up in the shop, the two of us and three workmen. They were magnificent hours of play, of invention, of freedom, such as we hadn't experienced together perhaps since childhood. Lila drew me into her frenzy.

We bought paste, paint, brushes. With extreme precision (she was demanding) we attached the black paper cutouts. We traced red or blue borders between the remains of the photograph and the dark clouds that were devouring it. Lila had always been good with lines and colors, but here she did something more, though I wouldn't have been able to say what it was; hour after hour it engulfed me.

For a while it seemed to me that she had fashioned that occasion to bring to an effective end the years that had begun with the designs for the shoes, when she was still the girl Lina Cerullo. And I still think that much of the pleasure of those days was derived from the resetting of the conditions of her, or our, life, from the capacity we had to lift ourselves above ourselves, to isolate ourselves in the pure and simple fulfillment of that sort of visual synthesis. We forgot about Antonio, Nino, Stefano, the Solaras, my problems with school, her pregnancy, the tensions between us. We suspended time, we isolated space, there remained only the play of glue, scissors, paper, paint: the play of shared creation.

But there was something else. I was soon reminded of the word Michele had used: *erase*. Likely, yes, very likely the black stripes did set the shoes apart and make them more visible: young Solara wasn't stupid, he knew how to look. But at times, and with growing intensity, I felt that that wasn't the true goal of our pasting and painting. Lila was happy, and she was drawing me deeper and deeper into her fierce happiness, because she had suddenly found, perhaps without even realizing it, an opportunity that allowed her to *portray* the fury she directed against herself, the insurgence, perhaps for the first time in her life, of the need—and here the verb used by Michele was appropriate—to erase herself.

Today, in the light of many subsequent events, I'm quite sure that that is really what happened. With the black paper, with the green and purple circles that Lila drew around certain parts of her body, with the blood-red lines with which she sliced and said she was slicing it, she completed her own self-destruction *in an image*, presented to the eyes of all in the space bought by the Solaras to display and sell *her* shoes.

It's likely that it was she who provoked in me that impression, who motivated it. While we worked, she began to talk about when she had begun to realize that she was now Signora Carracci. At first I didn't really understand what she was saying, her observations seemed to me banal. When, as girls, of course, we were in love, we would try out the sound of our name joined to the last name of the beloved. I, for example, still have a notebook from the first year of high school in which I practiced signing myself Elena Sarratore, and I clearly remember how I would very faintly whisper that name. But it wasn't what Lila meant. I soon realized that she was confessing exactly the opposite, a game like mine had never occurred to her. Nor, she said, had the formula of her new designation at first made much of an impression: *Raffaella Cerullo Carracci*. Nothing exciting, nothing serious. In the beginning, that "Carracci" had been no more absorbing than an exercise in logical analysis, of the sort that Maestra Oliviero had hammered into us in elementary school. What was it, an indirect object of place? Did it mean that she now lived not with her parents but with Stefano? Did it mean that the new house where she was going to live would have on the door a brass plate that said "Carracci"? Did it mean that if I were to write to her I would no longer address the letter to Raffaella Cerullo but to Raffaella Carracci? Did it mean that in everyday usage *Cerullo* would soon disappear from *Raffaella Cerullo Carracci*, and that she herself would define herself, and sign, only as Raffaella Carracci, and that her children would have to make an effort to recall their mother's surname, and that her grandchildren would be completely ignorant of their grandmother's surname?

Yes. A custom. Everything according to the rules, then. But

Lila, as usual, hadn't stopped there, she had soon gone further. As we worked with brushes and paints, she told me that she had begun to see in that formula an indirect object of place to which, as if *Cerullo Carracci* somehow indicated that Cerullo *goes toward Carracci, falls into it, is sucked up by it, is dissolved in it.* And, from the abrupt assignment of the role of speech maker at her wedding to Silvio Solara, from the entrance into the restaurant of Marcello Solara, wearing on his feet, no less, the shoes that Stefano had led her to believe he considered a sacred relic, from her honeymoon and the beatings, up until that installation—in the void that she felt inside, the living thing determined by Stefano—she had been increasingly oppressed by an unbearable sensation, a force pushing down harder and harder, crushing her. That impression had been getting stronger, had prevailed. Raffaella Cerullo, overpowered, had lost her shape and had dissolved inside the outlines of Stefano, becoming a subsidiary emanation of him: *Signora Carracci.* It was then that I began to see in the panel the traces of what she was saying. "It's a thing that's still going on," she said in a whisper. And meanwhile we pasted paper, laid on color. But what were we really doing, what was I helping her do?

The workmen, in great bewilderment, attached the panel to the wall. We were sad but we didn't say so; the game was over. We cleaned the shop thoroughly. Lila changed her mind once again about the position of a sofa, of an ottoman. Finally we withdrew together to the door and contemplated our work. She burst out laughing as I had never heard her laugh, a free, self-mocking laugh. I, on the other hand, was so enthralled by the upper part of the panel, where Lila's head no longer was, that I couldn't take in the whole. All you could see, at the top, was a very vivid eye, encircled by midnight blue and red.

27.

The day of the opening Lila arrived in Piazza dei Martiri sitting in the convertible next to her husband. When she got out, I saw in her the uncertain gaze of someone who is afraid something bad is going to happen. The overexcitement of the days of the panel had dissipated; she had again taken on the sickly look of a woman who is unwillingly pregnant. Yet she was carefully dressed, she seemed to have stepped out of a fashion magazine. She immediately left Stefano and dragged me off to look at the shopwindows of Via dei Mille.

We walked for a while. She was tense, she kept asking me if anything was out of place.

"Do you remember," she said suddenly, "the girl dressed all in green, the one with the derby?"

I remembered. I remembered the uneasiness we had felt when we saw her, on that same street, years before, and the fight between our boys and the local boys, and the intervention of the Solaras, and Michele with the iron bar, and the fear. I realized that she wanted to hear something soothing, I said:

"It was just a matter of money, Lila. Today it's all changed, you're much prettier than the girl in green."

But I thought: It's not true, I'm lying to you. There was something malevolent in the inequality, and now I knew it. It acted in the depths, it dug deeper than money. The cash of two grocery stores, and even of the shoe factory and the shoe store, was not sufficient to hide our origin. Lila herself, even if she had taken from the cash drawer more money than she had taken, even if she had taken millions, thirty, even fifty, couldn't do it. I had understood this, and finally there was something that I knew better than she did, I had learned it not on those streets but outside the school, looking at the girl who came to meet Nino. She was superior to us, just as she was, unwittingly. And this was unendurable.

We returned to the shop. The afternoon went on like a kind of marriage feast: food, sweets, a lot of wine; all the guests in the clothes they had worn to Lila's wedding, Fernando, Nunzia, Rino, the entire Solara family, Alfonso, we girls, Ada, Carmela, and I. There was a crowd of cars haphazardly parked, there was a crowd in the shop, the clamor of voices grew louder. The entire time, Gigliola and Pinuccia competed to act like the proprietor, each striving harder than the other, and both worn out by the strain. The panel with Lila's picture loomed over everything. Some paused to look at it with interest, some gave it a skeptical glance or even laughed. I couldn't take my eyes off it. Lila was no longer recognizable. What remained was a seductive, tremendous form, the image of a one-eyed goddess who thrust her beautifully shod feet into the center of the room.

In the crush I was amazed by Alfonso, who was lively, cheerful, elegant. I had never seen him like that, at school or in the neighborhood or in the grocery, and Lila herself pondered him for a long time, perplexed. I said to her, laughing, "He's not himself anymore."

"What happened to him?"

"I don't know."

Alfonso was the true good news of that afternoon. Something that had been silent in him awakened, in the brightly lit shop. It was as if he had unexpectedly discovered that this part of the city made him feel good. He became unusually active. We saw him arrange this object and that, start up conversations with the stylish people who came in out of curiosity, who examined the shoes or grabbed a pastry and a glass of vermouth. At a certain point he joined us and in a self-assured tone praised effusively the work we had done on the photograph. He was in a state of such mental freedom that he overcame his timidity and said to his sister-in-law, "I've always known you were dangerous," and he kissed her on both cheeks.

I stared at him perplexed. Dangerous? What had he perceived, in the panel, that had escaped me? Was Alfonso capable of seeing beyond appearances? Did he know how to look with imagination? Is it possible, I wondered, that his real future is not in studying but in this affluent part of the city, where he'll be able to use the little he's learning in school? Ah yes, he concealed inside himself another person. He was different from all the boys of the neighborhood, and mainly he was different from his brother, Stefano, who, sitting on an ottoman in a corner, was silent but ready to respond with a tranquil smile to anyone who spoke to him.

Evening fell. Suddenly a bright light flared outside. The Solaras, grandfather, father, mother, sons, rushed out to see, gripped by a noisy familial enthusiasm. We all went out into the street. Above the windows and the entrance shone the word "SOLARA."

Lila grimaced, she said to me, "They gave in on that, too."

She pushed me reluctantly toward Rino, who seemed happiest of all, and said to him, "If the shoes are Cerullo, why is the shop Solara?"

Rino took her by the arm and said in a low voice, "Lina, why do you always want to be a pain in the ass? You remember the mess you got me into in this very square? What am I supposed to do, you want another mess? Be satisfied for once. We are here, in the center of Naples, and we are the masters. Those shits who wanted to beat us up less than three years ago—do you see them now? They stop, they look in the windows, they go in, they take a pastry. Isn't that enough for you? Cerullo shoes, Solara shop. What do you want to see up there, Carracci?"

Lila was evasive, saying to him, without aggression, "I'm perfectly calm. Enough to tell you that you'd better not ask me for anything ever again. What do you think you're doing? Do you borrow money from Signora Solara? Does Stefano borrow money from her? Are you both in debt to her, and so you always say yes? From now on, every man for himself, Rino."

She abandoned us, headed straight toward Michele Solara, in a playfully flirtatious way. I saw that she went off with him to the square, they walked around the stone lions. I saw that her husband followed her with his gaze. I saw that he didn't take his eyes off her all the while she and Michele walked, talking. I saw that Gigliola grew furious, she whispered in Pinuccia's ear and they both stared at her.

Meanwhile the shop emptied, someone turned off the large, luminous sign. The square darkened for a few seconds, then the street lamps regained their strength. Lila left Michele laughing, but as she entered the shop her face was suddenly drained of life, she shut herself in the back room where the toilet was.

Alfonso, Marcello, Pinuccia, and Gigliola began to straighten up. I went to help.

Lila came out of the bathroom and Stefano, as if he had been waiting in ambush, immediately grabbed her by the arm. She wriggled free, irritated, and joined me. She was very pale. She whispered, "I've had some blood. What does it mean, is the baby dead?"

28.

Lila's pregnancy lasted scarcely more than ten weeks; then the midwife came and scraped away everything. The next day she went back to work in the new grocery with Carmen Peluso. This marked the beginning of a long period in which, sometimes gentle, sometimes fierce, she stopped running around, having apparently decided to compress her whole life into the orderliness of that space fragrant with mortar and cheese, filled with sausages, bread, mozzarella, anchovies in salt, hunks of *cicoli*, sacks overflowing with dried beans, bladders stuffed with lard.

This behavior was greatly appreciated in particular by Stefano's mother, Maria. As if she had recognized in her daughter-in-law something of herself, she suddenly became more affectionate, and gave her some old earrings of red gold. Lila accepted them with pleasure and wore them often. For a while her face remained pale, she had pimples on her forehead, her eyes were sunk deep into the sockets, the skin was stretched so tight over her cheekbones that it seemed transparent. Then she revived and put even more energy into promoting the shop. Already by Christmastime the profits had risen and within a few months surpassed those of the grocery in the old neighborhood.

Maria's appreciation grew. She went more and more often to give her daughter-in-law a hand, rather than her son, whose failed paternity—along with the pressures of business—had made him surly, or her daughter, who had started working in the store in Piazza dei Martiri and had strictly forbidden her mother to appear, so as not to make a bad impression with the clientele. The old Signora Carracci even took the young Signora Carracci's side when Stefano and Pinuccia blamed her for her inability, or unwillingness, to keep a baby inside her.

"She doesn't want children," Stefano complained.

"Yes," Pinuccia supported him, "she wants to stay a girl, she doesn't know how to be a wife."

Maria reproached them both harshly: "Don't even think such things, Our Lord gives children and Our Lord takes them away, I don't want to hear that nonsense."

"You be quiet," her daughter cried, in annoyance. "You gave that bitch the earrings I liked."

Their arguments, Lila's reactions, soon became neighborhood gossip, which spread, and even I heard it. But I didn't pay much attention, the school year had begun.

It started right off in a way that amazed me most of all. I did well from the first days, as if, with the departure of Antonio, the disappearance of Nino, maybe even Lila's decisive commitment to managing the grocery, something in my head had relaxed. I found that I remembered with precision everything I had learned badly in my first year; I answered the teachers' questions with ready intelligence. Not only that. Professor Galiani, maybe because she had lost Nino, her most brilliant student, redoubled her interest in me and said that it would be stimulating and instructive for me to go to a march for world peace that started in Resina and continued on to Naples. I decided to have a look, partly out of curiosity, partly out of fear that Professor Galiani would be offended, and partly because the march went along the *stradone*, skirting the neighborhood, and it wouldn't take much effort. But my mother wanted me to take my brothers. I argued, I protested, and was late. I arrived with them at the railway bridge, and down below saw the people marching; they occupied the whole street, preventing the cars from passing. They were normal people and weren't really marching but walking, carrying banners and signs. I wanted to find Professor Galiani, to be seen, and I ordered my brothers to wait on the bridge. It was a terrible idea: I couldn't find the professor, and, as soon as I turned my back, they joined some other children who were throwing stones at the demonstrators and yelling insults. In a sweat I rushed to get them, and hurried them away, terrified by the idea that the far-sighted Professor Galiani had picked them out and recognized that they were my brothers.

Meanwhile the weeks passed, there were new classes and the textbooks to buy. It seemed pointless to show the list of books to my mother so that she would negotiate with my father and get money from him, I knew that there was no money. In addition, there was no news of Maestra Oliviero. Between August and September, I had gone twice to visit her in the hospital, but the first time I had found her asleep and the second I discovered that she had been discharged but had not returned home. Feeling desperate, in early November I went to ask the neighbor about her, and learned that, because of her health, she had gone to a sister in Potenza, and who knew if she would ever return to Naples, to the neighborhood, to her job. At that point I decided to ask Alfonso if, when his brother had bought the books for him, we could somehow arrange things so that I could use his. He was enthusiastic and proposed that we should study together, maybe at Lila's house, which, ever since she had started working at the grocery, was empty from seven in the morning until nine at night. We resolved to do that.

But one morning Alfonso said to me, somewhat annoyed, "Go and see Lila in the grocery today, she wants to see you." He knew why, but she had sworn him to silence and it was impossible to get the secret out of him.

In the afternoon I went to the new grocery. Carmen, with a mixture of sadness and joy, wanted to show me a card from some city in Piedmont that Enzo, her fiancé, had sent her. Lila had also received a card, from Antonio, and for a moment I thought she had wanted me to come there just to show it to me. But she didn't show it to me or tell me what he had written. She dragged me into the back of the shop and asked, in a tone of amusement:

"You remember our bet?"

I nodded yes.

"You remember that you lost?"

I nodded yes.

"You remember that you now have to pass with the best grades?"

I nodded yes.

She pointed to two large packages tied up in wrapping paper. In them were the school books.

29.

They were very heavy. At home, I was very excited to discover that they were not the used, often ill-smelling volumes that in the past the teacher had got for me but were brand-new, fragrant with fresh ink, and conspicuous among them were the dictionaries—Zingarelli, Rocci, and Calonghi-Georges—which the teacher had never been able to acquire.

My mother, who had a word of contempt for anything that happened to me, burst into tears as she watched me unwrap the packages. Surprised, intimidated by that unusual reaction, I went to her, caressed her arm. It's difficult to say what had moved her: maybe her sense of impotence in the face of our poverty, maybe the generosity of the grocer's wife, I don't know. She calmed down quickly, muttered something incomprehensible, and became engrossed in her duties.

In the little room where I slept with my sister and brothers I had a small, rough table, riddled with worm holes, where I usually did my homework. On it I arranged all the books, and, seeing them lined up there, against the wall, I felt charged with energy.

The days began to fly by. I gave back to Professor Galiani the books she had lent me for the summer, she gave me others, which were even more difficult. I read them diligently on Sundays, but I didn't understand much. I ran my eyes along the lines, I turned the pages, and yet the style annoyed me, the meaning escaped me. That year, my fourth year of high school, between studying and difficult readings, I was exhausted, but it was the exhaustion of contentment.

One day Professor Galiani asked me, "What newspaper do you read, Greco?"

That question provoked the same uneasiness I had felt talking to Nino at Lila's wedding. The professor took it for granted that I normally did something that at my house, in my environment, was not at all normal. How could I tell her that my father didn't buy the newspaper, that I had never read one? I didn't have the heart, and my mind raced to remember if Pasquale, who was a Communist, read one. A useless effort. Then I thought of Donato Sarratore and I remembered Ischia, the Maronti, I remembered that he wrote for *Roma*. I answered:

"I read *Roma*."

The professor gave an ironic half smile, and the next day began handing on her newspapers. She bought two, sometimes three, and after school she would give me one. I thanked her and went home upset by what seemed to me still more homework.

At first I left the paper around the house, and put off reading it until I had finished my homework, but at night it had disappeared, my father had grabbed it to read in bed or in the bathroom. So I got in the habit of hiding it among my books, and took it out only at night, when everyone was sleeping. Sometimes it was *Unità*, sometimes *Il Mattino*, sometimes *Corriere della Sera*, but all three were difficult for me, it was like having to follow a comic strip whose preceding episodes you didn't know. I hurried from one column to the next, more out of duty than out of real curiosity, hoping, as in all things imposed by school, that what I didn't understand today I would, by sheer persistence, understand tomorrow.

In that period I saw little of Lila. Sometimes, right after school, before I rushed off to do my homework, I went to the new grocery. I was starving, she knew it, and would make me a generously stuffed sandwich. While I devoured it, I would articulate, in good Italian, statements I had memorized from Professor Galiani's books and newspapers. I would mention, let's say, "the atrocious reality of the Nazi extermination camps," or "what men were able to do and what they can do today as well," or "the atomic threat and the obligation to peace," or the fact that "as a result of subduing the forces of nature with the tools that we invent, we find ourselves today at the point where the force of our tools has become a greater concern than the forces of nature," or "the need for a culture that combats and eliminates suffering," or the idea that "religion will disappear from men's consciousness when, finally, we have constructed a world of equals, without class distinctions, and with a sound scientific conception of society and of life." I talked to her about these and other things because I wanted to show her that I was sailing toward passing with high marks, and because I didn't know who else to say them to, and because I hoped she would respond so that we could resume our old habit of discussion. But she said almost nothing, in fact she seemed embarrassed, as if she didn't really understand what I was talking about. Or if she made a remark, she concluded by digging up an old obsession that now—I didn't know why—had started working inside her again. She began to talk about the origin of Don Achille's money, and of the Solaras', even in the presence of Carmen, who immediately agreed. But as soon as a customer came in she stopped, she became very polite and efficient, she sliced, weighed, took money.

Once, she left the cash drawer open and, staring at the money, said, angrily, "I earn this with my labor and Carmen's. But nothing in there is mine, Lenù, it's made with Stefano's money. And Stefano to make money started with his father's money. Without what Don Achille put under the mattress, working the black market and loan-sharking, today there would not be this and there would not be the shoe factory. Not only that. Stefano, Rino, my father would not have sold a single shoe without the money and the connections of the Solara family, who are also loan sharks. Is it clear what I've got myself into?"

Clear, but I didn't understand the point of those discussions.

"It's water under the bridge," I said, and reminded her of the conclusions she had come to when she was engaged to Stefano. "What you're talking about is what's behind us, we are something else."

But although she had invented that theory, she did not seem convinced by it. She said to me, and I have a vivid memory of the phrase, which was in dialect:

"I don't like what I've done and what I'm doing."

I thought that she must be spending time with Pasquale, who had always had opinions like that. I thought that maybe their relationship had been strengthened by the fact that Pasquale was engaged to Ada, who worked in the old grocery, and was the brother of Carmen, who worked with her in the new one. I went home dissatisfied, struggling to hold off an old childhood feeling, from the period when I suffered because Lila and Carmela had become friends and tried to exclude me. I calmed myself down by studying until very late.

One night as I was reading *Il Mattino*, my eyes heavy with sleep, a short, unsigned article jolted me awake like an electric charge. I couldn't believe it—the article was about the shop in Piazza dei Martiri and it praised the panel that Lila and I had created.

I read and reread it, I can still recall a few lines: "The young women who manage the friendly shop in Piazza dei Martiri did not want to reveal the name of the artist. A pity. Whoever invented that anomalous mixture of photography and color has an avant-garde imagination that, with sublime ingenuity but also with unusual energy, subdues the material to the urgent needs of an intimate, potent grief." Otherwise, it had generous praise for the shoe store, "an important sign of the dynamism that, in recent years, has invested Neapolitan entrepreneurial endeavors."

I didn't sleep a wink.

After school I hurried to find Lila. The shop was empty,

Carmen had gone home to her mother, Giuseppina, who wasn't well, Lila was on the phone with a local supplier who had not delivered mozzarella or provolone or I don't remember what. I heard her shout, curse, I was upset. I thought maybe the man at the other end was old, he would be insulted, he would send one of his sons to take revenge. I thought: Why does she always overdo it? When she got off the phone she gave a snort of contempt and turned to me to apologize: "If I don't act like that, they won't even listen to me."

I showed her the newspaper. She gave it a distracted glance, said, "I know about it." She explained that it had been an initiative of Michele Solara's, carried out as usual without consulting anyone. Look, she said, and went to the cash register, took out of the drawer a couple of creased clippings, handed them to me. Those, too, were about the shop in Piazza dei Martiri. One was a small article in *Roma*, whose author lavished praise on the Solaras, but made not the slightest mention of the panel. The other was an article spread over three columns, in *Napoli Notte*, and in it the shop sounded like a royal palace. The space was described in an extravagant Italian that praised the furnishings, the splendid illumination, the marvelous shoes, and, above all, "the kindness, the sweetness, and the grace of the two seductive Nereids, Miss Gigliola Spagnuolo and Miss Giuseppina Carracci, marvelous young women upon whom rests the fate of an enterprise that stands high among the flourishing commercial activities of our city." You had to get to the end to find a mention of the panel, which was dismissed in a few lines. The author of the article called it "a crude mess, an out-of-tune note in a place of majestic refinement."

"Did you see the signature?" Lila asked, teasingly.

The article in *Roma* was signed "d.s." and the article in *Napoli Notte* bore the signature of Donato Sarratore, Nino's father.

"Yes."

"And what do you say?"

"What should I say?"

"Like father like son, you should say."

She laughed mirthlessly. She explained that, seeing the growing success of Cerullo shoes and the Solara shop, Michele had decided to publicize the business and had distributed a few gratuities here and there, thanks to which the city newspapers had promptly come out with admiring articles. Advertising, in other words. Paid for. Pointless even to read. In those articles, she said, there was not a single true word.

I was disappointed. I didn't like the way she belittled the newspapers, which I was diligently trying to read, sacrificing sleep. And I didn't like her emphasis on the relationship between Nino and the author of the two articles. What need was there to associate Nino with his father, a pompous fabricator of factitious phrases?

30.

Yet it was thanks to those phrases that in a short time the Solaras' shop and Cerullo shoes became more successful. Gigliola and Pinuccia boasted a lot about how they had been quoted in the papers, but the success did not diminish their rivalry and each went on to give herself the credit for the shop's fortunes, and began to consider the other an obstacle to further successes. On a single point they continued to agree: Lila's panel was an abomination. They were rude to anyone who, in a refined little voice, stopped in just to have a look at it. And they framed the articles from *Roma* and *Napoli Notte*, but not the one from *Il Mattino*.

Between Christmas and Easter, the Solaras and the Carraccis made a lot of money. Stefano, especially, drew a sigh of relief. The new grocery and the old one were prospering, the Cerullo shoe factory was working at full capacity. In addition, the shop in Piazza dei Martiri revealed what he had always known, and that is that the shoes Lila had designed years before sold well not only on the Rettifilo, Via Foria, and Corso Garibaldi but were coveted by the wealthy, those who casually reached for their wallets. An important market, therefore, which had to be consolidated and expanded.

As proof of that success, in the spring some good imitations of Cerullo shoes began to appear in the shopwindows of the outlying neighborhoods. These shoes were essentially identical to Lila's, but slightly modified by a fringe, a stud. Protests, threats immediately blocked their circulation: Michele Solara straightened things out. But he didn't stop there, he soon reached the conclusion that new models had to be designed. For that reason, one evening in the shop in Piazza dei Martiri, he summoned his brother Marcello, the Carraccis, Rino, and, naturally, Gigliola and Pinuccia. Surprisingly, Stefano showed up without Lila, he said that his wife was sorry, she was tired.

Her absence did not please the Solara brothers. If Lila isn't here, Michele said, making Gigliola nervous, what the fuck are we talking about. But Rino immediately interrupted. He asserted, lying, that he and his father had begun some time ago to think of new models and planned to introduce them at a trade show that was to be held in Arezzo in September. Michele didn't believe him, and became still more irritable. He said that they had to come out with products that were really innovative and not with normal stuff. Finally he turned to Stefano:

"Your wife is necessary, you've got to make her come."

Stefano answered with startling hostility: "My wife works hard all day in the grocery store and at night she has to stay home, she has to think of me."

"All right," Michele said, with a grimace, spoiling for a moment his handsome boy's face. "But see if she can think of us, too, a little."

The evening left everyone unhappy, but Pinuccia and Gigliola in particular. For different reasons, they found the importance that Michele gave Lila intolerable, and in the following days their disgruntlement became a dark mood that at the slightest opportunity gave rise to a quarrel.

At that point—I think it was March—an accident happened; I don't really know how. One afternoon, during one of their daily disagreements, Gigliola slapped Pinuccia. Pinuccia complained to Rino, who, believing at the time that he was riding the crest of a wave as high as a house, came to the shop with a proprietary air and told Gigliola off. Gigliola reacted aggressively and he went so far as to threaten to fire her.

"Starting tomorrow," he said to her, "you can go and stuff ricotta in the cannoli again."

Then Michele showed up. Smiling, he led Rino outside, to the square, to indicate the sign over the door.

"My friend," he said, "the shop is called Solara and you have no right to come here and tell my girlfriend: I'm firing you."

Rino retaliated by reminding him that everything in the shop belonged to his brother-in-law, and that he made the shoes himself, so he certainly did have the right. Inside, meanwhile, Gigliola and Pinuccia, each feeling protected by her own fiancé, had already started fighting again. The two young men hurried back inside, tried to calm them down, and couldn't. Michele lost patience and cried that he would fire them both. Not only that: he let slip that he would have Lila manage the shop.

Lila?

The shop?

The two girls were silent and the idea left even Rino speechless. Then the discussion started up again, this time focused on that outrageous statement. Gigliola, Pinuccia, and Rino were allied against Michele—what's wrong, what use to you is Lina, we're making money here, you can't complain, I thought up all the shoe styles, she was a child, what could she invent—and the tension increased. Who knows how long the quarreling would have gone on if the accident I mentioned hadn't happened. Suddenly, and it's unclear how, the panel—the panel with the strips of black paper, the photograph, the thick patches of color—let out a rasping sound, a kind of sick breath, and burst into flame. Pinuccia had her back to the photograph when it happened. The fire blazed up behind her as if from a secret hearth and licked her hair, which crackled and would have burned completely if Rino hadn't quickly extinguished it with his bare hands.

31.

Both Rino and Michele blamed Gigliola for the fire, because she smoked secretly and so had a tiny lighter. According to Rino, Gigliola had done it on purpose: while they were all occupied by their wrangling, she had set fire to the panel, which, loaded with paper, glue, paint, had instantly burst into flames. Michele was more circumspect: Gigliola, he knew, continuously toyed with the lighter and so, unintentionally, caught up in the argument, hadn't realized that the flame was too close to the photograph. But the girl couldn't bear either the first hypothesis or the second, and with a fiercely combative look blamed Lila herself, that is, she blamed the disfigured image, which had caught fire spontaneously, like the Devil, who, attempting to corrupt the saints, assumed the features of a woman, but the saints called on Jesus, and the demon was transformed into flames. She added, in confirmation of her version, that Pinuccia herself had told her that her sister-in-law had the ability not to stay pregnant, and, in fact, if she was unsuccessful she would let the child drain out, rejecting the gifts of the Lord.

This gossip grew worse when Michele Solara began to go regularly to the new grocery store. He spent a lot of time joking with Lila, joking with Carmen, so that Carmen hypothesized that he came for her and on the one hand was afraid that someone would tell Enzo, doing his military service in Piedmont, while on the other she was flattered and began to flirt. Lila instead made fun of the young Solara. She heard the rumors spread by his fiancée and so she said to him: "You'd better go, we're witches here, we're very dangerous."

But when I went to see her, during that period, I never found her truly cheerful. She assumed an artificial tone and was sarcastic about everything. Did she have a bruise on her arm? Stefano had caressed her too passionately. Were her eyes red from crying? Those were tears of happiness, not grief. Be careful of Michele, he liked to hurt people? No, she said, all he has to do is touch me and he'll burn: it's I who hurt people.

On that last point there had always been modest agreement. But Gigliola especially had no doubts by now: Lila was a witch-whore, she had cast a spell on her fiancé; that's why he wanted her to manage the shop in Piazza dei Martiri. And for days, jealous, desperate, she wouldn't go to work. Then she decided to talk to Pinuccia, they became allies, and moved to the offensive. Pinuccia worked on her brother, insisting that he was a happy cuckold, and then she attacked Rino, her fiancé, telling him that he wasn't a boss but Michele's servant. So one evening Stefano and Rino waited for Michele outside the bar, and when he appeared they made a very general speech that in substance, however, meant: leave Lila alone, you're making her waste time, she has to work. Michele immediately got the message and replied coldly:

"What the fuck are you saying?"

"If you don't understand it means you don't want to understand."

"No, my fine friends, it's you who don't want to understand

our commercial needs. And if you won't understand them, I necessarily have to see to them."

"Meaning?" Stefano asked.

"Your wife is wasted in the grocery."

"In what sense?"

"In Piazza dei Martiri she would make in a month what your sister and Gigliola couldn't make in a hundred years."

"Explain yourself."

"Lina needs to command, Ste'. She needs to have a responsibility. She should invent things. She ought to start thinking right away about the new shoe styles."

They argued and finally, amid a thousand fine distinctions, came to an agreement. Stefano absolutely refused to let his wife go and work in Piazza dei Martiri: the new grocery was going well and to take Lila out of there would be foolish; but he agreed to have her design new models right away, at least for winter. Michele said that not to let Lila run the shoe store was stupid, and with a vaguely threatening coolness he put off the discussion until after the summer; he considered it a done deal that she would start designing new shoes.

"They have to be chic," he urged, "you have to insist on that point."

"She'll do what she wants, as usual."

"I can advise her, she'll listen to me," said Michele.

"There's no need."

I went to see Lila shortly after that agreement, and she spoke to me about it herself. I had just come from school, the weather was already getting hot, and I was tired. She was alone in the grocery and for the moment she seemed as if relieved. She said that she wouldn't design anything, not even a sandal, not even a slipper.

"They'll get mad."

"What can I do about it?"

"It's money, Lila."

"They already have enough."

It was her usual sort of obstinacy, I thought. She was like that, as soon as someone told her to focus on something the wish to do so vanished. But I soon realized that it wasn't a matter of her character or even of disgust with the business affairs of her husband, Rino, and the Solaras, reinforced by the Communist arguments of Pasquale and Carmen. There was something more and she spoke slowly, seriously, about it.

"Nothing comes to mind," she said.

"Have you tried?"

"Yes. But it's not the way it was when I was twelve."

The shoes—I understood—had come out of her brain only that one time and they wouldn't again, she didn't have any others. That game was over, she didn't know how to start it again. The smell of leather repelled her, of skins, what she had done she no longer knew how to do. And then everything had changed. Fernando's small shop had been consumed by the new spaces, by the workers' benches, by three machines. Her father had as it were grown smaller, he didn't even quarrel with his oldest son, he worked and that was all. Even affections were as if deflated. If she still felt tender toward her mother when she came to the grocery to fill her shopping bags, free, as if they still lived in poverty, if she still gave little gifts to her younger siblings, she could no longer feel the bond with Rino. Ruined, broken. The need to help and protect him had diminished. Thus the motivations for the fantasy of the shoes had vanished, the soil in which they had germinated was arid. It was most of all, she said suddenly, a way of showing you that I could do something well even if I had stopped going to school. Then she laughed nervously, glancing obliquely at me to see my reaction.

I didn't answer, prevented by a strong emotion. Lila was like that? She didn't have my stubborn diligence? She drew out of herself thoughts, shoes, words written and spoken, complicated plans, rages and inventions, only to show *me* something of herself? Having lost that motivation, she was lost? Even the treatment to which she had subjected her wedding photograph—even that she would never be able to repeat? Everything, in her, was the result of the chaos of an occasion?

I felt that in some part of me a long painful tension was relaxing, and her wet eyes, her fragile smile moved me. But it didn't last. She continued to speak, she touched her forehead with a gesture that was customary with her, she said, regretfully, "I always have to prove that I can be better," and she added darkly, "When we opened this place, Stefano showed me how to cheat on the weight; and at first I shouted you're a thief, that's how you make money, and then I couldn't resist, I showed him that I had learned and immediately found my own ways to cheat and I showed him, and I was constantly thinking up new ones: I'll cheat you all, I cheat you on the weight and a thousand other things, I cheat the neighborhood, don't trust me, Lenù, don't trust what I say and do."

I was uneasy. In the space of a few seconds she had changed, already I no longer knew what she wanted. Why was she speaking to me like this now? I didn't know if she had decided to or if the words came out of her mouth unwittingly, an impetuous stream in which the intention of reinforcing the bond between us—a real intention—was immediately swept away by the equally real need to deny it specificity: you see, with Stefano I behave the way I do with you, I act like this with everyone, I'm beauty and the beast, good and evil. She interlaced her long thin fingers, clasped them tight, asked, "Did you hear that Gigliola says the photograph caught fire by itself?"

"It's stupid, Gigliola is mad at you."

She gave a little laugh that was like a shock, something in her twisted too abruptly.

"I have something that hurts here, behind the eyes, something is pressing. You see the knives there? They're too sharp—

I just gave them to the knife grinder. While I'm slicing salami I think how much blood there is in a person's body. If you put too much stuff in things, they break. Or they catch fire and burn. I'm glad the wedding picture burned. The marriage should burn, too, the shop, the shoes, the Solaras, everything."

I realized that, no matter how she struggled, worked, proclaimed, she couldn't get out of it: since the day of her wedding she had been pursued by an ever greater, increasingly ungovernable unhappiness, and I felt pity. I told her to be calm, she nodded yes.

"You have to try to relax."

"Help me."

"How."

"Stay near me."

"That's what I'm doing."

"It's not true. I tell you all my secrets, even the worst, you tell me hardly anything about yourself."

"You're wrong. The only person I don't hide anything from is you."

She shook her head no energetically, she said, "Even if you're better than me, even if you know more things, don't leave me."

32.

They pressured her, wearing her down, and so she pretended to give in. She told Stefano that she would design the new shoes, and at the first opportunity she also told Michele. Then she summoned Rino and spoke to him exactly as he had always wanted her to: "You design them, I can't. Design them with papa, you're in the business, you know how to do it. But until you put them on the market and sell them, don't tell anyone that I didn't do them, not even Stefano."

"And if they don't go well?"

"It will be my fault."

"And if they do well?"

"I'll say how things are and you'll get the credit you deserve."

Rino was very pleased with that lie. He set to work with Fernando, but every so often he went to Lila in complete secrecy to show her what he had in mind. She examined the styles and at first pretended to admire them, partly because she couldn't tolerate his anxious expression, partly to get rid of him quickly. But soon she herself marveled at how genuinely good the new shoes were—they resembled the ones now selling and yet were different. "Maybe," she said to me one day, in an unexpectedly lighthearted tone, "I really didn't think up those shoes, they really are my brother's work." And at that point she truly did seem to be rid of a weight. She rediscovered her affection for Rino, or rather she realized that she had exaggerated: that bond couldn't be dissolved, it would never be dissolved, whatever he did, even if a rat came out of his body, a skittish horse, any sort of animal. The lie—she hypothesized—has relieved Rino of the anxiety of being inadequate, and that has taken him back to the way he was as a boy, and now he is discovering that he knows his job, that he's good at it. As for Rino himself, he was increasingly satisfied with his sister's praise. At the end of every consultation, he asked in a whisper for the house key and, also in complete secrecy, went to spend an hour there with Pinuccia.

For my part, I tried to show her that I would always be her friend, and on Sundays I often invited her to go out with me. Once we ventured as far as the Mostra d'Oltremare neighborhood with two of my schoolmates, who were intimidated, however, when they found out that she had been married for more than a year, and behaved respectfully, sedately, as if I had compelled them to go out with my mother. One asked her hesitantly:

"Do you have a child?"

Lila shook her head no.

"They haven't come?"

She shook her head no.

From that moment on the evening was more or less a failure.

In mid-May I dragged her to a cultural club where, because Professor Galiani had urged me to, I felt obliged to go to a talk by a scientist named Giuseppe Montalenti. It was the first time we had had an experience of that type: Montalenti gave a kind of lesson, not for children but, rather, for the adults who had come to hear him. We sat at the back of the bare room and I was quickly bored. The professor had sent me but she hadn't shown up. I murmured to Lila, "Let's go." But Lila refused, she whispered that she wasn't bold enough to get up, she was afraid of disrupting the lecture. But it wasn't her type of worry; it was the sign of an unexpected submissiveness, or of an interest that she didn't want to admit. We stayed till the end. Montalenti talked about Darwin; neither of us knew who Darwin was. As we left, I said jokingly, "He said a thing that I already knew: you're a monkey."

But she didn't want to joke: "I don't want to ever forget it," she said.

"That you're a monkey?"

"That we're animals."

"You and I?"

"Everyone."

"But he said there are a lot of differences between us and the apes."

"Yes? Like what? That my mother pierced my ears and so I've worn earrings since I was born, but the mothers of monkeys don't, so their offspring don't wear earrings?"

A fit of laughter possessed us, as we listed differences, one after the other, each more ridiculous than the last: we were enjoying ourselves. But when we returned to the neighborhood our good mood vanished. We met Pasquale and Ada taking a walk on the *stradone* and learned from them that Stefano was looking everywhere for Lila, very upset. I offered to go home with her, she refused. Instead she agreed to let Pasquale and Ada take her in the car.

I found out the next day why Stefano had been looking for her. It wasn't because we were late. It wasn't even because he was annoyed that his wife sometimes spent her free time with me and not with him. It was something else. He had just learned that Pinuccia was often seen with Rino at his house. He had just learned that the two were together in his bed, that Lila gave them the keys. He had just learned that Pinuccia was pregnant. But what had most infuriated him was that when he slapped his sister because of the disgusting things she and Rino had done, Pinuccia shouted at him, "You're jealous because I'm a woman and Lina isn't, because Rino knows how to behave with women and you don't." Lila, seeing him so upset, listening to him—and recalling the composure he had always shown when they were engaged—had burst out laughing, and Stefano had gone for a drive, so as not to murder her. According to her, he had gone to look for a prostitute.

33.

The preparations for Rino and Pinuccia's wedding were carried out in a rush. I was not much concerned with it, I had my final class essays, the final oral exams. And then something else happened that caused me great agitation. Professor Galiani, who was in the habit of violating the teachers' code of behavior with indifference, invited me—me and no one else in the school—to her house, to a party that her children were giving. It was unusual enough that she lent me books and newspapers, that she had directed me to a march for peace and a demanding lecture. Now she had gone over the limit: she had taken me aside and given me that invitation. "Come as you like," she had said, "alone or with someone, with your boyfriend or without: the important thing is to come." Like that, a few days before the end of the school year, without worrying about how much I had to study, without worrying about the earthquake that it set off inside me.

I had immediately said yes, but I quickly discovered that I would never have the courage to go. A party at any professor's house was unthinkable, imagine at the house of Professor Galiani. For me it was as if I were to present myself at the royal palace, curtsey to the queen, dance with the princes. A great pleasure but also an act of violence, like a yank: to be dragged by the arm, forced to do a thing that, although it appeals to you, you know is not suitable—you know that, if circumstances did not oblige you, you would happily avoid doing it. Probably it didn't even occur to Professor Galiani that I had nothing to wear. In class I wore a shapeless black smock. What did she expect there was, the professor, under that smock: clothes and slips and underwear like hers? There was inadequacy, rather, there was poverty, poor breeding. I possessed a single pair of worn-out shoes. My only nice dress was the one I had worn to Lila's wedding, but now it was hot, the dress was fine for March but not for the end of May. And yet the problem was not just what to wear. There was the solitude, the awkwardness of being among strangers, kids with ways of talking among themselves, joking, with tastes I didn't know. I thought of asking Alfonso if he would go with me, he was always kind to me. But—I recalled—Alfonso was a schoolmate and Professor Galiani had addressed the invitation to me alone. What to do? For days I was paralyzed by anxiety, I thought of talking to the professor and coming up with some excuse. Then it occurred to me to ask Lila's advice.

She was as usual in a difficult period, she had a yellow bruise under one cheekbone. She didn't welcome the news.

"Why are you going there?"

"She invited me."

"Where does this professor live?"

"Corso Vittorio Emanuele."

"Can you see the sea from her house?"

"I don't know."

"What does her husband do?"

"A doctor at the Cotugno."

"And the children are still in school?"

"I don't know."

"Do you want one of my dresses?"

"You know they don't fit me."

"You just have a bigger bust."

"Everything of me is bigger, Lila."

"Then I don't know what to tell you."

"I shouldn't go?"

"It's better."

"O.K., I won't go."

She was visibly satisfied with that decision. I said goodbye, left the grocery, turned onto a street where stunted oleander bushes grew. But I heard her calling me, I turned back.

"I'll go with you," she said.

"Where?"

"To the party."

"Stefano won't let you."

"We'll see. Tell me if you want to take me or not."

"Of course I want to."

She became at that point so pleased that I didn't dare try to make her change her mind. But already on the way home I felt that my situation had become worse. None of the obstacles that prevented me from going to the party had been removed, and that offer of Lila's confused me even more. The reasons were tangled and I had no intention of enumerating them, but if I had I would have been confronted by contradictory statements. I was afraid that Stefano wouldn't let her come. I was afraid that Stefano would let her. I was afraid that she would dress in an ostentatious fashion, the way she had when she went to the Solaras. I was afraid that, whatever she wore, her beauty would explode like a star and everyone would be eager to grab a fragment of it. I was afraid that she would express herself in dialect, that she would say something vulgar, that it would become obvious that school for her had ended with an elementary-school diploma. I was afraid that, if she merely opened her mouth, everyone would be hypnotized by her intelligence and Professor Galiani herself would be entranced. I was afraid that the professor would find her both presumptuous and naïve and would say to me: Who is this friend of yours, stop seeing her. I was afraid she would understand that I was only Lila's pale shadow and would be interested not in me any longer but in her, she would want to see her again, she would undertake to make her go back to school.

For a while I avoided the grocery. I hoped that Lila would forget about the party, that the day would come and I would go almost secretly, and then I would tell her: you didn't let me know. Instead she soon came to see me, which she hadn't done for a long time. She had persuaded Stefano not only to take us but also to come and get us, and she wanted to know what time we were to be at the professor's house.

"What are you going to wear?" I asked anxiously.

"Whatever you wear."

"I'm going to wear a blouse and skirt."

"Then I will, too."

"And Stefano is sure that he'll take us and then come and get us?"

"Yes."

"How did you persuade him?"

She made a face, cheerfully, saying that by now she knew how to handle him. "If I want something," she whispered, as if she herself didn't want to hear, "I just have to act a little like a whore."

She said it like that, in dialect, and added other crude, self-mocking expressions, to make me understand the revulsion her husband provoked in her, the disgust she felt at herself. My anxiety increased. I should tell her, I thought, that I'm not going to the party, I should tell her that I changed my mind. I knew, naturally, that behind the appearance of the disciplined Lila, at work from morning to night, there was a Lila who was anything but submissive; yet, in particular now that I was assuming the responsibility of introducing her into the house of Professor Galiani, the recalcitrant Lila frightened me, seemed to me increasingly spoiled by her very refusal to surrender. What would happen if, in the presence of the professor, something made her rebel? What would happen if she decided to use the language she had just used with me? I said cautiously:

"There, please, don't talk like that."

She looked at me in bewilderment. "Like what?"

"Like now."

She was silent for a moment, then she asked, "Are you ashamed of me?"

34.

I wasn't ashamed of her, I swore it, but I hid from her the fact that I was afraid of having to be ashamed of myself for it.

Stefano took us in the convertible to the professor's house. I sat in the back, the two of them in front, and for the first time I was struck by the massive wedding rings on their hands, his and hers. While Lila wore a skirt and blouse, as she had promised, nothing excessive, and no makeup except some lipstick, he was dressed up, with a lot of gold, and a strong odor of shaving soap, as if he expected that at the last moment we would say to him: You come, too. We didn't. I confined myself to thanking him warmly several times, Lila got out of the car without saying goodbye. Stefano drove off with a painful screeching of tires.

We were tempted by the elevator, but then decided against it. We had never taken an elevator, not even Lila's new building had one, we were afraid of getting in trouble. Professor Galiani had said that her apartment was on the fourth floor, that on the door it said "Dott. Prof. Frigerio," but just the same we checked the name plates on every floor. I went ahead, Lila behind, in silence, flight after flight. How clean the building was, the doorknobs and the brass nameplates gleamed. My heart was pounding.

We identified the door first of all by the loud music coming from it, by the din of voices. We smoothed our skirts, I pulled down the slip that tended to rise up my legs, Lila straightened her hair with her fingertips. Both of us, evidently, were afraid of escaping ourselves, of erasing in a moment of distraction the mask of self-possession we had given ourselves. I pressed the bell. We waited, no one came to the door. I looked at Lila, I pressed the button again, longer. Quick footsteps, the door opened. A dark young man appeared, small in stature, with a handsome face and a lively gaze. He appeared to be around twenty. I said nervously that I was a student of Professor Galiani, and without even letting me finish, he laughed, exclaimed, "Elena?"

"Yes."

"In this house we all know you, our mother never misses a chance to torment us by reading us your papers."

The boy's name was Armando and that remark of his was decisive, it gave me a sudden sense of power. I still remember him fondly, there in the doorway. He was absolutely the first person to show me in a practical sense how comfortable it is to arrive in a strange, potentially hostile environment, and discover that you have been preceded by your reputation, that you don't have to do anything to be accepted, that your name is known, that everyone knows about you, and it's the others, the strangers, who must strive to win your favor and not you theirs. Used as I was to the absence of advantages, that unforeseen advantage gave me energy, an immediate self-confidence. My anxieties disappeared, I no longer worried about what Lila could or couldn't do. In the grip of my unexpected centrality, I even forgot to introduce my friend to Armando, nor, on the other hand, did he seem to notice her. He led me in as if I were alone, enthusiastically insisting on how much his mother talked about me, on how she praised me. I followed, self-deprecatingly, Lila closed the door.

The apartment was big, the rooms open and bright, the ceilings high and decorated with floral motifs. What struck me most was the books everywhere, there were more books in that house than in the neighborhood library, entire walls covered by floor-to-ceiling shelves. And music. And young people dancing freely in a large, brilliantly lighted room. And others talking, smoking. All of whom obviously went to school, and had parents who had gone to school. Like Armando: his mother a teacher, his father a surgeon, though he wasn't there that evening. The boy led us onto a small terrace: warm air, large sky, an intense odor of wisteria and roses mixed with that of vermouth and marzipan. We saw the city sparkling with lights, the dark plane of the sea. The professor called my name in greeting, it was she who reminded me of Lila behind me.

"Is she a friend of yours?"

I stammered something, I realized that I didn't know how to make introductions. "My professor. Her name is Lina. We went to elementary school together," I said. Professor Galiani spoke approvingly of long friendships, they're important, an anchorage, generic phrases uttered as she stared at Lila, who responded self-consciously in monosyllables, and who, when she realized that the professor's gaze had come to rest on the wedding ring, immediately covered it with her other hand.

"Are you married?"

"Yes."

"You're the same age as Elena?"

"I'm two weeks older."

Professor Galiani looked around, turned to her son: "Have you introduced them to Nadia?"

"No."

"What are you waiting for?"

"Take it easy, Mamma, they just got here."

The professor said to me, "Nadia is really eager to meet you. This fellow here is a rascal, don't trust him, but she's a good girl, you'll see, you'll be friends, she'll like you."

We left her alone to smoke. Nadia, I understood, was Armando's younger sister: sixteen years of being a pain in the ass—he described her with feigned animosity—she ruined my childhood. I jokingly alluded to the trouble that my younger sister and brothers had always given me, and I turned to Lila for confirmation, smiling. But she remained serious, she said nothing. We returned to the room with the dancers, which had darkened. A Paul Anka song, or maybe "What a Sky," who can remember anymore. The dancers held each other close, faint flickering shadows. The music ended. Even before someone reluctantly switched on the lights, I felt an explosion in my chest, I recognized Nino Sarratore. He was lighting a cigarette, the flame leaped up into his face. I hadn't seen him for almost a year, he seemed to me older, taller, more disheveled, more handsome. Meanwhile the electric light flooded the room and I also recognized the girl he had just stopped dancing with. She was the same girl I had seen long ago outside school, the refined, luminous girl, who had compelled me to comprehend my dullness.

"Here she is," said Armando.

It was Nadia, the daughter of Professor Galiani.

35.

Odd as it may seem, that discovery did not spoil the pleasure of finding myself there, in that house, among respectable people. I loved Nino, I had no doubt, I never had any doubt about that. And of course I should have suffered in the face of further proof that I would never have him. But I didn't. That he had a girlfriend, that the girlfriend was in every way better than me, I already knew. The novelty was that it was the daughter of Professor Galiani, who had grown up in that house, among those books. I immediately felt that the thing, instead of grieving me, calmed me, further justified their choosing each other, made it an inevitable movement, in harmony with the natural order of things. In other words, I felt as if suddenly I had before my eyes an example of symmetry so perfect that I had to enjoy it in silence.

But it wasn't only that. As soon as Armando said to his sister, "Nadia, this is Elena, mamma's student," the girl blushed and impetuously threw her arms around my neck, murmuring, "Elena, how happy I am to meet you." Then, without giving me time to say a single word, she went on to praise, without her brother's mocking tone, what I had written and how I wrote, in tones of such enthusiasm that I felt the way I did when her mother read a theme of mine in class. Or maybe it was even better, because there, present, listening to her, were the people I most cared about, Nino and Lila, and both could observe that in that house I was loved and respected.

I adopted a friendly demeanor that I had never considered

myself capable of, I immediately engaged in casual conversation, I came out with a fine, cultured Italian that didn't feel artificial, like the language I used at school. I asked Nino about his trip to England, I asked Nadia what books she was reading, what music she liked. I danced with Armando, with others, without a pause, even to a rock-and-roll song, during which my glasses flew off my nose but didn't break. A miraculous evening. At one point I saw that Nino exchanged a few words with Lila, invited her to dance. But she refused; she left the dancing room, and I lost sight of her. A long time passed before I remembered my friend. It took the slow waning of the dances, a passionate discussion between Armando, Nino, and a couple of other boys their age, a move, along with Nadia, to the terrace, partly because of the heat and partly to bring into the discussion Professor Galiani, who had stayed by herself, smoking and enjoying the cool air. "Come on," Armando said, taking me by the hand. I said, "I'll get my friend," and I freed myself. All hot, I went through the rooms looking for Lila. I found her alone in front of a wall of books.

"Come on, let's go out on the terrace," I said.

"To do what?"

"Cool off, talk."

"You go."

"Are you bored?"

"No, I'm looking at the books."

"See how many there are?"

"Yes."

I felt she was unhappy. Because she had been neglected. Fault of the wedding ring, I thought. Or maybe her beauty isn't recognized here, Nadia's counts more. Or perhaps it's she who, although she has a husband, has been pregnant, had a miscarriage, designed shoes, can make money—she who doesn't know who she is in this house, doesn't know how to be appreciated, the way she is in the neighborhood. I do. Suddenly I felt that the state of suspension that had begun the day of her wedding was over. I knew how to be with these people, I felt more at ease than I did with my friends in the neighborhood. The only anxiety was what Lila was provoking now by her withdrawal, by remaining on the margins. I drew her away from the books, dragged her onto the terrace.

While many of the guests were still dancing, a small group had formed around the professor, three or four boys and two girls. Only the boys talked. The sole woman who took part, and she did so with irony, was the professor. I saw right away that the older boys, Nino, Armando and one called Carlo, found it somehow improper to argue with her. They wished mainly to challenge each other, considering her the authority, bestower of the palm of victory. Armando expressed opinions contrary to his mother's but in fact he was addressing Nino. Carlo agreed with the professor but in refuting the others he strove to separate his arguments from hers. And Nino, politely disagreeing with the professor, contradicted Armando, contradicted Carlo. I listened spellbound. Their words were buds that blossomed in my mind into more or less familiar flowers, and then I flared up, mimicking participation; or they manifested forms unknown to me, and I retreated, to hide my ignorance. In this second case, however, I became nervous: I don't know what they're talking about, I don't know who this person is, I don't understand. They were sounds without sense, they demonstrated that the world of persons, events, ideas was endless, and the reading I did at night had not been sufficient, I would have to work even harder in order to be able to say to Nino, to Professor Galiani, to Carlo, to Armando: Yes, I understand, I know. The entire planet is threatened. Nuclear war. Colonialism, neocolonialism. The pieds-noirs, the O.A.S. and the National Liberation Front. The fury of mass slaughters. Gaullism, Fascism. France, Armée, Grandeur, Honneur. Sartre is a pessimist, but he counts on the Communist workers in Paris. The wrong direction taken by

France, by Italy. Opening to the left. Saragat, Nenni. Fanfani in London, Macmillan. The Christian Democratic congress in our city. The followers of Fanfani, Moro, the Christian Democratic left. The socialists have ended up in the jaws of power. We will be Communists, we with our proletariat and our parliamentarians, to get the laws of the center left passed. If it goes like that, a Marxist-Leninist party will become a social democracy. Did you see how Leone behaved at the start of the academic year? Armando shook his head in disgust: Planning isn't going to change the world, it will take blood, it will take violence. Nino responded calmly: Planning is an indispensable tool. The talk was tense, Professor Galiani kept the boys at bay. How much they knew, they were masters of the earth. At some point Nino mentioned America favorably, he said words in English as if he were English. I noticed that in the space of a year his voice had grown stronger, it was thick, almost hoarse, and he used it less rigidly than he had at Lila's wedding and, later, at school. He even spoke of Beirut as if he had been there, and Danilo Dolci and Martin Luther King and Bertrand Russell. He appeared to support an organization he called the World Brigade for Peace and rebuked Armando when he referred to it sarcastically. Then he grew excited, his voice rose. Ah, how handsome he was. He said that the world had the technical capability to eliminate colonialism, hunger, war from the face of the earth. I was overwhelmed by emotion as I listened, and, although I felt lost in the midst of a thousand things I didn't know—what were Gaullism, the O.A.S., social democracy, the opening to the left; who were Danilo Dolci, Bertrand Russell, the pieds-noirs, the followers of Fanfani; and what had happened in Beirut, what in Algeria—I felt the need, as I had long ago, to take care of him, to tend to him, to protect him, to sustain him in everything that he would do in the course of his life. It was the only moment of the evening when I felt envious of Nadia, who stood beside him like a minor but radiant divinity. Then I heard myself utter sentences as if it were not I who had decided to do so, as if another person, more assured, more informed, had decided to speak through my mouth. I began without knowing what I would say, but, hearing the boys, fragments of phrases read in Galiani's books and newspapers stirred in my mind, and the desire to speak, to make my presence felt, became stronger than timidity. I used the elevated Italian I had practiced in making translations from Greek and Latin. I was on Nino's side. I said I didn't want to live in a world at war. We mustn't repeat the mistakes of the generations that preceded us, I said. Today we should make war on the atomic arsenals, should make war on war itself. If we allow the use of those weapons, we will all become even guiltier than the Nazis. Ah, how moved I was, as I spoke: I felt tears coming to my eyes. I concluded by saying that the world urgently needed to be changed, that there were too many tyrants who kept peoples enslaved. But it should be changed by peaceful means.

I don't know if everyone appreciated me. Armando seemed unhappy and a blond girl whose name I didn't know stared at me with a small, mocking smile. But as I was speaking Nino nodded at me in agreement. And when Professor Galiani, just afterward, gave her opinion, she referred to me twice, and it was thrilling to hear, "As Elena rightly said." It was Nadia, though, who did the most wonderful thing. She left Nino and came over and whispered in my ear: "How clever you are, how brave." Lila, who was next to me, didn't say a word. But while the professor was still talking to me she gave me a tug and whispered, in dialect, "I'm falling asleep on my feet, find out where the telephone is and call Stefano?"

36.

How much that evening had hurt her I learned later from

her notebooks. She admitted that she had asked to go with me. She admitted she had thought she could at least for one evening get away from the grocery and be comfortable with me, share in that sudden widening of my world, meet Professor Galiani, talk to her. She admitted she thought she would find a way of making a good impression. She admitted she had been sure she would be attractive to the males, she always was. Instead she immediately felt voiceless, graceless, deprived of movement, of beauty. She listed details: even when we were next to each other, people chose to speak only to me; they had brought me pastries, a drink, no one had done anything for her; Armando had shown me a family portrait, something from the seventeenth century, he had talked to me about it for a quarter of an hour; she had been treated as if she weren't capable of understanding. They didn't want her. They didn't want to know anything about what sort of person she was. That evening for the first time it had become clear to her that her life would forever be Stefano, the grocery stores, the marriage of her brother and Pinuccia, the conversations with Pasquale and Carmen, the petty war with the Solaras. This she had written, and more, maybe that very night, maybe in the morning, in the store. There, for the entire evening, she had felt irrefutably lost.

But in the car, as we returned to the neighborhood, she didn't allude in the slightest to her feeling, she just became mean, treacherous. She began as soon as she got in the car, when her husband asked resentfully if we had had a good time. I let her answer, I was dazed by the effort, by excitement, by pleasure. And then she went on slowly to hurt me. She said in dialect that she had never been so bored in her life. It would have been better if we'd gone to a movie, she apologized to her husband, and—it was unusual, done evidently on purpose to wound me, to remind me: See, good or bad I have a man, while you've got nothing, you're a virgin, you know everything but

you don't know anything about this—she caressed the hand
that he kept on the gear shift. Even watching television, she
said, would have been more entertaining than spending time
with those disgusting people. There's not a thing there, an
object, a painting, that was acquired by them directly. The furniture is from a hundred years ago. The house is at least three
hundred years old. The books yes, some are new, but others
are very old, they're so dusty they haven't been opened since
who knows when, old law books, history, science, politics.
They've read and studied in that house, fathers, grandfathers,
great-grandfathers. For hundreds of years they've been, at the
least, lawyers, doctors, professors. So they all talk just so, so
they dress and eat and move just so. They do it because they
were born there. But in their heads they don't have a thought
that's their own, that they struggled to think. They know everything and they don't know a thing. She kissed her husband on
the neck, she smoothed his hair with her fingertips. If you were
up there, Ste', all you'd see is parrots going *cocorico, cocorico*.
You couldn't understand a word of what they were saying and
they didn't even understand each other. You know what the
O.A.S. is, you know what the opening to the left is? Next time,
Lenù, don't take me, take Pasquale, I'll show you, he'll put
them in their place in a flash. Chimpanzees that piss and shit
in the toilet instead of on the ground, and that's why they give
themselves a lot of airs, and they say they know what should be
done in China and in Albania and in France and in Katanga.
You, too, Lenù, I have to tell you: Look out, or you'll be the
parrots' parrot. She turned to her husband, laughing. You
should have heard her, she said. She made a little voice,
cheechee, cheechee. Show Stefano how you speak to those people? You and Sarratore's son: the same. *The world brigade for
peace; we have the technical capability; hunger, war.* But do you
really work that hard in school so you can say things just like
he does? *Whoever finds a solution to the problems is working*

for peace. Bravo. Do you remember how the son of Sarratore was able to find a solution: Do you remember, do you—and you pay attention to him? You, too, you want to be a puppet from the neighborhood who performs so you can be welcomed into the home of those people? You want to leave us alone in our own shit, cracking our skulls, while all of you go *cocorico cocorico*, hunger, war, working class, peace?

She was so spiteful, all the way home along Corso Vittorio Emanuele, that I was silent, and felt the poison that was transforming what had seemed to me an important moment of my life into a false step that had made me ridiculous. I struggled not to believe her. I felt she was truly hostile and capable of anything. She knew how to set the nerves of good people alight, in their breasts she kindled the fire of destruction. I felt that Gigliola and Pinuccia were right: it was she herself who in the photograph had blazed up like the devil. I hated her, and even Stefano noticed, and when he stopped at the gate and let me out on his side he said, "Bye, Lenù, good night, Lina's joking," and I muttered "Bye," and went in. Only when the car had left did I hear Lila shouting at me, re-creating the voice that in her view I had deliberately assumed at the Galiani house: "Bye, hey, bye."

37.

That night began the long, painful period that led to our first break and a long separation.

I had trouble recovering. There had been a thousand causes of tension up until that moment; her unhappiness and, at the same time, her yearning to dominate were constantly surfacing. But never, ever, ever had she so explicitly set out to humiliate me. I stopped dropping in at the grocery. Although she had paid for my schoolbooks, although we had made that bet, I didn't tell her that I had passed with all A's and two A-pluses. Just after school ended, I started working in a bookstore on Via Mezzocannone, and I disappeared from the neighborhood without telling her. The memory of the sarcastic tone of that night, instead of fading, became magnified, and my resentment, too, increased. It seemed to me that nothing could justify what she had done to me. It never occurred to me, as, in fact, it had on other occasions, that she had felt the need to humiliate me in order to better endure her own humiliation.

I soon had confirmation that I really had made a good impression at the party, and that made the separation easier. I was wandering along Via Mezzocannone during my lunch break when I heard someone call me. It was Armando, on his way to take an exam. I learned that he was studying medicine and that the exam was difficult but, just the same, before vanishing in the direction of San Domenico Maggiore, he stopped to talk, piling on compliments and starting in again on politics. In the evening he showed up in the bookstore, he'd gotten a high mark, and was happy. He asked for my telephone number, I said I didn't have a telephone; he asked if we could go for a walk the following Sunday, I said that on Sunday I had to help my mother in the house. He started talking about Latin America, where he intended to go right after graduating, to treat the destitute, and persuade them to take up arms against their oppressors, and he went on for so long that I had to send him away before the owner got irritated. In other words, I was pleased because he obviously liked me, and I was polite, but not available. Lila's words had indeed done damage. My clothes were wrong, my hair was wrong, my tone of voice was false, I was ignorant. Besides, with the end of school, and without Professor Galiani, I had lost the habit of reading the newspapers and, partly because money was tight, I didn't want to buy them out of my own pocket. Thus Naples, Italy, the world quickly went back to being a foggy terrain in which I could no longer orient myself. Armando talked, I nodded yes, but I understood little of what he was saying.

The next day there was another surprise. While I was sweeping the floor of the bookstore, Nino and Nadia appeared. They had heard from Armando where I worked and had come just to say hello. They invited me to go to the movies with them the following Sunday. I had to answer as I had answered Armando: it wasn't possible, I worked all week, and my mother and father wanted me home on my day off.

"But a little walk in the neighborhood—you could do that?"

"That, yes."

"So we'll come see you."

Since the owner was calling for me more impatiently than usual—he was a man of around sixty, the skin on his face seemed dirty, he was irascible, and had a dissolute look—they left right away.

Late in the morning on the following Sunday, I heard someone calling from the courtyard and I recognized Nino's voice. I looked out, he was alone. I quickly tried to make myself presentable and, without even telling my mother, happy and at the same time anxious, I ran down. When I found myself before him I could hardly breathe. "I only have ten minutes," I said, and we didn't go out to walk along the *stradone*, but wandered among the houses. Why had he come without Nadia? Why had he come all the way here if she couldn't? He answered my questions without my asking. Some relatives of Nadia's father were visiting and she had been obliged to stay home. He had wanted to see the neighborhood again but also to bring me something to read, the latest issue of a journal called *Cronache Meridionali*. He handed me the issue with a petulant gesture, I thanked him, and he started, incongruously, to criticize the review, and so I asked why he had decided to give it to me. "It's rigid," he said, and added, laughing, "Like Professor Galiani and Armando." Then he turned serious, he assumed a tone that was like an old man's. He said that he owed a great deal to our professor, that without her the period of high school would have been a waste of time, but that you had to be on guard, keep her at a distance. "Her greatest defect," he said emphatically, "is that she can't bear for someone to have an opinion different from hers. Take from her everything she can give you, but then go your own way." Then he returned to the review, he said that Galiani also wrote for it and suddenly, with no connection, he mentioned Lila: "Then, if possible, have her read it, too." I didn't tell him that Lila no longer read anything, that now she was Signora Carracci, that she had kept only her meanness from when she was a child. I was evasive, and asked about Nadia, he told me that she was taking a long car trip with her family, to Norway, and then would spend the rest of the summer in Anacapri, where her father had a family house.

"Will you go and see her?"

"Once or twice—I have to study."

"How's your mother?"

"Very well. She's going back to Barano this year, she's made up with the woman who owns the house."

"Will you go on vacation with your family?"

"I? With my father? Never ever. I'll be on Ischia but on my own."

"Where are you going?"

"I have a friend who has a house in Forio: his parents leave it to him for the whole summer, and we'll stay there and study. You?"

"I'm working at Mezzocannone until September."

"Even during the mid-August holiday?"

"No, for the holiday, no."

He smiled. "Then come to Forio, the house is big. Maybe Nadia will come for two or three days."

I smiled, nervously. To Forio? To Ischia? To a house with-

out adults? Did he remember the Maronti? Did he remember
that we had kissed there? I said I had to go in. "I'll stop by
again," he promised. "I want to know what you think of the
review." He added, in a low voice, his hands stuck in his pockets, "I like talking to you."

He had talked a lot, in fact. I was proud, thrilled, that he
had felt comfortable. I murmured, "Me, too," although I had
said little or nothing, and was about to go in when something
happened that disturbed us both. A cry cut the Sunday quiet
of the courtyard and I saw Melina at the window, waving her
arms, trying to attract our attention. When Nino also turned to
look, perplexed, Melina cried even louder, a mixture of joy and
anguish. She cried, Donato.

"Who is it?" Nino asked.

"Melina," I said, "do you remember?"

He made a grimace of uneasiness. "Is she angry with me?"

"I don't know."

"She's saying Donato."

"Yes."

He turned again to look toward the window where the
widow was leaning out, repeatedly calling that name.

"Do you think I look like my father?"

"No."

"Sure?"

"Yes."

He said nervously, "I'll go."

"You'd better."

He left quickly, shoulders bent, while Melina cried louder
and louder, increasingly agitated: Donato, Donato, Donato.

I also escaped, I went home with my heart pounding, and a
thousand tangled thoughts. Not a single feature of Nino's connected him to Sarratore: not his height, not his face, not his
manners, not even his voice or his gaze. He was an anomalous,
sweet fruit. How fascinating he was with his long, untidy hair.

How different from any other male form: in all Naples there was no one who resembled him. And he had respect for me, even if I still had my last year of high school to do and he was going to the university. He had come all the way to the neighborhood on a Sunday. He had been worried about me, he had come to put me on my guard. He had wanted to warn me that Professor Galiani was all well and good but even she had her flaws, and meanwhile he had brought me that journal in the conviction that I had the capacity to read it and discuss it, and he had even gone so far as to invite me to Ischia, to Forio, for the August holiday. Something impractical, not a real invitation, he himself knew perfectly well that my parents were not like Nadia's, they would never let me go; and yet he had invited me just the same, because in the words he said I heard other words, unsaid, like *I care a lot about seeing you, how I'd like to return to our talks at the Port, at the Maronti.* Yes, yes, I heard myself shouting in my head, I'd like it, too, I'll join you, in August I'll run away, no matter what.

I hid the review among my books. But at night, as soon as I was in bed, I looked at the table of contents and was startled. There was an article by Nino. An article by him in that very serious-looking magazine: almost a book, not the faded gray student magazine in which, two years earlier, he had suggested publishing my account of the priest, but important pages written by adults for adults. And yet there he was, Antonio Sarratore, name and last name. And I knew him. And he was only two years older than me.

I read, I didn't understand much, I reread. The article talked about Planning with a capital "P," Plan with a capital "P," and it was written in a complicated style. But it was a piece of his intelligence, a piece of his person, that, without boasting, quietly, he had given to me.

To me.

Tears came to my eyes, it was late when I put the magazine

down. Talk about it to Lila? Lend it to her? No, it was mine. I
didn't want to have a real friendship with her anymore, just
hello, trite phrases. She didn't know how to appreciate me.
Whereas others did: Armando, Nadia, Nino. They were my
friends, to them I owed my confidences. They had immediately
seen in me what she had hastened not to see. Because she had
the gaze of the neighborhood. She was able to see only the way
Melina did, who, locked in her madness, saw Donato in Nino,
took him for her former lover.

38.

At first I didn't want to go to Pinuccia and Rino's wedding,
but Pinuccia came herself to bring me the invitation and since
she treated me with exaggerated affection, and in fact asked
my advice about many things, I didn't know how to say no,
even though she didn't extend the invitation to the rest of my
family. It's not me who's discourteous, she apologized, but
Stefano. Not only had her brother refused to give her any of
the family's money so that she could buy a house (he had told
her that the investments he had made in the shoes and in the
new grocery had left him broke) but, since it was he who had
to pay for the wedding dress, the photographer, and the
refreshments, he had personally removed half the neighborhood from the guest list. It was extremely rude behavior, and
Rino was even more embarrassed than she was. His bride
would have liked a wedding as lavish as his sister's and a new
house, like hers, with a view of the railroad. Although he was
by now the proprietor of a shoe factory, he couldn't manage
with his own resources, but it was partly because he was a
spendthrift; he had just bought a Fiat 1100, he didn't have a
lira left. And so, after a lot of resistance, they had agreed to go
and live in Don Achille's old house, evicting Maria from the

bedroom. They intended to save as much as possible and, as soon as they could, buy an apartment nicer than Stefano and Lila's. My brother is a shit, Pinuccia said in conclusion, bitterly: when it comes to his wife he throws his money around, while for his sister he doesn't have a cent.

I avoided any comment. I went to the wedding with Marisa and Alfonso; he seemed to be just waiting for these worldly occasions to become someone else, not my usual classmate but a young man graceful in manner and appearance, with black hair, a heavy bluish beard showing on his cheeks, languid eyes, a suit that wasn't ill-fitting, as happened to other men, but showed off his slender yet sculpted body.

In the hope that Nino would be obliged to take his sister, I had very carefully studied his article and all of *Cronache Meridionali*. But by now Alfonso was Marisa's knight, he went to pick her up, he brought her home, and Nino didn't appear. I stayed close to the two of them, I wanted to avoid being alone with Lila.

In the church I glimpsed her in the first row, between Stefano and Maria; she was so beautiful, it was impossible to avoid looking at her. Later, at the wedding lunch, in the same restaurant on Via Orazio where her own reception was held, scarcely more than a year earlier, we met just once and exchanged wary words. Then I ended up at a table over on the side, with Alfonso, Marisa, and a fair-haired boy around thirteen, while she sat with Stefano at the bride and bridegroom's table, with the important guests. How many things had changed in a short time. Antonio wasn't there, Enzo wasn't there, both still doing their military service. The clerks from the groceries, Carmen and Ada, had been invited, but not Pasquale, or maybe he had chosen not to come, in order not to mix with people whom, as local gossip had it, partly joking, partly serious, he planned to murder with his own hands. His mother, Giuseppina Peluso, was also absent, as were Melina and her children. Instead, the Carraccis, the Cerullos, and the Solaras, business partners in various combinations, all sat together at the head table, along with the relatives from Florence, that is to say the metal merchant and his wife. I saw Lila talking to Michele, laughing in an exaggerated fashion. Every so often she looked in my direction, but I immediately turned away, with a mixture of irritation and distress. How much she laughed, too much. I thought of my mother: the way Lila was playing the married woman, the vulgarity of her manners, her dialect. She held Michele's attention completely, though next to him was his fiancée, Gigliola, pale and furious at being neglected. Only Marcello from time to time spoke soothingly to his future sister-in-law. Lila, Lila: she wanted to exceed and with her excesses make us all suffer. I noticed that Nunzia and Fernando also gave their daughter long, apprehensive looks.

The day went smoothly, apart from two episodes that apparently had no repercussions. Here's the first. Among the guests was Gino, the pharmacist's son, because he had recently become engaged to a second cousin of the Carraccis, a thin girl with brown hair worn close to her head and violet shadows under her eyes. As he got older he had become more detestable; I couldn't forgive myself for having been his girl-friend when I was younger. He had been devious then, and he remained devious, and, besides, he was in a situation that made him even more untrustworthy: he had failed his exams again. He hadn't even said hello to me for a long time, but he had continued to hang around Alfonso, at times he was friendly, at others he teased him with insults that always had sexual over-tones. That day, maybe out of envy (Alfonso had passed with good marks and, besides, was with Marisa, who was pretty, whose eyes sparkled), he was particularly unbearable. The fair-haired boy seated at our table, who was nice-looking and very shy, was the son of a relative of Nunzia's who had emigrated to

Germany and married a German. I was very nervous and didn't give him much encouragement to talk, but both Alfonso and Marisa had tried to put him at his ease. Alfonso in particular engaged him in conversation, did all he could if the waiters neglected him, and even took him out to the terrace for a view of the sea. Just as they came in and returned to the table, joking, Gino, with a laugh, left his fiancée, who tried to restrain him, and came to sit with us. He spoke to the boy in a low voice, indicating Alfonso:

"Watch out for that guy, he's a fag: this time he took you out to the terrace, next time it'll be the bathroom."

Alfonso turned fiery red but didn't react, he half-smiled, helplessly, and said nothing. It was Marisa who got angry:

"How dare you say such a thing!"

"I dare because I know."

"Tell me what you know."

"You're sure?"

"Yes."

"Then listen to what I'm telling you."

"Go ahead."

"My fiancée's brother stayed at the Carraccis' house once and had to sleep in the same bed with him."

"So?"

"He touched him."

"He who?"

"Him."

"Where's your fiancée?"

"Here she is."

"Tell that bitch I can prove that Alfonso likes girls, and I certainly don't know if she can say the same about you."

And at that point she turned to her boyfriend and kissed him on the lips: a passionate, public kiss—I would never have dared to do a thing like that in front of all those people.

Lila, who continued to look in my direction as if she were

monitoring me, was the first to see that kiss and she clapped her hands with spontaneous enthusiasm. Michele, too, applauded, laughing, and Stefano gave his brother a vulgar compliment, which was immediately expanded on by the metal merchant. All sorts of banter, in other words, but Marisa pretended not to notice. Squeezing Alfonso's hand tightly—her knuckles were white—she hissed at Gino, who had stared at the kiss with a blank expression, "Now get out of here, or I'll smack you."

The pharmacist's son got up without saying a word and went back to his table, where his girlfriend immediately whispered in his ear with an aggressive look. Marisa gave them both a last glance of contempt.

From that moment my opinion of her changed. I admired her courage, the stubborn capacity for love, the seriousness of her attachment to Alfonso. Here was another person I've neglected, I thought with regret, and wrongly so. How much my dependence on Lila had closed my eyes. How frivolous her applause had been, how it fit with the boorish amusement of Michele, of Stefano, of the metal merchant.

The second episode had as its protagonist Lila herself. The reception was now almost over. I had gotten up to go to the bathroom and was passing the bridal table when I heard the wife of the metal merchant laughing loudly. I turned. Pinuccia was standing and was shielding herself, because the woman was pulling up her wedding dress, baring her large, strong legs, and saying to Stefano, "Look at your sister's thighs, look at that butt and that stomach. You men of today like girls who resemble toilet brushes, but it's the ones like our Pinuccia whom God made just for bearing you children."

Lila, who was bringing a glass to her mouth, without a second's hesitation threw the wine in her face and on her silk dress. As usual, I thought, immediately anxious, she thinks she's entitled to do anything, and now all hell's going to break loose. I went out to the bathroom, locked myself in, stayed there as long as possible. I didn't want to see Lila's fury, I didn't want to hear it. I wanted to stay outside it, I was afraid of being dragged into her suffering, I was afraid of feeling obligated, out of long habit, to ally myself with her. Instead, when I came out, everything was calm. Stefano was chatting with the metal merchant and his wife, who was sitting stiffly in her stained dress. The orchestra played, couples danced. Only Lila wasn't there. I saw her outside the glass doors, on the terrace. She was looking at the sea.

39.

I was tempted to join her, I immediately changed my mind. She must be very upset and would surely be mean to me, which would make things even worse between us. I decided to return to my table when Fernando, her father, came up to me and asked timidly if I'd like to dance.

I didn't dare refuse, we danced a waltz in silence. He led me confidently around the room, among the tipsy couples, holding my hand too tight with his sweaty hand. His wife must have entrusted him with the task of telling me something important, but he couldn't get up his courage. Finally, at the end of the waltz, he muttered, addressing me, surprisingly, with formality: "If it's not too much trouble for you, talk to Lina a little, her mother is worried." Then he added awkwardly, "When you need shoes, come by, don't stand on ceremony," and he returned quickly to his table.

That hint at a kind of reward for my possibly devoting time to Lila bothered me. I asked Alfonso and Marisa to go, which they were happy to do. I felt Nunzia's gaze on me right up until we left the restaurant.

As the days passed, I began to lose confidence. I had thought that working in a bookstore meant having a lot of books available to me and time to read them, but I was unlucky. The owner treated me like a servant, he couldn't stand my being still for a moment: he forced me to unload boxes, pile them up, empty them, arrange the new books, rearrange the old ones, dust them, and he sent me up and down a ladder just so he could look under my skirt. Besides, Armando, after that first foray when he had seemed so friendly, hadn't showed up again. And Nino hadn't reappeared, either with Nadia or by himself. Had their interest in me been so short-lived? I began to feel solitude, boredom. The heat, the work, disgust at the bookseller's looks and his coarse remarks depressed me. The hours dragged. What was I doing in that dark cave, while along the sidewalk boys and girls filed past on their way to the mysterious university building, a place where I would almost certainly never go? Where was Nino? Had he gone to Ischia to study? He had left me the review, his article, and I had studied them as if for an examination, but would he ever come back to examine me? Where had I gone wrong? Had I been too reserved? Was he expecting me to seek him out and for that reason did not look for me? Should I talk to Alfonso, get in touch with Marisa, ask her about her brother? And why? Nino had a girlfriend, Nadia: What point was there in asking his sister where he was, what he was doing. I would make myself ridiculous.

Day by day the sense of myself that had so unexpectedly expanded after the party diminished, I felt dispirited. Get up early, hurry to Mezzocannone, slave all day, go home tired, the thousands of words learned in school packed into my head, unusable. I got depressed not only when I recalled conversations with Nino but also when I thought of the summers at the Sea Garden with the stationer's daughters, with Antonio. How stupidly our affair had ended, he was the only person who had truly loved me, there would never be anyone else. In bed at night, I recalled the odor of his skin, the meetings at the ponds, our kissing and petting at the old canning factory.

I was in this state of discouragement when, one evening, after dinner, Carmen, Ada, and Pasquale, who had one hand bandaged because he had injured it at work, came looking for me. We got ice cream, and ate it in the gardens. Carmen, coming straight to the point, asked me, somewhat aggressively, why I never stopped by the grocery anymore. I said I was working at Mezzocannone and didn't have time. Ada said, coldly, that if one is attached to a person one finds the time, but if that's how I was going to be, never mind. I asked, "Be how?" and she answered, "You have no feelings, just look how you treated my brother." I reminded her with an angry snap that it was her brother who had left me, and she replied, "Yes, anyone who believes that is lucky: there are people who leave and people who know how to be left." Carmen agreed: "Also friendships," she said. "You think they break off because of one person and instead, if you look hard, it's the other person's fault." At that point I got upset, I declared, "Listen, if Lina and I aren't friends anymore, it's not my fault." Here Pasquale intervened, he said, "Lenù, it's not important whose fault it is, it's important for us to support Lina." He brought up the story of his bad teeth, of how she had helped him, he talked about the money she still gave Carmen under the counter, and how she also sent money to Antonio, who, even if I didn't know and didn't want to know, was having a bad time in the Army. I tried cautiously to ask what was happening to my old boyfriend and they told me, in different tones of voice, some hostile, some less, that he had had a nervous breakdown, that he was ill, but that he was tough, he wouldn't give in, he would make it. *Lina, on the other hand.*

"What's wrong with Lina?"

"They want to take her to a doctor."

"Who wants to take her?"

"Stefano, Pinuccia, relatives."

"Why?"

"To find out why she's only gotten pregnant once and then never again."

"And she?"

"She acts like a madwoman, she doesn't want to go."

I shrugged my shoulders. "What can I do?"

"You take her."

40.

I talked to Lila. She started laughing, she said she would go to the doctor only if I swore that I wasn't angry with her.

"All right."

"Swear."

"I swear."

"Swear on your brothers, swear on Elisa."

I said that going to the doctor wasn't a big deal, but that if she didn't want to go I didn't care, she should do as she liked. She became serious.

"You don't swear, then."

"No."

She was silent for a moment, then she admitted, eyes lowered, "All right, I was wrong."

I made a grimace of irritation. "Go to the doctor and let me know."

"You won't come?"

"If I don't go in the bookseller will fire me."

"I'll hire you," she said ironically.

"Go to the doctor, Lila."

Maria, Nunzia, and Pinuccia took her to the doctor. All three insisted on being present at the examination. Lila was obedient, disciplined: she had never submitted to that type of examination, and the whole time she kept her lips pressed together, eyes

wide. When the doctor, a very old man who had been recom-
mended by the neighborhood obstetrician, said knowingly that
everything was in order, her mother and mother-in-law were
relieved, but Pinuccia darkened, asked:

"Then why don't children come and if they come why
aren't they born?"

The doctor noticed her spiteful tone and frowned.

"She's very young," he said. "She needs to get a little stronger."

Get stronger. I don't know if the doctor used exactly that
verb, yet that was reported to me and it made an impression. It
meant that Lila, in spite of the strength she displayed at all
times, was weak. It meant that children didn't come, or didn't
last in her womb, not because she possessed a mysterious
power that annihilated them but because, on the contrary, she
was an inadequate woman. My resentment faded. When, in the
courtyard, she told me about the torture of the medical examination, using vulgar expressions for both the doctor and the
three who accompanied her, I gave no signs of annoyance but
in fact took an interest: no doctor had ever examined me, not
even the obstetrician. Finally she said, sarcastically:

"He tore me with a metal instrument, I gave him a lot of
money, and to reach what conclusion? That I need strengthening."

"Strengthening of what sort?"

"I'm supposed to go to the beach and go swimming."

"I don't understand."

"The beach, Lenù, sun, salt water. It seems that if you go to
the beach you get stronger and children come."

We said goodbye in a good mood. We had seen each other
again and all in all we had felt good.

She came back the next day, affectionate toward me, irritated with her husband. Stefano wanted to rent a house at
Torre Annunziata and send her there for all July and all August
with Nunzia and Pinuccia, who also wanted to get stronger,

even though she didn't need to. They were already thinking how to manage with the shops. Alfonso would take care of Piazza dei Martiri, with Gigliola, until school began, and Maria would replace Lila in the new grocery. She said to me, desperate, "If I have to stay with my mother and Pinuccia for two months I'll kill myself."

"But you'll go swimming, lie in the sun."

"I don't like swimming and I don't like lying in the sun."

"If I could get stronger in your place, I'd leave tomorrow."

She looked at me with curiosity, and said softly, "Then come with me."

"I have to work at Mezzocannone."

She became agitated, she repeated that she would hire me, but this time she said it without irony. "Quit," she began to press me, "and I'll give you what the bookseller gives you." She wouldn't stop, she said that if I agreed, it would all become tolerable, even Pinuccia, with that bulging stomach that was already showing. I refused politely. I imagined what would happen in those two months in the burning-hot house in Torre Annunziata: quarrels with Nunzia, tears; quarrels with Stefano when he arrived on Saturday night; quarrels with Rino when he appeared with his brother-in-law, to join Pinuccia; quarrels especially with Pinuccia, continuous, muted or dramatic, sarcastic, malicious, and full of outrageous insults.

"I can't," I said firmly. "My mother wouldn't let me."

She went away angrily, our idyll was fragile. The next morning, to my surprise, Nino appeared in the bookstore, pale, thinner. He had had one exam after another, four of them. I, who fantasized about the airy spaces behind the walls of the university where well-prepared students and old sages discussed Plato and Kepler all day, listened to him spellbound, saying only, "How clever you are." And as soon as the moment seemed apt, I volubly if somewhat inanely praised his article in *Cronache Meridionali*. He listened to me seriously, without interrupting, so that at a certain point I no longer knew what to say to show him that I knew his text thoroughly. Finally he seemed content, he exclaimed that not even Professor Galiani, not even Armando, not even Nadia had read it with such attention. And he started to talk to me about other essays he had in mind on the same subject. I stood listening to him in the doorway of the bookshop, pretending not to hear the owner calling me. After a shout that was sharper than the others, Nino muttered, What does that shit want; he stayed a little longer, with his insolent expression, and, saying that he was leaving for Ischia the next day, held out his hand to me. I shook it—it was slender, delicate—and he immediately drew me toward him, just slightly, leaned over, brushed my lips with his. It was a moment, then he left me with a light gesture, a caress on the palm with his fingers, and went off toward the Rettifilo. I stood watching as he walked away without turning, walked like a distracted chieftain who feared nothing in the world because the world existed only to submit to him.

That night I didn't close my eyes. In the morning I got up early, I hurried to the new grocery. I found Lila just as she was pulling up the gate, Carmen hadn't yet arrived. I said nothing about Nino, I said only, in the tone of someone who is asking the impossible and knows it:

"If you go to Ischia instead of Torre Annunziata, I'll quit and come with you."

41.

We disembarked on the island the second Sunday in July, Stefano and Lila, Rino and Pinuccia, Nunzia and I. The two men, loaded down with bags, were apprehensive, like ancient heroes in an unknown land, uneasy without the armor of their cars, unhappy that they had had to rise early and forgo the neighborhood leisureliness of their day off. The wives, dressed in their Sunday best, were annoyed with them but in different ways: Pinuccia because Rino was too encumbered to pay attention to her, Lila because Stefano pretended to know what he was doing and where he was going, when it was clear that he didn't. As for Nunzia, she had the appearance of someone who feels that she is barely tolerated, and she was careful not to say anything inappropriate that might annoy the young people. The only one who was truly content was me, with a bag over my shoulder that held my few things, excited by the smells of Ischia, the sounds, the colors that, as soon as I got off the boat, corresponded precisely to the memories of that earlier vacation.

We arranged ourselves in two mini cabs, jammed-in bodies, sweat, luggage. The house, rented in a hurry with the help of a *salumi* supplier of Ischian origin, was on the road that led to a place called Cuotto. It was a simple structure and belonged to a cousin of the supplier, a thin woman, over sixty, unmarried, who greeted us with brusque efficiency. Stefano and Rino dragged the suitcases up a narrow staircase, joking but also cursing because of the effort. The owner led us into shadowy rooms stuffed with sacred images and small, glowing lamps. But when we opened the windows we saw, beyond the road, beyond the vineyards, beyond the palms and pine trees, a long strip of the sea. Or rather: the bedrooms that Pinuccia and Lila took—after some friction of the *yours is bigger; no, yours is bigger* type—faced the sea, while the room that fell to Nunzia had a sort of porthole, high up, so that we never discovered what was outside it, and mine, which was very small, and barely had space for the bed, looked out on a chicken coop sheltered by a forest of reeds.

There was nothing to eat in the house. On the advice of the owner we went to a trattoria, which was dark and had no other customers. We sat down dubiously, just to get fed, but in the end even Nunzia, who was distrustful of all cooking that was not her own, found that it was good and wanted to take something home so that she could prepare dinner that evening. Stefano didn't make the slightest move to ask for the check, and, after a mute hesitation, Rino resigned himself to paying for everyone. At that point we girls proposed going to see the beach, but the two men resisted, yawned, said they were tired. We insisted, especially Lila. "We ate too much," she said, "it'll do us good to walk, the beach is right here, do you feel like it, Mamma?" Nunzia sided with the men, and we returned to the house.

After a bored stroll through the rooms, both Stefano and Rino, almost in unison, said that they wanted to have a little nap. They laughed, whispered to each other, laughed again, and then nodded at their wives, who followed them unwillingly into the bedrooms. Nunzia and I remained alone for a couple of hours. We inspected the state of the kitchen, and found it dirty, which led Nunzia to start washing everything carefully: plates, glasses, silverware, pots. It was a struggle to get her to let me help. She asked me to keep track of a number of urgent requests for the owner, and when she herself lost count of the things that were needed, she marveled that I was able to remember everything, saying, "That's why you're so clever at school."

Finally the two couples reappeared, first Stefano and Lila, then Rino and Pinuccia. I again proposed going to see the beach, but there was coffee, joking, chatting, and Nunzia who began to cook, and Pinuccia who was clinging to Rino, making him feel her stomach, murmuring, stay, leave tomorrow morning, and so the time flew and yet again we did nothing. In the end the men had to rush, afraid of missing the ferry, and, cursing because they hadn't brought their cars, had to find someone to take them to the Port. They disappeared almost without saying goodbye. Pinuccia burst into tears.

In silence we girls began to unpack the bags, to arrange our things, while Nunzia insisted on making the bathroom shine. Only when we were sure that the men had not missed the ferry and would not return, did we relax, begin to joke. We had ahead of us a long week and only ourselves to worry about. Pinuccia said she was afraid of being alone in her room— there was an image of a grieving Madonna with knives in her heart that sparkled in the lamplight—and went to sleep with Lila. I shut myself in my little room to enjoy my secret: *Nino was in Forio, not far away, and maybe even the next day I would meet him on the beach*. I felt wild, reckless, but I was glad about it. There was a part of me that was sick of being a sensible person.

It was hot, I opened the window. I listened to the chickens pecking, the rustle of the reeds, then I became aware of the mosquitoes. I closed the window quickly and spent at least an hour going after them and crushing them with one of the books that Professor Galiani had lent me, *Complete Plays*, by a writer named Samuel Beckett. I didn't want Nino to see me on the beach with red spots on my face and body; I didn't want him to catch me with a book of plays—for one thing, I had never set foot in a theater. I put aside Beckett, stained by the black or bloody silhouettes of the mosquitoes, and began to read a very complicated text on the idea of nationhood. I fell asleep reading.

42.

In the morning Nunzia, who felt committed to looking after us, went in search of a place to do the shopping and we headed to the beach, the beach of Citara, which for that entire long vacation we thought was called Cetara.

What pretty bathing suits Lila and Pinuccia displayed when

they took off their sundresses: one-piece, of course. The husbands, who as fiancés had been indulgent, especially Stefano,
now were against the two-piece; but the colors of the new fabrics were shiny, and the shape of the neckline, front and back,
ran elegantly over their skin. I, under an old long-sleeved blue
dress, wore the same faded bathing suit, now shapeless, that
Nella Incardo had made for me years earlier, at Barano. I
undressed reluctantly.

We walked a long way in the sun, until we saw steam rising
from some thermal baths, then turned back. Pinuccia and I
stopped often to swim, Lila didn't, although she was there for
that purpose. Of course, there was no Nino, and I was disappointed, I had been convinced that he would show up, as if by
a miracle. When the other two wanted to go back to the house,
I stayed on the beach, and walked along the shore toward
Forio. That night I was so sunburned that I felt I had a high
fever; the skin on my shoulders blistered and for the next few
days I had to stay in the house. I cleaned, cooked, and read,
and my energy pleased Nunzia, who couldn't stop praising me.
Every night, with the excuse that I had been in the house all
day to stay out of the sun, I made Lila and Pina walk to Forio,
which was some distance away. We wandered through the
town, had some ice cream. It's pretty here, Pinuccia complained, it's a morgue where we are. But for me Forio was also
a morgue: Nino did not appear.

Toward the end of the week I proposed to Lila that we
should visit Barano and the Maronti. Lila agreed enthusiastically, and Pinuccia didn't want to stay and be bored with
Nunzia. We left early. Under our dresses we wore our bathing
suits, and in a bag I carried our towels, sandwiches, a bottle of
water. My stated purpose was to take advantage of that trip to
say hello to Nella, Maestra Oliviero's cousin, whom I had stayed
with during my summer on Ischia. The secret plan, instead, was
to see the Sarratore family and get from Marisa the address of

the friend with whom Nino was staying in Forio. I was naturally afraid of running into the father, Donato, but I hoped that he was at work; and, in order to see the son, I was ready to run the risk of having to endure some obscene remark from him.

When Nella opened the door and I stood before her, like a ghost, she was stunned, tears came to her eyes. "It's happiness," she said, apologizing.

But it wasn't only that. I had reminded her of her cousin, who, she told me, wasn't comfortable in Potenza, was ill and wasn't getting better. She led us out to the terrace, offered us whatever we wanted, was very concerned with Pinuccia, and her pregnancy. She made her sit down, wanted to touch her stomach, which protruded a little. Meanwhile I made Lila go on a sort of pilgrimage: I showed her the corner of the terrace where I had spent so much time in the sun, the place where I sat at the table, the corner where I made my bed at night. For a fraction of a second I saw Donato leaning over me as he slid his hand under the sheets, touched me. I felt revulsion but this didn't keep me from asking Nella casually, "And the Sarratores?"

"They're at the beach."

"How's it going this year?"

"Ah, well . . . "

"They're too demanding?"

"Ever since he became more the journalist than the railroad worker, yes."

"Is he here?"

"He's on sick leave."

"And is Marisa here?"

"No, not Marisa, but except for her they're all here."

"All?"

"You understand."

"No, I swear, I don't understand anything."

She laughed heartily.

"Nino's here today, too, Lenù. When he needs money he shows up for half a day, then he goes back to stay with a friend who has a house in Forio."

43.

We left Nella, and went down to the beach with our things. Lila teased me mildly the whole way. "You're sneaky," she said, "you made me come to Ischia just because Nino's here, admit it." I wouldn't admit it, I defended myself. Then Pinuccia joined her sister-in-law, in a coarser tone, and accused me of having compelled her to make a long and tiring journey to Barano for my own purposes, without taking her pregnancy into account. From then on I denied it even more firmly, and in fact I threatened them both. I promised that if they said anything improper in the presence of the Sarratores I would take the boat and return to Naples that night.

I immediately picked out the family. They were in exactly the same place where they used to settle years before, and had the same umbrella, the same bathing suits, the same bags, the same way of basking in the sun: Donato belly up in the black sand, leaning on his elbows; his wife, Lidia, sitting on a towel and leafing through a magazine. To my great disappointment Nino wasn't under the umbrella. I scanned the water, and glimpsed a dark dot that appeared and disappeared on the rocking surface of the sea: I hoped it was him. Then I announced myself, calling aloud to Pino, Clelia, and Ciro, who were playing on the shore.

Ciro had grown; he didn't recognize me, and smiled uncertainly. Pino and Clelia ran toward me excitedly, and the parents turned to look, out of curiosity. Lidia jumped up, shouting my name and waving, Sarratore hurried toward me with a big welcoming smile and open arms. I avoided his embrace, saying only Hello, how are you. They were very friendly, I introduced

Lila and Pinuccia, mentioned their parents, said whom they had married. Donato immediately focused on the two girls. He began addressing them respectfully as Signora Carracci and Signora Cerullo, he remembered them as children, he began, with fatuous elaboration, to speak of time's flight. I talked to Lidia, asked politely about the children and especially Marisa. Pino, Clelia, and Ciro were doing well and it was obvious; they immediately gathered around me, waiting for the right moment to draw me into their games. As for Marisa, her mother said that she had stayed in Naples with her aunt and uncle, she had to retake exams in four subjects in September and had to go to private lessons. "Serves her right," she said darkly. "She didn't work all year, now she deserves to suffer."

I said nothing, but I doubted that Marisa was suffering: she would spend the whole summer with Alfonso in the store in Piazza dei Martiri, and I was happy for her. I noticed instead that Lidia bore deep traces of grief: in her face, which was losing its contours, in her eyes, in her shrunken breast, in her heavy stomach. All the time we talked she was glancing fearfully at her husband, who, playing the role of the kindly man, was devoting himself to Lila and Pinuccia. She stopped paying attention to me and kept her eyes glued to him when he offered to take them swimming, promising Lila that he would teach her to swim. "I taught all my children," we heard him say, "I'll teach you, too."

I never asked about Nino, nor did Lidia ever mention him. But now the black dot in the sparkling blue of the sea stopped moving out. It reversed direction, grew larger, I began to distinguish the white of the foam exploding beside it.

Yes, it's him, I thought anxiously.

Nino emerged from the water looking with curiosity at his father, who was holding Lila afloat with one arm and with the other was showing her what to do. Even when he saw me and recognized me, he continued to frown.

"What are you doing here?" he asked.

"I'm on vacation," I answered, "and I came by to see Signora Nella."

He looked again with annoyance in the direction of his father and the two girls.

"Isn't that Lina?"

"Yes, and that's her sister-in-law Pinuccia, I don't know if you remember her."

He rubbed his hair with the towel, continuing to stare at the three in the water. I told him almost breathlessly that we would be staying on Ischia until September, that we had a house not far from Forio, that Lila's mother was there, too, that on Sunday the husbands of Lila and Pinuccia would come. As I spoke it seemed to me that he wasn't even listening, but still I said, and in spite of Lidia's presence, that on the weekend I had nothing to do.

"Come see us," he said, and then he spoke to his mother: "I have to go."

"Already?"

"I have things to do."

"Elena's here."

Nino looked at me as if he had become aware of my presence only then. He rummaged in his shirt, which was hanging on the umbrella, took out a pencil and a notebook, wrote something, tore out the page, and handed it to me.

"I'm at this address," he said.

Clear, decisive as a movie actor. I took the page as if it were a holy relic.

"Eat something first," his mother begged him.

He didn't answer.

"And at least wave goodbye to Papa."

He changed out of his bathing suit, wrapping a towel around his waist, and went off along the shore without saying goodbye to anyone.

44.

We spent the entire day at the Maronti, I playing and swimming with the children, Pinuccia and Lila completely occupied by Donato, who took them for a walk all the way to the thermal baths. At the end Pinuccia was exhausted, and Sarratore showed us a convenient and pleasant way of going home. We went to a hotel that was built practically over the water, as if on stilts, and there, for a few lire, we got a boat, entrusting ourselves to an old sailor.

As soon as we set out, Lila said sarcastically, "Nino didn't give you much encouragement."

"He had to study."

"And he couldn't even say hello?"

"That's how he is."

"How he is is rude," Pinuccia interjected. "He's as rude as the father is nice."

They were both convinced that Nino hadn't been polite or pleasant, and I let them think it, I preferred prudently to keep my secrets. And it seemed to me that if they thought he was disdainful of even a really good student like me, they would more easily put up with the fact that he had ignored them and maybe they would even forgive him. I wanted to protect him from their rancor, and I succeeded: they seemed to forget about him right away, Pinuccia was enthusiastic about Sarratore's graciousness, and Lila said with satisfaction, "He taught me to float, and even how to swim. He's great."

The sun was setting. I thought of Donato's molestations, and shuddered. From the violet sky came a chilly dampness. I said to Lila, "He's the one who wrote that the panel in the Piazza dei Martiri shop was ugly."

Pinuccia had a smug expression of agreement.

Lila said, "He was right."

I became upset. "And he's the one who ruined Melina."

Lila answered, with a laugh, "Or maybe he made her feel good for once."

That remark wounded me. I knew what Melina had endured, what her children endured. I also knew Lidia's sufferings, and how Sarratore, behind his fine manners, hid a desire that respected nothing and no one. Nor had I forgotten that Lila, since she was a child, had witnessed the torments of the widow Cappuccio and how painful it had been for her. So what was this tone, what were those words—a signal to me? Did she want to say to me: you're a girl, you don't know anything about a woman's needs? I abruptly changed my mind about the secrecy of my secrets. I wanted immediately to show that I was a woman like them and knew.

"Nino gave me his address," I said to Lila. "If you don't mind, when Stefano and Rino come I'm going to see him."

Address. Go see him. Bold formulations. Lila narrowed her eyes, a sharp line crossed her forehead. Pinuccia had a malicious look, she touched Lila's knee, she laughed: "You hear? Lenuccia has a date tomorrow. And she has the address."

I flushed.

"Well, if you're with your husbands, what am I supposed to do?"

For a long moment there was only the noise of the engine and the mute presence of the sailor at the helm.

Lila said coldly, "Keep Mamma company. I didn't bring you here to have fun."

I restrained myself. We had had a week of freedom. That day, besides, both she and Pinuccia, on the beach, in the sun, during long swims, and thanks to the words that Sarratore knew how to use to inspire laughter and to charm, had forgotten themselves. Donato had made them feel like girl-women in the care of an unusual father, the rare father who doesn't punish you but encourages you to express your desires without guilt. And now that the day was over I, in declaring that I would have a Sunday to myself with a university student—what was I doing, was I reminding them both that that week in which their condition as wives was suspended was over and that their husbands were about to reappear? Yes, I had overdone it. Cut out your tongue, I thought.

45.

The husbands, in fact, arrived early. They were expected Sunday morning, but they appeared Saturday evening, very excited, with Lambrettas that they had, I think, rented at the Ischia Port. Nunzia prepared a lavish dinner. There was talk of the neighborhood, of the stores, of how the new shoes were coming along. Rino was full of self-praise for the models that he was perfecting with his father, but at an opportune moment he thrust some sketches under Lila's nose, and she examined them reluctantly, suggesting some modifications. Then we sat down at the table, and the two young men gorged themselves, competing to see who could eat more. It wasn't even ten when they dragged their wives to the bedrooms.

I helped Nunzia clear and wash the dishes. Then I shut myself in my room, I read a little. The heat in the closed room was suffocating, but I was afraid of the blotches I'd get from the mosquito bites, and I didn't open the window. I tossed and turned in the bed, soaked with sweat: I thought of Lila, of how, slowly, she had yielded. Certainly, she didn't show any particular affection for her husband; and the tenderness that I had sometimes seen in her gestures when they were engaged had disappeared. During dinner she had frequently commented with disgust at the way Stefano gobbled his food, the way he drank; but it was evident that some equilibrium, who knows how precarious, had been reached. When he, after some allusive remarks, headed toward the bedroom, Lila followed without delay, without saying go on, I'll join you later; she was resigned to an inevitable routine. Between her and her husband there was not the carnival spirit displayed by Rino and Pinuccia, but there was no resistance, either. Deep into the night I heard the noise of the two couples, the laughter and the sighs, the doors opening, the water coming out of the tap, the whirlpool of the flush, the doors closing. Finally I fell asleep.

On Sunday I had breakfast with Nunzia. I waited until ten for any of them to emerge; they didn't, I went to the beach. I stayed until noon and no one came. I went back to the house, Nunzia told me that the two couples had gone for a tour of the island on the Lambrettas, advising us not to wait for them for lunch. In fact they returned around three, slightly drunk, sunburned, all four full of enthusiasm for Casamicciola, Lacco Ameno, Forio. The two girls had shining eyes and immediately glanced at me slyly.

"Lenù," Pinuccia almost shouted, "guess what happened."

"What."

"We met Nino on the beach," Lila said.

My heart stopped.

"Oh."

"My goodness, he is really a good swimmer," Pinuccia said excitedly, cutting the air with exaggerated arm strokes.

And Rino: "He's not unlikable: he was interested in how shoes are made."

And Stefano: "He has a friend named Soccavo and he's the mortadella Soccavo: his father owns a sausage factory in San Giovanni a Teduccio."

And Rino again: "That guy's got money."

And again Stefano: "Forget the student, Lenù, he doesn't have a lira: aim for Soccavo, you'd be better off."

After a little more joking (*Would you look at that, Lenuccia is about to be the richest of all, She seems like a good girl and yet*), they withdrew again into the bedrooms.

I was incredibly disappointed. They had met Nino, gone swimming with him, talked to him, and without me. I put on my best dress—the same one, the one I'd worn to the wedding, even though it was hot—I carefully combed my hair, which had become very blond in the sun, and told Nunzia I was going for a walk.

I walked to Forio, uneasy because of the long, solitary distance, because of the heat, because of the uncertain result of my undertaking. I tracked down the address of Nino's friend, I called several times from the street, fearful that he wouldn't answer.

"Nino, Nino."

He looked out.

"Come up."

"I'll wait here."

I waited, I was afraid that he would treat me rudely. Instead he came out of the doorway with an unusually friendly expression. How disturbing his angular face was. And how pleasantly crushed I felt confronted by his long profile, his broad shoulders and narrow chest, that taut skin, the sole, dark covering of his thinness, merely bones, muscles, tendons. He said his friend would join us later; we walked through the center of Forio, amid the Sunday market stalls. He asked me about the bookstore on Mezzocannone. I told him that Lila had asked me to go with her on vacation and so I had quit. I didn't mention the fact that she was giving me money, as if going with her were a job, as if I were her employee. I asked him about Nadia, he said only: "Everything's fine." "Do you write to each other?" "Yes." "Every day?" "Every week." That was our conversation, already we had nothing more of our selves to share. We don't know anything about each other, I thought. Maybe I could ask how relations are with his father, but in what tone? And, besides, didn't I see with my own eyes that they're bad? Silence: I felt awkward.

But he promptly shifted onto the only terrain that seemed to justify our meeting. He said that he was glad to see me, all he could talk about with his friend was soccer and exam subjects. He praised me. Professor Galiani perceived it, he said, you're the only girl in the school who has any curiosity about things that aren't useful for exams and grades. He started to speak about serious subjects, we resorted immediately to a fine, impassioned Italian in which we knew we excelled. He started off with the problem of violence. He mentioned a peace demonstration in Cortona and related it skillfully to the beatings that had taken place in a piazza in Turin. He said he wanted to understand more about the link between immigration and industry. I agreed, but what did I know about those things? Nothing. Nino realized it, and he told me in great detail about an uprising of young southerners and the harshness with which the police had repressed them. "They call them *napoli*, they call them Moroccans, they call them Fascists, provocateurs, anarcho-syndicalists. But really they are boys whom no institution cares about, so neglected that when they get angry they destroy everything." Searching for something to say that would please him, I ventured, "If you don't have a solid knowledge of the problems and if you don't find lasting solutions, then naturally violence breaks out. But the people who rebel aren't to blame, it's the ones who don't know how to govern." He gave me an admiring look, and said, "That's exactly what I think."

I was really pleased. I felt encouraged and cautiously went on to some reflections on how to reconcile individuality and universality, drawing on Rousseau and other memories of the readings imposed by Professor Galiani. Then I asked, "Have you read Federico Chabod?"

I mentioned that name because he was the author of the book on the idea of nationhood that I had read a few pages of. I didn't know anything else, but at school I had learned to give the impression that I knew a lot. *Have you read Federico Chabod?* It was the only moment when Nino seemed to be annoyed. I realized that he didn't know who Chabod was and from that I got an electrifying sensation of fullness. I began to summarize the little I had learned, but I quickly realized that to know, to compulsively display what he knew, was his point of strength and at the same time his weakness. He felt strong if he took the lead and weak if he lacked words. He darkened, in fact he stopped me almost immediately. He sidetracked the conversation, he started talking about the Regions, about how urgent it was to get them approved, about autonomy and decentralization, about economic planning on a regional basis, all things I had never heard a word about. No Chabod, then: I left him the field. And I liked to hear him talk, read the passion in his face. His eyes brightened when he was excited.

We went on like that for at least an hour. Isolated from the shouting around us, its coarse dialect, we felt exclusive, he and I alone, with our vigilant Italian, with those conversations that mattered to us and no one else. What were we doing? A discussion? Practicing for future confrontations with people who had learned to use words as we had? An exchange of signals to prove to ourselves that such words were the basis of a long and fruitful friendship? A cultivated screen for sexual desire? I don't know. I certainly had no particular passion for those subjects, for the real things and people they referred to. I had no training, no habit, only the usual desire not to make a bad showing. It was wonderful, though—that is certain. I felt the way I did at the end of the year when I saw the list of my grades and read: passed. But I also understood that there was no comparison with the exchanges I had had with Lila years earlier, which ignited my brain, and in the course of which we tore the words from each other's mouth, creating an excitement that seemed like a storm of electrical charges. With Nino it was different. I felt that I had to pay attention to say what he wanted me to say, hiding from him both my ignorance and the few things that I knew and he didn't. I did this, and felt proud that he was trusting me with his convictions. But now something else happened. Suddenly he said, That's enough, grabbed my hand, exclaimed, like a fluorescent caption, *Now I'll take you to see a landscape that you'll never forget*, and dragged me to Piazza del Soccorso, without letting go, rather, he entwined his fingers in mine, so that, overwhelmed as I was by his clasp, I preserve no memory of the arc of the deep blue sea.

It truly overwhelmed me. Once or twice he disentangled his fingers to smooth his hair, but he immediately took my hand again. I wondered for a moment how he reconciled that intimate gesture with his bond with Professor Galiani's daughter. Maybe for him, I answered, it's merely how he thinks of the friendship between male and female. But the kiss on Via Mezzocannone? That, too, was nothing, new customs, new habits of youth; and anyway so slight, just the briefest contact. I should be satisfied with the happiness of right now, the chance of this vacation that I wanted: later I'll lose him, he'll leave, he has a destiny that can in no way be mine, too.

I was absorbed by these throbbing thoughts when I heard a roar behind me and noisy cries of my name. Rino and Stefano passed us at full speed on their Lambrettas, with their wives behind. They slowed down, turned back with a skillful maneuver. I let go of Nino's hand.

"And your friend?" Stefano asked, revving his engine.

"He'll be here soon."

"Say hello from me."

"Yes."

Rino asked, "Do you want to take Lenuccia for a spin?"

"No, thanks."

"Come on, you see she'd like to."

Nino flushed, he said, "I don't know how to ride a Lambretta."

"It's easy, like a bicycle."

"I know, but it's not for me."

Stefano laughed: "Rinù, he's a guy who studies, forget it."

I had never seen him so lighthearted. Lila sat close against him, with both arms around his waist. She urged him, "Let's go, if you don't hurry you'll miss the boat."

"Yes, let's go," cried Stefano, "tomorrow we have to work: not like you people who sit in the sun and go swimming. Bye, Lenù, bye, Nino, be good boys and girls."

"Nice to meet you," Rino said cordially.

They went off, Lila waved goodbye to Nino, shouting, "Please, take her home."

She's acting like my mother, I thought with a little annoyance, she's playing grownup.

Nino took me by the hand again and said, "Rino is nice, but why did Lina marry that moron?"

46.

A little later I also met his friend, Bruno Soccavo, who was around twenty, and very short, with a low forehead, black curly hair, a pleasant face but scarred by what must have been severe acne.

They walked me home, beside the wine-colored sea of twilight. Nino didn't take my hand again, even though Bruno left us practically alone: he went in front or lingered behind, as if he didn't want to disturb us. Since Soccavo never said a word to me, I didn't speak to him, either, his shyness made me shy. But when we parted, at the house, it was he who asked suddenly, "Will we meet tomorrow?" And Nino found out where we were going to the beach, he insisted on precise directions. I gave them.

"Are you going in the morning or the afternoon?"

"Morning and afternoon. Lina is supposed to swim a lot."

He promised they would come and see us.

I ran happily up the stairs of the house, but as soon as I came in Pinuccia began to tease me.

"Mamma," she said to Nunzia during dinner, "Lenuccia's going out with the poet's son, a skinny fellow with long hair, who thinks he's better than everybody."

"It's not true."

"It's very true, we saw you holding hands."

Nunzia didn't understand the teasing and took the thing with the earnest gravity that characterized her.

"What does Sarratore's son do?"

"University student."

"Then if you love each other you'll have to wait."

"There's nothing to wait for, Signora Nunzia, we're only friends."

"But if, let's say, you should happen to become engaged, he'll have to finish his studies first, then he'll have to find a job that's worthy of him, and only when he's found something will you be able to get married."

Here Lila interrupted, amused: "She's telling you you'll get moldy."

But Nunzia reproached her: "You mustn't speak like that to Lenuccia." And to console me she said that she had married Fernando at twenty-one, that she had had Rino at twenty-three. Then she turned to her daughter, and said, without malice, only to point out how things stood, "You, on the other hand, were married too young." That comment infuriated Lila and she went to her room. When Pinuccia knocked on the door, to go in to sleep, she yelled not to bother her, "you have your room." How in that atmosphere could I say: Nino and Bruno promised they'll come and see me on the beach? I gave it up. If it happens, I thought, fine, and if it doesn't why tell them. Nunzia, meanwhile, patiently invited her daughter-in-law into her bed, telling her not to be upset by her daughter's nerves.

The night wasn't enough to soothe Lila. On Monday she got up in a worse mood than when she had gone to bed. It's the absence of her husband, Nunzia said apologetically, but neither Pinuccia nor I believed it. I soon discovered that she was angry mainly at me. On the road to the beach she made me carry her bag, and once we were at the beach she sent me back twice, first to get her a scarf, then because she needed some nail scissors. When I gave signs of protest she nearly reminded me of the money she was giving me. She stopped in time, but not so that I didn't understand: it was like when someone is about to hit you and then doesn't.

It was a very hot day; we stayed in the water. Lila practiced hard to keep afloat, and made me stand next to her so that I could hold her up if necessary. Yet her spitefulness continued. She kept reproaching me, she said that it was stupid to trust me: I didn't even know how to swim, how could I teach her. She missed Sarratore's talents as an instructor, she made me swear that the next day we would go back to the Maronti. Still, by trial and error, she made a lot of progress. She learned every movement instantly. Thanks to that ability she had learned to make shoes, to dexterously slice salami and provolone, to cheat on the weight. She was born like that, she could have learned the art of engraving merely by studying the gestures of a goldsmith, and then been able to work the gold better than he. Already she had stopped gasping for breath, and was forcing composure on every motion: it was as if she were drawing her body on the transparent surface of the sea. Long, slender arms and legs hit the water in a tranquil rhythm, without raising foam like Nino, without the ostentatious tension of Sarratore the father.

"Is this right?"

"Yes."

It was true. In a few hours she could swim better than I could, not to mention Pinuccia, and already she was making fun of our clumsiness.

That bullying air dissipated abruptly when, around four in the afternoon, Nino, who was very tall, and Bruno, who came up to his shoulders, appeared on the beach, just as a cool wind rose, taking away the desire to swim.

Pinuccia was the first to make them out as they advanced along the shore, among the children playing with shovels and pails. She burst out laughing in surprise and said: Look who's coming, the long and the short of it. Nino and his friend, towels over their shoulder, cigarettes and lighters, advanced deliberately, looking for us among the bathers.

I had a sudden sense of power, I shouted, I waved to signal our presence. So Nino had kept his promise. So he had felt, already, the next day, the need to see me again. So he had come purposely from Forio, dragging along his mute companion, and since he had nothing in common with Lila and Pinuccia, it was obvious that he had taken that walk just for me, who alone was not married, or even engaged. I felt happy, and the more my happiness seemed justified—Nino spread his towel next to me, he sat down, he pointed to an edge of the blue fabric, and I, who was the only one sitting on the sand, quickly moved over—the more cordial and talkative I became.

Lila and Pinuccia instead were silent. They stopped teasing me, they stopped squabbling with each other; they listened to Nino as he told funny stories about how he and his friend had organized their life of study.

It was a while before Pinuccia ventured a few words, in a mixture of dialect and Italian. She said the water was nice and warm, that the man who sold fresh coconut hadn't come by yet, that she had a great desire for some. But Nino paid little attention, absorbed in his witty stories, and it was Bruno, more attentive, who felt it his duty not to ignore what a pregnant woman was saying: worried that the child might be born with a craving for coconut, he offered to go in search of some. Pinuccia liked his voice, choked by shyness but kind, the voice of a person who doesn't want to hurt anyone, and she eagerly began chatting with him, in a low voice, as if not to disturb.

Lila, however, remained silent. She took little interest in the platitudes that Pinuccia and Bruno were exchanging, but she didn't miss a word of what Nino and I were saying. That attention made me uneasy, and a few times I said I would be glad to take a walk to the fumaroles, hoping that Nino would say: let's go. But he had just begun to talk about the construction chaos on Ischia, so he agreed mechanically, then continued talking anyway. He dragged Bruno into it, maybe upset by the fact that he was talking to Pinuccia, and called on him as a witness to certain eyesores right next to his parents' house. Nino had a great need to express himself, to summarize his reading, to give shape to what he had himself observed. It was his way of putting his thoughts in order—talk, talk, talk—but certainly, I thought, also a sign of solitude. I proudly felt that I was like him, with the same desire to give myself an educated identity, to impose it, to say: Here's what I know, here's what I'm going to be. But Nino didn't leave me space to do it, even if occasionally, I have to say, I tried. I sat and listened to him, like the others, and when Pinuccia and Bruno exclaimed, "All right, we're going for a walk now, we're going to look for coconut," I gazed insistently at Lila, hoping that she would go with her sister-in-law, leaving me and Nino finally alone to face each other, side by side, on the same towel. But she didn't breathe, and when Pina realized that she was compelled to go for a walk by herself with a young man who was polite but nevertheless unknown, she asked me, in annoyance, "Lenù, come on, don't you want to walk?" I answered, "Yes, but let us finish our conversation, then maybe we'll join you." And she, displeased, went with Bruno toward the fumaroles: they were exactly the same height.

We continued to talk about how Naples and Ischia and all Campania had ended up in the hands of the worst people, who acted like the best people. "Marauders," Nino called them, his voice rising, "destroyers, bloodsuckers, people who steal suitcases of money and don't pay taxes: builders, lawyers for builders, Camorrists, monarcho-fascists, and Christian Democrats who behave as if cement were mixed in Heaven, and God himself, with an enormous trowel, were throwing blocks of it on the hills, on the coasts." But that the three of us were talking is an exaggeration. It was mainly he who talked, every so often I threw in some fact I had read in *Cronache Meridionali*. As for Lila, she spoke only once, and cautiously, when in the list of villains he included shopkeepers.

She asked, "Who are shopkeepers?"

Nino stopped in the middle of a sentence, looked at her in astonishment.

"Tradesmen."

"And why do you call them shopkeepers?"

"That's what they're called."

"My husband is a shopkeeper."

"I didn't mean to offend you."

"I'm not offended."

"Do you pay taxes?"

"I've never heard of them till now."

"Really?"

"Yes."

"Taxes are important for planning the economic life of a community."

"If you say so. You remember Pasquale Peluso?"

"No."

"He's a construction worker. Without all that cement he would lose his job."

"Ah."

"But he's a Communist. His father, also a Communist, in the court's opinion murdered my father-in-law, who had made money on the black market and as a loan shark. And Pasquale is like his father, he has never agreed on the question of peace, not even with the Communists, his comrades. But, even though my husband's money comes directly from my father-in-law's money, Pasquale and I are close friends."

"I don't understand what you're getting at."

Lila made a self-mocking face.

"I don't, either, I was hoping to understand by listening to the two of you."

That was it, she said nothing else. But in speaking she hadn't used her normal aggressive tone of voice, she seriously seemed to want us to help her understand, since the life of the neighborhood was a tangled skein. She had spoken in dialect most of the time, as if to indicate, modestly: I don't use tricks, I speak as I am. And she had summarized disparate things frankly, without seeking, as she usually did, a thread that would hold them together. And in fact neither she nor I had ever heard that word-formula loaded with cultural and political contempt: shopkeepers. And in fact neither she nor I knew anything about taxes: our parents, friends, boyfriends, husbands, relatives acted as if they didn't exist, and school taught nothing that had to do even vaguely with politics. Yet Lila still managed to disrupt what had until that moment been a new and thrilling afternoon. Right after that exchange, Nino tried to return to his subject but he faltered, he went back to telling funny anecdotes about life with Bruno. He said they ate only fried eggs and salami, he said that they drank a lot of wine. Then he seemed embarrassed by his own stories and appeared relieved when Pinuccia and Bruno, their hair wet, came back, eating coconut.

"That was really fun," Pina exclaimed, but with the air of

one who wants to say: You two bitches, you sent me off by myself with someone I don't even know.

When the two boys left I walked with them a little way, just to make it clear that they were my friends and had come because of me.

Nino said moodily, "Lina really got lost, what a shame."

I nodded yes, said goodbye, stood for a while with my feet in the water to calm myself.

When we got home, Pinuccia and I were lively, Lila thoughtful. Pinuccia told Nunzia about the visit of the two boys and appeared unexpectedly pleased with Bruno, who had taken the trouble to make sure that her child wasn't born with a craving for coconut. He's well brought up, she said, a student but not too boring: he seems not to care about how he's dressed but everything he has on, from his bathing suit to his shirt and his sandals, is expensive. She appeared curious about the fact that someone could be wealthy in a fashion different from that of her brother, Rino, the Solaras. She made a remark that struck me: At the bar on the beach he bought me this and that without showing off.

Her mother-in-law, who, for the entire length of that vacation, never went to the beach but took care of the shopping, the house, preparing dinner and also the lunch that we carried to the beach the next day, listened as if her daughter-in-law were recounting to her an enchanted world. Naturally she noticed immediately that her daughter was preoccupied, and kept glancing at her questioningly. But Lila was just distracted. She caused no trouble of any type, she allowed Pinuccia to sleep with her again, she wished everyone good night. Then she did something completely unexpected. I had just gone to bed when she appeared in the little room.

"Will you give me one of your books?" she asked.

I looked at her in bewilderment. She wanted to read? How long since she had opened a book, three, four years? And why now had she decided to start again? I took the volume of Beckett, the one I used to kill the mosquitoes, and gave it to her. It seemed the most accessible text I had.

47.

The week passed, between long waits and encounters that ended too quickly. The two boys kept to a rigorous schedule. They woke at six in the morning, they studied until lunchtime, at three they set out for their date with us, at seven they went home, had dinner, and resumed studying. Nino never came by himself. He and Bruno, although so different in every way, got along well, and especially when it came to us they seemed to gain confidence from each other's presence.

Pinuccia from the start did not share the hypothesis of their companionship. She claimed that they were neither particularly friendly nor particularly close. In her view it was a relationship that was sustained completely by the patience of Bruno, who was good-natured and so accepted without complaint the fact that Nino talked his head off from morning till night with all that nonsense that was constantly coming out of his mouth. "Nonsense, yes," she repeated, but then apologized, with a touch of sarcasm, for having described in that way the talk that I, too, liked so much. "You're students," she said, "and it's logical that you're the only ones who understand what you're saying; but wouldn't you agree, at least, that the rest of us get a little fed up?"

Those words pleased me greatly. They ratified in the presence of Lila, a mute witness, that between Nino and me there was a sort of exclusive relationship, in which it was hard to interfere. But one day Pinuccia said to Bruno and to Lila, in a disparaging tone, "Let's leave those two to act like intellectuals and go swimming, the water is lovely." *Act like intellectuals* was clearly a way of saying that the things we talked about didn't interest us seriously, it was an attitude, a performance. And while I didn't particularly mind that formulation, it annoyed Nino a lot, and he broke off in the middle of a sentence. He jumped to his feet, ran off and dived into the water, paying no attention to the temperature, splashed us as we started in, shivering and begging him to stop, then went on to fight with Bruno as if he wanted to drown him.

There, I thought, he's full of grand thoughts, but if he wants to he can also be lighthearted and fun. So why does he only show me his serious side? Has Professor Galiani convinced him that all I'm interested in is studying? Or is it me, do I create that impression, with my glasses, the way I speak?

From that moment I noticed with increasing bitterness that the afternoons slipped away, leaving words burdened with his anxiety to express himself and mine to anticipate a concept, to hear him say that he agreed with me. He never took me by the hand, never invited me to sit on the edge of his towel. When I saw Bruno and Pinuccia laughing at silly things I envied them, I thought: How much I would like to laugh with Nino like that—I don't want anything, I don't expect anything, I'd just like a little intimacy, even if it's polite, the way it is between Pinuccia and Bruno.

Lila seemed to have other problems. For the whole week she seemed tranquil. She spent a great part of the morning in the water, swimming back and forth, following a line parallel to the shore and a few meters away from it. Pinuccia and I kept her company, insisting on instructing her even though by now she swam much better than we did. But soon we got cold and went to lie on the hot sand, while she continued to exercise with steady arm strokes, feet kicking lightly, rhythmic mouthfuls of air as Sarratore the father had taught her. She always has to overdo it, Pinuccia grumbled in the sun, caressing her belly. And often I got up and shouted, "Enough swimming, you've been in the water too long, you'll catch cold." But Lila paid no attention and came out only when she was livid, her eyes white, her lips blue, her fingertips wrinkled. I waited for her on the shore with her towel, warmed in the sun; I put it around her shoulders and rubbed her energetically.

When the two boys, who didn't skip a single day, arrived, either we took another swim together—though Lila generally refused, she stayed on her towel, watching us from the shore— or we all went for a walk and she lagged behind, picking up shells, or, if Nino and I started talking about the world, she listened attentively but rarely said anything. In the meantime, small habits became established, and I was struck by her insistence that they be respected. For example, Bruno always arrived with cold drinks that he bought on the way, at a bar on the beach, and one day she pointed out to him that he had brought me a soda whereas usually I had orangeade; I said, "Thanks, Bruno, this is fine," but she made him go and exchange it. For example, Pinuccia and Bruno at a certain point in the afternoon went to get fresh coconut, and although they invited us to go with them, it never occurred to Lila to do so, or to me or Nino: it thus became completely normal for them to go off dry, return wet from a swim, and bring coconut, with the whitest flesh, and so if it seemed that they might forget Lila would say, "And where's the coconut today?"

Also, she was very interested in Nino's and my conversations. When there was too much talk about nothing in particular she would say to him, "Didn't you read anything interesting today?" Nino smiled, pleased, rambled a bit, then started on the subjects he cared about. He talked and talked, but there were never real frictions between us: I found myself almost always in agreement with him, and if Lila interrupted to make an objection she did it briefly, with tact, without ever accentuating the disagreement.

One afternoon he was quoting an article that was very critical of the functioning of the public schools, and he went on without a break to speak disparagingly of the elementary school in our neighborhood. I agreed, I recalled how Maestra Oliviero rapped us on the knuckles when we made a mistake and also the brutal competitions to see who was smartest that she subjected us to. But Lila, surprising me, said that elementary school for her had been extremely important, and she praised our teacher in an Italian I hadn't heard from her in a long time, so precise, so intense, that Nino didn't interrupt her to say what he thought, but listened to her attentively, and in the end made some generic remarks about the different requirements we have and about how the same experience can satisfy the needs of one and be insufficient for the needs of someone else.

There was also another case where Lila revealed a disagreement politely and in a cultivated Italian. I felt increasingly drawn to arguments based on the theory that the right kind of interventions, carried out over time, would resolve problems, eliminate injustices, and prevent conflicts. I had quickly learned that system of reasoning—I was always very good at that—and I applied it every time Nino brought up subjects about which he had read here and there: colonialism, neocolonialism, Africa. But one afternoon Lila said softly that there was nothing that could eliminate the conflict between the rich and the poor.

"Why?"

"Those who are on the bottom always want to be on top, those who are on top want to stay on top, and one way or another they always reach the point where they're kicking and spitting at each other."

"That's exactly why problems should be resolved before violence breaks out."

"And how? Putting everyone on top, putting everyone on the bottom?"

"Finding a point of equilibrium between the classes."

"A point where? Those from the bottom meet those from the top in the middle?"

"Let's say yes."

"And those on top will be willing to go down? And those on the bottom will give up on going any higher?"

"If people work to solve all the problems well, yes. You're not convinced?"

"No. The classes aren't playing cards, they're fighting, and it's a fight to the death."

"That's what Pasquale thinks," I said.

"I think so, too, now," she said calmly.

Apart from those few one-on-one exchanges, there were rarely, between Nino and Lila, words that were not mediated by me. Lila never addressed him directly, nor did Nino address her, they seemed embarrassed by one another. She appeared much more comfortable with Bruno, who, though quiet, managed, with his kindness, and the pleasant tone in which he would call her Signora Carracci, to establish a certain familiarity. For example, once when we all went in the water together— and Nino, surprisingly, did not go on one of the long swims that made me anxious—she turned to Bruno, and not to him, to show her after how many strokes she should take her head out of the water to breathe. He promptly gave her a demonstration. But Nino was annoyed that he hadn't been asked, given his mastery of swimming, and he interrupted, making fun of Bruno's short arms, his lack of rhythm. Then he showed Lila the right way. She observed him with attention and immediately imitated him. In the end Lila's swimming led Bruno to call her the Esther Williams of Ischia.

When the end of the week arrived—I remember it was a splendid Saturday morning, the air was still cool and the sharp odor of the pines accompanied us all the way to the beach—Pinuccia reasserted categorically, "Sarratore's son is really unbearable."

I defended Nino warily. I said in the tone of an expert that when a person studies, when he becomes interested in things, he feels the need to communicate those interests to others, and for Nino it was like that. Lila didn't seem convinced, she made a remark that sounded offensive to me: "If you removed from Nino's head the things he's read, you wouldn't find anything there."

I snapped, "It's not true. I know him and he has a lot of good qualities."

Pinuccia, on the other hand, agreed enthusiastically. But Lila, maybe because she didn't like that approval, said she hadn't explained well and reversed the meaning of the remark, as if she had formulated it only as a trial and now, hearing it, regretted it, and was grasping at straws to make up for it. He, she clarified, is habituating himself to the idea that only the big questions are important, and if he succeeds he will live his whole life only for those, without being disturbed by anything else: not like us, who think only of our own affairs—money, house, husband, children.

I didn't like that version, either. What was she saying? That for Nino feelings for individual persons would not count, that his fate was to live without love, without children, without marriage? I forced myself to say:

"You know he has a girlfriend he's very attached to? They write once a week."

Pinuccia interrupted: "Bruno doesn't have a girlfriend, but he's looking for his ideal woman and as soon as he finds her he'll get married and he wants to have a lot of children." Then, without obvious connection, she sighed: "This week has really flown by."

"Aren't you glad? Now your husband will be back," I replied.

She seemed almost offended by the possibility that I could imagine her feeling any annoyance at Rino's return.

She exclaimed, "Of course I'm glad."

Lila then asked me, "And are you glad?"

"That your husbands are returning?"

"No, you know what I meant."

I did know but I wouldn't admit it. She meant that the next day, Sunday, while they were involved with Stefano and Rino, I would be able to see the boys by myself, and in fact, almost certainly, Bruno, as he had the week before, would be minding his own business, and I would spend the afternoon with Nino. And she was right, that was what I was hoping. For days, before going to sleep, I had been thinking of the weekend. Lila and Pinuccia would have their conjugal pleasures, I would have the small happinesses of the unmarried girl in glasses who spends her life studying: a walk, being taken by the hand. Or who knows, maybe even more. I said, laughing, "What should I understand, Lila? You're the lucky ones, who are married."

48.

The day slid by slowly. While Lila and I sat calmly in the sun waiting until the time when Nino and Bruno would arrive with cool drinks, Pinuccia's mood began, for no reason, to darken. She kept uttering nervous remarks. Now she was afraid that they wouldn't come, now she exclaimed that we couldn't waste our time waiting for them to show up. When, punctually, the boys appeared with the drinks, she was surly, and said she felt tired. But a few minutes later, though still in a bad mood, she changed her mind and agreed, grumbling, to go get the coconut.

As for Lila, she did something I didn't like. For the whole week she had never said anything about the book I had lent her, and so I had forgotten about it. But as soon as Pinuccia and Bruno left, she didn't wait for Nino to start talking, and immediately asked him, "Have you ever been to the theater?"

"A few times."

"Did you like it?"

"It was all right."

"I've never been, but I've seen it on television."

"It's not the same thing."

"I know, but better than nothing."

And at that point she took out of her bag the book I had given her, the volume of Beckett's plays, and showed it to him.

"Have you read this?"

Nino took the book, examined it, admitted uneasily, "No."

"So there *is* something you haven't read."

"Yes."

"You should read it."

Lila began to talk to us about the book. To my surprise she was very deliberate, she talked the way she used to, choosing the words so as to make us see people and things, and also the emotion she gave them, portraying them anew, keeping them there, present, alive. She said that we didn't have to wait for nuclear war, in the book it was as if it had already happened. She told us at length about a woman named Winnie who at a certain point announced, *another happy day*, and she herself declaimed the phrase, becoming so upset that, in uttering it, her voice trembled slightly: *another happy day*, words that were insupportable, because nothing, nothing, she explained, in Winnie's life, nothing in her gestures, nothing in her head, was *happy*, not that day or the preceding days. But, she added, the biggest impression had been made on her by a Dan Rooney. Dan Rooney, she said, is blind but he's not bitter about it, because he believes that life is better without sight, and in fact he wonders whether, if one became deaf and mute, life would not be still more life, life without anything but life.

"Why did you like it?" Nino asked.

"I don't know yet if I liked it."

"But it made you curious."

"It made me think. What does it mean that life is more life without sight, without hearing, even without words?"

"Maybe it's just a gimmick."

"No, what gimmick. There's a thing here that suggests a thousand others, it's not a gimmick."

Nino didn't reply. He said only, staring at the cover of the book as if that, too, needed to be deciphered, "Have you finished it?"

"Yes."

"Will you lend it to me?"

That request disturbed me, I felt pained. Nino had said, I remembered it clearly, that he had little interest in literature, what he read was different. I had given that Beckett to Lila just because I knew that I couldn't use it in conversation with him. And now that she was talking about it he was not only listening but asked to borrow it.

I said, "It's Professor Galiani's, she gave it to me."

"Have you read it?" he asked me.

I had to admit that I hadn't, but I added right away, "I was thinking of starting tonight."

"When you're finished will you give it to me?"

"If it interests you so much," I said quickly, "you read it first."

Nino thanked me, scratched away with his nail the trace of a mosquito from the cover, said to Lila, "I'll read it overnight and tomorrow we can talk about it."

"Not tomorrow, we won't see each other."

"Why?"

"I'll be with my husband."

"Oh."

He seemed annoyed. I waited fearfully for him to ask me if the two of us would see each other. But he had a burst of impatience, he said, "I can't tomorrow, either. Bruno's parents arrive tonight and I have to go sleep in Barano. I'll be back on Monday."

Barano? Monday? I hoped that he would ask me to join him at the Maronti. But he was distracted, maybe his mind was still on Dan Rooney, who, not content with being blind, wished to become deaf and mute, too. He didn't ask me anything.

49.

On the way home I said to Lila, "If I lend you a book, which, besides, isn't mine, please don't take it to the beach. I can't give it back to Professor Galiani with sand in it."

"I'm sorry," she said, and cheerfully gave me a kiss on the cheek. She wanted to carry both my bag and Pinuccia's, maybe to ask forgiveness.

Slowly my mood cleared. I thought that Nino hadn't randomly alluded to the fact that he was going to Barano: he wanted me to know, and I decided independently to go and see him there. He's like that, I said to myself, with growing relief, he needs to be pursued: tomorrow I'll get up early and go. Pinuccia's ill humor, on the other hand, continued. Usually she was quick to get angry but quick to get over it, too, especially now that pregnancy had softened not only her body but also the rough edges of her character. Instead she became increasingly fretful.

"Did Bruno say something unpleasant?" I asked her.

"No."

"Then what happened?"

"Nothing."

"Do you not feel well?"

"I'm fine, I don't even know what's wrong with me."

"Go and get ready, Rino will be here."

"Yes."

But she continued to sit in her damp bathing suit, leafing distractedly through a photonovel. Lila and I got dressed up,

Lila especially decked herself out as if she were going to a party, and still Pinuccia did nothing. Then even Nunzia, who was laboring silently over the dinner preparations, said softly, "Pinù, what's the matter, sweetie, aren't you going to get dressed?" No answer. Only when we heard the roar of the Lambrettas and the voices of the two young men calling did Pina jump up and run to her room, crying, "Don't let them come in, please."

The evening was bewildering, for the husbands, too. Stefano, by now used to permanent conflict with Lila, found himself unexpectedly in the company of a girl who was very affectionate, yielding to caresses and kisses without her usual irritation; while Rino, accustomed to Pinuccia's clingy coquettishness, intensified by her pregnancy, was disappointed that his wife didn't come down the stairs to greet him, that he had to look for her in the bedroom, and when finally he embraced her, he immediately noticed the effort she made to act as if she were pleased. Not only that. While Lila laughed heartily when, after a few glasses of wine, the two men started in with the lively sexual allusions that indicated desire, Pinuccia, at a whispered remark from Rino, laughing, jerked away and hissed, in a half Italian, "Stop it, you're a boor." He got angry: "You call me a boor? Boor?" She resisted for a few minutes, then her lower lip trembled and she took refuge in her room.

"It's the pregnancy," Nunzia said, "you have to be patient."

Silence. Rino finished eating, then, fuming, went to his wife. He didn't come back.

Lila and Stefano decided to go out on the Lambretta to see the beach at night. They left laughing together, kissing. I cleared the table, as usual struggling with Nunzia, who didn't want me to lift a finger. We talked about when she had met Fernando and they fell in love, and she said something that made a deep impression. She said, "For your whole life you love people and you never really know who they are." Fernando was both good and bad, and she had loved him very much but she had also hated him. "So," she emphasized, "there's nothing to worry about: Pinuccia is in a bad mood but she'll get over it; and you remember how Lina came back from her honeymoon? Well, look at them now. Life is like that: one day you're getting hit, the next kissed."

I went to my room, I tried to finish Chabod, but I recalled how Nino had been charmed by the way Lila talked about that Rooney, and the desire to waste time with the idea of nationhood vanished. Even Nino is evasive, I thought, even with Nino it's hard to understand who he is. He seemed not to care about literature and yet Lila randomly picks up a book of plays, says two foolish things, and he becomes ardent about it. I rummaged among the books in search of other literary things, but I had none. I realized that a book was missing. Was that possible? Professor Galiani had given me six. Nino now had one, one I was reading, on the marble windowsill there were three. Where was the sixth?

I looked everywhere, even under the bed, and while I was looking I remembered that it was a book about Hiroshima. I was upset—surely Lila must have taken it while I was in the bathroom. What was happening to her? After years of shoes, engagement, love, grocery store, dealings with the Solaras, had she decided to revert to the person she had been in elementary school? Certainly there had already been a sign: she had wanted to make that bet, which, whatever its outcome, had surely been a way of demonstrating to me her wish to study. But had she followed up on that desire, had she actually done it? No. Yet had Nino's conversation been enough—six afternoons of sun on the sand—to revive in her the desire to learn, maybe compete again to be the best? Was that why she had sung the praises of Maestra Oliviero? Why had she found it wonderful that someone should become passionate for his whole life only about important things and not those of daily life? I left my room on tiptoe, opening the door carefully, so that it wouldn't squeak.

The house was silent, Nunzia had gone to sleep, Stefano and Lila weren't back yet. I went into their room: a chaos of clothes, shoes, suitcases. On a chair I found the volume, it was titled *Hiroshima the Day After*. She had taken it without asking my permission, as if my things were hers, as if what I was I owed to her, as if even Professor Galiani's attention to my education resulted from the fact that she, with a distracted gesture, with a tentative phrase, had put me in the position of gaining that privilege for myself. I thought of taking the book. But I was ashamed, I changed my mind, and left it there.

50.

It was a dull Sunday. I suffered from the heat all night, I didn't dare open the window for fear of the mosquitoes. I fell asleep, woke up, fell asleep again. Go to Barano? With what result? Spend the day playing with Ciro, Pino, and Clelia, while Nino took long swims or sat in the sun without saying a word, in mute conflict with his father. I woke up late, at ten, and as soon as I opened my eyes a sensation of loss, as if from a great distance, came over me and pained me.

I learned from Nunzia that Pinuccia and Rino had already gone to the beach, while Stefano and Lila were still sleeping. I soaked my bread in the caffelatte without wanting it, I conclusively gave up going to Barano. I went to the beach, anxious and sad.

I found Rino sleeping in the sun, his hair wet, his heavy body lying, stomach down, on the sand, and Pinuccia walking back and forth on the shore. I invited her to go toward the fumaroles, she refused rudely. I walked for a long time alone in the direction of Forio to calm myself.

The morning passed slowly. When I came back I went swimming, then lay in the sun. I had to listen to Rino and Pinuccia, who, as if I weren't there, were murmuring to each other phrases such as:

"Don't go."

"I have to work: the shoes have to be ready for the fall. Did you see them, do you like them?"

"Yes, but the things Lina made you add are ugly, take them off."

"No, they look good."

"You see? What I say counts for nothing with you."

"That's not true."

"It's very true, you don't love me anymore."

"I do love you, and you know how much I want you."

"No way, look at the belly I have."

"I'd give that belly ten thousand kisses. For the whole week all I do is think about you."

"Then don't go to work."

"I can't."

"Then I'll leave tonight, too."

"We've already paid our share, you have to have your vacation."

"I don't want it anymore."

"Why?"

"Because as soon as I fall asleep I have terrible dreams and I'm awake all night."

"Even when you sleep with my sister?"

"Even more, if your sister could kill me, she would."

"Go sleep with my mamma."

"Your mamma snores."

Pinuccia's tone of voice was unbearable. All day I tried to figure out the reasons for her complaints. That she didn't sleep much or very well was true. But that she wanted Rino to stay, or that she really wanted to leave with him, seemed to me a lie.

At one point I was convinced that she was trying to tell him something that she herself didn't know and so could express only in the form of peevishness. But then I forgot about it, I had other things to think about. Lila's exuberance, first of all.

When she appeared at the beach with her husband, she seemed happier than the night before. She wanted to show him how she had learned to swim, and together they headed away from the shore—out where it's deep, Stefano said, even though it was really only a few meters from the shore. With her elegant and precise strokes, and the rhythmic turn of the head to breathe that she had by now learned, moving her mouth away from the water, she immediately left him behind. Then she stopped to wait for him, laughing, until he caught up, clumsily flailing his arms, his head straight up, as he snorted at the water that sprayed in his face.

She was even livelier in the afternoon, when they went for a ride on the Lambretta. Rino wanted to drive around, too, and since Pinuccia refused—she was afraid of falling and losing the baby—he said to me, "You come, Lenù." It was my first such experience, with Stefano in the lead, Rino following, and the wind, and the fear of falling or crashing, and the increasing excitement, the strong odor that came from the sweaty back of Pinuccia's husband, and the swaggering self-confidence that pushed him to violate every rule and to respond to any protests according to the habits of the neighborhood, braking suddenly, threatening, always ready to fight to assert his right to do as he pleased. It was fun, a return to those feelings of a bad girl, very different from the ones Nino inspired in me when he appeared on the beach, in the afternoon, with his friend.

In the course of that Sunday I named the two boys often: I especially liked saying the name of Nino. I quickly noticed that both Pinuccia and Lila acted as if it hadn't been the three of us who spent time with Bruno and Nino, but only me. As a result, when their husbands said goodbye, hurrying off to catch the ferry, Stefano asked me to say hello to Soccavo's son for him, as if I were the only one who would have the opportunity to see him, and Rino teased me, with remarks like: Who do you like more, the son of the poet or the son of the mortadella maker? Who do you think is handsomer? as if his wife and sister had no basis for forming their own opinions.

Finally, the reactions of both to the departure of their husbands annoyed me. Pinuccia became cheerful, she wanted to wash her hair, which—she said aloud—was full of sand. Lila lounged about the house listlessly, then she lay down on her unmade bed, paying no attention to the mess in the room. When I went to say good night I saw that she hadn't even undressed: she was reading the book about Hiroshima, frowning, eyes narrowed. I didn't reproach her, I said only, perhaps a little sharply:

"How is it that you suddenly feel like reading again?"

"It's none of your business," she answered.

51.

On Monday Nino appeared, like a ghost evoked by my desire, not at four in the afternoon, as usual, but, surprisingly, at ten in the morning. We three girls had just arrived at the beach, resentful, each convinced that the others had spent too much time in the bathroom, Pinuccia particularly upset about how her hair had been ruined by her sleeping on it. It was she who spoke first, stern, almost aggressive. She asked Nino, even before he could explain to us, why in the world he had turned his schedule upside down:

"Why didn't Bruno come, he had better things to do?"

"His parents are still here, they're leaving at noon."

"Then he'll come?"

"I think so."

"Because if he's not coming I'm going back to sleep, with just the three of you I'll be bored."

And while Nino was telling us how terrible his Sunday in Barano had been, and so he had left early and, since he couldn't go to Bruno's, had come straight to the beach, she interrupted once or twice, asking in a whine: Who's going to go swimming with me? Since both Lila and I ignored her, she went into the water angrily by herself.

Never mind. We preferred to listen attentively to the list of wrongs that Nino suffered at the hands of his father. A cheater, he called him, a malingerer. He had settled himself in Barano, extending his leave from work on the ground of some feigned illness, which had been properly certified, however, by a health-service doctor who was a friend of his. "My father," he said in disgust, "is in everything and for everything the negation of the general interest." And then, without a break, he did something unpredictable. With a sudden movement that made me jump he leaned over and gave me a big, noisy kiss on the cheek, followed by the remark: "I'm really glad to see you." Then, slightly embarrassed, as if he had realized that with that effusiveness toward me he might be acting rudely toward Lila, he said: "May I also give you a kiss?"

"Of course," Lila answered, affably, and he gave her a light kiss, with no sound, a barely perceptible contact. After that he began to talk excitedly about the plays of Beckett: Ah, how he liked those guys buried in the ground up to their necks; and how beautiful the statement was about the fire that the present kindles inside you; and, even though among the thousand evocative things that Maddy and Dan Rooney said he had had a hard time picking out the precise point cited by Lila, well, the concept that life is felt more when you are blind, deaf, mute, and maybe without taste or touch was objectively interesting in itself. In his view it meant: Let's get rid of all the filters that prevent us from fully savoring our being here and now, real.

Lila appeared bewildered, she said that she had thought about it and that life in the pure state frightened her. She expressed herself with some emphasis, she exclaimed, "Life without seeing and without speaking, without speaking and listening, life without a covering, without a container, is shapeless." She didn't use exactly those words, but certainly she said "shapeless" and she said it with a gesture of revulsion. Nino repeated reluctantly, "shapeless," as if it were a curse word. Then he started talking again, even more overwrought, until, with no warning, he took off his shirt, revealing himself in all his dark thinness, grabbed us both by the hand, and dragged us into the water, as I cried happily, "No, no, no, I'm cold, no," and he answered, "*Here finally another happy day*," and Lila laughed.

So, I thought contentedly, Lila is wrong. So there certainly exists another Nino: not the gloomy boy, not the one who gets excited only when he's thinking about the general state of the world, but *this boy*, this boy who plays, who drags us furiously into the water, who mocks us, grips us, pulls us toward him, swims away, lets us reach him, lets us grab him, lets us push him under the water and pretends to be overpowered, pretends that we're drowning him.

When Bruno arrived things got even better. We all took a walk together and Pinuccia's good humor slowly returned. She wanted to swim again, she wanted to eat coconut. Starting then, and for the whole week that followed, we found it completely natural that the boys should join us on the beach at ten in the morning and remain until sunset, when we said, "We have to go or Nunzia will get mad," and they resigned themselves to going off to do some studying.

How intimate we were now. If Bruno called Lila Signora Carracci to tease her, she punched him playfully on the shoulder, chased him, threatening. If he showed too much reverence toward Pinuccia because she was carrying a child, Pinuccia linked arms with him, said, "Come on, let's run, I want a soda."

As for Nino, now he often took my hand, put an arm around my shoulders, and then put an arm around Lila's, too, he took her index finger, her thumb. The wary distances receded. We became a group of five friends who were having a good time doing little or nothing. We played games, whoever lost paid a fine. The fines were almost always kisses, but joke kisses, obviously: Bruno had to kiss Lila's sandy feet, Nino my hand, and then cheeks, forehead, ear, with a pop in the auricle. We also had long games of *tamburello*. The ball flew through the air and was sent back with a sharp crack against the taut hide of the tambourines; Lila was good, Nino, too. But most agile of all, most precise, was Bruno. He and Pinuccia always won, against Lila and me, against Lila and Nino, against Nino and me. They won partly because we had all developed a sort of automatic tenderness toward Pina. She ran, she jumped, she tumbled on the sand, forgetting her condition, and so we ended by letting her win, sometimes just to soothe her. Bruno reproached her gently, made her sit down, said, that's enough and cried, "Point for Pinuccia, excellent."

A thread of happiness thus began to extend through the hours and days. I no longer minded that Lila took my books, in fact it seemed to me a good thing. I didn't mind that, when the discussions got going, she more and more often said what she thought and Nino listened attentively and seemed to lack the words for a response. I found it thrilling, in fact, that in those circumstances he would suddenly stop talking to her and start up with me, as if that helped him rediscover his convictions.

That was what happened the time Lila showed off her reading on Hiroshima. A tense discussion arose, because Nino, I saw, was so critical of the United States and didn't like the fact that the Americans had a military base in Naples, but he was also attracted by their way of life, he said he wanted to study it, and he was disappointed when Lila said, more or less, that dropping atomic bombs on Japan had been a war crime, in fact more than a war crime—the war had scarcely anything to do with it—it had been a crime of pride.

"Can I remind you of Pearl Harbor?" he said hesitantly.

I didn't know what Pearl Harbor was but I discovered that Lila did. She told him that Pearl Harbor and Hiroshima were two things that couldn't be compared, that Pearl Harbor was a vile act of war and Hiroshima was an idiotic, fierce, vindictive horror, worse, much worse, than the Nazi massacres. And she concluded: the Americans should be tried like the worst criminals, those who do terrible things to terrorize the living and keep them on their knees. She was so passionate that Nino, instead of moving to the counterattack, was silent, very thoughtful. Then he turned to me, as if she weren't there. He said that the problem wasn't ferocity or revenge but the urgency to bring an end to the most atrocious of wars and, at the same time, by using that terrible new weapon, to all wars. He spoke in a low tone, looking me straight in the eyes, as if he were interested only in my agreement. It was a wonderful moment. He himself was wonderful, when he was like that. I was so filled with emotion that tears rose to my eyes and I had trouble repressing them.

Then Friday came again, a very hot day that we spent mostly in the water. And suddenly something went bad again.

We had just left the two boys and were going back to the house, the sun was low, the sky pinkish-blue, when Pinuccia, unexpectedly silent after many long hours of extravagant playfulness, threw her bag on the ground, sat down on the side of road, and began to cry with rage, small thin cries, almost a moaning.

Lila narrowed her eyes, stared at her as if she saw not her sister-in-law but something ugly for which she wasn't prepared. I went back, frightened, asked, "Pina, what's the matter, don't you feel well?"

"I can't bear this wet bathing suit."

"We all have wet bathing suits."

"It bothers me."

"Calm down, come on, aren't you hungry?"

"Don't tell me to calm down. You irritate me when you tell me to calm down. I can't stand you anymore, Lenù, you and your calm down."

And she started moaning again, and hitting her thighs.

I sensed that Lila was going on without waiting for us. I sensed that she had decided to do so not out of annoyance or indifference but because there was something in that behavior, something scorching, and if she got too close it would burn her. I helped Pinuccia get up, I carried her bag.

52.

Eventually she became quieter, but she spent the evening sulking, as if we had somehow offended her. When she was rude even to Nunzia, brusquely criticizing the way the pasta was cooked, Lila flared up and, breaking into a fierce dialect, dumped on her all the fantastic insults she was capable of. Pina decided to sleep with me that night.

She tossed and turned in her sleep. And with two people in the room the heat made it almost impossible to breathe. Soaked with sweat, I resigned myself to opening the window and was tormented by the mosquitoes. Then I couldn't sleep at all, I waited for dawn, I got up.

Now I, too, was in a bad mood, I had three or four disfiguring bites on my face. I went to the kitchen, Nunzia was washing our dirty clothes. Lila, too, was already up, she had had her bread-and-milk, and was reading another of my books, who knows when she had stolen it from me. As soon as she saw me, she gave me a searching glance and asked, with a genuine concern that I didn't expect: "How is Pinuccia?"

"I don't know."

"Are you angry?"

"Yes, I didn't sleep a wink, and look at my face."

"You can't see anything."

"*You* can't see anything."

"Nino and Bruno won't see anything, either."

"What does that have to do with it?"

"You still like Nino?"

"I've told you no a hundred times."

"Calm down."

"I am calm."

"Let's think about Pinuccia."

"You think about her, she's your sister-in-law, not mine."

"You're angry."

"Yes, I am."

The day was even hotter than the one before. We went to the beach apprehensively, the bad mood traveled from one to the other like an infection.

Halfway there Pinuccia realized she had forgotten her towel and had another attack of nerves. Lila kept going, head down, without even turning around.

"I'll go get it," I offered.

"No, I'm going back to the house, I don't feel like the beach."

"Do you feel sick?"

"I'm perfectly fine."

"Then what?"

"Look at the belly I've got."

I looked at her belly, I said to her without thinking: "What about me? Don't you see these bites on my face?"

She started yelling, she called me an idiot, and ran away to catch up with Lila.

Once at the beach she apologized, muttering, You're so good that sometimes you make me mad.

"I'm not good."

"I meant that you're clever."

"I'm not clever."

Lila, who was trying in any case to ignore us, staring at the sea in the direction of Forio, said coldly, "Stop it, they're coming."

Pinuccia started. "The long and the short of it," she murmured, with a sudden softness in her voice, and she put on some lipstick even though she already had enough.

The boys' mood was just as bad as ours. Nino had a sarcastic tone, he said to Lila, "Tonight the husbands arrive?"

"Of course."

"And what nice things will you do?"

"We'll eat, drink, and sleep."

"And tomorrow?"

"Tomorrow we'll eat, drink, and sleep."

"Do they stay Sunday night, too?"

"No, on Sunday we eat, drink, and sleep only in the afternoon."

Hiding behind a tone of self-mockery, I forced myself to say, "I'm free: I'm not eating or drinking or going to sleep."

Nino looked at me as if he were becoming aware of something he had never noticed, so that I passed a hand over my right cheek, where I had an especially big mosquito bite. He said to me seriously, "Good, we'll meet here tomorrow morning at seven and then climb the mountain. When we get back, the beach till late. What do you say?"

I felt in my veins the warmth of elation, I said with relief, "All right, at seven, I'll bring food."

Pinuccia asked, unhappily, "And us?"

"You have husbands," he said, and pronounced "husbands" as if he were saying toads, snakes, spiders, so that she got up abruptly and went to the water's edge.

"She's a little oversensitive at the moment," I said in apology, "but it's because of her interesting condition, usually she's not like that."

Bruno said in his patient voice, "I'll take her to get some coconut."

We watched him as, small but well proportioned, his chest powerful, his thighs strong, he moved over the sand at a steady pace, as if the sun had neglected to burn the grains he walked on. When Bruno and Pina set off for the beach bar, Lila said, "Let's go swimming."

53.

The three of us moved together toward the sea, me in the middle, between them. It's hard to explain the sudden sense of fullness that had possessed me when Nino said: We'll meet here tomorrow morning at seven. Of course I was sorry about the swings in Pinuccia's moods, but it was a weak sorrow, it couldn't dent my state of well-being. I was finally content with myself, with the long, exciting Sunday that awaited me; and at the same time I felt proud to be there, at that moment, with the people who had always been important in my life, whose importance couldn't be compared even to that of my parents, my siblings. I took them both by the hand, I gave a shout of happiness, I dragged them into the cold water, spraying icy splinters of foam. We sank as if we were a single organism.

As soon as we were underwater we let go of the chain of our fingers. I've never liked the cold of the water in my hair, on my head, in my ears. I re-emerged immediately, spluttering. But I saw that they were already swimming and I began to swim, in order not to lose them. I had trouble right away: I wasn't capable of swimming straight, head in the water, with steady strokes; my right arm was stronger than the left, and I veered right; I had to be careful not to swallow the salt water. I tried to keep up by not losing sight of them, in spite of my myopic vision. They'll stop, I thought. My heart was pounding, I slowed down, I finally stopped and floated, admiring their confident progress toward the horizon, side by side.

Maybe they were going too far. I, too, in the grip of enthusiasm, had ventured beyond the reassuring imaginary line that normally allowed me to return to the shore in a few strokes, and beyond which Lila herself had never gone. Now there she was, competing with Nino. Despite her inexperience she wouldn't give in, she wanted to stay even, she pushed on, farther and farther.

I began to worry. If her strength failed. If she felt ill. Nino is expert, he'll help her. But if he gets a cramp, if he collapses, too. I looked around, the current was dragging me to the left. I can't wait for them here, I have to go back. I glanced down, and it was a mistake. The azure immediately turned bluer, darkened like night, even though the sun was shining, the surface of the sea sparkled, and pure white shreds of cloud were stretching across the sky. I perceived the abyss, I sensed its liquidness, with nothing to hold on to, I felt it as a pit of the dead from which anything might rise up in a flash, touch me, grab me, sink its teeth into me, drag me to the bottom.

I tried to calm myself: I shouted Lila. My eyes without glasses were of no use, defeated by the sparkle of the water. I thought of my outing with Nino the following day. Slowly I turned around, on my back, paddling with legs and arms until I reached the shore.

I sat there, half in the water, half on the beach, I could just make out their heads, black dots like abandoned buoys on the surface of the sea, I felt relieved. Lila not only was safe but she had done it, she had stayed with Nino. How stubborn she is, how she overdoes it, how courageous she is. I got up, joined Bruno, who was sitting beside our things.

"Where's Pinuccia?" I asked.

He gave a timid smile that seemed to conceal a worry.

"She left."

"Where did she go?"

"Home, she says she has to pack her bags."

"Her bags?"

"She wants to go, she doesn't feel she can leave her husband alone for so long."

I took my things and, after insisting that he not lose sight of Nino and especially Lila, I left, still dripping wet, to try to find out what else was happening to Pina.

54.

It was a disastrous afternoon followed by an even more disastrous evening. I found that Pinuccia was really packing her bags and that Nunzia was unable to quiet her.

"You mustn't worry," she said to her soothingly, "Rino knows how to wash his underwear, he knows how to cook, and then there is his father, his friends. He doesn't think you're here to have fun, he understands that you're here to rest so that you'll have a fine healthy baby. Come, I'll help you tidy up everything. I never went on vacation, but today there's money, thank God, and although you mustn't waste it, a little comfort isn't a sin, you can afford it. So Pinù, please, child: Rino worked all week, he's tired, he's about to arrive. Don't let him find you like this, you know him, he'll worry, and when he worries he gets angry, and if he gets angry what's the result? The result is that you want to leave to stay with him, he has left to be with you, and now when you'll be together, and you ought to be happy, instead you're torturing each other. Does that seem nice to you?"

But Pinuccia was impervious to the arguments that Nunzia rattled off. Then I began to enumerate them, too, since we had reached the point where we were taking her many things out of the suitcases and she was putting them in, she cried, she calmed down, she started again.

Eventually Lila returned. She leaned against the doorpost and stood looking, with a frown, a long horizontal crease across her brow, at that disheveled image of Pinuccia.

"Everything all right?" I asked her.

She nodded yes.

"You're such a good swimmer now."

She said nothing.

She had the expression of someone who is forced to repress joy and fear at the same time. It was evident that the spectacle of Pinuccia was becoming increasingly intolerable to her. Her sister-in-law was again displaying her intention to depart, farewells, regret that she had forgotten this object or that, sighs for her Rinuccio, all interwoven, in a contradictory fashion, with regret for the sea, the smells of the gardens, the beach. And yet Lila said nothing, not one of her mean statements or even a sarcastic remark. Finally, the words came out of her mouth, not a call to order but the announcement of an imminent event that threatened us all: "They're about to arrive."

At that point Pinuccia collapsed disconsolate on the bed, next to the closed suitcases. Lila grimaced, went off to dress. She returned soon afterward in a clinging red dress, her black hair pulled back. She was the first to recognize the sound of the Lambrettas, she looked out the window, waved enthusiastically. Then, becoming serious, she turned to Pinuccia and in her most scornful voice hissed: "Go wash your face and take off that bathing suit."

Pinuccia looked at her without reacting. Something passed rapidly between the two girls, their secret feelings darted invisibly, infinitesimal particles shot at each other from the depths of themselves, a jolt and a trembling that lasted a long second;

I caught it, bewildered, but couldn't understand, while they did, they understood, in something they recognized each other, and Pinuccia knew that Lila knew, understood and wished to help her, even with contempt. So she obeyed.

55.

Stefano and Rino burst in. Lila was even more affectionate than the week before. She embraced Stefano, let him embrace her, gave a cry of joy when he took a case out of his pocket and she opened it and found a gold necklace with a pendant in the shape of a heart.

Naturally Rino, too, had brought a present for Pinuccia, who did her best to react as her sister-in-law had, but her painful fragility was visible in her eyes. So Rino's kisses and embraces and the gift had soon swept away the form of the happy wife within which she had so hastily enclosed herself. Her mouth started to tremble, the fountain of tears erupted, and she said, in a choked voice, "I've packed my bags. I don't want to stay here a minute longer, I want to be with you and only you, always."

Rino smiled, he was moved by all that love, he laughed. Then he said, "I also want to be with you and only you, always." Finally he understood that his wife was not just communicating how much she missed him, and how much she would always miss him, but that she really wanted to leave, that everything was ready for departure, and she was insisting on that decision with a real, unbearable grief.

They shut themselves in the bedroom to discuss it, but the discussion didn't last long, Rino came out, shouting at his mother, "Mamma, I want to know what happened." And without waiting for an answer, he turned aggressively to his sister: "If it's your fault by God I'll smash your face." Then he shouted at his wife, "That's enough, you're a pain in the ass, come out now, I'm tired, I want to eat."

Pinuccia reappeared with swollen eyes. When Stefano saw her, he made a playful attempt to defuse the situation, embracing his sister, and sighing, "Ah, love, you women drive us crazy for it." Then, as if suddenly recalling the primary cause of his own craziness, he kissed Lila on the lips, and in observing the unhappiness of the other couple he felt happy at how unexpectedly happy they were.

We all sat down at the table and Nunzia served us, one by one, in silence. But this time it was Rino who couldn't bear it, he yelled that he wasn't hungry anymore, he hurled the plate of spaghetti and clams into the middle of the kitchen. I was frightened, Pinuccia began to cry again. And even Stefano lost his composure and said to his wife, sharply: "Let's go, I'll take you to a restaurant." Amid the protests of Nunzia and even of Pinuccia they left the kitchen. In the silence that followed we heard the Lambretta setting off.

I helped Nunzia clean the floor. Rino got up, went to the bedroom. Pinuccia locked herself in the bathroom, but then she came out and joined her husband. She closed the door. Only then did Nunzia explode, forgetting her role of tolerant mother-in-law.

"Do you see how that bitch is making Rinuccio suffer? What's happened to her?"

I said I didn't know, and it was true, but I spent the evening consoling her by romanticizing Pinuccia's feelings. I said that if I were carrying a child in my belly I, like her, would have wanted to be with my husband always, to feel protected, to be sure that my responsibility as a mother was shared by his as a father. I said that if Lila was there to have a child, and it was clear that the cure was right, that the sea was doing her good—you had only to look at the happiness that lighted up her face when Stefano arrived—Pinuccia instead was already full of love and wished to give all that love to Rino every minute of the day and night, otherwise it weighed on her and she suffered.

It was a sweet hour, Nunzia and I in the kitchen that was tidy now, the dishes and the pots shining because of the care with which they had been washed. She said to me, "How well you speak, Lenù, it's clear that you'll have a wonderful future." Tears came to her eyes, she murmured that Lila should have gone to school, it was her destiny. "But my husband didn't want it," she added, "and I didn't know how to oppose him: there wasn't the money then, and yet she could have done as you did; instead she got married, she chose a different path and one can't go back, life takes us where it wants." She wished me happiness, "with a fine young man who has studied like you." She asked if I really liked the son of Sarratore. I denied it, but I confided to her that I was going the next day to climb the mountain with him. She was glad, she helped me make some sandwiches with salami and provolone. I wrapped them in paper, put them in the bag with my towel for swimming, and everything else I needed. She urged me to be prudent as always and we said good night.

I went to my room, read a little, but I was distracted. How lovely it would be to go out early in the morning, with the cool air, the scents. How much I loved the sea, and even Pinuccia, her tears, the evening's quarrel, the conciliatory love that, week by week, was increasing between Lila and Stefano. And how much I desired Nino. And how pleasant it was to have there with me, every day, him and my friend, the three of us content despite misunderstandings, despite the bad feelings that did not always remain silent in the dark depths.

I heard Stefano and Lila return. Their voices and laughter were muffled. Doors opened, closed, opened again. I heard the tap, the flush. Then I turned off the light, I listened to the faint rustle of the reeds, the scurrying in the henhouse, I fell asleep.

But I woke immediately, there was someone in my room.

"It's me," Lila whispered.

I felt her sitting on the edge of the bed, I was about to turn on the light.

"No," she said, "I'll stay only a moment."

I turned it on anyway, I sat up.

She was wearing a pale pink nightgown. Her skin was so darkened by the sun that her eyes seemed white.

"Did you see how far I went?"

"You were great, but I was worried."

She shook her head proudly and gave a little smile as if to say that the sea now belonged to her. Then she became serious.

"I have to tell you something."

"What?"

"Nino kissed me," she said, and she said it in one breath, like someone who, making a spontaneous confession, is trying to hide, even from herself, something more unconfessable. "He kissed me but I kept my lips closed."

56.

The account was detailed. She, exhausted by the long swim and yet satisfied that she had proved how proficient she was, had leaned against him so that it would be less effort to float. But Nino had taken advantage of her closeness and had pressed his lips hard against hers. She had immediately compressed her mouth and although he had tried to open it with the tip of his tongue he hadn't been able to. "You're crazy," she had said, pushing him away, "I'm married." But Nino had answered, "I've loved you long before your husband, ever since we had that competition in class." Lila had ordered him never to try it again and they had started swimming again toward the shore. "He pressed so hard he hurt my lips," she concluded, "and they still hurt."

She waited for me to react, but I managed not to ask questions or comment. When she told me not to go to the mountain with him unless Bruno came, too, I said coldly that if Nino had kissed me, I wouldn't have found anything bad about it, I wasn't married and didn't even have a boyfriend. "Only it's a pity," I added, "that I don't like him: kissing him would be like putting my mouth on a dead rat." Then I pretended to be unable to repress a yawn and she, after a look that seemed to be of affection and also of admiration, went to bed. I wept from the moment she left until dawn.

Today I feel some uneasiness in recalling how much I suffered, I have no sympathy for myself of that time. But in the course of that night it seemed to me that I had no reason to live. Why did Nino behave in that way? He kissed Nadia, he kissed me, he kissed Lila. How could he be the same person I loved, who was so serious, so thoughtful. The hours passed, but it was impossible for me to accept that he was as profound in confronting the great problems of the world as he was superficial in feelings of love. I began to question myself, I had made a mistake, I was deluded. Was it possible that I—short, too full-figured, wearing glasses, I diligent but not intelligent, I who pretended to be cultured, informed, when I wasn't— could have believed that he would like me even just for the length of a vacation? And, besides, had I ever really thought that? I examined my behavior scrupulously. No, I wasn't able to tell myself what my desires were with any clarity. Not only was I careful to hide them from others but I admitted them to myself in a skeptical way, without conviction. Why had I never told Lila plainly what I felt for Nino? And now, why had I not cried to her the pain she had caused me with that confidence in the middle of the night, why hadn't I revealed to her that, before kissing her, Nino had kissed me? What drove me to act like that? Did I keep my feelings muted because I was frightened by the violence with which, in fact, in my innermost self,

I wanted things, people, praise, triumphs? Was I afraid that that violence, if I did not get what I wanted, would explode in my chest, taking the path of the worst feelings—for example, the one that had driven me to compare Nino's beautiful mouth to the flesh of a dead rat? Why, then, even when I advanced, was I so quick to retreat? Why did I always have ready a gracious smile, a happy laugh, when things went badly? Why, sooner or later, did I always find plausible excuses for those who made me suffer?

Questions and tears. It was daybreak when I felt that I understood what had happened. Nino had sincerely believed that he loved Nadia. Of course, aware of my reputation with Professor Galiani, he had looked at me for years with sincere respect and liking. But now, at Ischia, he had met Lila and had understood that she had been since childhood—and would be in the future—his only true love. Ah yes, surely it had happened that way. And how could one reproach him? Where was the fault? In their history there was something intense, sublime: elective affinities. I called on poems and novels as tranquilizers. Maybe, I thought, studying has been useful to me just for this: to calm myself. She had kindled the flame in his breast, he had preserved it for years without realizing it: now that that flame had flared up, what could he do but love her. Even if she was married and therefore inaccessible, forbidden: marriage lasts forever, beyond death. Unless one violates it, condemning oneself to the infernal whirlwind until Judgment Day. It seemed to me, when dawn broke, that I had gained some clarity. Nino's love for Lila was an impossible love. Like mine for him. And only within that frame of unattainability did the kiss he had given her in the middle of the sea begin to seem utterable.

The kiss.

It hadn't been a choice, it had happened: especially since Lila knew how to make things happen. Whereas I don't, what will I do now. I'll go to our meeting. We'll climb Epomeo. Or no. I'll leave tonight with Stefano and Rino. I'll say that my mother wrote and needs me. How can I go climbing with him when I know that he loves Lila, that he kissed her. And how will I be able to see them together every day, swimming, going farther and farther out. I was exhausted, I fell asleep. I woke with a start, and found that the formulas running through my head really had tamed the suffering a little. I hurried to the meeting.

57.

I was sure that he wouldn't come, but when I got to the beach he was already there, and without Bruno. But I realized that he had no desire to look for the road to the mountain, to set out on unknown paths. He said that he was ready to go, if I really wanted to, but he predicted that in this heat we'd get unbearably exhausted and dismissed the idea that we'd ever find anything as worthwhile as a good swim. I began to worry, I thought he was on the verge of saying that he was going to go back and study. Instead, to my surprise, he proposed renting a boat. He counted and recounted the money he had, I took out my few cents. He smiled, he said gently, "You've taken care of the sandwiches, I'll do this." A few minutes later we were on the sea, he at the oars, I sitting in the stern.

I felt better. I thought maybe Lila had lied to me, that he hadn't kissed her. But in some part of myself I knew very well that it wasn't so: I sometimes lied, yes, even (or especially) to myself; she, on the other hand, as far as I could remember, had never done so. Besides, I had only to wait a while and it was Nino himself who explained things. When we were out on the water he let go of the oars and dived in, I did the same. He didn't swim the way he usually did, mingling with the undulating surface of the sea. Instead he dropped toward the bottom, disappeared, reappeared farther on, sank again. I was alarmed by the depth, and swam around the boat, not daring to go too far, until I got tired and clumsily pulled myself in. After a while he joined me, grabbed the oars, began to row energetically, following a line parallel to the coast, toward Punta Imperatore. So far we had remarked on the sandwiches, the heat, the sea, how wise we had been not to take the mule paths up Epomeo. To my increasing wonder he hadn't yet resorted to the subjects he was reading about in books, in journals, in newspapers, even though every so often, afraid of the silence, I threw out some remark that might set off his passion for the things of the world. But no, he had something else on his mind. And eventually he put down the oars, stared for a moment at a rock face, a flight of seagulls, then he said:

"Did Lina say anything to you?"

"About what?"

He pressed his lips together uneasily, and said, "All right, I'm going to tell you what happened. Yesterday I kissed her."

That was the beginning. We spent the rest of the day talking about the two of them. We went swimming again, he explored cliffs and caves, we ate the sandwiches, drank all the water I had brought, he wanted to teach me to row, but as for talking we couldn't talk about anything else. And what most struck me was that he didn't try even once, as he normally tended to do, to transform his particular situation into a general situation. Only he and Lila, Lila and he. He said nothing about love. He said nothing about the reasons one ends up being in love with one person rather than another. He questioned me, instead, obsessively about her and her relationship with Stefano.

"Why did she marry him?"

"Because she was in love with him."

"It can't be."

"I assure you it is."

"She married him for money, to help her family, to settle herself."

"If that was all she could have married Marcello Solara."

"Who's that?"

"A guy who has more money than Stefano and was crazy about her."

"And she?"

"Didn't want him."

"So you think she married the grocer out of love."

"Yes."

"And what's this business about going swimming to have children?"

"The doctor told her."

"But does she want them?"

"At first no, now I don't know."

"And he?"

"He yes."

"Is he in love with her?"

"Very much."

"And you, from the outside, do you think that everything's fine between them?"

"With Lina things are never fine."

"Meaning?"

"They had problems from the first day of their marriage, but it was because of Lina, who couldn't adjust."

"And now?"

"Now it's going better."

"I don't believe it."

He went around and around that point with growing skepticism. But I insisted: Lila never had loved her husband as in that period. And the more incredulous he appeared the more I piled it on. I told him plainly that between them nothing could happen, I didn't want him to delude himself. This, however, was of no use in exhausting the subject. It became increasingly clear that the more I talked to him in detail about Lila the more pleasant for him that day between sea and sky would be. It didn't matter to him that every word of mine made him suffer. It mattered that I should tell him everything I knew, the good and the bad, that I should fill our minutes and our hours with her name. I did, and if at first this pained me, slowly it changed. I felt, that day, that to speak of Lila with Nino could in the weeks to come give a new character to the relationship between the three of us. Neither she nor I would ever have him. But both of us, for the entire time of the vacation, could gain his attention, she as the object of a passion with no future, I as the wise counselor who kept under control both his folly and hers. I consoled myself with that hypothesis of centrality. Lila had come to me to tell me about Nino's kiss. He, starting out from the confession of that kiss, talked to me for an entire day. I would become necessary to both.

In fact Nino already couldn't do without me.

"You think she'll never be able to love me?" he asked at one point.

"She made a decision, Nino."

"What?"

"To love her husband, to have a child with him. She's here just for that."

"And my love for her?"

"When one is loved one tends to love in return. It's likely that she'll feel gratified. But if you don't want to suffer more, don't expect anything else. The more Lina is surrounded by affection and admiration, the crueler she can become. She's always been like that."

We parted at sunset and for a while I had the impression of having had a good day. But as soon as I was on the road home the anguish returned. How could I even think of enduring that torture, talking about Lila with Nino, about Nino with Lila, and, from tomorrow, witnessing their flirtations, their games, the clasps, the touching? I reached the house determined to announce that my mother wanted me back home. But as soon as I came in Lila assailed me harshly.

"Where have you been? We came to look for you. We need you, you've got to help us."

I discovered that they had not had a good day. It was Pinuccia's fault, she had tormented everyone. In the end she had cried that if her husband didn't want her at home it meant that he didn't love her and so she preferred to die with the child. At that point Rino had given in and taken her back to Naples.

58.

I understood only the next day what Pinuccia's departure meant. That evening her absence struck me as positive: no more whining, the house quieted down, time slithered away silently. When I withdrew into my little room and Lila followed me, the conversation was apparently without tension. I held my tongue, careful to say nothing of what I truly felt.

"Do you understand why she wanted to leave?" Lila asked me, speaking of Pinuccia.

"Because she wants to be with her husband."

She shook her head no, she said seriously, "She was becoming afraid of her own emotions."

"Which means?"

"She fell in love with Bruno."

I was amazed, I had never thought of that possibility.

"Pinuccia?"

"Yes."

"And Bruno?"

"He had no idea."

"You're sure?"

"Yes."

"How do you know?"

"Bruno's interested in you."

"Nonsense."

"Nino told me yesterday."

"He didn't say anything to me today."

"What did you do?"

"We rented a boat."

"You and he alone?"

"Yes."

"What did you talk about?"

"Everything."

"Even about the thing I told you about?"

"What thing?"

"You know."

"The kiss?"

"Yes."

"No, he didn't tell me anything."

Although I was dazed by the hours of sun and swimming, I managed not to say the wrong thing. When Lila went to bed I felt that I was floating on the sheet and that the dark little room was full of blue and reddish lights. Pinuccia had left in a hurry because she was in love with Bruno? Bruno wanted not her but me? I thought back to the relationship between Pinuccia and Bruno, I listened again to remarks, tones of voice, I saw again gestures, and I was sure that Lila was right. I suddenly felt great sympathy for Stefano's sister, for the strength she had shown in forcing herself to leave. But that Bruno was interested in me I wasn't convinced. He had never even looked at me. Beyond the fact that, if he had had the intention that Lila said, he would have come to the appointment and not Nino. Or at least they would have come together. And anyway, true or not, I didn't like him: too short, too curly-haired, no forehead, wolflike teeth. No and no. Stay in the middle, I thought. That's what I'll do.

The next day we arrived at the beach at ten and discovered that the boys were already there, walking back and forth along the shore. Lila explained Pinuccia's absence in a few words: she had to work, she had left with her husband. Neither Nino nor Bruno showed the least regret and this disturbed me. How could someone vanish like that, without leaving a void? Pinuccia had been with us for two weeks. We had all five walked together, we had talked, joked, gone swimming. In those fifteen days something had certainly happened that had marked her, she would never forget that first vacation. But we? We, who in different ways had meant a lot to her, in fact didn't feel her absence. Nino, for example, made no comment on that sudden departure. And Bruno confined himself to saying, gravely, "Too bad, we didn't even say goodbye." A minute later we were already speaking of other things, as if she had never come to Ischia, to Citara.

Nor did I like a sort of rapid readjustment of roles. Nino, who had always talked to me and Lila together (in fact very often to me alone), immediately began talking only to her, as if it were no longer necessary, now that we were four, to take on the burden of entertaining both of us. Bruno, who until the preceding Saturday had been occupied with Pinuccia and nothing else, now focused on me, in the same timid and solic-itous way, as if nothing distinguished us from each other, not even the fact that she was married and pregnant and I was not.

For the first walk that we took along the shore, we left as four, side by side. But soon Bruno spotted a shell turned up by a wave, said, "How pretty," and bent down to pick it up. Out of politeness I stopped to wait for him, and he gave me the shell, which was nothing special. Meanwhile Nino and Lila continued to walk, which transformed us into two couples tak-ing a walk on the water's edge, the two of them ahead, the two of us behind, they talking animatedly, I trying to make conver-

sation with Bruno while Bruno struggled to talk to me. I tried
to hurry, he held me back, against my will. It was difficult to
establish a real connection. His conversation was banal, I don't
know, about the sea, the sky, the seagulls, but it was evident
that he was playing a role, the one that he thought was right for
me. With Pinuccia he must have talked about other things,
otherwise it was hard to know how they had enjoyed spending
so much time together. Besides, even if he had touched on
more interesting subjects, it would have been hard to know
what he was saying. If he was asking the time or for a cigarette
or a drink of water, he had a direct tone of voice, clear pronunciation. But when he started with that role of the devoted
young man (*the shell, do you like it, look how pretty it is, I'll
give it to you*), he got tangled up, he spoke neither in Italian
nor in dialect, but in an awkward language that came to him in
an undertone, mumbled, as if he were ashamed of what he was
saying. I nodded my head yes but I didn't understand much,
and meanwhile I strained my ears to catch what Nino and Lila
were saying.

I imagined that he was talking about the serious subjects he
was studying, or that she was showing off the ideas she got
from the books she had taken from me, and I often tried to
catch up to join in their conversations. But every time I managed to get close enough to pick up some phrase, I was disoriented. He seemed to be telling her about his childhood in the
neighborhood, using intense, even dramatic tones; she listened
without interrupting. I felt intrusive, retreated, resolved to stay
behind to be bored by Bruno.

Even when we all decided to go swimming, I wasn't in time
to restore the old trio. Bruno without warning pushed me into
the water, I went under, got my hair wet when I didn't want to
get my hair wet. When I re-emerged, Nino and Lila were floating a few meters farther out and were continuing to talk, seriously. They stayed in the water much longer than we did, but

without going too far from the shore. They must have been so involved in what they were talking about that they gave up even the luxury of the long swim.

In the late afternoon Nino spoke to me for the first time. He asked roughly, as if he himself expected a negative answer: "Why don't we meet after dinner? We'll come and get you and take you home."

They had never asked us to go out in the evening. I gave Lila a questioning glance, but she looked away. I said, "Lila's mamma is at home, we can't leave her alone all the time."

Nino didn't answer nor did his friend intervene to help him out. But after the last swim, before parting, Lila said, "We're going to Forio tomorrow night to telephone my husband. We could get an ice cream together."

That remark of hers irritated me, but I was even more irritated by what happened next. As soon as the two boys had set off for Forio, and she was gathering up her things, she began to reproach me, as if I bore the blame for the entire day, hour by hour, micro-event upon micro-event, including that request of Nino's, and the clear contradiction between my answer and hers, in some indecipherable yet indisputable way.

"Why were you always with Bruno?"

"I?"

"Yes, you. Don't ever dare to leave me alone with that guy again."

"What are you talking about? It was you two who rushed ahead without stopping to wait for us."

"We? It was Nino who was rushing."

"You could have said that you had to wait for me."

"And you could have said to Bruno: Get going, otherwise we'll lose them. Do me a favor: since you like him so much, go out on your own business at night. Then you're free to say and do what you like."

"I'm here for you, not for Bruno."

"It doesn't look as though you're here for me, you're always doing what you please."

"If you don't want me here anymore I'll leave tomorrow morning."

"Yes? And tomorrow night I have to go and get ice cream with those two by myself?"

"Lila, it was you who said you wanted to get ice cream with them."

"Of necessity, I have to telephone Stefano, and what an impression we'd make if we meet them in Forio?"

We continued in this vein even at the house, after dinner, in Nunzia's presence. It wasn't a real quarrel, but an ambiguous exchange with spikes of malice in which we both tried to communicate something without understanding each other. Nunzia, who was listening in bewilderment, at a certain point said, "Tomorrow we'll have dinner and then I'll come, too, to get ice cream."

"It's a long way," I said. But Lila interrupted abruptly: "We don't have to walk. We'll take a mini cab, we're rich."

59.

The next day, to adjust to the boys' new schedule, we arrived at the beach at nine instead of ten, but they weren't there. Lila became anxious. We waited, they didn't appear at ten or later. Finally, in the early afternoon, they showed up, with a light-hearted conspiratorial air. They said that since they were going to spend the evening with us, they had decided to do their studying early. Lila's reaction stunned me in particular: she sent them away. Slipping into a violent dialect, she hissed that they could go and study when they liked, afternoon, evening, night, no one was holding them back. And since Nino and Bruno made an effort not to take her seriously and continued to smile as if those words had been just a witty remark, she put on her sundress, impetuously grabbed her bag, and set off toward the road with long strides. Nino ran after her but returned soon afterward with a grim face. Nothing to do, she was really enraged and wouldn't listen to reason.

"It will pass," I said, pretending to be calm, and I went swimming with them. I dried in the sun eating a sandwich, I chattered weakly, then I announced that I, too, had to go home.

"And tonight?" Bruno asked.

"Lina has to call Stefano, we'll be there."

But the outburst had upset me greatly. What did that tone, that behavior mean? What right had she to get angry at an appointment not kept? Why couldn't she control herself and treat the two young men as if they were Pasquale or Antonio or even the Solaras? Why did she behave like a capricious girl and not like Signora Carracci?

I got to the house out of breath. Nunzia was washing towels and bathing suits, Lila was in her room, sitting on the bed and, something that was also unusual, she was writing. The notebook was resting on her knees, her eyes narrowed, her brow furrowed, one of my books lying on the sheets. How long it was since I had seen her write.

"You overdid it," I said.

She shrugged. She didn't raise her eyes from the notebook, she continued to write all afternoon.

At night she decked herself out the way she did when her husband was arriving, and we drove to Forio. I was surprised that Nunzia, who never went out in the sun and was very white, had borrowed her daughter's lipstick to give a little color to her lips and her cheeks. She wanted to avoid—she said—seeming dead already.

We immediately ran into the two boys, who were standing in front of the bar like sentries beside a sentry box. Bruno was still in shorts, he had only changed his shirt. Nino was wearing long pants, a shirt of a dazzling white, and his unruly hair so forcibly tamed that he seemed less handsome to me. When they noticed Nunzia's presence, they stiffened. We sat under a canopy, at the entrance to the bar, and ordered spumoni. Nunzia, marveling at it, started talking and wouldn't stop. She spoke only to the boys. She praised Nino's mother, recalling how pretty she was; she told several stories of wartime, neighborhood events, and asked Nino if he remembered; when he said no, she replied, with absolute certainty, "Ask your mother, you'll see that she remembers." Lila soon gave signs of impatience, announced that it was time to telephone Stefano, and went into the bar, where the phone booths were. Nino grew silent and Bruno readily replaced him in the conversation with Nunzia. I noted, with annoyance, that he wasn't awkward the way he was when he talked to me alone.

"Excuse me a moment," Nino said suddenly. He got up, went into the bar.

Nunzia became agitated. She whispered in my ear, "He's not going to pay is he? I'm the oldest, so it's up to me."

Bruno heard her and said that it was already paid for, he was hardly going to let a lady pay. Nunzia resigned herself, went on to inquire about his father's sausage factory, bragged about her husband and son, who also had a factory—they had a shoe factory.

Lila didn't return. I was worried. I left Nunzia and Bruno chatting, and I, too, went into the bar. When had a telephone call to Stefano ever lasted so long? The two telephone booths were empty. I looked around me, but, standing still like that, I just bothered the owner's sons, who were waiting on the tables. I glimpsed a door left ajar to let in the air, opening onto a courtyard. I went out hesitantly, an odor of old tires mingled with the smell of the chicken coop. The courtyard was empty, but I noticed that on one side of the boundary wall there was an opening and, beyond it, a garden. I crossed the space, cluttered with rusty scrap iron, and before I entered the garden I saw Lila and Nino. The brightness of the summer night licked the plants. They were holding each other tight, they were kissing. He had one hand under her skirt, she was trying to push it away, but she went on kissing him.

I retreated quickly, trying not to make any noise. I went back to the bar, I told Nunzia that Lila was still on the telephone.

"Are they quarreling?"

"No."

I felt as if I were burning up, but the flames were cold and I felt no pain. She is married, I said to myself, she's been married scarcely more than a year.

Lila returned without Nino. She was impeccable, and yet I felt the disorder, in her clothes, in her body.

We waited a while, he didn't show up, I realized that I hated them both. Lila got up, said, "Let's go, it's late." When we were already in the cab that would take us back to the house, Nino arrived, running, and said goodbye cheerfully. "See you tomorrow," he cried, friendly as I had never seen him. I thought: the fact that Lila is married isn't an obstacle for him or for her, and that observation seemed to me so odiously true that it turned my stomach, and I brought a hand to my mouth.

Lila went to bed right away, I waited in vain for her to come and confess what she had done and what she proposed to do. Today, I believe that she didn't know herself.

60.

The days that followed clarified the situation further. Usually Nino arrived with a newspaper, a book: no more. Animated conversations about the human condition faded, were reduced to distracted phrases that sought an opening for more private words. Lila and Nino got in the habit of swimming far out together, until they were indistinguishable from the shore. Or they compelled us to long walks that consolidated the division into couples. And never, absolutely never, was I beside Nino, nor was Lila with Bruno. It became natural for the two of them to be behind. Whenever I turned around suddenly I had the impression of having caused a painful laceration: hands, mouths springing backward as if because of some nervous tic.

I suffered but, I have to admit, with a permanent undercurrent of disbelief that caused the suffering to come in waves. It seemed to me that I was watching a performance without substance: they were playing at being together, both knowing well that they were not and couldn't be: the one already had a girlfriend, the other was actually married. I looked at them at times like fallen divinities: once so clever, so intelligent, and now so stupid, involved in a stupid game. I planned to say to Lila, to Nino, to both of them: who do you think you are, come back to earth.

I couldn't do it. In the space of two or three days things changed further. They began to hold hands without hiding it, with an offensive shamelessness, as if they had decided that with us it wasn't worth pretending. They often quarreled jokingly, then grabbed each other, hit each other, held each other tight, tumbled on the sand together. When we were walking, if they spotted an abandoned hut, an old bath house reduced to its foundations, a path that got lost among the wild vegetation, they decided like children to go exploring and didn't invite us to follow. They went off with him in the lead, she behind, in silence. When they lay in the sun, they lessened the distance between them as much as possible. At first they were satisfied with the slight contact of shoulders, their arms, legs, feet just grazing. Later, returning from that interminable daily swim, they lay beside each other on Lila's towel, which was bigger, and soon, with a natural gesture, Nino put his arm around her shoulders, she rested her head on his chest. They even, once, went so far as to kiss on the lips, a light, quick kiss. I thought: she's mad, they're mad. If someone from Naples who knows Stefano sees them? If the supplier who got the house for us passes by? Or if Nunzia, now, should decide to make a visit to the beach?

I couldn't believe such recklessness, and yet time and time again they crossed the limit. Seeing each other during the day no longer seemed sufficient; Lila decided that she had to call Stefano every night, but she rudely rejected Nunzia's offer to go with us. After dinner she obliged me to go to Forio. She made a quick phone call to her husband and then we went walking, she with Nino, I with Bruno. We never returned home before midnight and the two boys came with us along the dark beach.

On Friday night, that is, the day before Stefano returned, she and Nino argued, unexpectedly, not in fun but seriously. We were eating ice cream at the table, Lila had gone to telephone. Nino, grim-faced, took out of his pocket a number of pages with writing on both sides and began to read, giving no explanation, but isolating himself from the dull conversation between Bruno and me. When she returned, he didn't even glance at her, he didn't put the pages back in his pocket, but went on reading. Lila waited half a minute, then asked in a lighthearted tone:

"Is it so interesting?"

"Yes," Nino said, without looking up.

"Then read aloud, we want to hear it."

"It's my business, it has nothing to do with the rest of you."

"What is it?" Lila asked, but it was clear that she knew already.

"A letter."

"From whom?"

"From Nadia."

With a sudden, lightning-like move, she reached out and

tore the pages from his grasp. Nino started, as if a giant insect had stung him, but he made no effort to get the letter back, even when Lila began to read it to us in declamatory tones, in a loud voice. It was a rather childish love letter, carrying on from line to line with sentimental variations on the theme of missing. Bruno listened silently, with an embarrassed smile, and I, seeing that Nino showed no sign of taking the thing as a joke, but was staring darkly at his sandaled, suntanned feet, whispered to Lila, "That's enough, give it back to him."

As soon as I spoke she stopped reading, but her expression of amusement lingered, and she didn't give the letter back.

"You're embarrassed, eh?" she asked. "You're the one to blame. How can you have a girlfriend who writes like that?"

Nino said nothing, he went on staring at his feet. Bruno interrupted, also lightheartedly: "Maybe, when you fall in love with someone, you don't make her take an exam to see if she can write a love letter."

But Lila didn't even turn to look at him, she spoke to Nino as if they were continuing in front of us one of their secret conversations:

"Do you love her? And why? Explain it to us. Because she lives on Corso Vittorio Emanuele in a house full of books and old paintings? Because she speaks in a simpering little voice? Because she's the daughter of the professor?"

Finally Nino roused himself and said abruptly, "Give me back those pages."

"I'll only give them back if you tear them up immediately, here, in front of us."

Countering Lila's tone of amusement Nino uttered grave monosyllables, with obvious aggressive undertones. "And then?"

"Then we'll all write Nadia a letter together in which you tell her you're leaving her."

"And then?"

"We'll mail it tonight."

He said nothing for a moment, then he agreed. "Let's do it."

Lila pointed to the pages in disbelief.

"You're really going to tear them up?"

"Yes."

"And you'll leave her?"

"Yes. But on one condition."

"Let's hear it."

"That you leave your husband. Now. Let's all of us go together to the phone and you'll tell him."

Those words provoked in me a violent emotion. At the time I didn't know why. As he spoke he raised his voice so unexpectedly that it cracked. And Lila's eyes, as she listened to him, suddenly narrowed to slits, following a mode of behavior that I knew well. Now she would change her tone. Now, I thought, she'll turn mean. She said to him, in fact: How dare you. She said to him: To whom do you think you're speaking. She said to him: "How can you think of putting this letter, your foolishness with that whore from a good family, on the same plane as me, my husband, my marriage and everything that is my life? You really think you're something, but you don't get the joke. In fact you don't understand a thing. Nothing, you heard me, and don't make that face. Let's go to bed, Lenù."

61.

Nino did nothing to restrain us, Bruno said, "See you tomorrow." We took a mini cab and returned to the house. But during the journey Lila began to tremble, she grabbed my hand and gripped it hard. She began to confess to me in a chaotic way everything that had happened between her and Nino. She had yearned for him to kiss her, she had let herself be kissed. She had wanted to feel his hands on her, she had let him. "I can't sleep. If I fall asleep I wake with a start, I look at the clock, I hope it's already day, that we have to go to the beach. But it's night, I can't sleep anymore, I have in my head all the words he said, all the ones that I can't wait to tell him. I resisted. I said: I'm not like Pinuccia, I can do what I like, I can start and stop, it's a game. I kept my lips pressed together, then I said to myself well, really, what's a kiss, and I discovered what it was, I didn't know—I swear to you that I didn't know—and now I can't do without it. I gave him my hand, I entwined my fingers with his, tight, and it seemed to me painful to let go. How many things I've missed that now are landing on me all at once. I go around like a girlfriend, when I'm married. I'm frantic, my heart is pounding here in my throat and in my temples. And I like everything. I like that he drags me into secluded places, I like the fear that someone might see us, I like the idea that they might see us. Did you do those things with Antonio? Did you suffer when you had to leave him and you couldn't wait to see him again? Is it normal, Lenù? Was it like that for you? I don't know how it began and when. At first I didn't like him: I liked how he talked, what he said, but physically no. I thought: How many things he knows, this man, I should listen, I should learn. Now, when he speaks, I can't even concentrate. I look at his mouth and I'm ashamed of looking at it, I turn my eyes in another direction. In a short time I've come to love everything about him: his hands, the delicate fingernails, that thinness, the ribs under his skin, his slender neck, the beard that he shaves badly so it's always rough, his nose, the hair on his chest, his long, slender legs, his knees. I want to caress him. And I think of things that disgust me, they really disgust me, Lenù, but I would like to do them to give him pleasure, to make him be happy."

I listened to her for a good part of the night, in her room, the door closed, the light out. She was lying on the window side and in the moon's glow the hair on her neck gleamed, and the curve of her hip. I was lying on the door side, Stefano's side, and I thought: Her husband sleeps here, every weekend, on this side of the bed, and draws her to him, in the afternoon, at night, and embraces her. And yet here, in this bed, she is telling me about Nino. The words for him take away her memory, they erase from these sheets every trace of conjugal love. She speaks of him and in speaking of him she calls him here, she imagines him next to her, and since she has forgotten herself she perceives no violation or guilt. She confides, she tells me things that she would do better to keep to herself. She tells me how much she desires the person I've desired forever, and she does so convinced that I— through insensitivity, through a less acute vision, through incapacity to grasp what she, instead, is able to grasp—have never truly understood that same person, never realized his qualities. I don't know if it's in bad faith or if she's really convinced—it's my fault, my tendency to conceal myself—that since elementary school I've been deaf and blind, so that it took her to discover, here on Ischia, the power unleashed by the son of Sarratore. Ah, how I hate this presumption of hers, it poisons my blood. Yet I don't know how to say to her, That's enough, I can't go to my room to cry in silence, but I stay here, and now and then I interrupt her, I try to calm her.

I pretended a detachment I didn't have. "It's the sea," I said to her, "the fresh air, the vacation. And Nino knows how to confuse you; the way he talks he makes everything look easy. But, unfortunately, tomorrow Stefano arrives and you'll see, Nino will seem like a boy to you. Which he really is, I know him well. To us he seems like somebody, but if you think how Professor Galiani's son treats him—you remember?—you understand immediately that we overestimate him. Of course, compared to Bruno he seems extraordinary, but after all he's only the son of a railroad worker who got it in his head to study. Remember that Nino was from the neighborhood, he comes from there. Remember that at school you were smarter, even if he was older. And then you see how he takes advantage of his friend, makes him pay for everything, drinks, ice cream."

It cost me to say those things, I considered them lies. And it was of little use: Lila grumbled, she objected hesitantly, I refuted her. Until she really got mad and began to defend Nino in the tone of someone who says: I'm the only one who knows what sort of person he is. She asked why I was always disparaging him. She asked me what I had against him. "He helped you," she said, "he even wanted to publish that nonsense of yours in a review. Sometimes I don't like you, Lenù, you diminish everything and everyone, even people who are lovable if you just look at them."

I lost control, I couldn't bear it anymore. I had spoken ill of the person I loved in order to do something to make her feel better and now she insulted me. Finally I managed to say, "Do what you like, I'm going to bed." But she immediately changed her tone, she embraced me, she hugged me tight, to keep me there, she whispered, "Tell me what to do." I pushed her away with annoyance, I whispered that she had to decide herself, I couldn't decide in her place. "Pinuccia," I said, "how did she do it? In the end she behaved better than you."

She agreed, we sang the praises of Pinuccia and abruptly she sighed: "All right, tomorrow I won't go to the beach and the day after I'll go back to Naples with Stefano."

62.

It was a terrible Saturday. She really didn't go to the beach, and I didn't go, either, but I thought only of Nino and Bruno, who were waiting for us in vain. And I didn't dare say: I'll make a quick trip to the sea, time for a swim and then I'll come back. Nor did I dare ask: What should I do, pack the suitcases, are we going, are we staying? I helped Nunzia clean the house, cook lunch and dinner, every so often checking on Lila, who didn't even get up. She stayed in bed reading and writing in her notebook, and when her mother called her to eat she didn't answer, and when she called her again she slammed the door of her room so violently that the whole house shook.

"Too much sea makes one nervous," Nunzia said, as we ate lunch alone.

"Yes."

"And she's not even pregnant."

"No."

In the late afternoon Lila left her bed, ate something, spent hours in the bathroom. She washed her hair, put on her makeup, chose a pretty green dress, but her face remained sullen. Still, she greeted her husband affectionately and he, seeing her, gave her a movie kiss, a long intense kiss, with Nunzia and I as embarrassed spectators. Stefano brought greetings from my family, said that Pinuccia had made no more scenes, recounted in minute detail how happy the Solaras were with the new shoe styles that Rino and Fernando were working on. Lila wasn't pleased by Stefano's reference to the new styles, and things between them were spoiled. Until that moment she had kept a forced smile on her face, but as soon as she heard the name of the Solaras she became aggressive, and said she didn't give a damn about those two, she wouldn't live her life according to what they thought about this or that. Stefano was disappointed, he frowned. He realized that the enchantment of the previous weeks was over, but he answered her with his usual agreeable half smile, he said that he was only telling her what had happened in the neighborhood, there was no need to take that tone. It was little use. Lila rapidly transformed the evening into a relentless conflict. Stefano couldn't say a word without hostile criticism from her. They went to bed squabbling and I heard them quarreling until I fell asleep.

I woke at dawn. I didn't know what to do: gather my things,

wait for Lila to make a decision; go to the beach, with the risk of running into Nino, something that Lila would not have forgiven; rack my brains all day as I was already doing, shut in my room. I decided to leave a note saying that I was going to the Maronti but would be back in the early afternoon. I wrote that I couldn't leave Ischia without seeing Nella. I wrote in good faith, but today I know what was going on in my mind: I wanted to trust myself to chance; Lila couldn't reproach me if I ran into Nino when he had gone to ask his parents for money.

The result was a muddled day and a modest waste of money. I hired a boat, to take me to the Maronti. I went to the place where the Sarratores usually camped and found only the umbrella. I looked around, and saw Donato, who was swimming, and he saw me. He waved in greeting, hurried out of the water, told me that his wife and children had gone to spend the day in Forio, with Nino. I was extremely disappointed, the situation was not only ironic, it was contemptuous; it had taken away the son and delivered me to the sickening patter of the father.

When I tried to get away to go and see Nella, Sarratore wouldn't let me go, he gathered up his things and insisted on coming with me. On the road he assumed a sentimental tone and without any embarrassment began to speak of what had happened between us years earlier. He asked me to forgive him, he murmured that one cannot command one's heart, he spoke in a melancholy tone of my beauty then and above all of my present beauty.

"What an exaggeration," I said, and, while I knew I should be serious and aloof, I began to laugh out of nervousness.

And though he was encumbered by the umbrella and his things, he would not relinquish a somewhat breathless, rambling discourse. He said that in substance the problem of youth was the lack of eyes to see oneself and feelings to feel about oneself with objectivity.

"There's the mirror," I replied, "and that is objective."

"The mirror? The mirror is the last thing you can trust. I'll bet that you feel less pretty than your two friends."

"Yes."

"And yet you are much, much more beautiful than they are. Trust me. Look what lovely blond hair you have. And what a bearing. You need to confront and resolve two problems only: the first is your bathing suit, it's not adequate to your potential; the second is the style of your glasses. This is really wrong, Elena: too heavy. You have such a delicate face, so remarkably shaped by the things you study. What you need is daintier glasses."

As I listened my irritation diminished; he was like a scientist of female beauty. Mainly he spoke with such detached expertise that at a certain point he led me to think: and if it's true? Maybe I don't know how to value myself. On the other hand where is the money to buy suitable clothes, a suitable bathing suit, suitable glasses? I was about to yield to a complaint about poverty and wealth when he said to me with a smile, "Besides, if you don't trust my judgment, you'll be aware, I hope, of how my son looked at you the time you came to see us."

Only then did I realize that he was lying to me. His words were intended to appeal to my vanity, to make me feel good and drive me toward him in the need for gratification. I felt stupid, wounded not by him, with his lies, but by my own stupidity. I cut him short with an increasing rudeness that froze him.

At the house I talked to Nella for a while, I told her that we might all be returning to Naples that night and I wanted to say goodbye.

"A pity that you're going."

"Ah yes."

"Eat with me."

"I can't, I have to go."

"But if you don't go, swear that you'll come again and not so short next time. Stay with me for a day, or even overnight, since you know there's the bed. I have so many things to tell you."

"Thanks."

Sarratore interrupted, he said, "We count on it, you know how much we love you."

I fled, also because there was a relative of Nella's who was going to the Port in a car and I didn't want to miss the ride.

Along the way Sarratore's words, surprisingly, even if I only rejected them, began to dig into me. No, maybe he hadn't lied. He knew how to see beyond appearances. He had really had a means of observing his son's gaze on me. And if I was pretty, if Nino seriously found me attractive—and I knew it was so: in the end he had kissed me, he had held my hand—it was time I looked at the facts for what they were: Lila had taken him from me; Lila had separated him from me to win him for herself. Maybe she hadn't done it on purpose, but still she had done it.

I decided suddenly that I had to find him, see him at all costs. Now that our departure was imminent, now that the force of seduction that Lila had exercised over him would no longer have a chance to fascinate him, now that she herself had decided to return to the life that was hers, the relationship between him and me could begin again. In Naples. In the form of friendship. At least we could meet to talk about her. And then we would return to our conversations, to our reading. I would demonstrate that I could get interested in his interests better than Lila, certainly, maybe even better than Nadia. Yes, I had to speak to him right away, tell him I'm leaving, tell him: let's see each other in the neighborhood, in Piazza Nazionale, in Mezzocannone, wherever you want, but as soon as possible.

I found a minicab, I took it to Forio, to Bruno's house. I called, no one looked out. I wandered through the town feeling more and more depressed, then I set out to walk along the beach. And this time chance apparently decided in my favor. I had been walking for a long time when I saw before me Nino: he was happy we had met, a barely controlled happiness. His eyes were too bright, his gestures excited, his voice over-wrought.

"I looked for the two of you yesterday and today. Where's Lina?"

"With her husband."

He took an envelope out of his pants pocket, he shoved it into my hand too forcefully.

"Can you give her this?"

I was annoyed. "It's pointless, Nino."

"Give it to her."

"Tonight we're leaving, we'll go back to Naples."

He had an expression of suffering, he said hoarsely, "Who decided?"

"She did."

"I don't believe it."

"It's true, she told me last night."

He thought for a moment, pointed to the envelope.

"Please, give her that anyway, right away."

"All right."

"Swear that you will."

"I told you, yes."

He walked with me for a long way, saying spiteful things about his mother and his brothers and sister. They tormented me, he said, luckily they went back to Barano. I asked him about Bruno. He made a gesture of irritation, he was studying, he said mean things about him as well.

"And you're not studying?"

"I can't."

His head sank between his shoulders, he grew melancholy. He began to talk about the mistakes one makes because a professor, as a result of his own problems, leads you to believe you're smart. He realized that the things he wanted to learn had never really interested him.

"What do you mean? Suddenly?"

"A moment is enough to change the direction of your life completely."

What was happening to him, with these banal words, I no longer recognized him. I vowed I would help him return to himself.

"You're upset now, and you don't know what you're saying," I said in my best sensible tone. "But as soon as you return to Naples we can see each other, if you want, and talk."

He nodded yes, but right afterward cried angrily, "I'm finished with the university, I want to find a job."

63.

He came with me almost to the house, so that I was afraid of meeting Stefano and Lila. I said goodbye in a hurry and went up the stairs.

"Tomorrow morning at nine," he shouted.

I stopped.

"If we leave I'll see you in the neighborhood. Look for me there."

Nino made a sign of no, decisively.

"You won't leave," he said, as if he were giving a threatening order to fate.

I gave him a final wave and hurried up the stairs sorry that I hadn't had a chance to examine what was in the envelope.

In the house I found an unpleasant atmosphere. Stefano and Nunzia were whispering together. Lila must be in the bathroom or the bedroom. When I went in they both looked at me resentfully. Stefano said grimly, without preamble, "Will you tell me what you and she are getting up to?"

"In what sense?"

"She says she's tired of Ischia, she wants to go to Amalfi."

"I don't know anything about it."

Nunzia intervened but not in her usual motherly way.

"Lenù, don't put wrong ideas in her head, you can't throw money out the window. What does Amalfi have to do with anything? We've paid to stay here until September."

I got mad, I said, "You are both mistaken: it's I who do what Lina wants, not the opposite."

"Then go and tell her to be reasonable," Stefano muttered. "I'll be back next week, we'll be together for the mid-August holiday and you'll see, I'll show you a good time. But now I don't want to hear any nonsense. Shit. You think I'll take you to Amalfi? And if you don't like Amalfi, where do I take you, to Capri? And then? Cut it out, Lenù."

His tone intimidated me.

"Where is she?" I asked.

Nunzia indicated the bedroom. I went to Lila sure that I would find the suitcases packed and her determined to leave, even at the risk of a beating. Instead she was in her slip, and was sleeping on the unmade bed. All around was the usual disorder, but the suitcases were piled in a corner, empty. I shook her.

"Lila."

She started, asked me right away with a look veiled by sleep: "Where have you been, did you see Nino?"

"Yes. This is for you."

I gave her the envelope reluctantly. She opened it, took out a sheet of paper. She read it and in a flash became radiant, as if an injection of stimulants had swept away drowsiness and despair.

"What does it say?" I asked cautiously.

"To me nothing."

"So?"

"It's for Nadia, he's leaving her."

She put the letter back in the envelope and gave it to me, urging me to keep it carefully hidden.

I stood, confused, with the envelope in my hands. Nino was leaving Nadia? And why? Because Lila had asked him to? So she would win? I was disappointed. He was sacrificing the daughter of Professor Galiani to the game that he and the wife of the grocer were playing. I said nothing, I stared at Lila while she got dressed, put on her makeup. Finally I said, "Why did you ask Stefano that absurd thing, to go to Amalfi? I don't understand you."

She smiled.

"I don't, either."

We left the room. Lila kissed Stefano affectionately, rubbing against him happily, and we decided to go with him to the Port, Nunzia and I in the minicab, he and Lila on the Lambretta. We had some ice cream while we waited for the boat. Lila was nice to her husband, gave him a thousand bits of advice, promised to telephone every night. Before he started up the gangplank he put an arm around my shoulders and whispered in my ear:

"I'm sorry, I was really angry. Without you I don't know how it would have ended, this time."

It was a polite statement, and yet I felt in it a sort of ultimatum that meant: Tell your friend, please, that if she goes too far again, it's all over.

64.

At the head of the letter was Nadia's address in Capri. As soon as the boat left the shore carrying Stefano away, Lila propelled us cheerfully to the tobacconist, bought a stamp, and, while I kept Nunzia busy, recopied the address onto the envelope and mailed it.

We wandered through Forio, but I was too nervous, and kept talking to Nunzia. When we returned to the house I drew Lila into my room and spoke plainly to her. She listened to me in silence, but with a distracted air, as if on the one hand she felt the gravity of the things I was saying and on the other had abandoned herself to thoughts that made every word meaningless. I said to her, "Lila, I don't know what you have in mind, but in my view you're playing with fire. Now Stefano has left happy and if you telephone him every night he'll be even happier. But be careful: he'll be back in a week and will stay until August 20th. Do you think you can go on like this? Do you think you can play with people's lives? Do you know that Nino doesn't want to study anymore, he wants to find a job? What have you put in his head? And why did you make him leave his girlfriend? Do you want to ruin him? Do you want to ruin both of you?"

At that last question she roused herself and burst out laughing, but somewhat artificially. She sounded amused, but who knows. She said I ought to be proud of her, she had made me look good. Why? Because she had been considered in every way finer than the very fine daughter of my professor. Because the smartest boy in my school and maybe in Naples and maybe in Italy and maybe in the world—according to what I said, naturally—had just left that very respectable young lady, no less, to please her, the daughter of a shoemaker, elementary-school diploma, wife of Carracci. She spoke with increasing sarcasm and as if she were finally revealing a cruel plan of revenge. I must have looked angry, she realized it, but for several minutes she continued in that tone, as if she couldn't stop herself. Was she serious? Was that her true state of mind at that moment? I exclaimed:

"Who are you putting on this show for? For me? Do you want to make me believe that Nino is ready to do anything, however crazy, to please you?"

The laughter disappeared from her eyes, she darkened, abruptly changed her tone.

"No, I'm lying, it's completely the opposite. I'm the one who's prepared to do anything, and it's never happened to me with anyone, and I'm glad that it's happening now."

Then, overcome by embarrassment, she went to bed without even saying goodnight.

I fell into a nervous half sleep, during which I convinced myself that the last little trickle of words was truer than the torrent that had preceded it.

During the week that followed I had the proof. First of all, as early as Monday I realized that Bruno, after Pinuccia's departure, really had begun to focus on me, and he now considered that the moment had arrived to behave toward me as Nino behaved with Lila. While we were swimming he clumsily pulled me toward him to kiss me, so that I swallowed a mouthful of water and had to return to the shore coughing. I was annoyed, he saw it. When he came to lie down in the sun next to me, with the air of a beaten dog, I made a kind but firm little speech, whose sense was: Bruno, you're very nice, but between you and me there can't be anything but a fraternal feeling. He was sad but he didn't give up. The same night, after the phone call to Stefano, we all went to walk on the beach and then we sat on the cold sand and stretched out to look at the stars, Lila resting on her elbows, Nino with his head on her stomach, I with my head on Nino's stomach, Bruno with his head on my stomach. We gazed at the constellations, praising the portentous architecture of the sky with trite formulas. Not all of us, Lila didn't. She was silent, but when we had exhausted the catalogue of worshipful wonder, she said that the spectacle of night frightened her, she saw no structure but only random shards of glass in a blue pitch. This silenced us all, and I was vexed: she had that habit of speaking last, which gave her time to reflect and allowed her to disrupt with a single remark everything that we had more or less thoughtlessly said.

"How can you be afraid," I exclaimed. "It's beautiful."

Bruno immediately agreed. Nino instead encouraged her: with a slight movement he signaled me to free his stomach, he sat up and began to talk to her as if they were alone. The sky, the temple, order, disorder. Finally they got up and, still talking, disappeared into the darkness.

I was lying down but leaning on my elbows. I no longer had Nino's warm body as a pillow, and the weight of Bruno's head on my stomach was irritating. I said excuse me, touching his hair. He sat up, grabbed me by the waist, pressed his face against my chest. I muttered no, but he pushed me down on the sand and searched for my mouth, pressing one hand hard against my breast. Then I shoved him away, forcefully, crying, Stop it, and this time I was unpleasant, I hissed, "I don't like you, how do I have to tell you?" He stopped, embarrassed, sat up. He said in a low voice: "Is it possible that you don't like me even a little?" I tried to explain that it wasn't a thing that could be measured, saying, "It's not a matter of more beauty or less, more liking or less; it's that some people attract me and others don't, it's nothing to do with how they are really."

"You don't like me?"

I said impatiently, "No."

But as soon as I uttered that monosyllable I burst into tears, while stammering things like "See, I'm crying for no reason, I'm an idiot, I'm not worth wasting time on."

He touched my cheek with his fingers and tried again to embrace me, murmuring: I want to give you so many presents, you deserve them, you're so pretty. I pulled away angrily, and shouted into the darkness, my voice cracking, "Lila, come back right now, I want to go home."

The two friends went with us to the foot of the stairs, then they left. As Lila and I went up I said in exasperation, "Go where

you like, do what you like, I'm not going with you anymore. It's
the second time Bruno has put his hands on me: I don't want
to be alone with him anymore, is that clear?"

65.

There are moments when we resort to senseless formulations
and advance absurd claims to hide straightforward feelings.
Today I know that in other circumstances, after some resistance,
I would have given in to Bruno's advances. I wasn't attracted to
him, certainly, but I hadn't been especially attracted to Antonio,
either. One becomes affectionate toward men slowly, whether
they coincide or not with whomever in the various phases of life
we have taken as the model of a man. And Bruno Soccavo, in
that phase of his life, was courteous and generous; it would have
been easy to harbor some affection for him. But the reasons for
rejecting him had nothing to do with anything really disagreeable about him. The truth was that I wanted to restrain Lila. I
wanted to be a hindrance to her. I wanted her to be aware of the
situation she was getting into and getting me into. I wanted her
to say to me: Yes, you're right, I'm making a mistake, I won't go
off in the dark with Nino anymore, I won't leave you alone with
Bruno; starting now I will behave as befits a married woman.

Naturally it didn't happen. She confined herself to saying,
"I'll talk to Nino about it and you'll see, Bruno won't bother
you anymore." So day after day we continued to meet the boys
at nine in the morning and separated at midnight. But on
Tuesday night after the call to Stefano, Nino said, "You've
never been to see Bruno's house. You want to come over?"

I immediately said no, I pretended I had a stomachache and
wanted to go home. Nino and Lila looked uncertainly at each
other, Bruno said nothing. I felt the weight of their discontent
and added, embarrassed, "Maybe another night."

Lila said nothing but when we were alone she exclaimed, "You can't make my life unhappy, Lenù." I answered, "If Stefano finds out that we went alone to their house, he'll be angry not just at you but also at me." And I didn't stop there. At home I stirred up Nunzia's displeasure and used it to urge her to reproach her daughter for too much sun, too much sea, staying out till midnight. I even went so far as to say, as if I wished to make peace between mother and daughter, "Signora Nunzia, tomorrow night come and have ice cream with us, you'll see we're not doing anything wrong." Lila became furious, she said that she had had a miserable life all year, always shut up in the grocery, and now she had the right to a little freedom. Nunzia also lost her temper: "Lina, what are you saying? Freedom? What freedom? You are married, you must be accountable to your husband. Lenuccia can want a little freedom, you can't." Her daughter went to her room and slammed the door.

But the next day Lila won: her mother stayed home and we went to telephone Stefano. "You must be here at eleven on the dot," Nunzia said, grumpily, addressing me, and I answered, "All right." She gave me a long, questioning look. By now she was alarmed: she was our guard but she wasn't guarding us; she was afraid we were getting into trouble, but she thought of her own sacrificed youth and didn't want to keep us from some innocent amusement. I repeated to reassure her: "At eleven."

The phone call to Stefano lasted a minute at most. When Lila came out of the booth Nino asked, "Are you feeling well tonight, Lenù? Come see the house?"

"Come on," Bruno urged me. "You can have a drink and then go."

Lila agreed, I said nothing. On the outside the building was old, shabby, but inside it had been renovated: the cellar white and well lighted, full of wine and cured meats; a marble staircase with a wrought-iron banister; sturdy doors on which gold handles shone; windows with gilded fixtures. There were a lot of rooms, yellow couches, a television; in the kitchen, cupboards painted aquamarine and in the bedrooms wardrobes that were like gothic churches. I thought, for the first time clearly, that Bruno really was rich, richer than Stefano. I thought that if ever my mother had known that the student son of the owner of Soccavo mortadella had courted me, and that I had been, no less, a guest at his house, and that instead of thanking God for the good fortune he had sent me and seeking to marry him I had rejected him twice, she would have beaten me. On the other hand it was precisely the thought of my mother, of her lame leg, that made me feel unfit even for Bruno. In that house I was intimidated. Why was I there, what was I doing there? Lila acted nonchalant, she laughed often; I felt as if I had a fever, a nasty taste in my mouth. I began to say yes to avoid the embarrassment of saying no. Do you want a drink of this, do you want to put on this record, do you want to watch television, do you want some ice cream. When, finally, I realized that Nino and Lila had disappeared, I was worried. Where had they gone? Was it possible that they were in Nino's bedroom? Possible that Lila was willing to cross even that limit? Possible that—I didn't want to think about it. I jumped up, I said to Bruno:

"It's late."

He was kind, but with an undertone of sadness. He murmured, "Stay a little longer." He said that the next day he had to leave very early, to attend a family celebration. He announced that he would be gone until Monday and those days without me would be a torment. He took my hand delicately, said that he loved me and other things like that. I gently took my hand away, he didn't try for any other contact. Instead, he spoke at length about his feelings for me, he who in general said little, and I had trouble interrupting him. When I did I said, "I really have to go," then, in a louder voice, "Lila, please come, it's quarter after ten."

Some minutes passed, the two reappeared. Nino and Bruno took us to a taxi, Bruno said goodbye as if he were going not to Naples for a few days but to America for the rest of his life. On the way home Lila, her tone pointed, as if she were delivering important news: "Nino told me that he has a lot of admiration for you."

"Not me," I answered right away, in a rude voice. And then I whispered: "What if you get pregnant?"

She said in my ear: "There's no danger. We're just kissing and holding."

"Oh."

"And anyway I don't stay pregnant."

"It happened once."

"I told you, I don't stay pregnant. He knows how to manage."

"He who?"

"Nino. He would use a condom."

"What's that?"

"I don't know, he called it that."

"You don't know what it is and you trust it?"

"It's something that he puts over it."

"Over where?"

I wanted to force her to name things. I wanted her to understand what she was saying. First she assured me that they were only kissing, then she spoke of him as someone who knew how not to get her pregnant. I was enraged, I expected that she would be ashamed. Instead she seemed pleased with everything that had happened to her and that would happen to her. So much so that when we got home she was nice to Nunzia, pointed out that we had returned early, got ready for bed. But she left her door open and when she saw me going to my room she called me, she said, "Stay here a minute, close the door."

I sat on the bed, but trying to make it clear that I was tired of her and everything.

"What do you have to tell me?"

She whispered, "I want to go and sleep at Nino's."

I was astonished.

"And Nunzia?"

"Wait, don't get mad. There's not much time left, Lenù. Stefano will arrive on Saturday, he'll stay for ten days, then we go back to Naples. And everything will be over."

"Everything what?"

"This, these days, these evenings."

We discussed it for a long time, she seemed very lucid. She murmured that nothing like this would ever happen to her again. She whispered that she loved him, that she wanted him. She used that verb, *amare*, that we had found only in books and in the movies, that no one used in the neighborhood, I would say it at most to myself, we all preferred *voler bene*. She no, she *loved*. She loved Nino. But she knew very well that that love had to be suffocated, every occasion for it to breathe had to be removed. And she would do it, she would do it starting Saturday night. She had no doubts, she would be capable of it, and I had to trust her. But the very little time that remained she wished to devote to Nino.

"I want to stay in a bed with him for a whole night and a whole day," she said. "I want to sleep holding him and being held, and kiss him when I feel like it, caress him when I feel like it, even while he's sleeping. Then that's it."

"It's impossible."

"You have to help me."

"How?"

"You have to convince my mother that Nella has invited us to spend two days at Barano and that we'll spend the night there."

I was silent for a moment. So she already had a project, she had a plan. Clearly she had worked it out with Nino, maybe he had even sent Bruno away on purpose. For how long had they been deciding the how, the where? No more speeches on neocapitalism, on neocolonialism, on Africa, on Latin America, on Beckett, on Bertrand Russell. Mere doodles. Nino no longer talked about anything. Their brilliant minds now were exercised only on how to deceive Nunzia and Stefano, using me.

"You're out of your mind," I said, furiously, "even if your mother believes you your husband never will."

"You persuade her to send us to Barano and I'll persuade her not to tell Stefano."

"No."

"Aren't we friends anymore?"

"No."

"You're not Nino's friend anymore?"

"No."

But Lila knew how to draw me in. And I was unable to resist: on the one hand I said that's enough, on the other I was depressed at the idea of not being part of her life, of the means by which she invented it for herself. What was that deception but another of her fantastic moves, which were always full of risks? The two of us together, allied with each other, in the struggle against all. We would devote the next day to overcoming Nunzia's opposition. The day after that we would leave early, together. At Forio we would separate. She would go to Bruno's house with Nino, I would take the boat for the Maronti. She would spend the whole day and the whole night with Nino, I would be at Nella's and sleep in Barano. The next day I would return to Forio for lunch, we would see each other at Bruno's, and together would return home. Perfect. The more her mind was ignited as, in minute detail, she planned how to make every part of the ruse add up, the more skillfully she ignited mine, too, and she hugged me, begged me. Here was a new adventure, *together*. Here was how *we* would take what life didn't want to give us. Here. Or would I rather that she be deprived of that joy, that Nino should suffer, that both should lose the light of reason and end up not capably managing their desire but being dangerously overwhelmed by it? There was a moment, that night, when, by following her along the thread of her arguments, I came to think that to support her in this undertaking, besides being an important milestone for our long sisterhood, was also the way of manifesting my love—she said friendship, but I desperately thought: love, love love—for Nino. And it was at that point that I said:

"All right, I'll help you."

66.

The next day I told Nunzia many lies that were so disgraceful I was ashamed. At the center of the lies I placed Maestra Oliviero, who was in Potenza, in goodness knows what terrible conditions, and it was my idea, not Lila's. "Yesterday," I said to Nunzia, "I met Nella Incardo, and she told me that her cousin, who is convalescing, has come to stay with her for a vacation at the seaside that will finally restore her health. Tomorrow night Nella's having a party for the teacher and she invited me and Lila, who were her best students. We would really like to go, but it will be late and so impossible. But Nella has said that we can sleep at her house."

"In Barano?" Nunzia asked, frowning.

"Yes, the party is there."

"You go, Lenù, Lila can't, her husband will get mad."

Lila threw in, "Let's not tell him."

"What do you mean?"

"Mamma, he's in Naples and I'm here, he'll never find out."

"One way or another things are always found out."

"Well, no."

"Yes, and that's enough. Lina, I don't want to discuss it further: if Lenuccia wants to go, fine, but you stay here."

We went on for a good hour, I making the point that the

teacher was very sick and this might be our last chance to show her our gratitude, and Lila pressing her like this: "How many lies have you told Papa, admit it, and not for bad reasons but for good ones, to have a moment to yourself, to do a just thing that he would never allow." Wavering, Nunzia first said that she had never told the tiniest lie to Fernando; then she admitted that she had told one, two, many; finally she cried with rage and at the same time maternal pride, "What happened when I conceived you, an accident, a hiccup, a convulsion, the lights went out, a bulb blew, the basin of water fell off the night table? Certainly there must have been something, if you were born so intolerable, so different from the others." And here she grew sad, she seemed to soften. But soon she was indignant again, she said you don't tell lies to a husband just to see a schoolteacher. And Lila exclaimed, "To Maestra Oliviero I owe the little I know, the only school I had was with her." And in the end Nunzia gave in. But she insisted on a precise timetable: Saturday at exactly two o'clock we were to be home again. Not a minute later. "If Stefano arrives early and doesn't find you? Really, Lina, don't put me in an ugly situation. Clear?"

"Clear."

We went to the beach. Lila was radiant, she embraced me, she kissed me, she said that she would be grateful for her whole life. But I already felt guilty about that evocation of Maestra Oliviero, whom I had placed at the center of a party, in Barano, imagining her as she was when, full of energy, she taught us, and not as, instead, she must be now, worse than when she was taken away in the ambulance, worse than when I had seen her in the hospital. My satisfaction in having invented an effective lie vanished, I lost the frenzy of complicity, I became resentful again. I asked myself why I supported Lila, why I covered for her: in fact she wanted to betray her husband, she wanted to violate the sacred bond of marriage, she wanted to tear off her condition of wife, she wanted to do a thing that would provoke Stefano, if he should find out, to bash her head in. Suddenly I remembered what she had done to the wedding-dress photograph and I felt sick to my stomach. Now, I thought, she is behaving in the same way, and not with a photograph but with the very person of Signora Carracci. And in this case, too, she pulls me in to help her. Nino is a tool, yes, yes. Like the scissors, the paste, the paint, he is being used to disfigure her. Toward what terrible act is she driving me? And why do I let myself be driven?

We found him waiting for us at the beach. He asked anxiously: "So?"

She said, "Yes."

They ran off to swim without even inviting me, and, besides, I wouldn't have gone. I felt chilled by anxiety, and then why swim, to stay near the shore alone, with my fear of the deep water?

There was some wind, some strips of cloud, the sea was a little rough. They dived in without hesitation, Lila with a long cry of joy. They were happy, full of their own romance, they had the energy of those who successfully seize what they desire, no matter the cost. Moving with determined strokes, they were immediately lost amid the waves.

I felt chained to an intolerable pact of friendship. How tortuous everything was. It was I who had dragged Lila to Ischia. I had used her to pursue Nino, hopelessly. I had relinquished the money from the bookstore on Via Mezzocannone for the money that she gave me. I had put myself in her service and now I was playing the role of the servant who comes to the aid of her mistress. I was covering for her adultery. I was preparing it. I was helping her take Nino, take him in my place, be fucked—yes, fucked—fucked by him for a whole day and a whole night, give him blow jobs. My temples began to throb, I kicked the sand with my heel once, twice, three times, it was a thrill to hear echoing in my head childhood words, overloaded with sex imagined in ignorance. High school disappeared, the wonderful sonority of the books disappeared, of the translations from Greek and Latin. I stared at the sparkling sea, and the long livid array of clouds that was moving from the horizon toward the blue sky, toward the white streak of condensation, and I could barely see them, Nino and Lila, black dots. I couldn't tell if they were swimming toward the mass of clouds on the horizon or turning back. I wished that they would drown and that death would take from them the joys of the next day.

67.

I heard someone calling me, I turned suddenly.

"So I had good eyesight," said a teasing male voice.

"I told you it was her," said a female voice.

I recognized them immediately, I sat up. It was Michele Solara and Gigliola, along with her brother, a boy of twelve called Lello.

I welcomed them warmly, even though I never said: Sit down. I hoped that for some reason they were in a hurry, that they would leave right away, but Gigliola spread her towel, along with Michele's, carefully on the sand, placed her purse on it, cigarettes, lighter, said to her brother: lie down on the hot sand, because the wind's blowing, your bathing suit's wet and you'll catch cold. What to do. I made an effort not to look toward the sea, as if in that way it wouldn't occur to them to look at it, and I paid happy attention to Michele, who started talking in his usual unemotional, careless tone. They had taken a holiday, it was too hot in Naples. Boat in the morning, boat in the evening, good air. Since Pinuccia and Alfonso were in the shop on Piazza dei Martiri, or, rather, no, Alfonso and Pinuccia, because Pinuccia didn't do much, while Alfonso was

great. It was on Pina's recommendation that they had decided
to come to Forio. You'll find them, she had said, just walk
along the beach. And in fact, they had walked and walked,
Gigliola had shouted: Isn't that Lenuccia? And here we are. I
kept saying what a pleasure, and meanwhile Michele got up
absent-mindedly, with his sandy feet on Gigliola's towel, so she
reproached him—"Pay a little attention"—but in vain. Now
that he had finished the story of why they were on Ischia, I
knew that the real question was about to arrive, I read it in his
eyes even before he said it:

"Where's Lina?"

"She's swimming."

"In this sea?"

"It's not too rough."

It was inevitable, both he and Gigliola turned to look at the
sea, with its curls of foam. But they did it distractedly, they were
settling themselves on the towels. Michele argued with the boy,
who wanted to go swimming again. "Stay here," he said, "you
want to drown?" He stuck a comic book in his hand, adding, to
his girlfriend, "We're never taking him again."

Gigliola complimented me profusely: "How well you look,
all tanned, and your hair is even lighter."

I smiled, I was self-deprecating, but I was thinking only:
I've got to find a way to get them out of here.

"Come rest at the house," I said. "Nunzia's there, she'll be
very happy."

They refused, they had to catch the boat in a couple of
hours, they preferred to have a little more sun and then they
would head off on their walk.

"So let's go to the bath house, we'll get something to eat
there," I said.

"Yes, but let's wait for Lina."

As always in tense situations, I undertook to blot out the time
with words, and I started off with a flurry of questions, anything

that came into my head: How was Spagnuolo the pastry maker, how was Marcello, if he'd found a girlfriend, what did Michele think of the shoe designs, and what did his father think and what did his mamma think of them, and what did his grandfather think. At one point I got up, I said, "I'll call Lina," and I went down to the water's edge, I began to shout: "Lina, come back, Michele and Gigliola are here," but it was useless, she didn't hear me. I went back, and started talking again to distract them. I hoped that Lila and Nino, returning to shore, would become aware of the danger before Gigliola and Michele saw them and avoid any intimate attitude. But though Gigliola listened to me, Michele wasn't even polite enough to pretend. He had come to Ischia purposely to see Lila and talk to her about the new shoes, I was sure of it, and he cast long glances at the sea, which was getting rougher.

Finally he saw her. He saw her as she came out of the water, her hand entwined in Nino's, a handsome couple who would not pass unobserved, both tall, both naturally elegant, shoulders touching, smiles exchanged. They were so entranced with themselves that they didn't immediately realize I had company. When Lila recognized Michele and pulled her hand away, it was too late. Maybe Gigliola didn't notice, and her brother was reading the comic book, but Michele saw and turned to look at me as if to read on my face the verification of what he had just had before his eyes. He must have found it, in the form of fear. He said gravely, in the slow voice that he assumed when he had to deal with something that required speed and decisiveness: "Ten minutes, just the time to say hello, and we'll go."

In fact they stayed more than an hour. Michele, when he heard Nino's last name—introducing him I placed great emphasis on the fact that he was our schoolmate in elementary school as well as my classmate in high school—asked the most irritating question:

"You're the son of the guy who writes for *Roma* and for *Napoli Notte*?"

Nino nodded unwillingly, and Michele stared at him for a long instant, as if he wanted to find in his eyes confirmation of that relationship. Then he did not speak to him again, he spoke only and always to Lila.

Lila was friendly, ironic, at times deceitful.

Michele said to her, "That blowhard your brother swears he thought up the new shoes."

"It's the truth."

"So that's why they're garbage."

"You'll see, that garbage will sell even better than the preceding."

"Maybe, but only if you come to the store."

"You already have Gigliola, who's doing great."

"I need Gigliola in the pastry shop."

"Your problem, I have to stay in the grocery."

"You'll see, you'll move to Piazza dei Martiri, *signò,* and you'll have carte blanche."

"Carte blanche, carte noir, get it out of your head, I'm fine where I am."

And so on in this tone, they seemed to be playing *tamburello* with their words. Every so often Gigliola or I tried to say something, mainly Gigliola, who was furious at the way her fiancé talked about her fate without even consulting her. As for Nino, he was—I realized—stunned, or perhaps astonished at how Lila, skillful and fearless, found the phrases, in dialect, to match Michele's.

Finally the young Solara announced that they had to go, they had an umbrella with their belongings quite far away. He said goodbye to me, he said goodbye warmly to Lila, repeating that he would expect her in the store in September. To Nino he said seriously, as if to a subordinate whom one asks to go and buy a pack of Nationals, "Tell your papa that he was wrong to write that he didn't like the way the store looked. When you take money, you have to write that everything's great, otherwise no more money."

Nino was caught by surprise, perhaps by humiliation, and didn't answer. Gigliola held out her hand, he gave her his mechanically. The couple went off, dragging the boy, who was reading the comic book as he walked.

68.

I was enraged, frightened, unhappy with my every word or gesture. As soon as Michele and Gigliola were far enough away I said to Lila, so that Nino could also hear me: "He saw you."

Nino asked uneasily, "Who is he?"

"A shit Camorrist who thinks he's God's gift," said Lila contemptuously.

I corrected her immediately, Nino should know: "He's one of her husband's partners. He'll tell Stefano everything."

"What everything," Lila protested, "there's nothing to tell."

"You know perfectly well that they'll tell on you."

"Yes? And who gives a damn."

"I give a damn."

"Don't worry. Because even if you won't help me, things will go as they should go."

And as if I weren't present, she went on to make arrangements with Nino for the next day. But while she, precisely because of that encounter with Michele Solara, seemed to have multiplied her energies, he seemed like a windup toy that has run down. He murmured:

"Are you sure you won't get yourself in trouble because of me?"

Lila caressed his cheek. "You don't want to anymore?"

The caress seemed to revive him. "I'm just worried for you."

We soon left Nino, we returned home. Along the way I sketched catastrophic scenarios—"Michele will talk to Stefano tonight, Stefano will rush over here tomorrow morning, he won't find you at home, Nunzia will send him to Barano, he won't find you at Barano, either, you'll lose everything, Lila, listen to me, you'll ruin not only yourself but you'll ruin me, too, my mother will kill me"—but she confined herself to listening absent-mindedly, smiling, repeating in varying formulations a single idea: I love you, Lenù, and I will always love you; so I hope that you feel at least once in your life what I'm feeling at this moment.

Then I thought: so much the worse for you. We stayed home that night. Lila was nice to her mother, she wanted to cook, she wanted her to be served, she cleared, washed the dishes, sat on her lap, put her arms around her neck, resting her forehead against hers with an unexpected sadness. Nunzia, who wasn't used to those kindnesses and must have found them embarrassing, at a certain point burst into tears and amid her tears uttered a phrase convoluted by anxiety: "Please, Lina, no mother has ever had a daughter like you, don't make me die of sorrow."

Lila made fun of her affectionately and took her to her room. In the morning she dragged me out of bed; part of me was so anguished that it didn't want to get up and be conscious of the day. In the mini cab to Forio, I laid out other terrible scenarios that left her completely indifferent. "Nella's gone"; "Nella really has guests and has no room for me"; "The Sarratores decide to come here to Forio to visit their son." She continued to reply in a joking tone: "If Nella's gone, Nino's mother will welcome you"; "If there's no room you'll come back and sleep at our house"; "If the whole Sarratore family knocks at the door of Bruno's house we won't open it." And we went on like that until, a little before nine, we arrived at our destination. Nino was at the window waiting, he hurried to open the door. He gave me a nod of greeting, he drew Lila inside.

What until that door could still be avoided from that moment became an unstoppable mechanism. In the same cab, at Lila's expense, I was taken to Barano. On the way I realized that I couldn't truly hate them. I felt bitterness toward Nino, I certainly had some hostile feelings toward Lila, I could even wish death on both of them, but almost as a kind of incantation that was capable, paradoxically, of saving all three of us. Hatred no. Rather, I hated myself, I despised myself. I was there, I was there on the island, the air stirred by the cab's movement assailed me with the intense odors of the vegetation from which night was evaporating. But it was a mortified presence, submissive to the demands of others. I was living in them, unobtrusively. I couldn't cancel out the images of the embraces, kisses in the empty house. Their passion invaded me, disturbed me. I loved them both and so I couldn't love myself, feel myself, affirm myself with a need for life of *my own*, one that had the same blind, mute force as theirs. So it seemed to me.

69.

I was greeted by Nella and the Sarratore family with the usual enthusiasm. I assumed my humblest mask, the mask of my father when he collected tips, the elaborate mask of my forebears—always fearful, always subordinate, always pleasingly willing—by which to avoid danger, and I went from lie to lie in a pleasant manner. I said to Nella that if I had decided to come and disturb her it wasn't by choice but necessity. I said that the Carraccis had guests, that there was no room for me that night. I said that I hoped I hadn't presumed too much in showing up like this, unexpectedly, and that if there were difficulties I would return to Naples for a few days.

Nella embraced me, fed me, swearing that to have me in the house was an immense pleasure for her. I refused to go to the beach with the Sarratores, although the children protested. Lidia insisted that I join them soon and Donato declared that he would wait for me so we could swim together. I stayed with Nella, helped her straighten the house, cook lunch. For a moment everything weighed on me less: the lies, the images of the adultery that was taking place, my complicity, a jealousy that couldn't be defined because I felt at the same time jealous of Lila who was giving herself to Nino, of Nino who was giving himself to Lila. In the meantime, Nella, talking about the Sarratores, seemed less hostile. She said that husband and wife had found an equilibrium and since they were getting along they gave her less trouble. She told me about Maestra Oliviero: she had telephoned her in order to tell her that I had come to see her, and she had been very tired but more optimistic. For a while, in other words, there was a tranquil flow of news. But a few remarks were enough, an unexpected detour, and the weight of the situation I was involved in returned forcefully.

"She praised you a lot," Nella said, speaking of Maestra Oliviero, "but when she found out that you came to see me with your two married friends she asked a lot of questions, especially about Signora Lina."

"What did she say?"

"She said that in her entire career as a teacher she never had such a good student."

The evocation of Lila's old primacy disturbed me.

"It's true," I admitted.

But Nella made a grimace of absolute disagreement, her eyes lit up.

"My cousin is an exceptional teacher," she said, "and yet in my view this time she is wrong."

"No, she's not wrong."

"Can I tell you what I think?"

"Of course."

"It won't upset you?"

"No."

"I didn't like Signora Lina. You are much better, you're prettier and more intelligent. I talked about it with the Sarratores, too, and they agree with me."

"You say that because you love me."

"No. Pay attention, Lenù. I know that you are good friends, my cousin told me. And I don't want to interfere in things that have nothing to do with me. But a glance is enough for me to judge people. Signora Lina knows that you're better than her and so she doesn't love you the way you love her."

I smiled, pretending skepticism. "Does she hate me?"

"I don't know. But she knows how to wound, it's written in her face, it's enough to look at her forehead and her eyes."

I shook my head, I repressed my satisfaction. Ah, if it were all so straightforward. But I already knew—although not the way I do today—that between the two of us everything was more tangled. And I joked, laughed, made Nella laugh. I told her that Lila never made a good impression the first time. Since she was little she had seemed like a devil, and she really was, but in a good way. She had a quick mind and did well in whatever she happened to apply herself to: if she could have studied she would have become a scientist like Madame Curie or a great novelist like Grazia Deledda, or even like Nilde Iotti, the lover of Togliatti. And hearing those last two names, Nella exclaimed, oh Madonna, and ironically made the sign of the cross. Then she gave a little laugh, then another, and she couldn't contain herself, she wanted to whisper a secret, a very funny thing that Sarratore had said to her. Lila, according to him, had an almost ugly beauty, a type that males are, yes, enchanted by but also fear.

"What fear?" I asked, also in a low voice.

And she, in an even lower voice, "The fear that their thingy won't function or it will fall off or she'll pull out a knife and cut it off."

She laughed, her chest heaved, her eyes became teary. She couldn't contain herself for quite some time and I felt an unease I had never felt with her before. It wasn't my mother's laughter, the obscene laughter of the woman who knows. In Nella's there was something chaste and yet vulgar, it was the laugh of an aging virgin that assailed me and pushed me to laugh, too, but in a forced way. A smart woman like her, I said to myself, why does this amuse her? And meanwhile I saw myself growing old, with that laugh of malicious innocence in my breast. I thought: I'll end up laughing like that, too.

70.

The Sarratores arrived for lunch. They left a trail of sand on the floor, an odor of sea and sweat, a lighthearted reproach because the children had waited for me in vain. I set the table, cleared, washed the dishes, followed Pino, Clelia, and Ciro to the edge of a thicket to help them cut reeds to make a kite. With the children I was happy. While their parents rested, while Nella napped on a lounge chair on the terrace, the time slipped by, the kite absorbed me completely, I scarcely thought of Nino and Lila.

In the late afternoon we all went to the beach, even Nella, to fly the kite. I ran back and forth on the beach followed by the three children, who were silent, amazed, when the kite appeared to rise and they cried out when they saw it hit the sand after an unexpected pirouette. I kept trying but I couldn't make it fly, in spite of the instructions that Donato shouted to me from under the umbrella. Finally, all sweaty, I gave up, and said to Pino, Clelia, and Ciro, "Ask Papa." Dragged by his children, Sarratore came and checked the weave of the reeds, the blue tissue paper, the thread, then he studied the wind and began to run backward, leaping energetically despite his heavy body. The children ran beside him in their excitement, and I also revived, I began to run along with them, until their expanding happiness was transmitted to me, too. Our kite traveled higher and higher, it flew, there was no need to run, you had only to hold the string. Sarratore was a good father. He demonstrated that with his help Ciro could hold it, and Clelia, and Pino, and even me. He handed it to me, in fact, but he stood behind me, he breathed on my neck and said, "Like that, good, pull a little, let it go," and it was evening.

We had dinner, the Sarratore family went for a walk in the town, husband, wife, and three children, sunburned and dressed up. Although they urged me to come, I stayed with Nella. We cleaned up, she helped me make the bed in the usual corner of the kitchen, we sat on the terrace in the cool air. The moon wasn't visible, in the dark sky there were swells of white clouds. We talked about how pretty and intelligent the Sarratore children were, and Nella fell asleep. Then, suddenly, the day, the night that was beginning, fell on me. I left the house on tiptoe, I went toward the Maronti.

Who knows if Michele Solara had kept to himself what he had seen. Who knows if everything was going smoothly. Who knows if Nunzia was already asleep in the house on the road in Cuotto or was trying to calm her son-in-law who had arrived unexpectedly on the last boat, hadn't found his wife and was furious. Who knows if Lila had telephoned her husband and, reassured that he was in Naples, far away, in the apartment in the new neighborhood, was now in bed with Nino, without fear, a secret couple, a couple intent on enjoying the night. Everything in the world was in precarious balance, pure risk, and those who didn't agree to take the risk wasted away in a corner, without getting to know life. I understood suddenly why I hadn't had Nino, why Lila had had him. I wasn't capa-

ble of entrusting myself to true feelings. I didn't know how to
be drawn beyond the limits. I didn't possess that emotional
power that had driven Lila to do all she could to enjoy that day
and that night. I stayed behind, waiting. She, on the other
hand, seized things, truly wanted them, was passionate about
them, played for all or nothing, and wasn't afraid of contempt,
mockery, spitting, beatings. She deserved Nino, in other
words, because she thought that to love him meant to try to
have him, not to hope that he would want her.

I made the dark descent. Now the moon was visible amid
scattered pale-edged clouds; the evening was very fragrant, and
you could hear the hypnotic rhythm of the waves. On the beach
I took off my shoes, the sand was cold, a gray-blue light
extended as far as the sea and then spread over its tremulous
expanse. I thought: yes, Lila is right, the beauty of things is a
trick, the sky is the throne of fear; I'm alive, now, here, ten steps
from the water, and it is not at all beautiful, it's terrifying; along
with this beach, the sea, the swarm of animal forms, I am part
of the universal terror; at this moment I'm the infinitesimal par-
ticle through which the fear of every thing becomes conscious
of itself; I; I who listen to the sound of the sea, who feel the
dampness and the cold sand; I who imagine all Ischia, the
entwined bodies of Nino and Lila, Stefano sleeping by himself
in the new house that is increasingly not so new, the furies who
indulge the happiness of today to feed the violence of tomorrow. Ah, it's true, my fear is too great and so I hope that everything will end soon, that the figures of the nightmares will con-
sume my soul. I hope that from this darkness packs of mad dogs
will emerge, vipers, scorpions, enormous sea serpents. I hope
that while I'm sitting here, on the edge of the sea, assassins will
arrive out of the night and torture my body. Yes, yes, let me be
punished for my insufficiency, let the worst happen, something
so devastating that it will prevent me from facing tonight,
tomorrow, the hours and days to come, reminding me with

always more crushing evidence of my unsuitable constitution. Thoughts like that I had, the frenzied thoughts of girlish discouragement. I gave myself up to them, for I don't know how long. Then someone said, "Lena," and touched my shoulder with cold fingers. I started, an icy grip seized my heart and when I turned suddenly and recognized Donato Sarratore, the breath burst in my throat like the sip of a magic potion, the kind that in poems revives strength and the urge to live.

71.

Donato told me that Nella had awakened, found that I wasn't in the house, and was worried. Lidia, too, was a little alarmed, so she had asked him to go and look for me. The only one who had found it normal that I wasn't in the house was him. He had reassured the two women, he had said, "Go to sleep, surely she's gone to enjoy the moon on the beach." Yet to please them, out of prudence, he had come on a reconnaissance. And in fact here I was, sitting and listening to the sea's breath, contemplating the divine beauty of the sky.

He spoke like that, more or less. He sat beside me, he murmured that he knew me as he knew himself. We had the same sensitivity to beautiful things, the same need to enjoy them, the same need to search for the right words to say how sweet the night was, how magical the moon, how the sea sparkled, how two souls were able to meet and recognize each other in the darkness, in the fragrant air. As he spoke I heard clearly the ridiculousness of his trained voice, the crudeness of his poeticizing, the sleazy lyricizing behind which he concealed his eagerness to put his hands on me. But I thought: Maybe we really are made of the same clay, maybe we really are condemned, blameless, to the same, identical mediocrity. So I rested my head on his shoulder, I murmured, "I'm cold." And he quickly put an arm around my waist, pulled me slowly closer to him, asked me if it was better like that. I answered, "Yes," a whisper, and Sarratore lifted my chin with thumb and index finger, placed his lips lightly on mine, asked, "How's that?" Then he pressed me with little kisses that grew in intensity as he continued to murmur: "And like that, and like that, are you still cold, is it better like that, is it better?" His mouth was warm and wet, I welcomed it on mine with increasing gratitude, so that the kiss lasted longer and longer, his tongue grazed mine, collided with it, sank into my mouth. I felt better. I realized that I was regaining ground, that the ice was ceding, melting, that the fear was forgetting itself, that his hands were taking away the cold but slowly, as if it were made of very thin layers and Sarratore had the ability to peel them away with cautious precision, one by one, without tearing them, and that his mouth, too, had that capacity, and his teeth, his tongue, and he therefore knew much more about me than Antonio had ever learned, that in fact he knew what I myself didn't know. I had a hidden me—I realized—that fingers, mouth, teeth, tongue were able to discover. Layer after layer, that me lost every hiding place, was shamelessly exposed, and Sarratore showed that he knew how to keep it from fleeing, from being ashamed, he knew how to hold it as if it were the absolute reason for his affectionate motility, for his sometimes gentle, sometimes fevered pressures. The entire time, I didn't once regret having accepted what was happening. I had no second thoughts and I was proud of myself, I wanted it to be like that, I imposed it on myself. I was helped, perhaps, by the fact that Sarratore progressively forgot his flowery language, that, unlike Antonio, he claimed no intervention from me, he never took my hand to touch him, but confined himself to convincing me that he liked everything about me, and he applied himself to my body with the care, the devotion, the pride of the man absorbed in demonstrating how thoroughly he knows women. I didn't even hear him say *you're a virgin*, probably he was so sure of my condition that he would have been surprised by the opposite. When I was overwhelmed by a need for pleasure so demanding and so egocentric that it canceled out not only the entire world of sensation but also his body, in my eyes old, and the labels by which he could be classified—*father of Nino, railway worker-poet-journalist, Donato Sarratore*—he was aware of it and penetrated me. I felt that he did it delicately at first, then with a clear and decisive thrust that caused a rip in my stomach, a stab of pain immediately erased by a rhythmic oscillation, a sliding, a thrusting, an emptying and filling me with jolts of eager desire. Until suddenly he withdrew, turned over on his back on the sand and emitted a sort of strangled roar.

We were silent, the sea returned, the tremendous sky, I felt stunned. That impelled Sarratore again toward his coarse lyricism, he thought he had to lead me back to myself with tender words. But I managed to tolerate at most a couple of phrases. I got up abruptly, shook the sand out of my hair, off my whole body, straightened myself. When he ventured, "Where can we meet tomorrow?" I answered in Italian, in a calm voice, self-assured, that he was mistaken, he must never look for me again, not at Cetara or in the neighborhood. And when he smiled skeptically, I told him that what Antonio Cappuccio, Melina's son, could do to him was nothing in comparison to what Michele Solara, a person I knew well, would do. I need only say a word and Solara would make things very hard for him. I told him that Michele was eager to bash his face in, because he had taken money to write about the shop on Piazza dei Martiri but hadn't done his job well.

All the way back I continued to threaten him, partly because he had returned to his sugary-sweet little phrases and I wanted him to understand clearly my feelings, partly because I was amazed at how the tonality of threat, which since I was a child I had used only in dialect, came easily to me also in the Italian language.

72.

I was afraid I would find the two women awake but they were both asleep. They weren't so worried that they would lose sleep, they considered me sensible, they trusted me. I slept deeply.

The next day I woke up cheerful and even when Nino, Lila, and what had happened at the Maronti came back to me, in fragments, I still felt good. I chatted a long time with Nella, had breakfast with the Sarratores, didn't mind the falsely paternal kindness with which Donato treated me. Not for a moment did I think that sex with that rather conceited, vain, garrulous man had been a mistake. Yet to see him there at the table, to listen to him, and recognize that it was he who had deflowered me, disgusted me. I went to the beach with the whole family, I went swimming with the children, I left behind me a wake of fondness. I arrived punctually at Forio.

I called Nino, he appeared immediately. I refused to go in, partly because we had to leave as soon as possible, partly because I did not want to preserve images of rooms that Nino and Lila had inhabited by themselves for almost two days. I waited, Lila didn't come. Suddenly my anxiety returned, I imagined that Stefano had been able to leave in the morning, that he was disembarking several hours earlier than expected, and in fact was already on his way to the house. I called again, Nino returned, he indicated that I had to wait just another minute. They came down a quarter of an hour later, they embraced and kissed for a long time in the entrance. Lila ran toward me, but she stopped suddenly, as if she had forgotten something, and went back and kissed him again. I looked away uneasily and the idea that there was something wrong with me, that I lacked a true capacity for involvement, regained strength. Yet the two of them again seemed to me so handsome, perfect in every movement, that to cry, "Lina, hurry up," was almost to disfigure a fantastical image. She seemed drawn away by a cruel force, her hand ran slowly from his shoulder, along the arm, to the fingers, as if in the movement of a dance. Finally she joined me.

We hardly spoke during the ride in the mini cab.

"Everything all right?"

"Yes. And you?"

"Fine."

I said nothing about myself, nor did she about herself. But the reasons for that reticence were very different. I had no intention of putting into words what had happened to me: it was a bare fact, it had to do with my body, its physiological reactivity. That for the first time a tiny part of another body had entered it seemed to me irrelevant: the nighttime mass of Sarratore communicated to me nothing except a sensation of alienness, and it was a relief that it had vanished like a storm that never arrives. It seemed to me clear, instead, that Lila was silent because she didn't have words. I felt she was in a state without thoughts or images, as if in detaching herself from Nino she had forgotten in him everything of herself, even the capacity to say what had happened to her, what was happening. This difference between us made me sad. I tried to search in my experience on the beach for something equivalent to her sorrowful-happy disorientation. I also realized that at the Maronti, in Barano, I had left nothing, not even that new self that had been revealed. I had taken everything with me, and so I didn't feel the urgency, which I read in Lila's eyes, in her half-closed mouth, in her clenched fists, to go back, to be reunited with the person I had had to leave. And if on the surface my condition might seem more solid, more compact, here instead, beside Lila, I felt sodden, earth too soaked with water.

73.

Fortunately I didn't read her notebooks until later. There were pages and pages about that day and night with Nino, and what those pages said was exactly what I hadn't had and couldn't say. Lila wrote not even a word about sexual pleasures, nothing that might be useful in comparing her experience with mine. She talked instead about love and she did so in a surprising way. She said that from the day of her marriage until those days on Ischia she had been, without realizing it, on the point of dying. She described minutely a sensation of imminent death: lack of energy, lethargy, a strong pressure in the middle of her head, as if between the brain and the skull there was an air bubble that was continually expanding, the impression that everything was moving in a hurry to leave, that the speed of every movement of persons and things was excessive and hit her, wounded her, caused her physical pain in her stomach and in her eyes. She said that all this was accompanied by a dulling of the senses, as if they had been wrapped in cotton wool, and her wounds came not from the real world but from a hollow space between her body and the mass of cotton wool in which she felt she was wrapped. She admitted on the other hand that imminent death seemed to her so assured that it took away her respect for everything, above all for herself, as if nothing counted anymore and everything deserved to be ruined. At times she was overwhelmed by a mania to express herself with no mediation: express herself for the last time, before becoming like Melina, before crossing the *stradone* just as a truck was coming, and be hit, dragged away. Nino had changed that state, he had snatched her away from death. And he had done it when he had asked her to dance, at Professor Galiani's house, and she had refused, frightened by that offer of salvation. Then, on Ischia, day by day, he had assumed the power of the savior. He had restored to her the capacity to feel. He had above all brought back to life her sense of herself. Yes, brought to life. Lines and lines and lines had at their center the concept of resurrection: an ecstatic rising, the end of every bond and yet the inexpressible pleasure of a new bond, a revival that was also a revolt: he and she, she and he together learned life again, banished its poison, reinvented it as the pure joy of thinking and living.

This, more or less. Her words were very beautiful, mine are only a summary. If she had confided it to me then, in the taxi, I would have suffered even more, because I would have recognized in her fulfillment the reverse of my emptiness. I would have understood that she had come to something that I thought I knew, that I had believed I felt for Nino, and that, instead, I didn't know, and perhaps would never know, except in a weak, muted form. I would have understood that she wasn't playing a summer game for fun but that a violent feeling was growing inside her and would overwhelm her. Instead, as we were returning to Nunzia after our violations, I couldn't get away from the usual confused sense of disparity, the impression—recurrent in our story—that I was losing something and she was gaining. So occasionally I felt the need to even the score, to tell her how I had lost my virginity between sea and sky, at night, on the beach at the Maronti. I couldn't tell her the name of Nino's father, I thought, I could invent a sailor, a smuggler of American cigarettes, and tell her what had happened to me, tell her how good it had been. But I realized that to tell her about me and my pleasure didn't matter to me, I would tell my story only to induce her to tell hers and find out how much pleasure she had had with Nino and compare it with mine and feel—I hoped—in the lead. Luckily I sensed that she would never do it and that I would only have stupidly exposed myself. I remained silent, as she did.

74.

Once we were home Lila found words again, along with an overexcited expansiveness. Nunzia welcomed us, greatly relieved by our return and yet hostile. She said she hadn't closed an eye, she had heard inexplicable noises in the house, had been afraid of ghosts and murderers. Lila embraced her and Nunzia almost pushed her away.

"Did you have fun?" she asked.

"A lot of fun, I want to change everything."

"What do you want to change?"

Lila laughed. "I'll think about it and let you know."

"Let your husband know first of all," Nunzia said, in an unexpectedly sharp tone.

Her daughter looked at her in amazement, a pleased, and perhaps slightly moved, amazement, as if the suggestion seemed to her right and urgent.

"Yes," she said, and went to her room, then to the bathroom.

She came out after a while and, still in her slip, motioned me to come to her room. I went reluctantly. She gazed at me with feverish eyes, she spoke rapidly, almost breathlessly: "I want to study what he studies."

"He's at the university, the subjects are difficult."

"I want to read the same books as him, I want to understand the things he thinks, I want to learn not for the university but for him."

"Lila, don't act crazy: we said that you would see him this time and that's all. What's wrong with you, calm down, Stefano is about to get here."

"Do you think, if I work hard, I can understand the things he understands?"

I couldn't take it anymore. What I already knew and what I nevertheless was hiding from myself became at that moment perfectly clear: she, too, now saw in Nino the only person able to save her. She had taken possession of my old feeling, had made it her own. And, knowing what she was like, I had no doubts: she would knock down every obstacle and continue to the end. I answered harshly.

"No. It's complicated stuff, you're too behind in everything, you don't read a newspaper, you don't know who's in the government, you don't even know who runs Naples."

"And do you know those things?"

"No."

"He thinks you know them, I told you, he thinks a lot of you."

I felt myself flushing, I muttered, "I'm trying to learn, and when I don't know I pretend to know."

"Even pretending to know, one gradually learns. Can you help me?"

"No, and no, Lila, it's not something you should do. Leave him alone, because of you he's already saying that he wants to stop going to the university."

"He'll study, he was born for that. And yet there are a lot of things that even he doesn't know. If I study the things he doesn't know, I'll tell him when he needs them and so I'll be useful to him. I have to change, Lenù, immediately."

I burst out again: "You're married, you have to get him out of your head, you're not right for what he needs."

"Who is right?"

I wanted to wound her, I said, "Nadia."

"He left her for me."

"So everything's fine? I don't want to listen to you anymore, you're both out of your minds, do what you like."

I went to my room, consumed by unhappiness.

75.

Stefano arrived at the usual time. We all three greeted him

with false cheerfulness, and he was polite but a little tense, as if behind his benign expression he had a worry. Since his vacation was to begin that day, I was surprised that he hadn't brought any luggage. Lila didn't seem to notice, but Nunzia did and asked him, "You look preoccupied, Ste', is something worrying you? Is your mamma well? And Pinuccia? And how are things with the shoes? What do the Solaras say, are they pleased?" He said that everything was fine, and we had dinner, but the conversation was forced. First Lila made an effort to seem in a good mood, but when Stefano responded with monosyllables and no sign of affection she became annoyed and was silent. Only Nunzia and I tried every possible means to keep the silence from becoming permanent. When we got to the fruit Stefano, with a half smile, said to his wife:

"You go swimming with Sarratore's son?"

My breath failed. Lila answered with irritation: "Sometimes. Why?"

"How many times? One, two three, five, how many? Lenù, do you know?"

"Once," I said, " he came by two or three days ago and we all went swimming together."

Stefano, still with the half smile on his face, turned to his wife.

"And you and the son of Sarratore are so intimate that when you come out of the water you hold hands?"

Lila stared straight into his face: "Who told you that?"

"Ada."

"And who told Ada?"

"Gigliola."

"And Gigliola?"

"Gigliola saw you, bitch. She came here with Michele, they came to visit you. And it's not true that you and that piece of shit went swimming with Lenuccia, you went by yourselves and you were holding hands."

Lila got up, she said calmly, "I'm going out, I'm going for a walk."

"You're not going anywhere: sit down and answer."

Lila remained standing. She said suddenly, in Italian and with an expression that looked like weariness but which—I realized—was contempt: "How stupid I was to marry you, you're worthless. You know that Michele Solara wants me in his shop, you know that for that reason Gigliola would kill me if she could, and what do you do, you believe her? I don't want to listen to you anymore, you let yourself be manipulated like a puppet. Lenù, will you come with me?"

She was about to move toward the door and I started to get up, but Stefano leaped up and grabbed her by the arm, said to her, "You're not going anywhere. You will tell me if it's true or not that you went swimming by yourself with the son of Sarratore, if it's true or not that you go around holding hands."

Lila tried to free herself, but she couldn't. She whispered, "Let go of my arm, you make me sick."

Nunzia at that point intervened. She reproached her daughter, said she could not allow herself to say that terrible thing to Stefano. But right afterward, with a surprising energy, she nearly shouted at her son-in-law to stop it, Lila had already answered, it was envy that made Gigliola say those things, the daughter of the pastry maker was treacherous, she was afraid of losing her place in Piazza dei Martiri, she wanted to get rid of Pinuccia, too, and be the sole mistress of the shop, she who knew nothing about shoes, who didn't even know how to make pastries, while everything—everything, everything—was due to Lila, including the success of the new grocery store, and so her daughter didn't deserve to be treated like that, no, she didn't deserve it.

She was truly enraged: her face was alight, wide-eyed, at a one point she seemed to be suffocating, as she added point to point without taking a breath. But Stefano didn't listen to a word. His mother-in-law was still speaking when he yanked Lila toward the bedroom, yelling: "You will now answer me, immediately," and when she insulted him grossly and grabbed the door of a cupboard to resist, he pulled her with such force that the door opened, the cupboard tottered dangerously, with a sound of plates and glasses rattling, and Lila almost flew through the kitchen and hit the wall of the hall that led to their room. A moment later her husband had grabbed her again and, holding her by the arm, but as if he were steadying a cup by the handle, pushed her into the bedroom and closed the door.

I heard the key turn in the lock, that sound terrified me. I had seen with my own eyes, in those long moments, that Stefano really was inhabited by the ghost of his father, that the shadow of Don Achille could swell the veins of his neck and the blue network under the skin of his forehead. But, although I was frightened, I felt that I couldn't stay still, sitting at the table, like Nunzia. I grabbed the doorknob and began to shake it, to pound the wooden door with my fist, begging, "Stefano, please, it's not true, leave her alone. Stefano, don't hurt her." But by now he was sealed within his rage, I could hear him yelling that he wanted the truth, and since Lila didn't respond—in fact, it was as if she were no longer in the room—he seemed to be talking to himself and meanwhile hitting himself, striking himself, breaking things.

"I'm going to call the landlady," I said to Nunzia, and I ran down the stairs. I wanted to ask the woman if she had another key or if her grandson was there, a large man who could have broken down the door. But I knocked in vain, the woman wasn't there, or if she was she didn't open the door. Meanwhile Stefano's shouts shattered the walls, spread through the street, through the reeds, toward the sea, and yet they seemed to find no ears but mine, no one looked out of the neighboring houses, no one came running. All that came was Nunzia's pleas, in a low tone, alternating with the threat that if Stefano continued to hurt her daughter she would tell Fernando and Rino every-thing, and they, as God was her witness, would kill him.

I ran back, I didn't know what to do. I hurled myself with all the weight of my body against the door, I cried that I had called the police, they were coming. Then, since Lila still showed no signs of life, I shrieked: "Lila, are you all right? Please, Lila, tell me you're all right." Only then did we hear her voice. She spoke not to us but to her husband, coldly:

"You want the truth? Yes, the son of Sarratore and I go swimming and we hold hands. Yes, we go into the deep sea and kiss each other and touch each other. Yes, I've been fucked by him a hundred times and so I discovered that you're a shit, that you're worthless, that you only demand disgusting things that make me throw up. Is that what you want? Are you happy?"

Silence. After those words Stefano didn't take a breath, I stopped pounding on the door, Nunzia stopped crying. Outside noises returned, the cars passing, some distant voices, the hens beating their wings.

Some minutes passed and it was Stefano who began speak-ing again, but so softly that we couldn't hear what he was say-ing. I realized, though, that he was looking for a way to calm down: short, disconnected phrases, show me that you're done, be good, stop it. Lila's confession must have seemed so unbear-able that he had ended by taking it as a lie. He had seen in it something she resorted to in order to hurt him, an exaggera-tion equivalent to a solid punch to bring his feet back to the ground, words that in short meant: if you still don't realize what groundless things you're accusing me of, now I'm going to make it clear to you, you just listen.

But to me Lila's words seemed as terrible as Stefano's blows. I felt that if the excessive violence he repressed behind his polite manners and his meek face terrified me, I now couldn't bear her courage, that audacious impudence that allowed her to cry out the truth as if it were a lie. Every single word that she had addressed to Stefano had returned him to his senses, because he considered it a lie, but had pierced me painfully, because I knew the truth. When the voice of the grocer reached us more clearly, both Nunzia and I felt that the worst had passed, Don Achille was withdrawing from his son and returning him to his gentle, pliable side. And Stefano, restored to the part of himself that had made him a successful shop-keeper, was bewildered, he didn't understand what had happened to his voice, his hands, his arms. Even though the image of Lila and Nino holding hands probably persisted in his mind, what Lila had evoked for him with that hail of words could not help but have the flashing features of unreality.

The door didn't open, the key didn't turn in the lock until it was day. But Stefano's voice became sad, a depressed pleading, and Nunzia and I waited outside for hours, keeping each other company with despondent, barely heard remarks. Whispered words inside, whispered words outside. "If I tell Rino," Nunzia murmured, "he'll kill him, surely he'll kill him." And I whispered, as if I believed her: "Please, don't tell him." But meanwhile I thought: Rino, and even Fernando, after the wedding never moved a finger for Lila; not to mention that ever since she was born they've hit her whenever they wanted. And then I said to myself: men are all made of the same clay, only Nino is different. And I sighed, while my resentment grew stronger: now it's absolutely clear that Lila will have him, even if she's married, and together they'll get out of this filth, while I will be here forever.

76.

At the first light of dawn Stefano came out of his bedroom, Lila didn't. He said, "Pack your bags, we're leaving."

Nunzia couldn't contain herself and bitterly pointed out the damage he had done to the landlady's things, saying that he would have to compensate her. He answered—as if many of the words she had shouted at him hours earlier had stayed in his mind and he felt the need to dot the "i"s—that he always paid and would continue to pay. "I paid for this house," he enumerated in a tired voice, "I paid for your vacation, everything you, your husband, your son have I've given you: so don't be a pain in the neck, pack the bags and let's go."

Nunzia didn't say another word. A little later Lila came out of the room in a yellow dress with long sleeves and big dark glasses, like a movie star. She didn't say a word to us. She didn't at the Port, or on the boat, or even when we reached the neighborhood. She went home with her husband without saying goodbye.

As for me, I decided that from that moment on I would live for myself only, and as soon as we returned to Naples that was what I did, I imposed on myself an attitude of absolute detachment. I didn't look for Lila, I didn't look for Nino. I accepted without argument the scene that my mother made, as she accused me of having gone to play the lady on Ischia without thinking about how we needed money at home. Even my father, although he praised my healthy appearance, the golden blond of my hair, did the same: as soon as my mother attacked me in his presence, he backed her up. "You're a grownup," he said, "you see what you have to do."

Earning money was, in fact, an urgent necessity. I could have demanded from Lila what she had promised me in compensation for my coming to Ischia, but after that decision to cut myself off from her, and especially after the brutal words that Stefano had addressed to Nunzia (and in some way also to me), I didn't do it. For the same reason I absolutely ruled out the idea of her buying my school books, as she had the year before. When I saw Alfonso I asked him to tell her that I had already taken care of the books, and closed the discussion.

But after the August holiday I presented myself again at the bookstore on Mezzocannone, and partly because I had been an efficient and disciplined salesclerk, partly because of my looks, which had been improved by the sun and the sea, the owner, after some resistance, gave me back my job. He insisted, however, that I should not quit when school started but continue to work, if only in the afternoons, for the entire period of schoolbook sales. I agreed and spent long hours in the bookstore greeting teachers who came with bags full of books they had received free from publishing houses, to sell for a few lire, and students who sold their tattered used books for even less.

I lived through a week of pure anguish when my period didn't come. Afraid that Sarratore had made me pregnant, I was in despair; I was polite on the outside, grim inside. I spent sleepless nights, but didn't ask advice or comfort from anyone, I kept it all to myself. Finally, one afternoon in the bookstore I went to the dirty toilet and found the blood. It was one of the rare moments of well-being during that time. My period seemed a sort of symbolic cancellation of Sarratore's incursion into my body.

In early September it occurred to me that Nino must have returned from Ischia and I began to fear and hope that he would come by at least to say hello. But he didn't show up on Via Mezzocannone or in the neighborhood. As for Lila, I saw her only a couple of times, on Sunday, when, beside her husband in the car, she drove by on the *stradone*. Those few seconds were enough to enrage me. What had happened. How she had arranged things for herself. She continued to have everything, to keep everything: the car, Stefano, the house with the bathroom and the telephone and the television, the nice clothes, the prosperity. And who could say what plans she was devising in the secrecy of her mind. I knew how she was made and I said to myself that she wouldn't give up Nino even if Nino gave up her. But I chased away those thoughts and forced myself to respect the pact I had made with myself: to plan my life without them and learn not to suffer for it. To that end I concentrated on training myself to react little or not at all. I learned to reduce my emotions to the minimum: if the owner reached out his hands I repulsed him without indignation; if the customers were rude I made the best of it; even with my mother I managed to stay submissive. I said to myself every day: I am what I am and I have to accept myself; I was born like this, in this city, with this dialect, without money; I will give what I can give, I will take what I can take, I will endure what has to be endured.

77.

Then school began again. Only when I entered the classroom on the first of October did I realize that I was in my last year of high school, that I was eighteen years old, that the years of school, in my case already miraculously long, were about to end. So much the better. Alfonso and I talked a lot about what we would do after we graduated. He knew as much as I did. We'll take a civil-service exam, he said, but in fact we didn't have clear ideas on what the exams entailed; we said *sit the exam, pass the exam*, but the concept was vague: did you have to do a written exercise, take an oral test? And what did you get once you'd taken it, a salary?

Alfonso confided that he was thinking of getting married, once he had taken the exam and gained a post.

"To Marisa?"

"Yes, of course."

Sometimes I asked him warily about Nino, but he didn't like Nino, they didn't even say hello to each other. He had never understood what I found in him. He's ugly, he said, all out of proportion, skin and bone. Marisa, on the other hand, seemed pretty to him. But he immediately added, careful not to wound me, "You're pretty, too." He liked beauty, and especially appreciated care for one's body. He himself was attentive to his appearance, he smelled of the barber, he bought clothes, he lifted weights every day. He told me that he had a good time at the shop in Piazza dei Martiri. It wasn't like the grocery. There you could be elegant, in fact you had to be. There you could speak Italian, the people were respectable, had gone to school. There, even when you were on your knees in front of the customers, men and women, trying on the shoes, you could do it with pleasant manners, like the knight in a courtly love story. But unfortunately he wouldn't be able to stay in the shop.

"Why?"

"Well . . . "

At first he was vague and I didn't insist. Then he told me that Pinuccia was staying home now because she didn't want to get tired, she had a belly like a torpedo; and anyway it was clear that once she had the baby she wouldn't have time to work. This in theory should have cleared a path for him, the Solaras were pleased with him, maybe he would be able to establish himself there after he graduated. But it wasn't possible, and here suddenly the name of Lila came up. Just hearing it my stomach flared up.

"What does she have to do with it?"

I knew she had returned from the vacation like a madwoman. She still wasn't pregnant, the swimming had been of no use, she was behaving oddly. Once she had broken all the flowerpots on her balcony. She said she was going to the grocery, instead she left Carmen alone and went walking around. Stefano woke up at night and she wasn't in bed: she was wandering through the house, she read and wrote. Then suddenly she calmed down. Or rather she focused her entire capacity to spoil Stefano's life on a single objective: for Gigliola to work in the new grocery, and she in Piazza dei Martiri.

I was amazed.

"It's Michele who wants her in the shop," I said, "but she doesn't want to go."

"Once. Now she's changed her mind, she's moving heaven and earth to get herself there. The only obstacle is Stefano, he's against it. But of course in the end my brother does what she wants."

I asked no other questions, I wanted in no way to be reabsorbed into Lila's affairs. But for a while I surprised myself by wondering: what could she have in mind, why all of a sudden does she want to go and work in the city? Then I forgot about it, taken up by other problems: the bookstore, school, the class interrogations, the textbooks. Some I bought, most I stole from the bookstore without too many scruples. I began studying rigorously again, mainly at night. In the afternoon, in fact, until Christmas vacation, when I quit, I was busy at the bookstore. And right after that Professor Galiani herself arranged a couple of private pupils for me, and I worked hard for them. Between school, lessons, and study, there was no room for anything else.

When at the end of the month I gave my mother the money I earned, she put it in her pocket without saying anything, but in the morning she got up early to make breakfast for me, sometimes even a beaten egg, which she devoted such care to—while I was still in bed half asleep, I heard the *clack clack* of the spoon against the cup as she beat in the sugar—that it melted in my mouth like a cream, the sugar completely dissolved. As for the teachers at school, it seemed that they couldn't help considering me a brilliant student, as if the sluggish operation of the entire dusty scholastic machine had decided it. I had no trouble defending my position as first in the class and, with Nino gone, I ranked among the best in the whole school. But I soon realized that although Professor Galiani continued to be very generous, she blamed me for some offense that kept her from being as friendly as she had been in the past. For example, when I gave her back her books she was annoyed, because they were sandy, and took them away without promising to give me others. For example, she no longer offered me her newspapers, and for a while I forced myself to buy *Il Mattino*, then I stopped, it bored me, it was a waste of money. For example, she never invited me to her house, although I would have liked to see her son Armando again. Yet she continued to praise me publicly, to give me high grades, to advise me about important lectures and even films that were shown in a parish hall in Port'Alba. Until once, near Christmas vacation, she called as school was letting out and we walked some way together. Bluntly she asked what I knew about Nino.

"Nothing," I said.

"Tell me the truth."

"It's the truth."

It slowly emerged that Nino, after the summer, had not been in touch either with her or with her daughter.

"He broke up with Nadia in a very unpleasant way," she said, with the resentment of a mother. "He sent her a few lines in a letter from Ischia and caused her a lot of suffering." Then she contained herself and added, resuming her role as a professor again: "Never mind, you're all young, suffering helps one grow."

I nodded yes, she asked me: "Did he leave you, too?"

I turned red. "Me?"

"Didn't you see each other on Ischia?"

"Yes, but there was nothing between us."

"Really?"

"Absolutely."

"Nadia is convinced that he left her for you."

I denied it forcefully, I said I would be happy to see Nadia and tell her that between me and Nino there had never been anything and never would be. She was pleased, she assured me that she would report that. I didn't mention Lila, naturally, and not only because I had decided to mind my own business but also because to talk about it would have depressed me. I tried to change the subject, but she returned to Nino. She said that various rumors were circulating about him. There were some who said that not only had he not taken his exams in the autumn but he had stopped studying; and there were some who swore they had seen him one afternoon on Via Arenaccia, alone, completely drunk, lurching along, and every so often taking a swig from a bottle. But not everyone, she concluded, found him likable and maybe there were people who enjoyed spreading nasty rumors about him. If, however, they were true, what a pity.

"Surely they're lies," I said.

"Let's hope so. But it's hard to keep up with that boy."

"Yes."

"He's very smart."

"Yes."

"If you have a way of finding out what's happening, let me know."

We parted. I hurried off to give a Greek lesson to a girl in middle school who lived in Parco Margherita. But it was difficult. The large, permanently semi-dark room where I was greeted respectfully held heavy furniture, rugs with hunting scenes, old photographs of high-ranking soldiers, and various other signs of a long history of authority and ease that produced in my pale fourteen-year-old pupil a dullness of body and intelligence, and in me a feeling of impatience. That day I had to struggle to supervise declensions and conjugations. The picture of Nino as Professor Galiani had evoked him kept returning to my mind: worn jacket, tie flying, long legs staggering, the empty bottle that after the last swallow shattered on the stones of Via Arenaccia. What had happened between him and Lila, after Ischia? Contrary to my predictions, she had evidently seen her mistake, it was all over, she had returned to herself. Nino hadn't: from a studious youth with a well-formulated response to everything he had become a vagrant, undone by the pain of love for the grocer's wife. I thought of asking Alfonso again if he had news. I thought of going to Marisa myself and asking her about her brother. But soon I forced the idea out of my mind. It will pass, I said to myself. Has he come to see me? No. Has Lila come to see me? No. Why should I worry about him, or her, when they don't care about me? I continued the lesson and went on my way.

78.

After Christmas I found out from Alfonso that Pinuccia had given birth, she had had a boy, named Fernando. I went to see her, thinking that I would find her in bed, happy, with the baby at her breast. Instead, she was up, but in nightgown and slippers, sulking. She rudely sent away her mother, who said to her, "Get in bed, don't tire yourself," and when she led me to the cradle she said grimly, "Nothing ever works out for me, look how ugly he is, it upsets me just to look at him, let alone touch him." And although Maria, standing in the doorway, murmured, like a soothing formula, "What are you talking about, Pina, he's beautiful," she continued to repeat angrily, "He's ugly, he's uglier than Rino, that whole family is ugly." Then she drew in her breath and exclaimed desperately, with tears in her eyes, "It's my fault, I made a bad choice of a husband, but when you're a girl you don't think about it, and now look at what a child I've had, he has a pug nose just like Lina." Then, with no interruption, she began to insult her sister-in-law grossly.

I learned from her that Lila, the whore, had already in two weeks done and redone as she liked the shop in Piazza dei Martiri. Gigliola had had to give in, she had returned to the Solaras' pastry shop; she herself, Pinuccia, had had to give in, chained to the child until goodness knows when; they had all had to give in, Stefano above all, as usual. And now, every day, Lila was up to something new: she went to work dressed up as if she were Mike Bongiorno's assistant, and if her husband wouldn't take her in the car she had no scruples about getting Michele to drive her; she had spent who knows how much for two paintings that you couldn't understand what they were of, and had hung them in the shop for who knows what purpose; she had bought a lot of books and, instead of shoes, she put those on the shelf; she had fitted out a sort of living room, with couches, chairs, ottomans, and a crystal bowl where she kept chocolates from Gay Odin, available to whoever wanted them, free, as if she were there not to notice the stink of the customers' feet but to play the great lady in her castle.

"And it's not only that," she said, "there's something even worse."

"What?"

"You know what Marcello Solara did?"

"No."

"You remember the shoes that Stefano and Rino gave him?"

"The ones made exactly the way Lina designed them?"

"Yes, a wretched shoe, Rino always said that the water got in."

"Well, what happened?"

Pina overwhelmed me with a laborious, sometimes confused story, involving money, treacherous plots, deception, debts. Marcello, dissatisfied with the new models made by Rino and Fernando—and certainly in agreement with Michele—had had shoes like those manufactured, but not in the Cerullo factory, in another factory, in Afragola. Then, at Christmas, he had distributed them under the Solara name in the stores, including the one on Piazza dei Martiri.

"And he could do that?"

"Of course, they're his: my brother and my husband, those two shits, gave them to him, he can do what he likes."

"So?"

"So," she said, "now there are Cerullo shoes and Solara shoes circulating in Naples. And the Solara shoes are selling really well, better than the Cerullos. And all the profit is the Solaras'. So Rino is extremely upset, because he expected some competition, of course, but not from the Solaras themselves, his partners, and with a shoe he made with his own hands and then stupidly threw away."

I remembered Marcello when Lila threatened him with the shoemaker's knife. He was slower than Michele, more timid. What need had he to be so offensive? The Solaras had numerous businesses, some legitimate, others not, and they were getting bigger every day. They had had powerful friendships since the days of their grandfather, they did favors and received them. Their mother was a loan shark and had a book that struck fear into half the neighborhood, maybe now the Cerullos and the Carraccis, too. For Marcello, then, and for his brother, the shoes and the shop on Piazza dei Martiri were only one of the many wells into which their family dipped, and surely not among the most important. So why?

Pinuccia's story began to disturb me. Behind the appearance of money I felt something depressing. Marcello's love for Lila was over, but the wound had remained and become infected. No longer dependent, he felt free to hurt those who had humiliated him in the past. "Rino," Pinuccia in fact said, "went with Stefano to protest, but it was pointless." The Solaras had treated them contemptuously, they were people used to doing what they wanted, her brother and husband might as well have been talking to themselves. Finally Marcello had said vaguely that he and his brother were thinking of an entire Solara line that would repeat, with variations, the features of the shoe that had been made as a trial. And then he had added, without a clear connection, "Let's see how your new products go and if it's worth the trouble to keep them on the market." Understood? Understood. Marcello wanted to eliminate the Cerullo brand, replace it with Solara, and thus cause not insignificant economic damage to Stefano. I have to get out of the neighborhood, out of Naples, I said to myself, what do I care about their quarrels? But in the meantime I asked:

"And Lina?"

Pinuccia's eyes blazed.

"She's the real problem."

Lina had laughed at that story. When Rino and her husband got angry she made fun of them: "You gave him those shoes, not me; you did business with the Solaras, not me. If you two are idiots, what can I do?" She wouldn't cooperate, you couldn't tell where she stood, with the family or with the Solaras. So when Michele again insisted that he wanted her in Piazza dei Martiri, she had suddenly said yes, and had tormented Stefano to let her go.

"And why in the world did Stefano give in?" I asked.

Pinuccia let out a long sigh of impatience. Stefano had given in because he hoped that Lila, seeing that Michele valued her so much, and seeing that Marcello had always had a weakness for her, would manage to settle things. But Rino didn't trust his sister, he was frightened, he couldn't sleep at night. He liked the old shoe that he and Fernando had thrown away and that Marcello had had made in its original form; it sold well. What would happen if the Solaras began to deal with Lila directly and if she, a bitch since the day she was born, after refusing to design new shoes for the family, went on to design shoes for them?

"It won't happen," I said to Pinuccia.

"Did she tell you?"

"No, I haven't seen her since the summer."

"So?"

"I know what she's like. Lina gets curious about a thing and she's utterly caught up in it. But once she's done it, the desire goes away, she doesn't care about it anymore."

"You're sure?"

"Yes."

Maria was content with those words of mine, she clung to them to soothe her daughter.

"You hear?" she said. "Everything is fine, Lenuccia knows what she's talking about."

But in fact I knew nothing, the less pedantic part of me was well aware of Lila's unpredictability, so I couldn't wait to get out of that house. What do I have to do with it, I thought, with these wretched stories, with the petty vendetta of Marcello Solara, with this struggle and worry over money, cars, houses, furniture and knickknacks and vacations? And how could Lila, after Ischia, after Nino, go back to jousting with those thugs? I'll get my diploma, I'll take the entrance exams, I'll win. I'll get out of this muck, go as far away as possible. I said, softening toward the baby, whom Maria was now holding in her arms: "How cute he is."

79.

But I couldn't resist. I put it off for a long time and finally I gave in: I asked Alfonso if one Sunday we could go for a walk, he and Marisa and I. Alfonso was pleased, we went to a pizzeria on Via Foria. I asked about Lidia, the children, especially Ciro, and then I asked what Nino was up to. She answered reluctantly, talking about her brother upset her. She said that he had gone through a long period of madness, and her father, whom she adored, had had a difficult time with him; Nino had gone so far as to lay hands on him. What the cause of the madness was they never found out: he didn't want to study anymore, he wanted to leave Italy. Then suddenly it was over: he returned to himself and had just begun to take his exams.

"So he's all right?"

"Who knows."

"He's happy?"

"As far as somebody like him is capable of being happy, yes."

"And all he does is study?"

"You mean does he have a girlfriend?"

"No, of course not, I mean does he go out, does he have fun, does he go dancing."

"How should I know, Lenù? He's always out. Now he's obsessed with movies, novels, art, and the rare times he comes by the house he starts arguing with Papa, just to insult him and quarrel with us."

I felt relieved that Nino had come to his senses, but I was also bitter. Movies, novels, art? How quickly people changed, with their interests, their feelings. Well-made phrases replaced by well-made phrases, time is a flow of words coherent only in appearance, the one who piles up the most is the one who wins. I felt stupid, I had neglected the things I liked to conform to what Nino liked. Yes, yes, resign yourself to what you are, each on his own path. I only hoped that Marisa would not tell him that she had seen me and that I had asked about him. Not even to Alfonso, after that evening, did I mention Nino or Lila.

I withdrew even more into my duties, I multiplied them in order to cram my days and nights. That year I studied obsessively, punctiliously, and I even took on a new private lesson, for a lot of money. I imposed on myself an iron discipline, much harsher than what I had enforced since childhood. A marking of time, a straight line that went from dawn until late at night. In the past there had been Lila, a continuous happy detour into surprising lands. Now everything I was I wanted to get from myself. I was almost nineteen, I would never again depend on someone, and I would never again miss someone.

The last year of high school slipped by like a single day. I struggled with astronomical geography, with geometry, with trigonometry. It was a sort of race to know everything, when in fact I took it for granted that my inadequacy was constitutional and so couldn't be eliminated. Yet I liked to do my best. I didn't have time to go to the movies? I learned titles and plots. Hadn't been to the archeological museum? I ran through it in half a day. Hadn't been to the picture gallery of Capodimonte? I made a flying visit, two hours and done. I had too much to do, in short. What did I care about shoes and the shop on Piazza dei Martiri? I never went there.

Sometimes I met Pinuccia, disheveled-looking, as she pushed Fernando in his carriage. I stopped a moment, listened absent-mindedly to her complaints about Rino, Stefano, Lila, Gigliola, everyone. Sometimes I ran into Carmen, who was increasingly bitter about how badly things had been going in the new grocery since Lila left, abandoning her to the oppression of Maria and Pinuccia, and I let her vent for a few minutes about how she missed Enzo Scanno, how she counted the days as she waited for him to finish his military service, how her brother Pasquale slaved, between his construction work and his Communist activities. Sometimes I ran into Ada, who had begun to hate Lila, while she was very pleased with Stefano, and spoke of him tenderly, and not only because he had recently increased her salary but also because he was a hard worker, available to everyone, and didn't deserve that wife who treated him like dirt.

It was she who told me that Antonio had been discharged early because of a severe nervous breakdown.

"What happened?"

"You know what he's like, he already had a breakdown with you."

It was a mean statement that wounded me, I tried not to think about it. One Sunday in winter I ran into Antonio and scarcely recognized him, he was so thin. I smiled at him, expecting him to stop, but he seemed not to notice me and kept going. I called him, he turned, with a disoriented smile.

"Hello, Lenù."

"Hello, I'm so glad to see you."

"Me, too."

"What are you doing?"

"Nothing."

"You're not going back to the workshop?"

"There's no job."

"You're good, you'll find something somewhere else."

"No, if I don't get better I can't work."

"What's wrong with you?"

"Fear."

He said it just like that: fear. In Cordenons, one night, while he was on guard duty, he had remembered a game that his father played when he was still alive and he himself was very small: with a pen his father would draw eyes and mouths on the five fingers of his left hand, and then he would move them and make them talk as if they were people. It was such a sweet game that, as he remembered it, tears came to his eyes. But that night, during his shift, he had had the impression that his father's hand had entered his and that now he had real people inside his fingers, tiny but fully formed, who were laughing and singing. That was the source of the fear. He banged his hand against the sentry box until it bled, but the fingers went on laughing and singing, without stopping, not for an instant. He recovered only when his shift was over and he went to sleep. A little rest and the next morning it was gone. But the terror that the illness in his hand would return remained. In fact it did return, and, with increasing frequency, his fingers began to laugh and sing even in the daytime. Until he had gone mad and they had sent him to the doctor.

"It's gone now," he said, "but it could always start again."

"Tell me how I can help you."

He thought for a while, as if he were really evaluating a series of possibilities. He muttered, "No one can help me."

I immediately understood that he no longer felt anything for me, I had definitively gone out of his mind. So after that encounter I got in the habit of going every Sunday to his windows and calling. We would take a walk around the courtyard, talking about this and that, and when he said he was tired we said goodbye. Sometimes Melina came down with him, garishly made up, and he and his mother and I walked. Sometimes we met Ada and Pasquale and took a longer walk, but then it was generally the three of us who talked, Antonio was silent. In other words it became a peaceful routine. I went with him to the funeral of Nicola Scanno, the fruit-and-vegetable seller, who died suddenly of pneumonia; Enzo came home on leave but wasn't in time to see him alive. We also went together to console Pasquale, Carmen, and their mother, Giuseppina, when they learned that their father, the former carpenter who had killed Don Achille, had died in prison from a heart attack. And we were together also when we learned that Don Carlo Resta, the seller of soap and various household items, had been beaten to death in his cellar. We talked about it for a long time, the whole neighborhood talked about it, the talk spread truths and cruel rumors, someone said that the beating wasn't enough and they had stuck a file in his nose. Some vagrants were blamed for the crime, people who had stolen the day's cash. But Pasquale, later, told us he had heard rumors that in his view were well founded: Don Carlo was in debt to the mother of the Solaras, because he had the vice of gambling and went to her so that he could pay his debts.

320 · ELENA FERRANTE

"So what?" asked Ada, who was always skeptical when her fiancé came up with reckless hypotheses.

"So he wouldn't pay what he owed the loan shark and they had him murdered."

"Come on, you always talk such nonsense."

It's likely that Pasquale was exaggerating, but, first of all, no one knew who had killed Don Carlo Resta, and, second, it was, precisely, the Solaras who took over the shop, along with its stock, for very little money, even though they left Don Carlo's wife and oldest son there to manage it.

"Out of generosity," said Ada.

"Because they're bastards," said Pasquale.

I don't remember if Antonio made comments on that episode. He was crushed by his illness, which Pasquale's speeches in some way made more acute. It seemed to him that the dysfunction of his body was spreading to the whole neighborhood and was manifested in the bad things that happened.

The worst thing for us happened on a warm Sunday in the spring, when Pasquale and Ada and he and I were waiting in the courtyard for Carmela, who had gone up to get a pullover. Five minutes passed; Carmen looked out the window, shouted to her brother: "Pasquà, I can't find mamma. The door of the bathroom is locked from the inside but she doesn't answer."

Pasquale took the stairs two at a time and we followed. We found Carmela standing anxiously in front of the bathroom door, and Pasquale knocked, politely, again and again, but no one answered. Antonio then said to his friend, indicating the door: don't worry, I'll put it back in place, and, grabbing the handle, he practically tore it off.

The door opened. Giuseppina Peluso had been a radiant woman, energetic, hardworking, kindly, capable of confronting all adversities. She had continued, without fail, to occupy herself with her imprisoned husband, whose arrest—I remembered—she had opposed with all her strength, when he

was accused of killing Don Achille Carracci. She had thought-
fully accepted Stefano's invitation to spend New Year's Eve
together four years earlier, pleased with that reconciliation
between the families. And she had been happy when her
daughter found work, thanks to Lila, in the grocery in the new
neighborhood. But now, with her husband dead, evidently she
was worn out, she had become in a short time a tiny woman,
skin and bone, without her old vigor. She had unfastened the
lamp in the bathroom, a metal plate hanging on a chain, and
had attached a clothesline to the hook set in the ceiling. Then
she had hanged herself by the neck.

Antonio saw her first and burst into tears. It was easier to
calm Giuseppina's children, Carmen and Pasquale, than him.
He repeated to me, horrified: Did you see that her feet were
bare and that the nails were long and that on one foot there
was fresh red nail polish and not on the other? I hadn't noticed
but he had. He had returned from military service more convinced than before, in spite of his nervous breakdown, that his
job was to be the man in every situation, the one who hurls
himself into danger, fearlessly, and resolves every problem. But
he was fragile. For weeks after that episode, he saw Giuseppina
in every dark corner of the house, and he got worse, so I neglected some of my obligations to help him calm down. He was
the only person in the neighborhood I saw more or less regularly until I took my graduation exams. I had just a glimpse of
Lila, next to her husband, at Giuseppina's funeral, while she
hugged Carmen, who was sobbing. She and Stefano had sent a
large wreath on whose violet ribbon the condolences of the
Carracci spouses could be read.

80.

It wasn't because of the exams that I stopped seeing Antonio.

The two things happened to coincide, because just then he came to see me, rather relieved, to tell me that he had accepted a job from the Solara brothers. I didn't like it, it seemed to me another sign of his illness. He hated the Solaras. He had scuffled with them as a boy to defend his sister. He, Pasquale, and Enzo had beaten up Marcello and Michele and destroyed their car. But the main thing was that he had left me because I went to ask Marcello for his help in getting Antonio out of military service. Why, then, had he succumbed like that? He gave me confused explanations. He said that in the Army he had learned that if you are a simple soldier you owe obedience to anyone who wears stripes. He said that order is better than disorder. He said he had learned how you come up behind a man and kill him before he has even heard you arrive. I understood that the illness had something to do with it but that the real problem was poverty. He had presented himself at the bar to ask for work. And Marcello had treated him a little roughly but then had offered him a fixed amount each month—he put it like that—without, however, a precise duty, only to be available.

"Available?"

"Yes."

"Available for what?"

"I don't know."

"Forget it, Antò."

He didn't. And because of that job he ended up quarreling with both Pasquale and Enzo, who had returned from military service more taciturn than before, more inflexible. Illness or not, neither of them could forgive Antonio for that decision. Pasquale, although he was engaged to Ada, went so far as to threaten him, he said that, brother-in-law or not, he didn't want to see him anymore.

I quickly got away from these problems and concentrated on my graduation exam. While I studied day and night, sometimes, overwhelmed by the heat, I thought again about the previous summer, before Pinuccia left, when Lila, Nino, and I were a happy trio, or at least so it seemed to me. But I repressed every image, and even the faintest echo of a word: I allowed no distractions.

The exam was a crucial moment of my life. In a couple of hours I wrote an essay on the role of Nature in the poetry of Giacomo Leopardi, putting in, along with lines I knew by heart, finely written reworkings from the textbook of Italian literary history; but, most important, I handed in my Latin and Greek tests when my schoolmates, including Alfonso, had barely started on it. This attracted the attention of the examiners, in particular of an old, extremely thin teacher, with a pink suit and freshly coiffed, pale-blue hair, who kept smiling at me. But the real turning point took place during the oral exams. I was praised by all the professors, but in particular I gained the approval of the examiner with the blue hair. She had been struck by my essay not only because of what I said but because of how I said it.

"You write very well," she said, with an accent I didn't recognize, but anyway far from Neapolitan.

"Thank you."

"Do you really think that nothing is fated to last, not even poetry?"

"That's what Leopardi thinks."

"You're sure?"

"Yes."

"And what do you think?"

"I think that beauty is a sham."

"Like the Leopardian garden?"

I didn't know anything about Leopardian gardens, but I answered, "Yes. Like the sea on a calm day. Or like a sunset. Or like the sky at night. It's like face powder patted on over the horror. If you take it away, we are left alone with our fear."

The sentences came easily, I uttered them with an inspired cadence. And, besides, I wasn't improvising, it was an adaptation of what I had written in the essay.

"What faculty do you intend to choose?"

I didn't know much about faculties, that meaning of the term was barely familiar to me. I was evasive:

"I'll sit the civil-service exam."

"You won't go to the university?"

My cheeks burned, as if I were unable to hide a sin.

"No."

"You need to work?"

"Yes."

I was dismissed, I returned to Alfonso and the others. But a little later the professor came up to me in the hallway, and talked for a long time about a kind of college in Pisa, where, if you passed an exam like the one I had already done, you studied free.

"If you come back here in a couple of days, I'll give you all the necessary information."

I listened, but the way you do when someone is talking to you about something that will never really concern you. And when, two days later, I went back to school, only out of fear that the professor would be offended and give me a low grade, I was struck by the very precise information that she had transcribed for me on a sheet of foolscap. I never met her again, I don't even know her name, and yet I owe her a great deal. Continuing to address me formally, she unaffectedly gave me a dignified farewell embrace.

The exams were over, I passed with an A average. Alfonso also did well, with a B average. Before leaving forever, with no regrets, the run-down gray building whose only merit, in my eyes, was that Nino, too, had been there, I caught sight of Professor Galiani and went to say goodbye. She congratulated me on my results but without enthusiasm. She didn't offer me books for the summer, she didn't ask what I would do now that

I had my high-school diploma. Her distant tone upset me, I thought that things between us had been settled. What was the trouble? Once Nino had left her daughter and had fallen out of touch, was I to be associated with him forever, the same clay: insubstantial, unserious, unreliable? I was used to being liked by everyone, to wrapping that liking around me like shining armor; I was disappointed, and I think that her indifference had an important role in the decision I then made. Without talking about it to anyone (who could I ask advice from, anyway, if not Professor Galiani?) I applied for admission to the Pisa Normale. I immediately started doing everything I possibly could to earn money. Since the upper-class families whose children I had given lessons to all year were happy with me and my reputation as a good teacher had spread, I was able to fill the August days with new students who had to retake, in September, their exams in Latin, Greek, history, philosophy, and even mathematics. At the end of the month I found myself rich, I had amassed seventy thousand lire. I gave fifty to my mother, who reacted with a violent gesture, she almost tore the money from my hand and stuffed it in her bra, as if we were not in the kitchen of our house but on the street and she was afraid of being robbed. I didn't tell her that I had kept twenty thousand lire for myself.

Not until the day before my departure did I tell my family that I was going to Pisa to take exams. "If they accept me," I announced, "I'll go there to study and I won't have to spend a lira for anything." I spoke with great decisiveness, in Italian, as if it were not a subject that could be reduced to dialect, as if my father, my mother, my siblings shouldn't and couldn't understand what I was about to do. In fact they confined themselves to listening uneasily, it seemed to me that in their eyes I was no longer me but a stranger who had come to visit at an inconvenient time. Finally my father said, "Do what you have to do but be careful, we can't help you." And he went to bed. My little sister asked if she could come with me. My mother, instead, said nothing, but before she vanished she left five thousand lire on the table for me. I stared at it for a long time, without touching it. Then, overcoming my scruples about how I wasted money to satisfy my whims, I thought, it's my money, and I took it.

For the first time, I left Naples, left Campania. I discovered that I was afraid of everything: afraid of taking the wrong train, afraid of having to pee and not knowing where to do it, afraid that it would be night and I wouldn't be able to orient myself in an unfamiliar city, afraid of being robbed. I put all my money in my bra, as my mother did, and spent hours in a state of wary anxiety that coexisted seamlessly with a growing sense of liberation.

Everything went well. Except the exam, it seemed. The professor with the blue hair hadn't told me that it would be much more difficult than the graduation exam. The Latin, especially, seemed complex, but really that was only the beginning: every test was the occasion for an extremely painstaking investigation of my skills. I held forth, I stammered, I often pretended to have the answer on the tip of my tongue. The professor of Italian treated me as if even the sound of my voice irritated him: *You, miss, do not make a logical argument when you write but flit from one thing to another; I see, miss, that you launch recklessly into subjects in which you are completely ignorant of the issues of critical method.* I was depressed, I quickly lost confidence in what I was saying. The professor realized it and, looking at me ironically, asked me to talk about something I had read recently. I suppose he meant something by an Italian writer, but I didn't understand and clung to the first support that seemed to me secure, that is to say the conversation we had had the summer before, on Ischia, on the beach of Citara, about Beckett and about Dan Rooney, who, although he was blind, wanted to become deaf and mute as well. The professor's ironic expression changed slowly to bewilderment. He cut me off me quickly and delivered me to the history professor. He was just as bad. He subjected me to an endless and exhausting list of questions formulated with the utmost precision. I had never felt so ignorant as I did at that moment, not even in the worst years of school, when I had done so badly. I was able to answer everything, dates, events, but only in an approximate way. As soon as he pressed me with even more exacting questions I gave up. Finally he asked me, disgusted, "Have you ever read something that is not simply the school textbook?"

I said, "I've studied the idea of nationhood."

"Do you remember the name of the author of the book?"

"Federico Chabod."

"Let's hear what you understood."

He listened to me attentively for several minutes, then abruptly dismissed me, leaving me with the certainty that I had said a lot of nonsense.

I cried and cried, as if I had carelessly lost somewhere the most promising part of myself. Then I said that despair was stupid, I had always known that I wasn't really smart. Lila, yes, she was smart, Nino, yes, he was smart. I was only presumptuous and had been justly punished.

Instead I found out that I had passed the exam. I would have a place of my own, a bed that I didn't have to make at night and unmake in the morning, a desk and all the books I needed. I, Elena Greco, the daughter of the porter, at nineteen years old was about to pull myself out of the neighborhood, I was about to leave Naples. By myself.

81.

A series of whirlwind days began. A few things to wear, a very few books. My mother's sullen words: "If you earn money, send it to me by mail; now who's going to help your brothers with their homework? They'll do badly at school because of you. But go, leave, who cares: I've always known that you thought you were better than me and everybody else." And then my father's hypochondriac words: "I have a pain here, who knows what it is, come to your papa, Lenù, I don't know if you'll find me alive when you get back." And then my brothers' and sister's insistent words: "If we come to see you can we sleep with you, can we eat with you?" And Pasquale, who said to me, "Be careful where all this studying leads, Lenù. Remember who you are and which side you're on." And Carmen, who couldn't get over the death of her mother, and was fragile, started crying as she said goodbye. And Alfonso, who was stunned and murmured, "I knew you'd keep studying." And Antonio, who instead of listening to what I was saying about where I was going, and what I was going to do, kept repeating, "I'm really feeling good now, Lenù, it's all gone, it was going into the Army that made me ill." And then Enzo, who confined himself to taking my hand and squeezing it so hard that it hurt for days. And finally Ada, who said only, "Did you tell Lina, did you tell her?" and she gave a little laugh, and insisted, "Tell her, she'll die of envy."

I imagined that Lila had already heard from Alfonso, from Carmen, from her husband, whom Ada had certainly told, that I was going to Pisa. If she didn't come to congratulate me, I thought, it's likely that the news really has disturbed her. On the other hand, if she didn't know, to go deliberately to tell her, when for more than a year we had scarcely said hello, seemed to me out of place. I didn't want to flaunt the good fortune that she hadn't had. So I set aside the question and devoted myself to the last preparations. I wrote to Nella to tell her what had happened and ask for the address of Maestra Oliviero, so that I could give her the news. I visited a cousin of my father, who had promised me an old suitcase. I made the rounds of some of the houses where I had taught and where I had to collect my final payment.

It seemed to me an occasion to give a kind of farewell to
Naples. I crossed Via Garibaldi, went along the Tribunali, at
Piazza Dante took a bus. I went up to the Vomero, first to Via
Scarlatti, then to the Santarella. Afterward I descended in the
funicular to Piazza Amedeo. I was greeted with regret and, in
some cases, affection by the mothers of my students. Along
with the money they gave me coffee and almost always a small
gift. When my rounds were over, I realized that I was a short
distance from Piazza dei Martiri.

I turned onto Via Filangieri, uncertain what to do. I
recalled the opening of the shoe store, Lila all dressed up like
a rich lady, how she was gripped by the anxiety of not having
truly changed, of not having the same refinement as the girls of
that neighborhood. I, on the other hand, I thought, really have
changed. I'm still wearing the same shabby clothes, but I've
got my high-school diploma and I'm about to go and study in
Pisa. I've changed not in appearance but deep inside. The
appearance will come soon and it won't be just appearance.

I felt pleased with that thought, that observation. I stood in
front of an optician's window, I studied the frames. Yes, I'll
have to change my glasses, the ones I have overwhelm my face,
I need lighter frames—I picked out a pair with large, round
thin rims. Put up my hair. Learn to use makeup. I left the window and arrived at Piazza dei Martiri.

Many shops at that hour had their shutters lowered halfway;
the Solaras' was three-quarters down. I looked around. What
did I know of Lila's new habits? Nothing. When she worked in
the new grocery she didn't go home for lunch, even though the
house was nearby. She stayed in the shop and ate something
with Carmen or talked to me when I came by after school.
Now that she worked in Piazza dei Martiri, it was even more
unlikely that she would go home for lunch: it would be pointless, besides the fact that there wasn't enough time. Maybe she
was in a café, maybe walking along the sea with the assistant

she surely had. Or maybe she was inside resting. I knocked on
the shutter with my open hand. No answer. I knocked again.
Nothing. I called, I heard steps inside, Lila's voice asked,
"Who is it?"

"Elena."

"Lenù," I heard her exclaim.

She pulled up the shutter, she appeared before me. It was a
long time since I'd seen her, even from a distance, and she
seemed changed. She wore a white blouse and a tight blue
skirt, her hair and makeup were done with the usual care. But
her face was as if broadened and flattened, her entire body
seemed to me broader and flatter. She pulled me inside, lowered the shutter. The place, gaudily illuminated, had changed,
it really did seem not like a shoe store but like a living room.
She said with a tone of such genuineness that I believed her:
"What a wonderful thing has happened to you, Lenù, and how
happy I am that you came to say goodbye." She knew about
Pisa, of course. She embraced me warmly, she kissed me on
both cheeks, her eyes filled with tears, she repeated, "I'm really
happy." Then she called, turning to the door of the bathroom:

"Come, Nino, you can come out, it's Lenuccia."

My breath failed. The door opened and Nino appeared, in
his usual pose, head lowered, hands in pockets. But his face
was furrowed by tension. "Hello," he murmured. I didn't
know what to say and offered him my hand. He shook it without energy. Lila meanwhile went on to tell me many important
things in a brief series of sentences: they had been secretly seeing each other for almost a year; she had decided for my good
not to involve me further in a deception that, if discovered,
would cause trouble for me as well; she was two months pregnant, she was about to confess everything to Stefano, she
wanted to leave him.

82.

Lila spoke in a tone I knew well, of determination, with which she strove to eliminate emotion, and she confined herself to rapidly and almost disdainfully summarizing events and actions, as if she were afraid that allowing herself merely a tremor in her voice or lower lip would cause everything to lose its outlines and overflow, inundating her. Nino sat on the couch looking down, making at most a nod of assent. They held hands.

She said that their meetings there in the shop, amid all the anxieties, had ended the moment she had the urine analysis and discovered the pregnancy. Now she and Nino needed their own house, their own life. She wanted to share with him friendships, books, lectures, movies, theater, music. "I can't bear living apart anymore," she said. She had hidden some money and was negotiating for a small apartment in Campi Flegrei, twenty thousand lire a month. They would hide there, waiting for the baby to be born.

How? Without a job? With Nino who had to study? I couldn't control myself, I said:

"What need is there to leave Stefano? You're good at telling lies, you've told him so many, you can perfectly well continue."

She looked at me with narrow eyes. She had clearly perceived the sarcasm, the bitterness, even the contempt that those words contained behind the appearance of friendly advice. She also noticed that Nino had abruptly raised his head, that his mouth was half open as if he wanted to say something, but he contained himself in order to avoid an argument. She replied, "Lying was useful in order not to be killed. But now I would prefer to be killed rather than continue like this."

When I said goodbye, wishing them well, I hoped for *my* sake that I wouldn't see them again.

83.

The years at the Normale were important, but not for the story of our friendship. I arrived at the university very timid and awkward. I immediately realized I spoke a bookish Italian that at times was almost absurd, especially when, right in the middle of a much too carefully composed sentence, I needed a word and transformed a dialect word into Italian to fill the gap: I began to struggle to correct myself. I knew almost nothing about etiquette, I spoke in a loud voice, I chewed noisily; I became aware of other people's embarrassment and tried to restrain myself. In my anxiety to appear friendly I interrupted conversations, gave opinions on things that had nothing to do with me, assumed manners that were too familiar: so I endeavored to be polite but distant. Once a girl from Rome, answering a question of mine I don't remember what about, parodied my inflections and everyone laughed. I felt wounded, but I laughed, too, and gaily emphasized the dialectal accent as if I were the one making fun of myself.

In the first weeks I fought the desire to go home by burrowing inside my usual meek diffidence. But from within that I began to distinguish myself and gradually became liked. Students male and female, janitors, professors liked me, and though it might have appeared effortless, in fact I worked hard. I learned to subdue my voice and gestures. I assimilated rules of behavior, written and unwritten. I kept my Neapolitan accent as much under control as possible. I managed to demonstrate that I was smart and deserving of respect by never appearing arrogant, by being ironic about my ignorance, by pretending to be surprised at my good results. Above all I avoided making enemies. When one of the girls appeared hostile, I would focus my attention on her, I was friendly yet restrained, obliging but tactful, and my attitude didn't change even when she softened and was the one who sought me out. I did the same with the professors. Naturally with them I behaved more circumspectly, but my goal was the same: to be appreciated, to gain approval and affection. I approached the most aloof, the most severe, with serene smiles and an air of devotion.

I took the exams as scheduled, studying with my usual fierce self-discipline. I was terrified by the idea of failing, of losing what immediately seemed to me, in spite of the difficulties, paradise on earth: a space of my own, a bed of my own, a desk, a chair, books and more books, a city a world away from the neighborhood and Naples, around me only people who studied and who tended to discuss what they studied. I applied myself with such diligence that no professor ever gave me less than an A, and within a year I became one of the most promising students, whose polite greetings could be met with kindness.

There were only two difficult moments, both in the first few months. The girl from Rome who had made fun of my accent assailed me one morning, yelling at me in front of other girls that money had disappeared from her purse, and I must give it back immediately or she would report me to the dean. I realized that I couldn't respond with an accommodating smile. I slapped her violently and heaped insults on her in dialect. They were all frightened. I was classified as a person who always made the best of things, and my reaction disoriented them. The girl from Rome was speechless, she stopped up her nose, which was bleeding, a friend took her to the bathroom. A few hours later they both came to see me and the one who had accused me of being a thief apologized—she had found her money. I hugged her, said that her apologies seemed genuine, and I really thought so. The way I had grown up, I would never have apologized, even if I had made a mistake.

The other serious difficulty had to do with the opening party, which was to be held before Christmas vacation. It was a sort of dance for the first-year students that everyone essentially had to attend. The girls talked about nothing else: the boys, who lived in Piazza dei Cavalieri, would come, it was a great moment of intimacy between the university's male and female divisions. I had nothing to wear. It was cold that autumn; it snowed a lot, and the snow enchanted me. But then I discovered how troublesome the ice in the streets could be, hands that, without gloves, turned numb, feet with chilblains. My wardrobe consisted of two winter dresses made by my mother a couple of years earlier, a worn coat inherited from an aunt, a big blue scarf that I had made myself, a single pair of shoes, with a half heel, that had been resoled many times. I had enough problems with my clothes, I didn't know how to deal with that party. Ask my classmates? Most of them were having dresses made just for the occasion, and it was likely that they had something among their everyday clothes that would have been fine for me. But after my experience with Lila I couldn't bear the idea of trying on someone else's clothes and discovering that they didn't fit. Pretend to be sick? I was tempted by that solution but it depressed me: to be healthy, and desperate to be a Natasha at the ball with Prince Andrei or Kuryagin, and instead to be sitting alone, staring at the ceiling, while listening to the echo of the music, the sound of voices, the laughter. In the end I made a choice that was probably humiliating but that I was sure I wouldn't regret: I washed my hair, put it up, put on some lipstick, and wore one of my two dresses, the one whose only merit was that it was dark blue.

I went to the party, and at first I felt uncomfortable. But my outfit had the advantage of not arousing envy; rather, it produced a sense of guilt that encouraged camaraderie. In fact many sympathetic girls kept me company and the boys often asked me to dance. I forgot how I was dressed and even the state of my shoes. Besides, that night I met Franco Mari, a rather ugly but very amusing boy with a quick intelligence, insolent and profligate. He was a year older than me, and from a wealthy family in Reggio Emilia, a militant Communist but critical of the Party's social-democratic leanings. I happily spent a lot of my little free time with him. He gave me everything: clothes, shoes, a new coat, glasses that didn't obscure my eyes and my whole face, books about politics, because that was the subject dearest to him. I learned from him terrible things about Stalinism and he urged me to read Trotsky; as a result I developed an anti-Stalinist sensibility and the conviction that in the U.S.S.R. there was neither socialism nor even Communism: the revolution had been truncated and needed to be started up again.

He took me on my first trip abroad. We went to Paris, to a conference of young Communists from all over Europe. I hardly saw Paris: we spent all our time in smoky places. I was left with an impression of streets much more colorful than those of Naples and Pisa, irritation at the sound of the police sirens, and amazement at the widespread presence of blacks on the streets and in the meeting rooms; Franco gave a long speech, in French, that was much applauded. When I told Pasquale about my political experience, he wouldn't believe that I—*really, you*, he said—had done a thing like that. Then he was silent, embarrassed, when I showed off my reading, declaring that I was now a Trotskyite.

From Franco I also got many habits that were later reinforced by the instructions and conversations of some of the professors: to use the word "study" even if I was reading a book of science fiction; to compile very detailed note cards on every text I studied; to get excited whenever I came upon passages in which the effects of social inequality were well described. He was very attached to what he called my reeducation and I willingly let myself be reeducated. But to my great regret I couldn't fall in love. I loved him, I loved his restless body, but I never felt that he was indispensable. The little that I felt was gone in a short time, when he lost his place at the

Normale: he failed an exam and had to leave. For several months we wrote to each other. He tried to reenter the Normale; he said that he was doing it only to be near me. I encouraged him to take the exam, he failed. We wrote occasionally, and then for a long time I had no news of him.

84.

This is more or less what happened to me between the end of 1963 and the end of 1965. How easy it is to tell the story of myself without Lila: time quiets down and the important facts slide along the thread of the years like suitcases on a conveyor belt at an airport; you pick them up, put them on the page, and it's done.

It's more complicated to recount what happened to her in those years. The belt slows down, accelerates, swerves abruptly, goes off the tracks. The suitcases fall off, fly open, their contents scatter here and there. Her things end up among mine: to accommodate them, I am compelled to return to the narrative concerning me (and that had come to me unobstructed), and expand phrases that now sound too concise. For example, if Lila had gone to the Normale in my place would she ever have decided simply to make the best of things? And the time I slapped the girl from Rome, how much did her behavior influence me? How did she manage—even at a distance—to sweep away my artificial meekness, how much of the requisite determination did she give me, how much did she dictate even the insults? And the audacity, when, amid a thousand doubts and fears, I brought Franco to my room—where did that come from if not from her example? And the sense of unhappiness, when I realized that I didn't love him, when I observed the coldness of my feelings, what was its origin if not, by comparison, the capacity to love that she had demonstrated and was demonstrating?

Yes, it's Lila who makes writing difficult. My life forces me to imagine what hers would have been if what happened to me had happened to her, what use she would have made of my luck. And her life continuously appears in mine, in the words that I've uttered, in which there's often an echo of hers, in a particular gesture that is an adaptation of a gesture of hers, in my *less* which is such because of her *more*, in my *more* which is the yielding to the force of her *less*. Not to mention what she never said but let me guess, what I didn't know and read later in her notebooks. Thus the story of the facts has to reckon with filters, deferments, partial truths, half lies: from it comes an arduous measurement of time passed that is based completely on the unreliable measuring device of words.

I have to admit, for example, that everything about Lila's sufferings escaped me. Because she had taken Nino, because with her secret arts she had become pregnant by him and not by Stefano, because for love she was on the point of carrying out an act inconceivable in the environment we had grown up in—abandoning her husband, throwing away the comfort so recently acquired, running the risk of being murdered along with her lover and the child she carried in her womb—I considered her happy, with that tempestuous happiness of novels, films, and comic strips, the only kind that at that time truly interested me, that is to say not conjugal happiness but the happiness of passion, a furious confusion of evil and good that had befallen her and not me.

I was mistaken. Now I return to the moment when Stefano took us away from Ischia, and I know for certain that the moment the boat pulled out from the shore and Lila realized that she would no longer find Nino waiting for her on the beach in the morning, would no longer debate, talk, whisper with him, that they would no longer swim together, no longer kiss and caress and love each other, she was violently scarred by suffering. Within a few days the entire life of Signora Carracci—

balances and imbalances, strategies, battles, wars and alliances, troubles with suppliers and customers, the art of cheating on the weight, the devotion to piling up money in the drawer of the cash register—dematerialized, lost truth. Only Nino was concrete and true, and she who wanted him, who desired him day and night, who clung to her husband in the darkness of the bedroom to forget the other even for a few moments. A terrible fraction of time. It was in those very moments that she felt most strongly the need to have him, and so clearly, with such a precision of detail, that she pushed Stefano away like a stranger and took refuge in a corner of the bed, weeping and shouting insults, or she ran to the bathroom and locked herself in.

85.

At first she thought of sneaking out at night and returning to Forio, but she realized that her husband would find her right away. Then she thought of asking Alfonso if Marisa knew when her brother would return from Ischia, but she was afraid that her brother-in-law would tell Stefano she had asked that question and she let it go. She found in the telephone book the number of the Sarratore house and she telephoned. Donato answered. She said she was a friend of Nino, he cut her off in an angry tone, hung up. Out of desperation she returned to the idea of taking the boat, and had nearly made up her mind, when, one afternoon in early September, Nino appeared in the doorway of the crowded grocery, unshaved and totally drunk.

Lila restrained Carmen, who had jumped up to chase out the disorderly youth, in her eyes a crazy stranger. "I'll take care of it," she said, and dragged him away. Precise gestures, cold voice, the certainty that Carmen Peluso hadn't recognized the son of Sarratore, now very different from the child who had gone to elementary school with them.

She acted fast. She appeared normal, like a woman who knows how to solve every problem. In truth, she no longer knew where she was. The shelves stacked with goods had faded, the street had lost every definition, the pale façades of the new apartment buildings had dissolved; but most of all she didn't feel the risk she was running. Nino Nino Nino: she felt only joy and desire. He was before her again, finally, and his every feature loudly proclaimed that he had suffered and was suffering, had looked for her and wanted her, so much that he tried to grab her, kiss her on the street.

She took him to her house, it seemed to her the safest place. Passersby? She saw none. Neighbors? She saw none. They began to make love as soon as she closed the door of the apartment behind her. She felt no scruple. She felt only the need to grab Nino, immediately, hold him, keep him. That need didn't diminish even when they calmed down. The neighborhood, the neighbors, the grocery, the streets, the sounds of the trains, Stefano, Carmen waiting, perhaps anxious, slowly returned, but only as objects to be arranged hastily, so that they would not get in the way, but with enough care so that, piled up haphazardly, they would not suddenly fall.

Nino reproached her for having left without warning him, he held her tight, he still wanted her. He demanded that they go away immediately, together, but then he didn't know where. She answered yes yes yes, and shared his madness in everything, although, unlike him, she felt the time, the real seconds and minutes that, slipping by, magnified the danger of being surprised. So, lying with him on the floor, she looked at the lamp hanging from the ceiling just above them, like a threat, and if before she had been preoccupied only with having Nino right away, no matter what might come crashing down, now she thought about how to keep him close to her without the lamp detaching itself from the ceiling, without the floor cleaving in two, with him forever on one side, her on the other.

"Go."

"No."

"You're mad."

"Yes."

"Please, I'm begging you, go."

She convinced him. She waited for Carmen to say something, for the neighbors to gossip maliciously, for Stefano to return from the other grocery and beat her. It didn't happen, and she was relieved. She increased Carmen's pay, she became affectionate toward her husband, she invented excuses that allowed her to meet Nino secretly.

86.

At first the larger problem was not the possibility of gossip that would ruin everything but him, the beloved. Nothing mattered to him except to clutch her, kiss her, bite her, penetrate her. It seemed that he wanted, that he needed, to live his whole life with his mouth on her mouth, inside her body. And he couldn't tolerate the separations, he was frightened by them, he feared that she would vanish again. So he stupefied himself with alcohol, he didn't study, he smoked constantly. It was as if for him there was nothing in the world but the two of them, and if he resorted to words he did it only to cry to her his jealousy, to tell her obsessively how intolerable he found it that she continued to live with her husband.

"I've left everything," he murmured wearily, "and you don't want to leave anything."

"What are you thinking of doing?" she then asked him.

Nino was silent, disoriented by the question, or he became enraged, as if the situation offended him. He said desperately, "You don't want me anymore."

But Lila wanted him, wanted him again and again, but she

also wanted something else, and right away. She wanted him to return to studying, she wanted him to continue to stimulate her mind the way he had on Ischia. The phenomenal child of elementary school, the girl who had charmed Maestra Oliviero, who had written *The Blue Fairy*, had reappeared and was stirring with new energy. Nino had found her under the pile of dirt where she had ended up and pulled her out. That girl was now urging him to be once more the studious youth he had been and allow her to develop the power to sweep away Signora Carracci. Which she gradually did.

I don't know what happened: Nino must have perceived that in order not to lose her he had to be something more than a furious lover. Or maybe not, maybe he simply felt that passion was emptying him. The fact is that he began studying again. And Lila at first was content: he slowly recovered, became as she had known him on Ischia, which made him even more essential to her. She had again not only Nino but also something of his words, his ideas. He read Smith unhappily, she, too, tried to do it; he read Joyce even more unhappily, she tried, too. She bought the books that he mentioned to her the rare times they managed to meet. She wanted to talk about them, there was never a chance.

Carmen, who was increasingly bewildered, didn't understand what could be so urgent when Lila, with one excuse or another, was absent for several hours. She observed her frowning, so immersed in reading a book or writing in her notebooks that she seemed not to see or hear anything, as she left the burden of the customers to Carmen, even during the grocery's busiest hours. Carmen had to say, "Lina, please, can you help me?" Only then did she look up, run a fingertip over her lips, say yes.

As for Stefano, he fluctuated between anxiety and acquiescence. While he quarreled with his brother-in-law, his father-in-law, the Solaras, and was upset because, in spite of all that swimming in the sea, children didn't come, here was his wife being sarcastic about the troubles with the shoes, and wrapped up in novels, journals, newspapers until late into the night: this mania had returned, as if real life no longer interested her. He observed her, he didn't understand or didn't have the time or the wish to understand. After Ischia, a part of him, the most aggressive, in the face of those alternating attitudes of rejection and peaceful estrangement, was inciting him to a new clash and a definitive explanation. But another part, more prudent, perhaps afraid, restrained the first, pretended not to notice, thought: better like this than when she's being a pain in the ass. And Lila, who had grasped that thought, tried to make it last in his mind. At night, when they both returned home from work, she was not hostile toward her husband. But after dinner and some talk she withdrew cautiously into reading, a mental space inaccessible to him, inhabited only by her and Nino.

What did he become for her in that period? A sexual yearning that kept her in a state of permanent erotic fantasy; a blazing up of her mind that wanted to be at the same level as his; above all an abstract plan for a secret couple, hiding in a kind of refuge that was to be part bungalow for two hearts, part workshop of ideas on the complexity of the world, he present and active, she a shadow glued to his footsteps, cautious prompter, fervent collaborator. The rare times that they were able to be together not for a few minutes but for an hour, that hour was transformed into an inexhaustible flow of sexual and verbal exchanges, a complete well-being that, at the moment of separation, made the return to the grocery and to Stefano's bed unbearable.

"I can't take it anymore."

"Me neither."

"What can we do?"

"I don't know."

"I want to be with you always."

Or at least, she added, for a few hours every day.

But how to carve out time, safe and regular? Seeing Nino at home was extremely dangerous, seeing him in the street even more so. Not to mention that at times Stefano telephoned the grocery and she wasn't there, and to come up with a plausible explanation was difficult. So, caught between Nino's impatience and her husband's complaints, instead of regaining a sense of reality and telling herself clearly that she was in a situation with no way out, Lila began to act as if the real world were a backdrop or a chessboard, and you had only to shift a painted screen, move a pawn or two, and you would see that the game, the only thing that really counted, *her* game, *the game of the two of them*, could continue to be played. As for the future, the future became the day after and then the next and then the one after that. Or sudden images of massacre and blood, which were very frequent in her notebooks. She never wrote *I will die murdered*, but she noted local crime news, sometimes she reinvented it. In these stories of murdered women she emphasized the murderer's rage, the blood everywhere. And she added details that the newspapers didn't report: eyes dug out of their sockets, injuries caused by a knife to the throat or internal organs, the blade that pierced a breast, nipples cut off, the stomach ripped open from the bellybutton down, the blade that scraped across the genitals. It was as if she wanted to take the power away even from the realistic possibility of violent death by reducing it to words, to a form that could be controlled.

87.

It was in that perspective of a game with possibly mortal outcomes that Lila inserted herself into the conflict between her brother, her husband, and the Solara brothers. She used

Michele's conviction that she was the most suitable person to manage the commercial situation in Piazza dei Martiri. She abruptly stopped saying no and after quarrelsome negotiations as a result of which she obtained absolute autonomy and a substantial weekly salary, as if she were not Signora Carracci, she agreed to go and work in the shoe store. She didn't care about her brother, who felt threatened by the new Solara brand and saw her move as a betrayal; or about her husband, who at first was furious, threatened her, then drove her to complicated mediations in his name with the two brothers concerning debts contracted with their mother, sums of money to receive and to give. She also ignored the sugary words of Michele, who constantly hovered around her, to supervise, without appearing to, the reorganization of the shop, and at the same time pressed to get new shoe models directly from her, passing over Rino and Stefano.

Lila had perceived for a long time that her brother and her father would be swept away, that the Solaras would appropriate everything, that Stefano would stay afloat only if he became more dependent on their dealings. But if before that prospect made her indignant, now, she wrote in her notebooks, the situation left her completely indifferent. Of course, she was sad about Rino, she was sorry that his role as a boss was already declining, especially since he was married and had a child. But in her eyes the bonds of the past now had little substance, her capacity for affection had taken a single path, every thought, every feeling had Nino at its center. If before her motivation was to make her brother rich, now it was only to please Nino.

The first time she went to the shop in Piazza dei Martiri to see what to do with it she was struck by the fact that on the wall where the panel with her wedding photograph had been you could still see the yellowish-black stain from the flames that had destroyed it. That trace upset her. I don't like any part of what happened to me and what I did before Nino, she thought. And it suddenly occurred to her that there, in that space at the center of the city, and for reasons that were obscure to her, every crucial development in her war had occurred. There, the evening of the fight with the youths of Via dei Mille, she had decided conclusively that she had to escape poverty. There she had repented of that decision and had defaced her wedding photograph and had insisted that the defacement, as defacement, should be featured in the shop as a decoration. There she had discovered the signs that her pregnancy was about to end. There, now, the shoe enterprise was failing, swallowed up by the Solaras. And there, too, her marriage would end, she would tear off Stefano and his name, along with all that derived from it. What a mess, she said to Michele Solara, pointing out the burn marks. Then she went out to the sidewalk to look at the stone lions in the center of the square, and was afraid of them.

She had it all painted. In the bathroom, which had no windows, she reopened a walled-up door that had once led to an interior courtyard and installed a half window of frosted glass that could let in some light. She bought two paintings that she had seen in a gallery in Chiatamone and had liked. She hired a salesgirl, not from the neighborhood but a girl from Materdei who had studied to be a secretary. She arranged that the afternoon closing hours, from one until four, should be for her and for the assistant a period of absolute repose, for which the girl was always grateful. She held off Michele, who, although he supported every innovation sight unseen, nonetheless insisted on knowing the details of what she was doing, what she spent.

In the neighborhood, meanwhile, the decision to go to work in Piazza dei Martiri isolated her more than she already had been. A girl who had made a good marriage and had gained, out of nowhere, a comfortable life, a pretty girl who could be mistress of her own house, a house owned by her husband—why did she jump out of bed in the morning and remain far from home all day, in the city, employed by others, complicating Stefano's life, and her mother-in-law's, who because of her had to go back to work in the new grocery? Pinuccia and Gigliola especially, each in her way, threw on Lila all the mud they were capable of, and this was predictable. Less predictable was Carmen, who adored Lila for all she had done for her, but who, as soon as Lila left the grocery, withdrew her affection as if she were pulling back a hand grazed by an animal's claws. She didn't like the abrupt change from friend-colleague to servant in the clutches of Stefano's mother. She felt betrayed, abandoned to fate, and couldn't control her resentment. She even began to argue with her fiancé, Enzo, who didn't approve of her bitterness, he shook his head and, in his laconic way, rather than defend Lila, assigned her, in a few words, a sort of inviolability, the privilege of having reasons that were always just and indisputable.

"Everything I do is no good, everything she does is good," Carmen hissed bitterly.

"Who said so?"

"You: Lina thinks, Lina does, Lina knows. And I? I whom she went off and left there? But naturally she was right to leave and I am wrong to complain. Is it true? Is that what you think?"

"No."

But in spite of that pure and simple monosyllable, Carmen wasn't convinced, she suffered. She sensed that Enzo was tired of everything, even of her, and this enraged her even more: ever since his father died, since he had returned from the Army, he did what he had to do, led his usual life, but meanwhile he was studying at night—he had started during his military service—to get some sort of diploma. Now he was shut up in his head, roaring like a beast—roaring inside, outside silent—and Carmen couldn't bear it, she especially couldn't stand that he became a little animated only when he talked about that bitch, and she shouted at him, and began to cry, screaming:

"Lina makes me sick, because she doesn't give a damn about anyone, but you like that, I know. While if I acted the way she acts, you'd smash my face."

Ada, on the other hand, had long since aligned herself with her employer, Stefano, against the wife who harassed him, and when Lila went to the center of town to be the luxury saleswoman she simply became more treacherous. She said bad things about her to anyone, openly, straight out, but she was angry mainly with Antonio and Pasquale. "She has always taken you in, you men," she said, "because she knows how to get you, she's a whore." She said it just like that, irately, as if Antonio and Pasquale were the representatives of all the insufficiency of the male sex. She insulted her brother, who didn't side with her, she screamed at him: "You're silent because you take money from the Solaras, too, you're both employees of the company, and I know you're ordered around by a woman, you help her put the shop in order, she says move this and move that and you obey." And she was even worse with her fiancé, Pasquale, with whom she was increasingly at odds, constantly criticizing him, saying, "You're dirty, you stink." He apologized, he had just finished work, but Ada continued to attack him, every chance she got, so that Pasquale, to live in peace, gave in on the subject of Lila; the alternative was to break the engagement, although—it should be said—that was not the only reason. He had often been angry with both his fiancée and his sister for having forgotten all the benefits they had gained from Lila's rise, but when, one morning, he saw our friend in the Giulietta with Michele Solara, who was driving her to Piazza dei Martiri, dressed like a high-class prostitute, all made up, he admitted that he couldn't understand how, without a real economic need, she could sell herself to a man like that.

Lila, as usual, paid no attention to the hostility that was growing around her; she devoted herself to the new job. And soon sales rose sharply. The shop became a place where people went to buy, but also to chat with that lively, very pretty young woman, whose conversation sparkled, who kept books among the shoes, who read those books, who offered you little chocolates along with the intelligent talk, and who, moreover, never seemed to want to sell Cerullo shoes or Solara shoes to the wife or daughters of the lawyer or the engineer, to the journalist for *Mattino*, to the young or old dandy who was wasting time and money at the Club; rather, she wanted them to make themselves comfortable on the couch and the ottomans and chat about this and that.

The only obstacle, Michele. He was often in the way during work hours and once he said in that ironic, insinuating tone he had, "You have the wrong husband, Lina. I was right: look how well you move among the people who can be useful to us. You and I together in a few years would take over Naples and do what we like with it."

At that point he tried to kiss her.

She pushed him away, he wasn't offended. He said, in amusement, "That's all right, I know how to wait."

"Wait where you like, but not here," she said, "because if you wait here I'll go back to the grocery tomorrow."

Michele's visits diminished while Nino's secret visits increased. For months he and Lila had, finally, in the shop on Piazza dei Martiri, a life of their own, which lasted for three hours a day, except Sundays and holidays, and those were unbearable. He came in through the door of the bathroom at one o'clock, as soon as the assistant pulled the gate three-quarters of the way down and went off, and he left by that same door at four, exactly, before the assistant returned. On the rare occasions that there was some problem—a couple of times Michele arrived with Gigliola and there were particularly tense situations when Stefano showed up—Nino shut himself in the bathroom and sneaked out by the door that opened to the courtyard.

I think for Lila that was a tumultuous trial period for a happy existence. On the one hand she enthusiastically played the part of the young woman who gave the shoe store an eccentric touch, on the other she read for Nino, studied for Nino, reflected for Nino. And even the people of some prominence with whom she became acquainted in the shop seemed to her mainly connections to be used to help him.

During that period, Nino published an article in *Il Mattino* on Naples that gave him modest fame in university circles. I didn't know about it, and luckily: if they had included me in their story as they had on Ischia I would have been so severely scarred that I would never have managed to recover. And it wouldn't have taken me long to figure out that many of the lines in that article—not the most erudite, but those few intuitions that did not require great expertise, only an inspired moment of contact between things that were very distant from one another—were Lila's, and that the tonality of the writing in particular belonged to her. Nino had never been able to write in such a fashion nor was he able to later. Only she and I could write like that.

88.

Then she discovered that she was pregnant and decided to put an end to the deception of Piazza dei Martiri. One Sunday in the late autumn of 1963 she refused to go to lunch at her mother-in-law's, as they usually did, and devoted herself to cooking with great care. While Stefano went to get pastries at the Solaras', bringing some to his mother and sister to be forgiven for his Sunday desertion, Lila put in the suitcase bought for her honeymoon some underwear, a few dresses, a pair of winter shoes, and hid it behind the door of the living room. Then she washed all the pots that she had gotten dirty, set the table in the kitchen, took a carving knife out of a drawer and put it on the sink, covered by a towel. Finally, waiting for her husband to return, she opened the window to get rid of the cooking smells, and stood there looking at the trains and the shining tracks. The cold dissipated the warmth of the apartment, but it didn't bother her, it gave her energy.

Stefano returned, they sat down at the table. Irritated because he had been deprived of his mother's good cooking, he didn't say a single word in praise of the lunch but was harsher than usual toward his brother-in-law, Rino, and more affectionate than usual toward his nephew. He kept calling him *my sister's son*, as if Rino's contribution had been of little account. When they got to the pastries, he ate three, she none. Stefano carefully wiped the cream off his mouth and said, "Let's go to bed for a while."

Lila answered, "Starting tomorrow I'm not going to the shop anymore."

Stefano immediately understood that the afternoon was taking a bad turn. "Why?"

"Because I don't feel like it."

"Did you fight with Michele and Marcello?"

"No."

"Lina, don't talk nonsense, you know very well that your brother and I are just one step from a violent clash with them, don't complicate things."

"I'm not complicating anything. But I'm not going there anymore."

Stefano was silent and Lila saw that he was worried, that he wanted to escape without examining the matter. Her husband was afraid she was about to reveal to him some insult on the part of the Solaras, an unforgivable offense to which, once he knew about it, he would have to react, leading to an irrevocable rupture. Which he couldn't afford.

"All right," he said, when he made up his mind to speak, "don't go, go back to the grocery."

She answered, "I don't feel like the grocery, either."

Stefano looked at her in bewilderment. "You want to stay home? Good. You wanted to work, I never asked you. Is that true or not?"

"It's true."

"Then stay home, I'd be glad to have you at home."

"I don't want to stay home, either."

He was close to losing his calm, the only way he knew to expel anxiety.

"If you don't want to stay home, either, am I allowed to know what the fuck you want?"

Lila answered, "I want to go."

"Go where?"

"I don't want to stay with you anymore, I want to leave you."

The only thing Stefano could do was start laughing. Those words seemed to him so enormous that for a few minutes he seemed relieved. He pinched her cheek, he said with his usual half smile that they were husband and wife and that husband and wife don't leave each other, he promised that the following Sunday he would take her to the Amalfi Coast, so they could relax a little. But she answered calmly that there was no reason to stay together, that she had been wrong from the start, that even when they were engaged she had liked him only a little, that she now knew clearly that she had never loved him and that to be supported by him, to help him make money, to sleep with him were things that she could no longer tolerate. It was at the end of that speech that she received a blow that knocked her off her chair. She got up while Stefano moved to grab her, she ran to the sink, seized the knife that she had put under the

dishtowel. She turned to him just when he was about to hit her
again.

"Do it and I'll kill you the way they killed your father," she
said.

Stefano stopped, stunned by that reference to the fate of his
father. He muttered things like "All right, kill me, do what you
want." And he made a gesture of boredom and yawned, an
uncontrollable yawn, his mouth wide open, that left his eyes
bright and shining. He turned his back on her and, still muttering resentfully—"Go on, go, I've given you everything, I've
yielded in every way, and you repay me like this, me, who
raised you out of poverty, who made your brother rich, your
father, and your whole shitty family"—went to the table and
ate another pastry.

Then he left the kitchen, retreated to the bedroom, and
from there he cried suddenly, "You can't even imagine how
much I love you."

Lila placed the knife on the sink, she thought: he doesn't
believe that I'm leaving him; he wouldn't even believe that I
have someone else, he can't. Yet she got up her courage and
went to the bedroom to confess to him about Nino, to tell him
she was pregnant. But her husband was sleeping, he had fallen
asleep as if wrapped in a magic cape. So she put on her coat,
took the suitcase, and left the apartment.

89.

Stefano slept all day. When he woke up and realized that his
wife wasn't there he pretended not to notice. He had behaved
like that since he was a boy, when his father terrorized him by
his mere presence and he, in reaction, had trained himself to
that half smile, to slow, tranquil gestures, to a controlled distance from the world around him, to keep at bay both fear and

the desire to tear open his chest with his bare hands and, pulling it apart, rip out the heart.

In the evening he went out and did something rash: he went to Ada's windows, and though he knew she was supposed to be at the movies or somewhere with Pasquale, he called her, kept calling her. Ada looked out, both happy and alarmed. She had stayed home because Melina was raving more than usual and Antonio, ever since he had gone to work for the Solaras, was always out, he didn't have a schedule. Her fiancé was there keeping her company. Stefano went up just the same, and, without ever mentioning Lila, spent the evening at the Cappuccio house talking politics with Pasquale and about matters connected to the grocery with Ada. When he got home he pretended that Lila had gone to her parents' and before he went to bed he shaved carefully. He slept heavily all night.

The trouble began the next day. The assistant at Piazza dei Martiri told Michele that Lila hadn't shown up. Michele telephoned Stefano and Stefano told him that his wife was sick. The illness lasted for days, so Nunzia stopped by to see if her daughter needed her. No one opened the door, she went back in the evening, Stefano had just returned from work and was sitting in front of the television, which was at high volume. He swore, he went to open the door, invited her in. As soon as Nunzia said, "How is Lina?" he answered that she had left him, then he burst into tears.

Both families hurried over: Stefano's mother, Alfonso, Pinuccia with the baby, Rino, Fernando. For one reason or another they were all frightened, but only Maria and Nunzia were openly worried about Lila's fate and wondered where she had gone. The others quarreled for reasons that had little to do with her. Rino and Fernando, who were angry at Stefano because he had done nothing to prevent the closing of the shoe factory, accused him of having never understood Lila and said he had been very wrong to send her to the Solaras' shop.

Pinuccia got angry and yelled at her husband and her father-in-law that Lila had always been a hothead, that she wasn't Stefano's victim, Stefano was hers. When Alfonso ventured that they should turn to the police, ask at the hospitals, feelings flared up even more, they all criticized him as if he had insulted them: Rino in particular cried that the last thing they needed was to become the laughingstock of the neighborhood. It was Maria who said softly, "Maybe she's gone to stay with Lenù for a while." That hypothesis caught on. They continued to quarrel, but they all pretended, except Alfonso, to believe that Lila, because of Stefano, and the Solaras, had decided to go to Pisa. "Yes," Nunzia said, calming down, "she always does that, as soon as she has a problem she goes to Lenù." At that point, they all started to get angry about that reckless journey, all by herself, on the train, far away, without telling anyone. And yet that Lila was with me seemed so plausible and at the same time so reassuring that it immediately became a fact. Only Alfonso said, "I'll leave tomorrow and go see," but he was immediately checked by Pinuccia, "Where are you going when you have to work," and by Fernando, who muttered, "Leave her alone, let her calm down."

The next day that was the version that Stefano gave to anyone who asked about Lila: "She went to Pisa to see Lenù, she wants to rest." But that afternoon Nunzia was gripped again by anxiety, she went to see Alfonso and asked if he had my address. He didn't have it, no one did, only my mother. So Nunzia sent Alfonso to her, but my mother, out of her natural hostility toward everyone or to safeguard my studies from distraction, gave him an incomplete version (it's likely that she herself had it that way: writing was hard for my mother, and we both knew that she would never use that address). In any case Nunzia and Alfonso together wrote me a letter in which they asked in a very roundabout way if Lila was with me. They addressed it to the University of Pisa, nothing else, only my

name and surname, and its arrival was much delayed. I read it,
I became even angrier with Lila and Nino, I didn't answer.

Meanwhile, the day after Lila's so-called departure, Ada, in
addition to working in the old grocery store, in addition to
attending to her entire family and the needs of her fiancé, also
began to tidy up Stefano's house and to cook for him, which
put Pasquale in a bad mood. They quarreled, he said to her,
"You're not paid to be a servant," and she answered, "Better
to be a servant than waste time arguing with you." On the
other hand, to keep the Solaras happy Alfonso was quickly
sent to Piazza dei Martiri, where he felt at his ease: he left early
in the morning dressed as if he were going to a wedding and
returned at night very pleased: he liked spending the day in the
center. As for Michele, who with the disappearance of Signora
Carracci had become intractable, he called Antonio and said to
him: "Find her for me."

Antonio muttered, "Naples is big, Michè, and so is Pisa,
and even Italy. Where do I begin?"

Michele answered, "With Sarratore's oldest son." Then he
gave him the look he reserved for people he considered worth
less than nothing and said, "Don't you dare tell anyone about
this search or I'll put you in the insane asylum at Aversa and
you'll never get out. Everything you know, everything you see,
you will tell me alone. Is that clear?"

Antonio nodded yes.

90.

That people, even more than things, lost their boundaries
and overflowed into shapelessness is what most frightened Lila
in the course of her life. The loss of those boundaries in her
brother, whom she loved more than anyone in her family, had
frightened her, and the disintegration of Stefano in the passage

from fiancé to husband terrified her. I learned only from her notebooks how much her wedding night had scarred her and how she feared the potential distortion of her husband's body, his disfigurement by the internal impulses of desire and rage or, on the contrary, of subtle plans, base acts. Especially at night she was afraid of waking up and finding him formless in the bed, transformed into excrescences that burst out because of too much fluid, the flesh melted and dripping, and with it everything around, the furniture, the entire apartment and she herself, his wife, broken, sucked into that stream polluted by living matter.

When she closed the door behind her and, as if she were inside a white cloud of steam that made her invisible, took the metro to Campi Flegrei, Lila had the impression that she had left a soft space, inhabited by forms without definition, and was finally heading toward a structure that was capable of containing her fully, all of her, without her cracking or the figures around her cracking. She reached her destination along desolate streets. She dragged the suitcase to the third floor of a working-class apartment building, and into a shoddy, dark two-room apartment furnished with old, cheap furniture, a bathroom where there was only a toilet and sink. She had done it all herself, Nino had to prepare for his exams and he was also working on a new article for *Il Mattino* and on transforming the other into an essay that had been rejected by *Cronache Meridionali*, but that a journal called *Nord e Sud* said it was eager to publish. She had seen the apartment, had rented it, had given three payments in advance. Now, as soon as she entered, she felt enormously cheerful. She discovered with surprise the pleasure of having abandoned those she thought would have to be part of her forever. Pleasure, yes, she wrote just that. She didn't feel in the least the loss of the new neighborhood's comforts, she didn't smell the odor of mold, didn't see the stain of dampness in a corner of the bedroom, didn't notice the gray light that struggled to enter through the window, wasn't depressed by a place that immediately foretold a return to the poverty of her childhood. Instead, she felt as if she had magically disappeared from a place where she suffered, and had reappeared in a place that promised happiness. She was again fascinated, I think, by erasing herself: enough with everything she had been; enough with the *stradone*, shoes, groceries, husband, Solaras, Piazza dei Martiri; enough even with me, bride, wife, gone elsewhere, lost. All that remained of her self was the lover of Nino, who arrived that evening.

He was visibly overcome by emotion. He embraced her, kissed her, looked around disoriented. He barred doors and windows as if he feared sudden incursions. They made love, in a bed for the first time after the night in Forio. Then he got up, he started studying, he complained often about the weak light. She also got out of bed and helped him review. They went to sleep at three in the morning, after revising together the new article for *Il Mattino*, and they slept in an embrace. Lila felt safe, although it was raining outside, the windows shook, the house was alien to her. How new Nino's body was, long, thin, so different from Stefano's. How exciting his smell was. It seemed to her that she had come from a world of shadows and had arrived in a place where finally life was real. In the morning, as soon as she put her feet on the floor, she had to run to the toilet to throw up. She closed the door so that Nino wouldn't hear.

91.

They lived together for twenty-three days. The relief at having left everything increased from moment to moment. She didn't miss any of the comforts she had enjoyed after her marriage, and separation from her parents, her younger siblings, Rino, her nephew didn't sadden her. She never worried that the money would run out. The only thing that seemed to matter was that she woke up with Nino and fell asleep with him, that she was beside him when he studied or wrote, that they had lively discussions in which the jumble of thoughts in her head poured out. At night they went to a movie together, or chose a book presentation, or a political debate, and often they stayed out late, returning home on foot, clinging to one another to protect themselves from the cold or the rain, squabbling, joking.

Once they went to hear a writer named Pasolini, who also made films. Everything that had to do with him caused an uproar and Nino didn't like him, he twisted his mouth, said, "He's a fairy, all he does is make a lot of noise," so he had resisted, he would have preferred to stay home and study. But Lila was curious and she dragged him there. The talk was held in the same club where I had gone once, in obedience to Professor Galiani. Lila was enthusiastic when she came out, she pushed Nino toward the writer, she wanted to talk to him. But Nino was nervous and did his best to get her away, especially when he realized that on the sidewalk across the street there were youths shouting insults. "Let's go," he said, worried, "I don't like him and I don't like the fascists, either." But Lila had grown up amid violence, she had no intention of sneaking off; he tried to pull her toward an alley and she wriggled free, she laughed, she responded to the insults with insults. She gave in abruptly when, just as a real fight was starting, she recognized Antonio. His eyes and his teeth shone as if they were made of metal, but unlike the others he wasn't shouting. He seemed too busy hitting people to be aware of her, but the thing ruined the evening for her anyway. On the way home she felt some tension with Nino: they didn't agree about what Pasolini had said, they seemed to have gone to different places to hear different people. But it wasn't only that. That night he regretted the long exciting period of the furtive meetings in the shop on Piazza dei

Martiri and at the same time perceived that something about Lila disturbed him. She noticed his distraction, his irritation, and to avoid further tension did not say that among the attackers she had seen a friend of hers from the neighborhood, Melina's son.

From then on Nino seemed less and less inclined to take her out. First he said that he had to study, and it was true, then he let slip that on various public occasions she had been excessive.

"In what sense?"

"You exaggerate."

"Meaning?"

He made a resentful list: "You make comments out loud; if someone tells you to be quiet you start arguing; you bother the speakers with your own monologues. It's not done."

Lila had known that it wasn't done, but she had believed that now, with him, everything was possible, bridging gaps with a leap, speaking face to face with people who counted. Hadn't she been able to talk to influential types, in the Solaras' shop? Hadn't it been thanks to one of the customers that he had published his first article in *Il Mattino*? And so? "You're too timid," she said. "You still don't understand that you're better than they are and you'll do much more important things." Then she kissed him.

But the following evenings Nino, with one excuse or another, began to go out alone. And if he stayed home instead and studied, he complained of how much noise there was in the building. Or he grumbled because he had to go and ask his father for money, and Donato would torment him with questions like: Where are you sleeping, what are you doing, where are you living, are you studying? Or, in the face of Lila's ability to make connections between very different things, instead of being excited as usual he shook his head, became irritable.

After a while he was in such a bad mood, and so behind

with his exams, that in order to keep studying he stopped going to bed with her. Lila said, "It's late, let's go to sleep," he answered with a distracted, "You go, I'll come later." He looked at the outline of her body under the covers and desired its warmth but was also afraid of it. I haven't yet graduated, he thought, I don't have a job; if I don't want to throw my life away I have to apply myself; instead I'm here with this person who is married, who is pregnant, who vomits every morning, who prevents me from being disciplined. When he found out that *Il Mattino* wouldn't publish the article he was really upset. Lila consoled him, told him to send it to other newspapers. But then she added, "Tomorrow I'll call."

She wanted to call the editor she had met in the Solaras' shop and find out what was wrong. He stammered, "You won't telephone anyone."

"Why?"

"Because that shit was never interested in me but in you."

"It's not true."

"It's very true, I'm not a fool, you just make problems for me."

"What do you mean?"

"I shouldn't have listened to you."

"What did I do?"

"You confused my ideas. Because you're like a drop of water, *ting ting ting*. Until it's done your way, you won't stop."

"You thought of the article and wrote it."

"Exactly. And so why did you make me redo it four times?"

"*You* wanted to rewrite it."

"Lina, let's be very clear: choose something of your own that you like, go back to selling shoes, go back to selling salami, but don't desire to be something you're not by ruining me."

They had been living together for twenty-three days, a cloud in which the gods had hidden them so that they could enjoy each other without being disturbed. Those words wounded her deeply, she said, "Get out."

He quickly pulled his coat on over his sweater and slammed the door behind him.

Lila sat on the bed and thought: he'll be back in ten minutes, he left his books, his notes, his shaving cream and razor. Then she burst into tears: how could I have thought of living with him, of being able to help him? It's my fault: to free my head, I even made him write something wrong.

She went to bed and waited. She waited all night, but Nino didn't come back, not the morning after or the one after that.

92.

What I am now recounting I learned from various people at various times. I begin with Nino, who left the house in Campi Flegrei and took refuge with his parents. His mother treated him better, much better, than the prodigal son. With his father, on the other hand, he was quarreling within an hour, the insults flew. Donato yelled at him in dialect that he could either leave home or stay there, but the thing he absolutely could not do was to disappear for a month without telling anyone and then return only to swipe some money as if he had earned it himself.

Nino retreated to his room and had many arguments with himself. Although he already wanted to run back to Lina, ask her pardon, cry to her that he loved her, he assessed the situation and became convinced that he had fallen into a trap, not his fault, not Lina's fault, but the fault of desire. Now, for example, he thought, I can't wait to go back to her, cover her with kisses, assume my responsibilities; but a part of me knows perfectly well that what I did today on a wave of disappointment is true and right: Lina isn't right for me, Lina is pregnant, what's in her womb scares me; so I must absolutely not return, I have to go to Bruno, borrow some money, leave Naples as Elena did, study somewhere else.

He deliberated all night and all the next day, now pierced by a need for Lila, now clinging to chilling thoughts that evoked her crude ingenuousness, her too intelligent ignorance, the force with which she drew him into her thoughts, which seemed like insights but were, instead, muddled.

In the evening he telephoned Bruno and, in a frenzy, left to go see him. He ran through the rain to the bus stop, barely caught the right bus before it left. But suddenly he changed his mind and got off at Piazza Garibaldi. He took the metro to Campi Flegrei, he couldn't wait to embrace Lila, take her standing up, right away, as soon as he was in the house, against the entrance wall. That now seemed the most important thing, then he would think what to do.

It was dark, he walked with long strides in the rain. He didn't even notice the dark silhouette coming toward him. He was shoved so violently that he fell down. A long series of blows began, punching and kicking, kicking and punching. The person who hit him kept repeating, but not angrily:

"Leave her, don't see her and don't touch her again. Repeat: I will leave her. Repeat: I won't see her and I won't touch her again. You piece of shit: you like it, eh, taking other men's wives. Repeat: I was wrong, I'll leave her."

Nino repeated obediently, but his attacker didn't stop. He fainted more out of fear than out of pain.

93.

It was Antonio who beat up Nino, but he reported almost none of this to his boss. When Michele asked if he had found Sarratore's son he answered yes. When he asked with evident anxiety if that track had led to Lila he said no. When he asked him if he had had information about Lila he said he couldn't find her and the only thing he could absolutely rule out was that Sarratore's son had anything to do with Signora Carracci.

He was lying, of course. He had found Nino and Lila fairly soon, by chance, the night he had had the job of brawling with the Communists. He had smashed a few faces and then had left the fight to follow the two who had fled. He had discovered where they lived, he had understood that they were living together, and in the following days he had studied everything they did, how they lived. Seeing them he had felt both admiration and envy. Admiration for Lila. How is it possible, he had said to himself, that she abandoned her house, a beautiful house, and left her husband, the groceries, the cars, the shoes, the Solaras, for a student without a cent who keeps her in a place almost worse than the old neighborhood? What is it with that girl: courage, or madness? Then he concentrated on his envy of Nino. What hurt him most was that Lila and I both liked the skinny, ugly bastard. What was it about the son of Sarratore, what was his advantage? He had thought about it night and day. He was gripped by a kind of morbid obsession that affected his nerves, especially in his hands, so that he was constantly interlacing them, pressing them together as if he were praying. Finally he had decided that he had to free Lila, even if at that moment, perhaps, she had no desire to be freed. But—he had said to himself—it takes time for people to understand what's good and what's bad, and helping them means doing for them what in a particular moment of their life they aren't capable of doing. Michele Solara hadn't ordered him to beat up Sarratore's son, no: he had not told Michele the most important thing and so there was no reason to go that far; beating him up had been his own decision, and he had made it partly because he wanted to get Nino away from Lila and give her back what she had incomprehensibly thrown away, and partly for his own enjoyment, because of an exasperation he felt not toward Nino, an insignificant limp agglomerate of effeminate flesh and bone, too long and breakable, but toward what we two girls had attributed and did attribute to him.

I have to admit that when, some time afterward, he told me that story I seemed to understand his motivations. It moved me, I caressed his cheek to console him for his savage feelings. And he reddened, he was flustered; to show me that he wasn't a beast he said, "Afterward I helped him." He had picked up Sarratore's son, taken him, half dazed, to a pharmacy, left him at the entrance, and returned to the neighborhood to talk to Pasquale and Enzo.

They had agreed to meet him reluctantly. They no longer considered him a friend, especially Pasquale, even though he was his sister's fiancé. But Antonio didn't care, he pretended not to notice, he behaved as if their hostility because he had sold himself to the Solaras were a gripe that made no dent in their friendship. He said nothing about Nino, he focused on the fact that he had found Lila and that they had to help her.

"Do what?" Pasquale had asked, aggressively.

"Go home to her own house: she didn't go to see Lenuccia, she's living in a shitty place in Campi Flegrei."

"By herself?"

"Yes."

"And why in the world did she decide to do that?"

"I don't know, I didn't talk to her."

"Why?"

"I found her on behalf of Michele Solara."

"You're a shit fascist."

"I'm nothing, I did a job."

"Bravo, now what do you want?"

"I haven't told Michele that I found her."

"And so?"

"I don't want to lose my job, I have to think of earning a living. If Michele finds out that I lied to him he'll fire me. You go get her and bring her home."

Pasquale had insulted him grossly again, but even then Antonio scarcely reacted. He became upset only when his future brother-in-law said that Lila had done well to leave her husband and all the rest: if she had finally gotten out of the Solaras' shop, if she realized that she had made a mistake in marrying Stefano, he certainly wouldn't be the one who brought her back.

"You want to leave her in Campi Flegrei by herself?" Antonio asked, bewildered. "Alone and without a lira?"

"Why, are we rich? Lina is a grownup, she knows what life is: if she made that decision she has her reasons, let's leave her in peace."

"But she helped us whenever she could."

At that reminder of the money Lila had given them Pasquale was ashamed. He had stammered some trite stuff about rich and poor, about the condition of women in the neighborhood and outside it, about the fact that if it was a matter of giving her money he was ready. But Enzo, who until then had been silent, broke in with a gesture of annoyance, and said to Antonio, "Give me the address, I'm going to see what she intends to do."

94.

He did go, the next day. He took the metro, got out at Campi Flegrei, and looked for the street, the building.

Of Enzo at that time I knew only that he couldn't tolerate anything anymore: the whining of his mother, the burden of his siblings, the Camorra in the fruit-and-vegetable market, the rounds with the cart, which earned less and less, Pasquale's Communist talk, and even his engagement to Carmen. None of it. But since he was reserved by nature, it was difficult to get an idea of what type of person he was. From Carmen I had learned that he was secretly studying on his own, he wanted to get an engineering diploma. It must have been on the same occasion—Christmas?—that Carmen told me he had kissed her only four times since he returned from military service, in the spring. She added, with irritation, "Maybe he's not a man."

That was what we often said, we girls, when someone didn't care much about us: that he wasn't a man. Enzo was, wasn't he? I didn't know anything about the dark depths that men could have, none of us did, and so for any confusing manifestation we had recourse to that formula. Some, like the Solaras, like Pasquale, Antonio, Donato Sarratore, even Franco Mari, my boyfriend at the Normale, wanted us in ways that were different—aggressive, subordinate, heedless, attentive—but that they wanted us there was no doubt. Others, like Alfonso, Enzo, Nino, had—according to equally diverse attitudes—an aloof self-possession, as if between us and them there were a wall and the work of scaling it were our job. In Enzo, after the Army, this characteristic had become accentuated, and he not only did nothing to please women but did nothing to please the entire world. He was short, and yet his body seemed to have become even smaller, as if through a sort of self-compression: it had become a compact block of energy. The skin over the bones of his face was stretched like an awning, and he had reduced motion to the pure compass of his legs, no other part of him moved, not arms or neck or head, not even his hair, which was a reddish-blond helmet. When he decided to go and see Lila he told Pasquale and Antonio, not in order to discuss it but in the form of a brief statement that served to cut off any discussion. Nor when he arrived at Campi Flegrei did he display any uncertainty. He found the street, found the doorway, went up the stairs, and rang with determination at the right door.

95.

When Nino did not return in ten minutes or an hour or even the next day, Lila turned spiteful. She felt not abandoned but humiliated, and although she had admitted to herself that she wasn't the right woman for him, she still found it unbearable that he, disappearing from her life after only twenty-three days, had brutally confirmed it. In a rage she threw away everything he had left: books, underwear, socks, a sweater, even a pencil stub. She did it, she regretted it, she burst into tears. When finally the tears stopped, she felt ugly, swollen, stupid, cheapened by the bitter feelings that Nino, Nino whom she loved and by whom she believed she was loved in return, was provoking. The apartment seemed suddenly what it was, a squalid place through whose walls all the noises of the city reached her. She became aware of the bad smell, of the cockroaches that came in under the stairwell door, the stains of dampness on the ceiling, and felt for the first time that childhood was clutching at her again, not the childhood of dreams but the childhood of cruel privations, of threats and beatings. In fact suddenly she discovered that one fantasy that had comforted us since we were children—to become rich—had evaporated from her mind. Although the poverty of Campi Flegrei seemed to her darker than in the neighborhood of our games, although her situation was worse because of the child she was expecting, although in a few days she had used up the money she had brought, she discovered that wealth no longer seemed a prize and a compensation, it no longer spoke to her. The creased and evil-smelling paper money—piling up in the drawer of the cash register when she worked in the grocery, or in the colored metal box of the shop in Piazza dei Martiri—that in adolescence replaced the strongboxes of our childhood, overflowing with gold pieces and precious stones, no longer functioned: any remaining glitter was gone. The relationship between money and the possession of things had disappointed her. She wanted nothing for herself or for the child she would have. To be rich for her meant having Nino, and since Nino was gone she felt poor, a poverty that no money could obliterate. Since there was no remedy for that new condition—she had made too many mistakes since she was a child, and they had all converged in that last mistake: to believe that the son of Sarratore couldn't do without her as she couldn't without him, and that theirs was a unique, exceptional fate, and that the good fortune of loving each other would last forever and would extinguish the force of any other necessity—she felt guilty and decided not to go out, not to look for him, not to eat, not to drink, but to wait for her life and that of the baby to lose their outlines, any possible definition, and she found that there was nothing left in her mind, not even a trace of the thing that made her spiteful, that is to say the awareness of abandonment.

Then someone rang at the door.

She thought it was Nino: she opened it. It was Enzo. Seeing him didn't disappoint her. She thought he had come to bring her some fruit—as he had done many years earlier, as a child, after he was defeated in the competition created by the principal and Maestra Oliviero, and had thrown a stone at her—and she burst out laughing. Enzo considered the laughter a sign of illness. He went in, but left the door open out of respect, he didn't want the neighbors to think she was receiving men like a prostitute. He looked around, he glanced at her disheveled state, and although he didn't see what still didn't show, that is, the pregnancy, he deduced that she really needed help. In his serious way, completely without emotion, he said, even before she managed to calm down and stop laughing:

"We're going now."

"Where?"

"To your husband."

"Did he send you?"

"No."

"Who sent you?"

"No one sent me."

"I'm not coming."

"Then I'll stay here with you."

"Forever?"

"Until you're persuaded."

"And your job?"

"I'm tired of it."

"And Carmen?"

"You are much more important."

"I'll tell her, then she'll leave you."

"I'll tell her, I've already decided."

From then on he spoke distantly, in a low voice. She answered him laughing, in a teasing way, as if none of their words were real, as if they were speaking in fun of a world, of people, of feelings that hadn't existed for a long time. Enzo realized that, and for a while he said nothing more. He went through the house, found Lila's suitcase, filled it with the things in the drawers, in the closet. Lila let him do it, because she considered him not the flesh-and-blood Enzo but a shadow, in color, as in the movies, who although he spoke was nevertheless an effect of the light. Having packed the suitcase, Enzo confronted her again and made a very surprising speech. He said, in his concentrated yet detached way,

"Lina, I've loved you since we were children. I never told you because you are very beautiful and very intelligent, and I am short, ugly, and worthless. Now return to your husband. I don't know why you left him and I don't want to know. I know only that you can't stay here, you don't deserve to live in filth. I'll take you to the entrance of the building and wait: if he treats you badly, I'll come up and kill him. But he won't, he'll be glad you've come back. But let's make a pact: in the case that you can't come to an agreement with your husband, I brought you back to him and I will come and get you. All right?"

Lila stopped laughing, she narrowed her eyes, she listened to him attentively for the first time. Interactions between Enzo and her had been very rare until that moment, but the times I had been present they had always amazed me. There was something indefinable between them, originating in the confusion of childhood. She trusted Enzo, I think, she felt she could count on him. When the young man took the suitcase and headed toward the door, which had remained open, she hesitated a moment, then followed him.

96.

Enzo did wait under Lila and Stefano's windows the night he took her home, and, if Stefano had beaten her, he probably would have gone up and killed him. But Stefano didn't beat her; he welcomed her into her home, which was clean and tidy. He behaved as if his wife really had gone to stay with me in Pisa, even if there was no evidence that that was what had happened. Lila, on the other hand, did not take refuge in that excuse or any other. The following day, when she woke up, she said reluctantly, "I'm pregnant," and he was so happy that when she added, "The baby isn't yours," he burst out laughing, with genuine joy. When she angrily repeated that phrase, once, twice, three times, and even tried to hit him with clenched fists, he cuddled her, kissed her, murmuring, "Enough, Lina, enough, enough, I'm too happy. I know that I've treated you badly but now let's stop, don't say mean things to me," and his eyes filled with tears of joy.

Lila knew that people tell themselves lies to defend against the truth of the facts, but she was amazed that her husband was able to lie to himself with such joyful conviction. On the other hand she didn't care, by now, about Stefano or about herself, and after again repeating for a while, without emotion, "The baby isn't yours," she withdrew into the lethargy of pregnancy. He prefers to put off the pain, she thought, and all right, let him do as he likes: if he doesn't want to suffer now, he'll suffer later.

She went on to make a list of what she wanted and what she didn't want: she didn't want to work in the shop in Piazza dei Martiri or in the grocery; she didn't want to see anyone, friends, relatives, especially the Solaras; she wished to stay home and be a wife and mother. He agreed, sure that she would change her mind in a few days. But Lila secluded herself in the apartment, without showing any interest in Stefano's business, or that of her brother and her father, or in the affairs of his relatives or of her own relatives.

A couple of times Pinuccia came with her son, Fernando, whom they called Dino, but she didn't open the door.

Once Rino came, very upset, and Lila let him in, listened to all his chatter about how angry the Solaras were about her disappearance from the shop, about how badly things were going with Cerullo shoes, because Stefano thought only of his own affairs and was no longer investing. When at last he was silent, she said, "Rino, you're the older brother, you're a grownup, you have a wife and son, do me a favor: live your life without constantly turning to me." He was hurt and he went away depressed, after a complaint about how everyone was getting richer while he, because of his sister, who didn't care about the family, the blood of the Cerullos, but now felt she was a Carracci, was in danger of losing the little he had gained.

It happened that even Michele Solara went to the trouble of coming to see her—in the beginning even twice a day—at times when he was sure that Stefano wouldn't be there. But she never let him in, she sat silently in the kitchen, almost without breathing, so that once, before he left, he shouted at her from the street: "Who the fuck do you think you are, whore, you had an agreement with me and you didn't keep it."

Lila welcomed willingly only Nunzia and Stefano's mother, Maria, both of whom followed her pregnancy closely. She stopped throwing up but her complexion remained gray. She had the impression of having become large and inflated inside rather than outside, as if within the wrapping of her body every organ had begun to fatten. Her stomach seemed a bubble of flesh that was expanding because of the baby's breathing. She was afraid of that expansion, she feared that the thing she was most afraid of would happen: she would break apart, overflow. Then suddenly she felt that the being she had inside, that absurd modality of life, that expanding nodule that at a certain point would come out of her sex like a puppet on a string— suddenly she loved it, and through it the sense of herself returned. Frightened by her ignorance, by the mistakes she could make, she began to read everything she could find about what pregnancy is, what happens inside the womb, how to prepare for the birth. She hardly went out at all in those months. She stopped buying clothes or objects for the house, she got in the habit instead of having her mother bring at least a couple of newspapers and Alfonso some journals. It was the only money she spent. Once Carmen showed up to ask for money and she told her to ask Stefano, she had none; the girl went away discouraged. She didn't care about anyone anymore, only the baby.

The experience wounded Carmen, who became even more resentful. She still hadn't forgiven Lila for breaking up their alliance in the new grocery. Now she couldn't forgive her for not opening her purse. But mainly she couldn't forgive her because—as she began to gossip to everyone—she had done as she liked: she had vanished, she had returned, and yet she continued to play the part of the lady, to have a nice house, and now even had a baby coming. The more of a slut you are, the better off you are. She, on the other hand, who labored from morning to night with no gratification—only bad things happened to her, one after the other. Her father died in jail. Her mother died in that way she didn't even want to think about. And now Enzo as well. He had waited for her one night outside the grocery and told her that he didn't want to continue the engagement. Just like that, very few words, as usual, no explanation. She had run weeping to her brother, and Pasquale had met Enzo to ask for an explanation. But Enzo had given none, so now they didn't speak to each other.

When I returned from Pisa for Easter vacation and met Carmen in the gardens, she vented. "I'm an idiot," she wept, "waiting for him the whole time he was a soldier. An idiot slaving from morning to night for practically nothing." She said she was tired of everything. And with no obvious connection she began to insult Lila. She went so far as to ascribe to her a relationship with Michele Solara, who had often been seen wandering around the Carracci house. "Adultery and money," she hissed, "that's how she gets ahead."

Not a word, however, about Nino. Miraculously, the neighborhood knew nothing of that. During the same period, Antonio told me about beating him up, and about how he had sent Enzo to retrieve Lila, but he told only me, and I'm sure that for his whole life he never spoke a word to anyone else. But I learned something from Alfonso: insistently questioned, he told me he had heard from Marisa that Nino had gone to study in Milan. Thanks to them, when on Holy Saturday I ran into Lila on the *stradone*, completely by chance, I felt a subtle pleasure at the idea that I knew more than she about the facts of her life, and that from what I knew it was easy to deduce how little good it had done her to take Nino away from me.

Her stomach was already quite big, it was like an excrescence on her thin body. Even her face didn't show the florid beauty of pregnant women; it was ugly, greenish, the skin stretched over the prominent cheekbones. We both tried to pretend that nothing had happened.

"How are you?"

"Well."

"Can I touch your stomach?"

"Yes."

"And that matter?"

"Which?"

"The one on Ischia."

"It's over."

"Too bad."

"What are you doing?"

"I study, I have a place of my own and all the books I need. I even have a sort of boyfriend."

"A sort?"

"Yes."

"What's his name?"

"Franco Mari."

"What does he do?"

"He's also a student."

"Those glasses really suit you."

"Franco gave them to me."

"And the dress?"

"Also him."

"He's rich?"

"Yes."

"I'm glad."

"And how is the studying going?"

"I work hard, otherwise they'll send me away."

"Be careful."

"I'm careful."

"Lucky you."

"Well."

She said her due date was in July. She had a doctor, the one who had sent her to bathe in the sea. A doctor, not the obstetrician in the neighborhood. "I'm afraid for the baby," she said. "I don't want to give birth at home." She had read that it was better to go to a clinic. She smiled, she touched her belly. Then she said something that wasn't very clear.

"I'm still here just for this."

"Is it nice to feel the baby inside?"

"No, it repulses me, but I'm pleased to carry it."

"Was Stefano angry?"

"He wants to believe what's convenient for him."

"That is?"

"That for a while I was a little crazy and ran away to you in Pisa."

I pretended not to know anything, feigning amazement: "In Pisa? You and me?"

"Yes."

"And if he asks, should I say that's what happened?"

"Do as you like."

We said goodbye, promising to write. But we never wrote and I did nothing to find out about the birth. Sometimes a feeling stirred in me that I immediately repressed to keep it from becoming conscious: I wanted something to happen to her, so the baby wouldn't be born.

97.

In that period I often dreamed of Lila. Once she was in bed in a lacy green nightgown, her hair was braided, which was something she had never done, she held in her arms a little girl dressed in pink, and she kept saying, in a sorrowful voice, "Take a picture but only of me, not of the child." Another time she greeted me happily and then called her daughter, who had

my name. "Lenù," she said, "come and say hello to your aunt."
But a fat old giantess appeared, and Lila ordered me to
undress her and wash her and change her diaper and swad-
dling. On waking I was tempted to look for a telephone and try
to call Alfonso to find out if the baby had been born without
any problems, if she was happy. But I had to study or maybe I
had exams, and I forgot about it. When, in August, I was free
of both obligations, it happened that I didn't go home. I wrote
some lies to my parents and went with Franco to Versilia, to an
apartment belonging to his family. For the first time I wore a
two-piece bathing suit: it fit in one fist and I felt very bold.

It was at Christmas that I heard from Carmen how difficult
Lila's delivery had been.

"She almost died," she said, "so in the end the doctor had
to cut open her stomach, otherwise the baby couldn't be
born."

"She had a boy?"

"Yes."

"Is he well?"

"He's lovely."

"And she?"

"She's lost her figure."

I learned that Stefano wanted to give his son the name of his
father, Achille, but Lila was opposed to it, and the yelling of
husband and wife, which hadn't been heard for a long time,
echoed throughout the clinic, so that the nurses had repri-
manded them. In the end the child was called Gennaro, that is,
Rino, like Lila's brother.

I listened, I didn't say anything. I felt unhappy, and to cope
with my unhappiness I imposed on myself an attitude of
reserve. Carmen noticed:

"I'm talking and talking, but you don't say a word, you
make me feel like the TV news. Don't you give a damn about
us anymore?"

"Of course I do."

"You've gotten pretty, even your voice has changed."

"Did I have an ugly voice?"

"You had the voice that we have."

"And now?"

"You have it less."

I stayed in the neighborhood for ten days, from December 24, 1964, to January 3, 1965, but I never went to see Lila. I didn't want to see her son, I was afraid of recognizing in his mouth, in his nose, in the shape of his eyes or ears something of Nino.

At my house now I was treated like an important person who had deigned to stop by for a quick hello. My father observed me with pleasure. I felt his satisfied gaze on me, but if I spoke to him he became embarrassed. He didn't ask what I was studying, what was the use of it, what job I would have afterward, and not because he didn't want to know but out of fear that he wouldn't understand my answers. My mother instead moved angrily through the house, and, hearing her unmistakable footsteps, I thought of how I had been afraid of becoming like her. But, luckily, I had outdistanced her, and she felt it, she resented me for it. Even now, when she spoke to me, it was as if I were guilty of terrible things: in every situation I perceived in her voice a shadow of disapproval, but, unlike in the past, she never wanted me to do the dishes, clean up, wash the floors. There was some uneasiness also with my sister and brothers. They tried to speak to me in Italian and often corrected their own mistakes, ashamed. But I tried to show them that I was the same as ever, and gradually they were persuaded.

At night I didn't know how to pass the time, my old friends were no longer a group. Pasquale had terrible relations with Antonio and avoided him at all costs. Antonio didn't want to see anyone, partly because he didn't have time (he was constantly being sent here and there by the Solaras), partly because he didn't know what to talk about: he couldn't talk about his work and he didn't have a private life. Ada, after the grocery, either hurried home to take care of her mother and siblings or was tired and depressed, and went to bed, so that she hardly ever saw Pasquale, and this made him very anxious. Carmen now hated everything and everyone, maybe even me: she hated the job in the new grocery, the Carraccis, Enzo, who had left her, her brother, who had confined himself to quarreling about it and hadn't beaten him up. Yes, Enzo. Enzo, finally—whose mother, Assunta, was now seriously ill, and who, when he wasn't laboring to earn money during the day, was taking care of her, and at night, too, and yet, surprisingly, had managed to get his engineer's diploma—Enzo was never around. I was curious at the news that he had accomplished that very difficult goal of getting a diploma by studying on his own. Who would have imagined, I thought. Before returning to Pisa I made a big effort and persuaded him to take a short walk. I was full of congratulations for his achievement, but he had only a disparaging expression. He had reduced his vocabulary so far that I did all the talking, he said almost nothing. I remember only one phrase, which he uttered before we separated. I hadn't mentioned Lila until that moment, not even a word. And yet, as if I had talked exclusively about her, he said suddenly,

"Anyway, Lina is the best mother in the whole neighborhood."

That *anyway* put me in a bad mood. I had never thought of Enzo as particularly sensitive, but on that occasion I was sure that, walking beside me, he had *felt*—felt as if I had proclaimed it aloud—the long mute list of wrongs that I attributed to our friend, as if my body had angrily articulated it without my knowing.

98.

For love of little Gennaro, Lila began to go out again. She put the baby, dressed in blue or white, in the cumbersome, enormous, and expensive carriage that her brother had given her and walked alone through the new neighborhood. As soon as Rinuccio cried, she went to the grocery and nursed him, amid the enthusiasm of her mother-in-law, the tender compliments of the customers, and the annoyance of Carmen, who lowered her head, and said not a word. Lila fed the baby as soon as he cried. She liked feeling him attached to her, she liked feeling the milk that ran out of her into him, pleasantly emptying her breast. It was the only bond that gave her a sense of well-being, and she confessed in her notebooks that she feared the moment when the baby would separate from her.

When the weather turned nice, she started going to the gardens in front of the church, since in the new neighborhood there were only bare streets with a few bushes or sickly saplings. Passersby stopped to look at the baby and praised him, which pleased her. If she had to change him, she went to the old grocery, where, as soon as she entered, the customers greeted Gennaro warmly. Ada, however, with her smock that was too tidy, the lipstick on her thin lips, her pale face, her neat hair, her commanding ways even toward Stefano, was increasingly impudent, acting like a servant-mistress, and, since she was busy, she did everything possible to let Lila understand that she, the carriage, and the baby were in the way. But Lila took little notice. The surly indifference of her husband confused her more: in private, inattentive but not hostile to the baby, in public, in front of the customers who spoke in tender childish voices and wanted to hold him and kiss him, he didn't even look at him, in fact he made a show of disinterest. Lila went to the rear of the shop, washed Gennaro, quickly dressed him again, and went back to the gardens. There she examined her son lovingly, searching for signs of Nino in his face, and wondering if Stefano had seen what she couldn't.

But soon she forgot about it. In general the days passed over her without provoking the least emotion. She mostly took care of her son, the reading of a book might last weeks, two or three pages a day. In the gardens, if the baby was sleeping, every so often she let herself be distracted by the branches of the trees that were putting out new buds, and she wrote in one of her battered notebooks.

Once she noticed that there was a funeral in the church, and when, with the baby, she went to see, she discovered that it was the funeral of Enzo's mother. She saw him, stiff, pale, but she didn't offer her condolences. Another time she was sitting on a bench with the carriage beside her, bent over a large volume with a green spine, when a skinny old woman appeared before her, leaning on a cane; her cheeks seemed to be sucked into her throat by her very breathing.

"Guess who I am."

Lila had trouble recognizing her, but finally the woman's eyes, in a flash, recalled the imposing Maestra Oliviero. She jumped up full of emotion, about to embrace her, but the teacher drew back in annoyance. Lila then showed her the baby, said proudly, "His name is Gennaro," and since everyone praised her son she expected that the teacher would, too. But Maestra Oliviero completely ignored the child, she seemed interested only in the heavy book that her former pupil was holding, a finger in the pages to mark her place.

"What is it?"

Lila became nervous. The teacher's looks had changed, her voice, everything about her, except her eyes and the sharp tones, the same tones as when she had asked her a question in the classroom. So she, too, showed that she hadn't changed, she answered in a lazy yet aggressive way: "The title is *Ulysses*."

"Is it about the Odyssey?"

"No, it's about how prosaic life is today."

"And so?"

"That's all. It says that our heads are full of nonsense. That we are flesh, blood, and bone. That one person has the same value as another. That we want only to eat, drink, fuck."

The teacher reproached her for that last word, as in school, and Lila posed as an insolent girl, and laughed, so that the old woman became even sterner, asked her how the book was. She answered that it was difficult and she didn't completely understand it.

"Then why are you reading it?"

"Because someone I knew read it. But he didn't like it."

"And you?"

"I do."

"Even if it's difficult?"

"Yes."

"Don't read books that you can't understand, it's bad for you."

"A lot of things are bad for you."

"You're not happy?"

"So-so."

"You were destined for great things."

"I've done them: I'm married and I've had a baby."

"Everyone can do that."

"I'm like everyone."

"You're wrong."

"No, you are wrong, and you always were wrong."

"You were rude as a child and you're rude now."

"Clearly you weren't much of a teacher as far as I'm concerned."

Maestra Oliviero looked at her carefully and Lila read in her face the anxiety of being wrong. The teacher was trying to find in her eyes the intelligence she had seen when she was a child, she wanted confirmation that she hadn't been wrong.

She thought: I have to remove from my face every sign that makes her right, I don't want her to preach to me how I'm wasted. But meanwhile she felt exposed to yet another examination, and, contradictorily, she feared the result. She is discovering that I am stupid, she said to herself, her heart pounding harder, she is discovering that my whole family is stupid, that my forebears were stupid and my descendants will be stupid, that Gennaro will be stupid. She became upset, she put the book in her bag, she grabbed the handle of the carriage, she said nervously that she had to go. Crazy old lady, she still believed she could rap me on the knuckles. She left the teacher in the gardens, small, clutching her cane, consumed by an illness that she would not give in to.

99.

Lila began to be obsessed with stimulating her son's intelligence. She didn't know what books to buy and asked Alfonso to find out from the booksellers. Alfonso brought her a couple of volumes and she dedicated herself to them. In her notebooks I found notes on how she was reading the difficult texts: she struggled to advance, page by page, but after a while she lost the thread, she thought of something else; yet she forced her eye to keep gliding along the lines, her fingers turned the pages automatically, and by the end she had the impression that, even though she hadn't understood, the words had nevertheless entered her brain and inspired thoughts. Starting there, she reread the book and, reading, corrected her thoughts or amplified them, until the text was no longer useful, she looked for others.

Her husband came home at night and found that she hadn't cooked dinner, that she had the baby playing games she had invented herself. He got angry, but she, as had happened for a long time, didn't react. It was as if she didn't hear him, as if the house were inhabited only by her and her son, and when she got up and started cooking she did it not because Stefano was hungry but because she was.

In those months their relationship, after a long period of mutual tolerance, began to deteriorate again. Stefano told her one night that he was tired of her, of the baby, of everything. Another time he said that he had married too young, without understanding what he was doing. But once she answered, "I don't know what I'm doing here, either, I'll take the baby and go," and he, instead of telling her to get out, lost his temper, as he hadn't for a long time, and hit her in front of the child, who stared at her from the blanket on the floor, dazed by the uproar. Her nose dripping blood and Stefano shouting insults at her, Lila turned to her son laughing, told him in Italian (she had been speaking to him only in Italian for a long time), "Papa's playing, we're having fun."

I don't know why, but at a certain point she began to take care of Dino, her nephew. It's possible that it began because she needed to compare Gennaro to another child. Or maybe not, maybe she felt a qualm that she was devoting all her attention only to her own son and it seemed right to take care of her nephew as well. Pinuccia, although she still considered Dino the living proof of the disaster that her life was, and was always yelling at him, and sometimes hit him ("Will you stop it, will you stop it? What do you want from me, you want to make me crazy?"), was resolutely opposed to having Lila take him to her house to play mysterious games with little Gennaro. She said to her angrily: "You take care of raising your son and I'll take care of mine, and instead of wasting time take care of your husband, otherwise you'll lose him." But here Rino intervened.

It was a terrible time for Lila's brother. He fought constantly with his father, who wanted to close the shoe factory because he was sick of working only to enrich the Solaras and, not understanding that it was necessary to go on at all costs, regretted his old workshop. He fought constantly with Michele and Marcello, who treated him like a petulant boy and when the problem was money spoke directly to Stefano. And mainly he fought with Stefano, shouting and insulting, because his brother-in-law wouldn't give him a cent and, according to him, was now negotiating secretly to deliver the whole shoe business into the hands of the Solaras. He fought with Pinuccia, who accused him of having led her to believe he was a big shot when really he was a puppet who could be manipulated by anyone, by his father, by Stefano, by Marcello and Michele. So, when he realized that Stefano was mad at Lila because she was being too much a mamma and not enough a wife, and that Pinuccia wouldn't entrust the child to her sister-in-law for even an hour, he began, defiantly, to take the baby to his sister himself, and since there was less and less work at the shoe factory, he got in the habit of staying, sometimes for hours, in the apartment in the new neighborhood to see what Lila did with Gennaro and Dino. He was fascinated by her maternal patience, by the way the children played, by the way his son, who at home was always crying or sat listlessly in his playpen like a sad puppy, with Lila became eager, quick, seemed happy.

"What do you do to them?" he asked admiringly.

"I make them play."

"My son played before."

"Here he plays and learns."

"Why do you spend so much time on it?"

"Because I read that everything we are is decided now, in the first years of life."

"And is mine doing well?"

"You see him."

"Yes, I see, he's better than yours."

"Mine is younger."

"Do you think Dino is intelligent?"

"All children are, you just have to train them."

"Then train them, Lina, don't get tired of it immediately the way you usually do. Make him very intelligent for me."

But one evening Stefano came home early and especially irritable. He found his brother-in-law sitting on the kitchen floor and, instead of confining himself to a harsh look because of the mess, his wife's lack of interest, the attention given to the children instead of to him, said to Rino that this was his house, that he didn't like seeing him around every day wasting time, that the shoe factory was failing precisely because he was so idle, that the Cerullos were unreliable—in other words, Get out immediately or I'll kick your ass.

There was a commotion. Lila cried that he mustn't speak like that to her brother, Rino threw in his brother-in-law's face everything that until that moment he had only hinted at or had prudently kept to himself. Gross insults flew. The two children, abandoned in the confusion, began grabbing each other's toys, crying, especially the smaller one, who was overpowered by the bigger one. Rino shouted at Stefano, his neck swollen, his veins like electric cables, that it was easy to be the boss with the goods that Don Achille had stolen from half the neighborhood, and added, "You're nothing, you're just a piece of shit, your father at least knew how to commit a crime, you don't even know that."

It was a terrible moment, which Lila watched in terror. Stefano seized Rino by the hips with both hands, like a ballet dancer with his partner, and although they were of the same height, the same build, although Rino struggled and yelled and spit, Stefano picked him up with a prodigious force and hurled him against a wall. Right afterward he took him by the arm and dragged him across the floor to the door, opened it, pulled him to his feet and threw him down the stairs, even though Rino tried to resist, even though Lila had roused herself and was clinging to Stefano, begging him to calm down.

It didn't end there. Stefano whirled around, and she realized that he wanted to do to Dino the same thing he had done to his father, throw him like an object down the stairs. So she flew at him, from behind, and, grabbing his face, scratched him, crying, "He's a child, Ste', he's a child." He froze, and said softly, "I'm fucking fed up with everything, I can't take it anymore."

100.

A complicated period began. Rino stopped going to his sister's house, but Lila didn't want to give up keeping Rinuccio and Dino together, so she got in the habit of going to her brother's house, but in secret from Stefano. Pinuccia endured it, sullenly, and at first Lila tried to explain to her what she was doing: exercises in reactivity, games of skill, she went so far as to confide in her that she would have liked to involve all the neighborhood children. But Pinuccia said simply, "You're a lunatic and I don't give a damn what nonsense you get up to. You want to take the child? You want to kill him, you want to eat him like the witches? Go ahead, I don't want him and I never did, your brother has been the ruin of my life and you are the ruin of my brother's life." Then she cried, "That poor devil is perfectly right to cheat on you."

Lila didn't react.

She didn't ask what that remark meant, in fact she made a careless gesture, one of those gestures that you make to brush away a fly. She took Rinuccio and, although she was sorry to be deprived of her nephew, she did not return.

But in the solitude of her apartment she discovered that she was afraid. She absolutely didn't care if Stefano was paying some whore, in fact she was glad—she didn't have to submit at night when he approached her. But after that remark of

Pinuccia's she began to worry about the baby: if her husband had taken another woman, if he wanted her every day and every hour, he might go mad, he might throw her out. Until that moment the possibility of a definitive break in her marriage had seemed to her a liberation; now instead she was afraid of losing the house, the money, the time, everything that allowed her to bring up the child in the best way.

She hardly slept. Maybe Stefano's rages were not only the sign of a constitutional lack of equilibrium, the bad blood that blew the lid off good-natured habits: maybe he really was in love with someone else, as had happened to her with Nino, and he couldn't stand to stay in the cage of marriage, of paternity, even of groceries and other dealings. She felt she had to make up her mind to confront the situation, if only to control it, and yet she delayed, she gave it up, she counted on the fact that Stefano enjoyed his lover and left her in peace. Ultimately, she thought, I just have to hold out for a couple of years, long enough for the child to grow up and be educated.

She organized her day so that he would always find the house in order, dinner ready, the table set. But, after the scene with Rino, he did not return to his former mildness, he was always disgruntled, always preoccupied.

"What's wrong?"

"Money."

"Money and that's all?"

Stefano got angry: "What does *and that's all* mean?"

For him there was no other problem, in life, but money. After dinner he did the accounts and cursed the whole time: the new grocery wasn't taking in cash as it used to; the Solaras, especially Michele, were acting as if the shoe business were all theirs and the profits weren't to be shared anymore; without saying anything to him, Rino, and Fernando, they were having the old Cerullo models made by cheap shoemakers on the outskirts, and meanwhile they were having new Solara styles

designed by artisans who in fact were simply making tiny variations in Lila's; in this way the small enterprise of his father-in-
law and brother-in-law really was being ruined, dragging him
down with it, the one who had invested in it.

"Understand?"

"Yes."

"So try not to be a pain in the ass."

But Lila wasn't convinced. She had the impression that her
husband was deliberately amplifying problems that were real
but old, in order to hide from her the true, new reasons for his
outbursts and his increasingly explicit hostility toward her. He
blamed her for all sorts of things, and especially for having
complicated his relations with the Solaras. Once he yelled at
her, "What did you do to that bastard Michele, I'd like to
know?"

And she answered, "Nothing."

And he: "It can't be, in every discussion he brings you up
but he screws me: try to talk to him and find out what he
wants, otherwise I ought to smash your faces, both of you."

And Lila, impulsively: "If he wants to fuck me what should
I do, let him fuck me?"

A moment later she was sorry she had said that—sometimes
contempt prevailed over prudence—but now she had done it
and Stefano hit her. The slap counted little, it wasn't even with
his hand open, as usual, he hit her with the tips of his fingers.
Rather, what he said right afterward, disgusted, carried more
weight:

"You read, you study, but you're vulgar: I can't bear people
like you, you make me sick."

From then on he came home later and later. On Sunday,
instead of sleeping until midday as usual, he went out early and
disappeared for the whole day. At the least hint from her of
concrete family problems, he got angry. For example, on the
first hot days she was preoccupied about a vacation at the

beach for Rinuccio, and she asked her husband how they should organize it. He answered: "You take the bus and go to Torregaveta."

She ventured: "Isn't it better to rent a house?"

He: "Why, so you can be a whore from morning to night?"

He left, and didn't return that night.

Everything became clear soon afterward. Lila went to the city with the child, she was looking for a book that she had found quoted in another book, but she couldn't find it. After much searching she went on to Piazza dei Martiri, to ask Alfonso, who was still happily managing the shop, if he could find it. She ran into a handsome young man, very well dressed, one of the handsomest men she had ever seen, his name was Fabrizio. He wasn't a customer, he was a friend of Alfonso's. Lila stayed to talk to him, she discovered that he knew a lot. They discussed literature, the history of Naples, how to teach children, something about which Fabrizio, who worked at the university, was very knowledgeable. Alfonso listened in silence the whole time and when Rinuccio began to whine he calmed him. Then some customers arrived, Alfonso went to take care of them. Lila talked to Fabrizio a little more; it was a long time since she had felt the pleasure of a conversation that excited her. When the young man had to leave, he kissed her with childish enthusiasm, then did the same with Alfonso, two big smacking kisses. He called to her from the doorway: "It was lovely talking to you."

"For me, too."

Lila was sad. While Alfonso continued to wait on customers, she remembered the people she had met in that place, and Nino, the lowered shutter, the shadowy light, the pleasant conversations, the way he arrived secretly, exactly at one, and disappeared at four, after they made love. It seemed to her an imaginary time, a bizarre fantasy, and she looked around uneasily. She didn't feel nostalgia for it, she didn't feel nostalgia for Nino. She felt only that time had passed, that what had been important was important no longer, that the tangle in her head endured and wouldn't come untangled. She took the child and was about to leave when Michele Solara came in.

He greeted her enthusiastically, he played with Gennaro, he said that the baby was just like her. He invited her to a bar, bought her a coffee, decided to take her home in his car. Once they were in the car he said to her, "Leave your husband, right away, today. I'll take you and your son. I've bought a house on the Vomero, in Piazza degli Artisti. If you want I'll drive you there now, I'll show it to you, I took it with you in mind. There you can do what you like: read, write, invent things, sleep, laugh, talk, and be with Rinuccio. I'm interested only in being able to look at you and listen to you."

For the first time in his life Michele expressed himself without his teasing tone of voice. As he drove and talked he glanced at her obliquely, slightly anxious, to see her reactions. Lila stared at the street in front of her the whole way, trying, meanwhile, to take the pacifier out of Gennaro's mouth, she thought he used it too much. But the child pushed her hand away energetically. When Michele stopped—she didn't interrupt him—she asked:

"Are you finished?"

"Yes."

"And Gigliola?"

"What does Gigliola have to do with it? You say yes or no, and then we'll see."

"No, Michè, the answer is no. I didn't want your brother and I don't want you, either. First, because I don't like either of you; and second because you think you can do anything and take anything without regard."

Michele didn't react right away, he muttered something about the pacifier, like: Give it to him, don't let him cry. Then he said, threateningly, "Think hard about it, Lina. Tomorrow you may be sorry and you'll come begging to me."

"I rule it out."

"Yes? Then listen to me."

He revealed to her what everyone knew ("Even your mother, your father, and that shit your brother, but they tell you nothing in order to keep the peace"): Stefano had taken Ada as a lover, and not recently. The thing had begun before the vacation on Ischia. "When you were on vacation," he said, "she went to your house every night." With Lila's return the two had stopped for a while. But they hadn't been able to resist: they had started again, had left each other again, had gone back together when Lila disappeared from the neighborhood. Recently Stefano had rented an apartment on the Rettifilo, they saw each other there.

"Do you believe me?"

"Yes."

"And so?"

So what. Lila was disturbed not so much by the fact that her husband had a lover and that the lover was Ada but by the absurdity of every word and gesture of his when he came to get her on Ischia. The shouts, the blows, the departure returned to her mind.

She said to Michele: "You make me sick, you, Stefano, all of you."

101.

Lila suddenly felt that she was in the right and this calmed her. That evening she put Gennaro to bed and waited for Stefano to come home. He returned a little after midnight, and found her sitting at the kitchen table. Lila looked up from the book she was reading, said she knew about Ada, she knew how long it had been going on, and that it didn't matter to her at all. "What you have done to me I did to you," she said clearly, smiling, and repeated to him—how many times had she said it in the past, two, three?—that Gennaro wasn't his son. She concluded that he could do what he liked, sleep where and with whom he wanted. "The essential thing," she cried suddenly, "is that you don't touch me again."

I don't know what she had in mind, maybe she just wanted to get things out in the open. Or maybe she was prepared for anything and everything. She expected that he would confess, that then he would beat her, chase her out of the house, make her, his wife, be a servant to his lover. She was prepared for every possible aggression and the arrogance of a man who feels that he is the master and has money to buy whatever he wants. Instead, getting to words that would clarify and sanction the failure of their marriage was impossible. Stefano denied it. He said, menacing, but calm, that Ada was merely the clerk in his grocery, that whatever gossip circulated about them had no basis. Then he got mad and told her that if she said that ugly thing about his son again, as God was his witness he would kill her: Gennaro was the image of him, identical, and everyone confirmed it, to keep provoking him on this point was useless. Finally—and this was the most surprising thing—he declared to her, as he had done at other times in the past, without varying the formulas, his love. He said that he would love her forever, because she was his wife, because they had been married before the priest and nothing could separate them. When he came over to kiss her and she pushed him away, he grabbed her, lifted her up, carried her to the bedroom, where the baby's cradle was, tore off everything she had on and entered her forcibly, while she begged him in a low voice, repressing sobs: "Rinuccio will wake up, see us, hear us, please let's go in there."

102.

After that night Lila lost many of the small freedoms that remained to her. Stefano's behavior was completely contradictory. Since his wife now knew of his relationship with Ada, he abandoned all caution. Often he didn't come home to sleep; every other Sunday he went out in the car with his lover. In August, he went on a vacation with her: they went to Stockholm in the sports car, even though officially Ada had gone to Turin, to visit a cousin who worked at Fiat. At the same time, a sick form of jealousy exploded in him: he didn't want his wife to leave the house, he obliged her to do the shopping by phone and if she went out for an hour so that the baby could get some air he interrogated her on whom she had met, whom she had talked to. He felt more a husband than ever and he watched her. It was as if he feared that his betrayal of her authorized her to betray him. What he did in his encounters with Ada on the Rettifilo stirred his imagination and led him to detailed fantasies in which Lila did even more with her lovers. He was afraid of being made ridiculous by a possible unfaithfulness on her part, while he did nothing to hide his own.

He wasn't jealous of all men, he had a hierarchy. Lila quickly understood that in particular he was preoccupied by Michele, by whom he felt cheated in everything and as if kept in a position of permanent subjugation. Although she had never said anything about the time Solara had tried to kiss her, or of his proposal that she become his lover, Stefano had perceived that to insult him by taking his wife was an important move in the process of ruining him in business. But on the other hand the logic of business meant that Lila should behave at least a little cordially. As a result whatever she did he didn't like. At times he pressed her obsessively: "Did you see Michele, did you talk to him, did he ask you to design new shoes?" Sometimes he shouted at her: "You are not even to say hello to that shit, is that clear?" And he opened all her drawers, rummaged through them in search of evidence of her nature as a whore.

To further complicate the situation first Pasquale interfered, then Rino.

Pasquale naturally was the last to know, even after Lila, that his fiancée was Stefano's lover. No one told him, he saw them with his own eyes, late on a Sunday afternoon in September, coming out of a doorway on the Rettifilo embracing. Ada had told him that she had things to do with Melina and couldn't see him. Besides, he was always out at work or at his political meetings, and took little notice of his fiancée's distortions and evasions. Seeing them caused him terrible pain, complicated by the fact that, while his immediate impulse would have been to kill them both, his education as a militant Communist prohibited him. Pasquale had recently become secretary of the neighborhood section of the Party and although in the past, like all the boys we had grown up with, he had classified us when necessary as whores, he now felt—since he kept himself up to date, read *l'Unità*, studied booklets, presided over debates in the section—that he could no longer do that, in fact he made an effort to consider us women not inferior, generally speaking, to men, with our feelings, our ideas, our freedoms. Caught, therefore, between rage and broad-mindedness, the next night, still dirty from work, he went to Ada and told her that he knew everything. She appeared relieved and admitted it, cried, begged forgiveness. When he asked if she had done it for money, she answered that she loved Stefano and that she alone knew what a good and generous and kind person he was. The result was that Pasquale punched the kitchen wall in the Cappuccio house, and returned home weeping, his knuckles sore. Afterward he talked to Carmen all night, the sister and brother suffered together, one because of Ada, the other because of Enzo, whom she couldn't forget. Things really took a bad turn when Pasquale, although he had been betrayed, decided that he had to defend the dignity of both Ada and Lila. First he wanted to clarify things, and went to talk to Stefano; he made a complicated speech whose essence was that he should leave his wife and set up a household with his lover. Then he went to Lila and reproached her because she let Stefano trample on her rights as a wife and her feelings as a woman. One morning—it was six-thirty—Stefano confronted him just as he was leaving to go to work and good-naturedly offered him money so that he would stop bothering him, his wife, and Ada. Pasquale took the money, counted it, and threw it away, saying, "I've worked since I was a child, I don't need you," then, as if to apologize, he added that he had to go, otherwise he would be late and would be fired. But when he had gone some distance he had a second thought, he turned and shouted at the grocer, who was picking up the money scattered on the street: "You are worse than that fascist pig your father." They fought, savagely, they had to be separated or they would have murdered each other.

Then came the trouble from Rino. He couldn't bear the fact that his sister had stopped trying to make Dino a very intelligent child. He couldn't bear the fact that his brother-in-law not only wouldn't give him a cent but had even laid hands on him. He couldn't bear the fact that the relation between Stefano and Ada had become public knowledge, with all the humiliating consequences for Lila. And he reacted in an unexpected way. Since Stefano beat Lila, he began to beat Pinuccia. Since Stefano had a lover, he found a lover. He started, that is, on a persecution of Stefano's sister that mirrored what his sister was subjected to by Stefano.

This threw Pinuccia into despair: with tears, with entreaties, she begged him to end it. But no. If she merely opened her mouth Rino, blinded by rage, and frightening even Nunzia, shouted at her: "I should end it? I should calm down? Then go to your brother and tell him that he should leave Ada, that he should respect Lina, that we have to be a united family and that he should give me the money that he and the Solaras have cheated me of and are cheating me of." The result was that Pinuccia very often ran out of the house, looking battered, and went to the grocery, to her brother, and sobbed in front of Ada and the customers. Stefano dragged her into the rear of the shop and she listed all her husband's demands, but concluded, "Don't give that bastard anything, come home now and kill him."

103.

This was more or less the situation when I returned to the neighborhood for the Easter vacation. I had been living in Pisa for two and a half years, I was a very brilliant student, and returning to Naples for the holidays had become an ordeal that I submitted to in order to avoid arguments with my parents, especially with my mother. As soon as the train entered the station I became nervous. I feared that some accident would prevent me from returning to the Normale at the end of the vacation: a serious illness that obliged me to enter the chaos of a hospital, some dreadful event that forced me to stop studying because the family needed me.

I had been home for a few hours. My mother had just given me a malicious report on the ugly affairs of Lila, Stefano, Ada, Pasquale, Rino, on the shoe factory that was about to close, on how these were times when one year you had money, you thought you were somebody, you bought a sports car, and the next year you had to sell everything, you ended up in Signora Solara's red book and stopped acting like a big shot. And here she cut off her litany and said to me, "Your friend thought she really had arrived, the wedding of a princess, the big car, the new house, and yet today you are much smarter and much prettier than she is." Then she frowned, to repress her satisfaction, and handed me a note that, naturally, she had read, even though it was for me. Lila wanted to see me, she invited me to lunch the next day, Holy Friday.

That was not the only invitation I had, the days were full. Soon afterward Pasquale called me from the courtyard and, as if I were descending from an Olympus instead of from my parents' dark house, wanted to expound to me his ideas about women, to tell me how much he was suffering, find out what I thought of his behavior. Pinuccia did the same in the evening, furious with both Rino and Lila. Ada, unexpectedly, did the same the next morning, burning with hatred and a sense of injury.

With all three I assumed a distant tone. I urged Pasquale to be calm, Pinuccia to concern herself with her son, and Ada to try to understand if it was true love. In spite of the superficiality of the words, I have to say that she interested me most. While she spoke, I stared at her as if she were a book. She was the daughter of Melina the madwoman, the sister of Antonio. In her face I recognized her mother, and many features of her brother. She had grown up without a father, exposed to every danger, used to working. She had washed the stairs of our buildings for years, with Melina, whose brain had suddenly stopped functioning. The Solaras had picked her up in their car when she was a girl and I could imagine what they had done to her. It seemed therefore normal that she should fall in love with Stefano, the courteous boss. She loved him, she told me, they loved each other. "Tell Lina," she said, her eyes shining with passion, "that one cannot command one's heart, and that if she is the wife I am the one who has given and gives Stefano everything, every attention and feeling that a man could want, and soon children, too, and so he is mine, he no longer belongs to her."

I understood that she wanted to get everything possible for herself, Stefano, the grocery stores, the money, the house, the cars. And I thought it was her right to fight that battle, which we were all fighting, one way or another. I tried to make her calm down, because she was very pale, her eyes were inflamed. And I was happy to hear how grateful she was to me, I was pleased to be consulted like a seer, handing out advice in a good Italian that confused her, as it did Pasquale and Pinuccia. Here, I thought sarcastically, is the use of history exams, classical philology, linguistics, and the thousands of file cards with which I drill myself rigorously: to soothe them for a few hours. They considered me impartial, without malicious feelings or passions, sterilized by study. And I accepted the role that they assigned me without mentioning my own suffering, my audaciousness, the times I had risked everything by letting Franco come to my room or sneaking into his, the vacation we had taken by ourselves in Versilia, living together as if we were married. I felt pleased with myself.

But as the time for lunch approached, the pleasure gave way to uneasiness, I went to Lila's unwillingly. I was afraid that she would find a way to restore in a flash the old hierarchy, causing me to lose faith in my choices. I feared that she would point out Nino's features in little Gennaro to remind me that the toy that was supposed to be mine had fallen to her. But it wasn't like that. Rinuccio—so she called him more and more frequently—touched me immediately: he was a handsome dark boy, and Nino hadn't yet emerged in his face and body, his features recalled Lila and even Stefano, as if all three had produced him. As for her, I felt that she had rarely been more fragile than she was then. At the mere sight of me her eyes shone with tears and her whole body trembled, I had to hold her tight to quiet her.

I noticed that in order not to make a bad impression she had combed her hair in a hurry, in a hurry had put on a little lipstick and a dress of pearl-gray rayon from the time of her engagement, that she wore shoes with a heel. She was still beautiful, but it was as if the bones of her face had become larger, her eyes smaller, and under the skin blood no longer circulated but an opaque liquid. She was very thin, embracing her I felt her bones, the clinging dress showed her swollen stomach.

At first she pretended that everything was fine. She was happy that I was enthusiastic about the baby, she liked the way I played with him, she wanted to show me all the things that Rinuccio could say and do. She began, in an anxious way that was unfamiliar, to pour out the terminology she had picked up from the chaotic reading she had done. She cited authors I had never heard of, made her son show off in exercises that she had invented for him. I noticed that she had developed a sort of tic, an expression of her mouth: she opened it suddenly and then pressed her lips together as if to contain the emotion produced by the things she was saying. Usually the expression was accompanied by a reddening of her eyes, a rosy light that the contraction of her lips, like a spring mechanism, promptly helped to reabsorb. She kept repeating that if she had dedicated herself assiduously to every child in the neighborhood, in a generation everything would change, there would no longer be the smart and the incompetent, the good and the bad. Then she looked at her son and again burst out crying. "He's ruined the books," she said between her tears, as if it were Rinuccio who had done it, and she showed them to me, torn, ripped in half. I had trouble understanding that the guilty person was not the little boy but her husband. "He's got in the habit of rummaging among my things," she murmured, "he doesn't want me to have even a thought of my own and if he discovers that I've hidden even some insignificant thing he beats me." She climbed up on a chair and took from on top of the wardrobe in the bedroom a metal box, and handed it to me. "Here's everything that happened with Nino," she said, "and so many thoughts that have gone through my head in these years, and also things of mine and yours that we haven't said.

Take it away, I'm afraid that he'll find it and start reading. But I don't want him to, they aren't things for him, they aren't for anyone, not even for you."

104.

I took the box unwillingly, I thought: where will I put it, what can I do with it. We sat at the table. I marveled that Rinuccio ate by himself, that he used his own small set of wooden implements, that, after his initial shyness passed, he spoke to me in Italian without mangling the words, that he answered each of my questions directly, with precision, and asked me questions in turn. Lila let me talk to her son, she ate almost nothing, she stared at her plate, absorbed. At the end, when I was about to go, she said:

"I don't remember anything about Nino, about Ischia, about the shop in Piazza dei Martiri. And yet it seemed to me that I loved him more than myself. It doesn't even interest me to know what happened to him, where he went."

I thought she was sincere, and said nothing of what I knew.

"Infatuations," I said, "have this good thing about them: after a while they pass."

"Are you happy?"

"Pretty much."

"How beautiful your hair is."

"Oh well."

"You have to do me another favor."

"What?"

"I have to leave this house before Stefano, without even realizing it, kills me and the child."

"You're worrying me."

"You're right to be worried, I'm afraid."

"Tell me what to do."

"Go to Enzo. Tell him that I tried but I couldn't make it."

"I don't understand."

"It's not important for you to understand: you have to go back to Pisa, you have your things. Tell him this, that's all: *Lina tried but she couldn't make it.*"

She went with me to the door with the child in her arms. She said to her son, "Rino, say goodbye to Aunt Lenù."

The baby smiled, waved his hand goodbye.

105.

Before I left I went to see Enzo. When I said to him, "*Lina told me to tell you that she tried but she couldn't make it,*" not even the shadow of an emotion crossed his face, so I thought that the message left him completely indifferent. "Things are bad," I added. "On the other hand I don't really know what can be done." He pressed his lips together, assumed a grave expression. We said goodbye.

On the train I opened the metal box, even though I had sworn not to. There were eight notebooks. From the first lines I began to feel bad. In Pisa, the bad feeling increased, over days, over months. Every word of Lila's diminished me. Every sentence, even sentences written when she was still a child, seemed to empty out mine, not the ones of that time but the ones now. And yet every page ignited my thoughts, my ideas, my pages as if until that moment I had lived in a studious but ineffectual stupor. Those notebooks I memorized, and in the end they made me feel that the world of the Normale—the friends, male and female, who respected me, the affectionate looks of those professors who encouraged me to constantly do more—was part of a universe that was too protected and thus too predictable, compared with that tempestuous world that, in the conditions of life in the neighborhood, Lila had been able to explore in her hurried lines, on pages that were crumpled and stained. Every past effort of mine seemed without meaning. I was frightened, for months school went badly. I was alone, Franco Mari had lost his place at the Normale, I couldn't pull myself out of the feeling of pettiness that had overwhelmed me. At a certain point it became clear that soon I, too, would get a bad mark and be sent home. So one evening in late autumn, without a precise plan, I went out carrying the metal box. I stopped on the Solferino bridge and threw it into the Arno.

106.

During my last year in Pisa the perspective from which I had experienced the first three changed. I was possessed by an ungrateful dislike of the city, my classmates, the teachers, the exams, the frigid days, the political meetings on warm evenings near the Baptistery, the films at the film forum, the entire unchanging urban space: the Timpano, the Lungarno Pacinotti, Via XXIV May, Via San Frediano, Piazza dei Cavalieri, Via Consoli del Mare, Via San Lorenzo, routes that were the same and yet alien even when the baker said hello and the newspaper seller chatted about the weather, alien in the voices that I had neverthe-less forced myself to imitate from the start, alien in the color of the stone and the plants and the signs and the clouds or sky.

I don't know if it was because of Lila's notebooks. Certainly, right after reading them and long before throwing away the box that contained them, I became disenchanted. My first impression, that of finding myself part of a fearless battle, passed. The trepidation at every exam and the joy of passing it with the highest marks had faded. Gone was the pleasure of re-educating my voice, my gestures, my way of dressing and walk-ing, as if I were competing for the prize of best disguise, the mask worn so well that it was *almost* a face.

Suddenly I was aware of that *almost*. Had I made it? Almost. Had I torn myself away from Naples, the neighborhood? Almost. Did I have new friends, male and female, who came from cultured backgrounds, often more cultured than the one that Professor Galiani and her children belonged to? Almost. From one exam to the next, had I become a student who was well received by the solemn professors who questioned me? Almost. Behind the *almost* I seemed to see how things stood. I was afraid. I was afraid as I had been the day I arrived in Pisa. I was scared of anyone who had that culture without the *almost*, with casual confidence.

There were many people at the Normale who did. It wasn't just students who passed the exams brilliantly, in Latin or Greek or history. They were youths—almost all male, as were the outstanding professors and the illustrious names who had passed through that institution—who excelled because they knew, without apparent effort, the present and future use of the labor of studying. They knew because of the families they came from or through an instinctive orientation. They knew how a newspaper or a journal was put together, how a publishing house was organized, what a radio or television office was, how a film originates, what the university hierarchies were, what there was beyond the borders of our towns or cities, beyond the Alps, beyond the sea. They knew the names of the people who counted, the people to be admired and those to be despised. I, on the other hand, knew nothing, to me anyone whose name was printed in a newspaper or a book was a god. If someone said to me with admiration or with resentment: that's so-and-so, that's the son of so-and-so, that's that other so-and-so's granddaughter, I was silent or I pretended to know. I perceived, of course, that they were *truly* important names, and yet I had never heard them, I didn't know what they had done that was important, I didn't know the map of prestige. For example, I came to my exams very well prepared, but if the professor were suddenly to ask me, "Do you know from what works I derive the authority on the basis of which I teach this subject in this university?" I wouldn't know what to answer. But the others knew. So I moved among them fearful of saying and doing the wrong things.

When Franco Mari fell in love with me, that fear diminished. He instructed me, I learned to move in his wake. Franco was lively, attentive to others, insolent, bold. He felt so sure of having read the right books and thus of being right that he always spoke with authority. I had learned to express myself in private and, more rarely, in public, relying on his reputation. And I was successful, or at least was becoming so. Strengthened by his certainties, I was at times bolder than he, at times more effective. But, although I had made a lot of progress, I still worried that I wasn't up to it, that I would say the wrong thing, reveal how ignorant and inexperienced I was in precisely the things that everyone knew. And as soon as Franco, in spite of himself, went out of my life, the fear regained power. I had had the proof of what, deep down, I already knew. His wealth, his upbringing, his reputation, well known among the students, as a young militant on the left, his sociability, even his courage when he delivered carefully measured speeches against powerful people within and outside the university—all this had given him an aura that automatically extended to me, as his fiancée or girlfriend or companion, as if the pure and simple fact that he loved me were the public sanctioning of my talents. But as soon as he lost his place at the Normale his merits faded, and no longer shone on me. The students from good families stopped inviting me to Sunday outings and parties. Some began making fun of my Neapolitan accent again. The things he had given me were no longer in fashion, looked dated. I had quickly understood that Franco, his presence in my life, had masked my true condition but hadn't changed it, I hadn't really succeeded in fitting in. I was one of those who labored day and night, got excellent results, were even treated with congeniality and respect, but would never carry off with the proper manner the high level of those studies. I would always be afraid: afraid of saying the wrong thing, of using an exaggerated tone, of dressing unsuitably, of revealing petty feelings, of not having interesting thoughts.

107.

I have to say that it was a depressing period for other reasons as well. Everyone knew, in Piazza dei Cavalieri, that I went to Franco's room at night, that I had gone alone with him to Paris, to Versilia, and this had given me the reputation of an easy girl. It's complicated to explain what it cost me to adapt to the idea of sexual freedom that Franco ardently supported; I myself hid the difficulty to seem free and open-minded to him. Nor could I repeat in public the ideas that he had instilled in me as if they were gospel, that is to say that half virgins were the worst kind of woman, petit bourgeois who preferred to give you their ass than to do things properly. And I couldn't say that I had a friend, in Naples, who at sixteen was already married, who at eighteen had taken a lover, who had become pregnant by him, who had returned to her husband, who would do God knows what else—that, in other words, going to bed with Franco seemed to me a small thing, compared with Lila's turbulent affairs. I had had to put up with malicious remarks from the girls, crude ones from the boys, their persistent looks at my large bosom. I had had to reject bluntly the bluntness with which some offered to replace my former boyfriend. I had to resign myself to the fact that the youths responded to my rejections with vulgar remarks. I kept on with clenched teeth, I said to myself: it will end.

Then, one afternoon, as I was leaving a crowded café on Via

San Frediano with two girlfriends, one of my rejected suitors shouted at me, seriously, in front of everyone, "Hey, Naples, remember to bring me the blue sweater I left in your room." Laughter, I went out without responding. But I soon realized that I was being followed by a boy I had already noticed in classes because of his peculiar appearance. He was neither a shadowy young intellectual like Nino nor an easygoing youth like Franco. He wore glasses, was very shy, solitary, with a tangled mass of black hair, a clearly solid body, crooked feet. He followed me to the college, then finally he called to me: "Greco."

Whoever he was, he knew my surname. I stopped out of politeness. The young man introduced himself, Pietro Airota, and made an embarrassed, confused speech. He said that he was ashamed of his companions but that he also hated himself because he had been cowardly and hadn't intervened.

"Intervened to do what?" I asked sarcastically, but at the same time amazed that someone like him, stooping, with thick glasses, that ridiculous hair, and the aura, the language of someone who is always at his books, felt it his duty to be the knight in shining armor like the boys of the neighborhood.

"To defend your good name."

"I don't have a good name."

He stammered something that seemed to me a mixture of apology and goodbye, and went off.

The next day I looked for him, I began to sit next to him in classes, we took long walks together. He surprised me: he had already begun to work on his thesis, for example, and like me he was doing it in Latin literature; unlike me, he didn't say "thesis," he said "work"; and once or twice he said "book," a book that he was finishing and that he would publish right after graduating. Work, book? What was he saying? Although he was twenty-two he had a thoughtful tone, he resorted continuously to the most refined quotations, he acted as if he already had a position at the Normale or some other university.

"Will you really publish your thesis?" I asked once, in disbelief.

He looked at me with equal amazement: "If it's good, yes."

"Are all theses that come out well published?"

"Why not."

He was studying Bacchic rites, I the fourth book of the Aeneid. I said, "Maybe Bacchus is more interesting than Dido."

"Everything is interesting if you know how to work on it."

We never talked about everyday things, or the possibility that the U.S.A. would give nuclear arms to West Germany, or whether Fellini was better than Antonioni, as Franco had accustomed me to do, but only about Latin literature, Greek literature. Pietro had a prodigious memory: he knew how to connect texts that were very unlike one another and he quoted them as if he were looking at them, but without being pedantic, without pretension, as if it were the most natural thing between two people who were devoted to their studies. The more time I spent with him, the more I realized that he was really smart, smart in a way that I would never be, because where I was cautious only out of fear of making a mistake, he demonstrated a sort of easy inclination to deliberate thought, to assertions that were never rash.

Even after I'd been walking with him a couple of times on Corso Italia or between the Duomo and the Camposanto, I saw that things around me changed again. One morning a girl I knew said to me, with friendly resentment, "What do you do to men? Now you've conquered the son of Airota."

I didn't know who Airota the father was, but certainly my classmates became respectful again: I was invited to parties or dinner. At a certain point I even had the suspicion that they talked to me because I brought Pietro out with me, since he generally kept to himself, absorbed in his work. I began to ask questions, all directed toward finding out what the merits of my new friend's father were. I discovered that he taught Greek literature at the university in Genoa but was also a prominent figure in the socialist party. This information constrained me, I was afraid of saying or having said in Pietro's presence things that were naïve or wrong. While he went on talking to me about his thesis-book, I, fearful of saying something stupid, talked less about mine.

One Sunday he arrived at the college out of breath, he wanted me to have lunch with his family, father, mother, and sister, who had come to see him. I was immediately apprehensive, I dressed up as well as I could. I thought: I'll make a mistake with subjunctives, they'll find me clumsy, they're grand people, they'll have a big car and a driver, what will I say, I'll look like an idiot. But as soon as I saw them I relaxed. Professor Airota was a man of medium height in a rather rumpled gray suit, he had a broad face that showed signs of weariness, large eyeglasses: when he took off his hat I saw that he was completely bald. Adele, his wife, was a thin woman, not pretty but refined, elegant without pretension. The car was like the Solaras' Fiat 1100, before they bought the Giulietta, and, I discovered, it was not a chauffeur who drove it from Genoa to Pisa but Mariarosa, Pietro's sister, who was attractive, with intelligent eyes, and who immediately hugged and kissed me as if we had been friends for a long time.

"Do you always drive here from Genoa?" I asked.

"Yes, I like driving."

"Was it hard to get a license?"

"Not at all."

She was twenty-four and was working for a professor in the art-history department at the University of Milan, she was studying Piero della Francesca. She knew everything about me, that is, everything her brother knew, my scholarly interests and that was all. Professor Airota and his wife knew the same things.

I spent a wonderful morning with them; they put me at my

ease. Unlike Pietro, his father, mother, and sister conversed on a wide variety of subjects. At lunch, in the restaurant of the hotel where they were staying, Professor Airota and his daughter had, for example, affectionate skirmishes on political subjects that I had heard about from Pasquale, from Nino, and from Franco but of whose substance I knew almost nothing. Arguments like: you've been trapped by inter-class collaboration; you call it a trap, I call it mediation; mediation in which the Christian Democrats always and only win; the politics of the center left is difficult; if it's difficult, go back to being socialists; you're not reforming a thing; in our place what would you do; revolution, revolution, and revolution; revolution is taking Italy out of the Middle Ages, without us socialists in the government, the students who talk about sex in school would be in jail and so would those who distribute pacifist leaflets; I want to see how you'd manage with the Atlantic Pact; we were always against the war and against all imperialism; you govern with the Christian Democrats, but will you stay anti-American?

Like that, a swift back and forth: a polemical exercise that they both obviously enjoyed, maybe a friendly habit of long standing. I recognized in them, father and daughter, what I had never had and, I now knew, would always lack. What was it? I wasn't able to say precisely: the training, perhaps, to feel that the questions of the world were deeply connected to me; the capacity to feel them as crucial and not purely as information to display at an exam, in view of a good grade; a mental conformation that didn't reduce everything to my own individual battle, to the effort to be successful. Mariarosa was kind, and so was her father; their tones were controlled, without a trace of the verbal excesses of Armando, Professor Galiani's son, or of Nino; and yet they injected warmth into political formulas that on other occasions had seemed to me cold, remote, to be used only in an attempt not to make a bad impression. Following each other in rapid succession, they moved on, without interruption, to the bombing of North Vietnam, to the student revolts on various campuses, to the many breeding grounds of anti-imperialist struggle in Latin America and Africa. And the daughter now seemed to be more up to date than the father. How many things Mariarosa knew, she talked as if she had first-hand information, so that Airota at a certain point looked at his wife ironically, and Adele said to her, "You're the only one who hasn't chosen a dessert yet."

"I'll have chocolate cake," she said, breaking off with a graceful frown.

I looked at her in admiration. She drove a car, lived in Milan, taught at the university, stood up to her father without resentment. I, instead: I was frightened by the idea of opening my mouth, and, at the same time, humiliated by staying silent. I couldn't contain myself, I said hyperbolically, "The Americans, after Hiroshima and Nagasaki, should be brought to trial for crimes against humanity."

Silence. The whole family looked at me. Mariarosa exclaimed Bravo!, she took my hand, shook it. I felt encouraged and immediately bubbled over with words, scraps of old phrases memorized at various times. I talked about planning and rationalization, the socialist-Christian Democratic precipice, about neocapitalism, about organizational structures, about Africa, Asia, primary school, Piaget, collusion of the police and the courts, fascist rot in every manifestation of the state. I was muddled, breathless. My heart was pounding, I forgot who I was with and where I was. Yet I felt around me an atmosphere of increasing approval, and I was happy to have expressed myself, I seemed to have made a good impression. I was also glad that no one in that nice little family had asked me, as happened frequently, where I came from, what my father did, and my mother. I was I, I, I.

I stayed with them, talking, in the afternoon, too. And in the evening we all went for a walk, before going to dinner. At every step Professor Airota met people he knew. Even two of the university professors, with their wives, stopped to greet him warmly.

108.

But already the next day I felt bad. The time spent with Pietro's family had given me further proof that the hard work of the Normale was a mistake. Merit was not enough, something else was required, and I didn't have it nor did I know how to learn it. How embarrassing that jumble of agitated words was, without logical rigor, without composure, without irony, things that Mariarosa, Adele, Pietro were capable of. I had learned the methodical persistence of the researcher who checks even the commas, that, yes, and I proved it during exams, or with the thesis that I was writing. But in fact I remained naïve, even if almost too cultured, I didn't have the armor to advance serenely as they did. Professor Airota was an immortal god who had given his children magical weapons before the battle. Mariarosa was invincible. And Pietro perfect in his overcultivated courtesy. I? I could only remain near them, shine in their radiance.

Anxiety not to lose Pietro seized me. I sought him out, I clung to him, I was affectionate. But I waited in vain for him to declare himself. One night I kissed him, on the cheek, and finally he kissed me on the mouth. We began to meet in secluded places, at night, waiting for darkness. I touched him, he touched me, he didn't want to penetrate me. It was as if I had returned to the time of Antonio, and yet the difference was enormous. There was the excitement of going out in the evening with Airota's son, getting strength from him. Every so often I thought of calling Lila from a public telephone: I wanted to tell her that I had this new boyfriend and that almost certainly our graduation theses would be published, they would become books, just like real books, with the cover, the title, the name. I wanted to tell her it was possible that both he and I would teach in the university, his sister Mariarosa at twenty-four was already doing so. I also wanted to tell her: you're right, Lila, if they teach you properly from childhood, as an adult you have less trouble with everything, you are someone who seems to have been born already knowing. But in the end I gave it up. Why telephone her? To listen silently to her story? Or, if she let me speak, what would I tell her? I knew very well that what would surely happen to Pietro would never happen to me. Most important, I knew that, like Franco, he would soon disappear, and that after all it was better that way, because I didn't love him, I was with him in the dark alleys, in the meadows, only so that I would feel the fear less.

109.

Around Christmas vacation in 1966 I got a very bad flu. I telephoned a neighbor of my parents—finally even in the old neighborhood many people had a telephone—and told them I wasn't coming home for the vacation. Then I sank into desolate days of fever and coughing, while the college emptied, became silent. I ate nothing, I even had trouble drinking. One morning when I had fallen into an exhausted half-sleep, I heard loud voices, in my dialect, as when in the neighborhood the women leaned out the windows, arguing. From the darkest depths of my mind came the known footsteps of my mother. She didn't knock, she opened the door, she entered, loaded down with bags.

It was unimaginable. She had hardly ever left the neighborhood, at most to go to the center of the city. Outside of Naples, as far as I knew, she had never been. And yet she had got on the train, had traveled all night, and had come to my room to heap on me Christmas food that she had prepared ahead of time, quarrelsome gossip in a loud voice, orders that were supposed, as if by magic, to bring me back to health and allow me to leave with her in the evening: because she had to go, at home she had other children and my father.

She depleted me more than the fever. She shouted so much, moving objects, carelessly rearranging things, that I was afraid the dean would come. At one point I felt I was fainting, I closed my eyes, hoping she wouldn't follow me into the nauseating darkness I was being dragged into. But she didn't stop at anything. Always in motion through the room, helpful and aggressive, she told me about my father, my siblings, the neighbors, friends, and, naturally, about Carmen, Ada, Gigliola, Lila.

I tried not to listen but she pursued me: *Do you understand what she did, do you understand what happened?* And she shook me, touching an arm or a foot buried under the covers. I discovered that, in the state of fragility caused by the illness, I was more sensitive to everything I couldn't stand about her. I got angry—and I told her this—at how, with every word, she wanted to demonstrate that all my contemporaries, compared to me, had failed. "Stop it," I muttered. She paid no attention, she kept repeating, *You, on the other hand.*

But what wounded me most was to sense behind her pride as a mother the fear that things would suddenly change and I would again lose points, no longer give her occasion to boast. She did not much trust the stability of the world. So she force-fed me, dried the sweat, made me take my temperature I don't know how many times. Was she afraid I would die, depriving her of my trophy existence? Was she afraid that, being ill, I would give in, be in some way demoted, have to return home without glory? She spoke obsessively about Lila. She was so insistent that I suddenly perceived how highly she had regarded

414 - ELENA FERRANTE

her since she was a child. Even she, I thought, even my mother, realized that Lila is better than me and now she is surprised that I've left her behind, she believes and doesn't believe it, she's afraid of losing her position as *luckiest mother in the neighborhood*. Look how combative she is, look at the arrogance in her eyes. I felt the energy she gave off, and I thought that her lameness had required her to have greater strength than normal, in order to survive, imposing on her the ferocity with which she moved inside and outside the family. What, on the other hand, was my father? A weak little man, trained to be obliging, to hold out his hand discreetly to pocket small tips: certainly he would never have managed to overcome all the obstacles and arrive at this austere building. She had done it.

When she left and the silence returned, on the one hand I felt relieved, on the other, because of the fever, I was moved. I thought of her alone, asking every passerby if this was the right direction for the train station, her, walking, with her lame leg, in an unknown city. She would never spend the money for a bus, she was careful not to waste even five lire. But she would make it: she would buy the right ticket and take the right trains, traveling overnight on the uncomfortable seats, or even standing, all the way to Naples. There, after another long walk, she would arrive in the neighborhood, and start polishing and cooking, she would cut up the eel, and prepare the *insalata di rinforzo*, and the chicken broth, and the *struffoli*, without resting for a moment, filled with rage, but consoling herself by saying, in some part of her brain, "Lenuccia is better than Gigliola, than Carmen, than Ada, than Lina, than all of them."

110.

It was because of Gigliola, according to my mother, that Lila's situation had become even more intolerable. Everything began on a Sunday in April when the daughter of Spagnuolo the pastry maker invited Ada to the parish cinema. The following evening, after the stores closed, she again went to her and said, "What are you doing all alone? Come watch television at my parents' house and bring along Melina." One thing led to another, and she ended up dragging her along on evening outings with Michele Solara, her boyfriend. Five of them often went to the pizzeria: Gigliola, her younger brother, Michele, Ada, Antonio. The pizzeria was in the center, at Santa Lucia. Michele drove, Gigliola sat beside him, all dressed up, and in the back seat were Lello, Antonio, and Ada.

Antonio didn't like spending his free time with his boss, and at first he tried to tell Ada that he was busy. But when Gigliola reported that Michele was angry that he didn't show up, he sank his head between his shoulders and obeyed. The conversation was almost always between the two girls; Michele and Antonio didn't exchange a word, in fact Solara often left the table and went to talk to the owner of the pizzeria, with whom he had various dealings. Gigliola's brother ate pizza and was quietly bored.

The girls' preferred subject was the love between Ada and Stefano. They talked about the presents he had given her and was giving her, of the wonderful trip to Stockholm in August the year before (how many lies Ada had had to tell poor Pasquale), how in the grocery he treated her better than if she had been the owner. Ada softened, she talked and talked. Gigliola listened and every so often said things like "The Church, if you want, can annul a marriage."

Ada interrupted, scowling, "I know, but it's difficult."

"Difficult, not impossible. You have to go to the Sacra Rota."

"What's that?"

"I don't know exactly, but the Sacra Rota can wipe out everything."

"You're sure?"

"I read it."

Ada was very happy about that unexpected friendship. She had been living her story in silence, among many fears and much remorse. Now she discovered that talking about it did her good, proved she was right, erased her guilt. The only thing that spoiled her relief was her brother's hostility, and in fact when they got home all they did was quarrel. Once Antonio nearly hit her, he shouted at her, "Why the fuck do you tell your business to everybody? Do you realize you look like a whore and I'm the pimp?"

She said in the most antagonistic tone she was capable of: "You know why Michele Solara comes to dinner with us?"

"Because he's my boss."

"Oh yes, sure."

"Then why?"

"Because I'm with Stefano, who's important. If I waited for you, the daughter of Melina I would be and the daughter of Melina I would remain."

Antonio lost control, he said: "You're not *with* Stefano, you're Stefano's *whore*."

Ada burst into tears. "It's not true, Stefano loves only me."

One night things got even worse. They were at home, dinner was over. Ada was doing the dishes, Antonio was staring into space, their mother was humming an old song while she swept the floor too energetically. At some point Melina accidentally swept the broom over her daughter's feet. It was terrible. There was at the time a superstition—I don't know if it still exists—that if you sweep the broom over the feet of an unmarried girl she'll never get married. Ada saw her future in a flash. She leaped back as if she had been touched by a cockroach and the plate she was holding fell to the floor.

"You swept over my feet," she shrieked, leaving her mother astonished.

"She didn't do it on purpose," Antonio said.

"She did do it on purpose. You don't want me to get married, it's too useful for you to have me work for you, you want to keep me here my whole life."

Melina tried to embrace her daughter, saying no no, but Ada repulsed her rudely, so that she retreated, bumped into a chair, and fell on the floor amid the fragments of the broken plate.

Antonio rushed to help his mother, but Melina now was screaming in fear, fear of her son, of her daughter, of the things around her. And Ada screamed louder in return, saying, "I'll show you who I'm going to marry, and soon, because if Lina doesn't get out of the way by herself, I'll get her out, and off the face of the earth."

Antonio left the house, slamming the door. More desperate than usual, in the following days he tried to escape from that new tragedy in his life, he made an effort to be deaf and dumb, he avoided going past the old grocery, and if by chance he ran into Stefano Carracci he looked in another direction before the wish to beat him up overpowered him. His mind was troubled, he couldn't understand what was right and what wasn't. Had it been right not to hand Lila over to Michele? Had it been right to tell Enzo to take her home? If Lila hadn't returned to her husband, would his sister's situation be different? Everything happens by chance, he reasoned, without good and without ill. But at that point his brain got stuck and on the first occasion, as if to free himself from bad dreams, he went back to quarreling with Ada. He shouted at her, "He is a married man, bitch: he has a small child, you are worse than our mother, you don't have any sense of things." Ada then went to Gigliola, confided to her: "My brother is crazy, my brother wants to kill me."

So it was that one afternoon Michele called Antonio and sent him to do a long-term job in Germany. He didn't object, in fact he obeyed willingly, he left without saying goodbye to his sister or even to Melina. He took it for granted that in a foreign country, among people who spoke like the Nazis at the church cinema, he would be stabbed, or shot, and he was content. He considered it more tolerable to be murdered than to continue to observe the suffering of his mother and Ada without being able to do anything.

The only person he wanted to see before setting off on the train was Enzo. He found him busy: at the time he was trying to sell everything, the mule, the cart, his mother's little shop, a garden near the railroad. He wanted to give part of the proceeds to a maiden aunt who had offered to take care of his siblings.

"And you?" Antonio asked.

"I'm looking for a job."

"You want to change your life?"

"Yes."

"It's a good thing."

"It's a necessity."

"I, on the other hand, am what I am."

"Nonsense."

"It's true, but it's all right. Now I have to leave and I don't know when I'll be back. Every so often, please, could you cast an eye on my mother, my sister, and the children?"

"If I stay in the neighborhood, yes."

"We were wrong, Enzù, we shouldn't have taken Lina home."

"Maybe."

"It's all a mess, you never know what to do."

"Yes."

"Bye."

"Bye."

They didn't even shake hands. Antonio went to Piazza Garibaldi and got the train. He had a long, difficult journey, night and day, with many angry voices running through his veins. He felt extremely tired after just a few hours, his feet were tingling; he hadn't traveled since he returned from military service. Every so often he got out to get a drink of water from a fountain, but he was afraid the train would leave. Later he told me that at the station in Florence he felt so depressed that he thought: I'll stop here and go to Lenuccia.

111.

With the departure of Antonio the bond between Gigliola and Ada became very tight. Gigliola suggested to her what the daughter of Melina had had in mind for some time, that is, that she shouldn't wait any longer, the matrimonial situation of Stefano should be resolved. "Lina has to get out of that house," she said, "and you have to go in: if you wait too long, the enchantment will be broken and you'll lose everything, even the job in the grocery, because she'll regain ground and force Stefano to get rid of you." Gigliola went so far as to confide to her that she was speaking from experience, she had the same problem with Michele. "If I wait for him to make up his mind to marry me," she whispered, "I'll get old; so I'm tormenting him: either we marry by the spring of 1968 or I'm leaving and fuck him."

Thus Ada went on to envelop Stefano in a net of true, sticky desire that made him feel special, and meanwhile she murmured between kisses, "You have to decide, Ste', either me or her; I'm not saying you have to throw her out in the street with the child, that's your son, you have responsibilities; but do what lots of actors and important people do today: give her some money and that's it. Everybody in the neighborhood knows that I'm your real wife, so I want to stay with you, always."

Stefano said yes and hugged her tight in the uncomfortable narrow bed on the Rettifilo, but then he didn't do much, except return home to Lila and yell, because there were no clean socks, or because he had seen her talking to Pasquale or someone else.

At that point Ada began to despair. One Sunday morning she ran into Carmen, who spoke to her in accusatory tones of the working conditions in the two groceries. One thing led to another, they began to talk venomously about Lila, whom both of them, for different reasons, considered the origin of their troubles. Finally Ada couldn't resist and recounted her romantic situation, forgetting that Carmen was the sister of her former fiancé. And Carmen, who couldn't wait to be part of the network of gossip, listened willingly, often interrupted to fan the flames, tried with her advice to do as much damage to Ada, who had betrayed Pasquale, and to Lila, who had betrayed her. But, I should say, apart from the resentments, there was the pleasure of having something to do with a person, her childhood friend, who found herself in the role of lover of a married man. And although since childhood we girls of the neighborhood had wanted to become wives, growing up we had almost always sympathized with the lovers, who seemed to us more spirited, more combative, and, especially, more modern. On the other hand we hoped that the legitimate wife would get gravely ill and die (in general she was a very wicked or at least unfaithful woman), and that the lover would stop being a lover and crown her dream of love by becoming a wife. We were, in short, on the side of the violation, but only because it reaffirmed the value of the rule. As a result Carmen, although amid much devious advice, ended up by passionately taking Ada's side, her feelings were genuine, and one day she said to her, in all honesty: "You can't go on like this, you have to get rid of that bitch, marry Stefano, give him your own children. Ask the Solaras if they know anyone in the Sacra Rota."

Ada immediately added Carmen's suggestions to Gigliola's and one night, in the pizzeria, she turned directly to Michele: "Can you get to this Sacra Rota?"

He answered ironically, "I don't know, I can ask, one always finds a friend. But just take what's yours, that's the most urgent thing. And don't worry about anything: if someone gives you trouble, send him to me."

Michele's words were very important, Ada felt supported, never in her life had she felt so surrounded by approval. Yet Gigliola's hammering, Carmen's advice, that unexpected promise of protection on the part of an important male authority, and even her anger at the fact that in August Stefano wouldn't take a trip abroad as he had the year before but had only gone to the Sea Garden a few times, were not enough to push her to attack. It took a true, concrete new fact: the discovery that she was pregnant.

The pregnancy made Ada furiously happy, but she kept the news to herself, she didn't speak of it even to Stefano. One afternoon she took off her smock, left the grocery as if to go out for some fresh air, and instead went to Lila's house.

"Did something happen?" Signora Carracci asked in bewilderment as she opened the door.

Ada answered, "Nothing has happened that you don't already know."

She came in and told her everything, in the presence of the child. She began calmly, she talked about actors and also cyclists, she called herself a kind of "white lady"—like the lover of the famous cyclist Fausto Coppi—but more modern, and she mentioned the Sacra Rota to demonstrate that even the Church and God in certain cases where love is very strong would dissolve a marriage. Since Lila listened without interrupting, something that Ada would never have expected—rather, she hoped that she would say just half a word, so that she could beat her bloody—she got nervous and began to walk around the apartment, first to demonstrate that she had been in the house often and knew it well, and, second, to reproach her: "Look at this mess, dirty dishes, the dust, socks and underwear on the floor, it's not possible that that poor man has to live like this." Finally, in an uncontrollable frenzy, she began to pick the dirty clothes up off the bedroom floor, shrieking, "Starting tomorrow I'm coming here to tidy up. You don't even know how to make the bed, look here, Stefano can't bear the sheet to be folded like this, he told me he's explained it to you a thousand times and you pay no attention."

Here she stopped suddenly, confused, and said in a low voice, "You have to go, Lina, because if you don't I'll kill the child."

Lila managed to respond only, "You're behaving like your mother, Ada."

Those were the words. I imagine her voice now: she wasn't capable of emotional tones, she must have spoken as usual with cold malice, or with detachment. And yet years later she told me that, seeing Ada in the house in that state, she had remembered the cries of Melina, the abandoned lover, when the Sarratore family left the neighborhood, and she had seen again the iron that flew out the window and almost killed Nino. The long flame of suffering, which then had much impressed her, was flickering again in Ada; only now it wasn't the wife of Sarratore feeding it but her, Lila. A cruel game of mirrors that at the time escaped us all. But not her, and so it's likely that instead of resentment, instead of her usual determination to do harm, bitterness was triggered in her, and pity. Certainly she tried to take her hand, she said, "Sit down, I'll make you a cup of chamomile tea."

But Ada, in all Lila's words, from first to last, and above all in that gesture, saw an insult. She withdrew abruptly, she rolled her eyes in a striking way, showing the white, and when the pupils reappeared she shouted, "Are you saying that I'm mad? That I'm mad like my mother? Then you had better pay attention, Lina. Don't touch me, get out of the way, make yourself a chamomile. I'm going to clean up this disgusting house."

She swept, she washed the floors, she remade the bed, and she didn't say another word.

Lila followed her with her gaze, afraid that she would break, like an artificial body subjected to excessive acceleration. Then she took the child and went out, she walked around the new neighborhood for a long time, talking to Rinuccio, pointing out things, naming them, inventing stories. But she did it more to keep her anguish under control than to entertain the child. She went back to the house only when, from a distance, she saw Ada go out the front door and hurry off as if she were late.

112.

When Ada returned to work, out of breath and extremely agitated, Stefano, menacing but calm, asked her, "Where have you been?" She answered, in the presence of the customers waiting to be served, "To clean up your house, it was disgusting." And addressing the audience on the other side of the counter: "There was so much dust on the night table you could write in it."

Stefano said nothing, disappointing the customers. When the shop emptied and it was time to close, Ada cleaned, swept, always watching her lover out of the corner of her eye. Nothing happened, he did the accounts sitting at the cash register, smoking heavily aromatic American cigarettes. Once the last butt was out, he grabbed the handle to lower the shutter, but he lowered it from the inside.

"What are you doing?" Ada asked, alarmed.

"We'll go out on the courtyard side."

After that, he struck her in the face so many times, first with the palm of his hand, then the back, that she leaned against the counter in order not to faint. "How dare you go to my house?" he said in a voice strangled by the will not to scream. "How dare you disturb my wife and my son?" Finally he realized that his heart was nearly bursting and he tried to calm down. It was the first time he had hit her. He stammered, trembling, "Don't ever do it again." And he went out, leaving her bleeding in the shop.

The next day Ada didn't go to work. Battered as she was, she appeared at Lila's house, and Lila, when she saw the bruises on her face, told her to come in.

"Make me the chamomile," said Melina's daughter.

Lila made it for her.

"The baby is cute."

"Yes."

"Just like Stefano."

"No."

"He has the same eyes and the same mouth."

"No."

"If you have to read your books, go ahead, I'll take care of the house and Rinuccio."

Lila stared at her, this time almost amused, then she said, "Do what you like, but don't go near the baby."

"Don't worry, I won't do anything to him."

Ada set to work: she straightened, washed the clothes, hung them in the sun, cooked lunch, prepared dinner. At one point she stopped, charmed by the way Lila was playing with Rinuccio.

"How old is he?"

"Two years and four months."

"He's little, you push him too much."

"No, he does what he can do."

"I'm pregnant."

"What?"

"It's true."

"With Stefano?"

"Of course."

"Does he know?"

"No."

Lila then understood that her marriage really was almost over, but, as usual when she became aware that change was imminent, she felt neither resentment nor anguish nor worry. When Stefano arrived, he found his wife reading in the living room, Ada playing with the baby in the kitchen, the apartment full of good smells and shining like a large, single precious object. He realized that the beating had been of no use, he turned white, he couldn't breathe.

"Go," he said to Ada in a low voice.

"No."

"What's got into your head?"

"I'm staying here."

"You want me to go mad?"

"Yes, that makes two of us."

Lila closed the book, took the baby without saying anything and withdrew into the room where, a long time earlier, I had studied, and where Rinuccio now slept. Stefano whispered to his lover, "You'll ruin me, like this. It's not true that you love me, Ada, you want me to lose all my customers, you want to reduce me to a pauper, and you know that circumstances are already not good. Please, tell me what you want and I'll give it to you."

"I want to be with you always."

"Yes, but not here."

"Here."

"This is my house, there's Lina, there's Rinuccio."

"From now on I'm here, too: I'm pregnant."

Stefano sat down. In silence he gazed at Ada's stomach as she stood before him, as if he were seeing through her dress, her underpants, her skin, as if he were seeing the baby already formed, a living being, all ready, about to jump out. Then there was a knock at the door.

It was a waiter from the Bar Solara, a boy of sixteen who had just been hired. He told Stefano that Michele and Marcello wanted to see him right away. Stefano roused himself, at that moment he considered the demand a salvation, given the storm he had in the house. He said to Ada, "Don't move." She smiled, she nodded yes. He went out, got in the Solaras' car. What a mess I've got myself into, he thought. What should I do? If my father were alive he would break my legs with an iron bar. Women, debts, Signora Solara's red book. Something hadn't worked. Lina. She had ruined him. What the fuck do Marcello and Michele want, at this hour, so urgently?

They wanted, he discovered, the old grocery. They didn't say it but they let him understand it. Marcello spoke merely of another loan that they were willing to give him. But, he said, the Cerullo shoes have to come definitively to us, we're finished with that lazy brother-in-law of yours, he's not reliable. And we need a guarantee, an activity, a property, you think about it. That said, he left, he said he had things to do. At that point Stefano was alone with Michele. They talked for a long time to see if Rino and Fernando's factory could be saved, if he could do without what Marcello had called the guarantee.

But Michele shook his head, he said, "We need guarantees, scandals aren't good for business."

"I don't know what you mean."

"*I* know what I mean. Who do you love more, Lina or Ada?"

"It's none of your business."

"No, Ste', when it's a question of money your business is my business."

"What can I tell you: we're men, you know how it works. Lina is my wife, Ada is another thing."

"So you love Ada more?"

"Yes."

"Resolve the situation and then we'll talk."

Many very dark days passed before Stefano found a way of getting out of that chokehold. Quarrels with Ada, quarrels with Lila, work gone to hell, the old grocery often closed, the neighborhood that watched and committed to memory and still remembers. The handsome engaged couple. The convertible. Soraya is going by with the Shah of Persia, Jack and Jackie are going by. Finally Stefano resigned himself and said to Lila, "I've found you a nice place, suitable for you and Rinuccio."

"How generous you are."

"I'll come twice a week to see the baby."

"As far as I'm concerned you don't have to come see him, since he's not your son."

"You're a bitch, you're going to make me smash your face."

"Smash my face when you want, I've got a callus there. But you take care of your child and I'll take care of mine."

He fumed, he got angry, he really tried to hit her. Finally he said, "The place is on the Vomero."

"Where?"

"I'll take you tomorrow and show it to you, in Piazza degli Artisti."

Lila remembered in a flash the proposal Michele Solara had made long ago: "*I've bought a house on the Vomero, in Piazza degli Artisti. If you want I'll drive you there now, I'll show it to you, I took it with you in mind. There you can do what you like: read, write, invent things, sleep, laugh, talk, and be with Rinuccio. I'm interested only in being able to look at you and listen to you.*"

She shook her head in disbelief, she said to her husband, "You really are a piece of shit."

113.

Now Lila is barricaded in Rinuccio's room, thinking what to do. She'll never go back to her mother and father's house: the weight of her life belongs to her, she doesn't want to become a child again. She can't count on her brother: Rino is beside himself, he's angry with Pinuccia in order to get revenge on Stefano, and has begun to quarrel also with his mother-in-law, Maria, because he's desperate, he has no money and a lot of debts. She can count only on Enzo: she trusted and trusts him, even though he never showed up and in fact he seems to have disappeared from the neighborhood. She thinks: he promised that he'll get me out of here. But sometimes she hopes he won't keep his promise, she's afraid of making trouble for him. She's not worried about a possible fight with Stefano, her husband has now given her up, and then he's a coward, even if he has the strength of a wild beast. But she is afraid of Michele Solara. Not today, not tomorrow, but when I'm not even thinking about it anymore he'll appear and if I don't submit he'll make me pay, and he'll make anyone who's helped me pay. So it's better for me to go away without involving anyone. I have to find a job, anything, enough to earn what I need to feed him and give him a roof.

Just thinking of her son saps her strength. What ended up in Rinuccio's head: images, words. She worries about the voices that reach him, unmonitored. I wonder if he heard mine, while I carried him in my womb. I wonder how it was imprinted in his nervous system. If he felt loved, if he felt rejected, was he aware of my agitation. How does one protect a child. Nourishing him. Loving him. Teaching him things. Acting as a filter for every sensation that might cripple him forever. I've lost his real father, who doesn't know anything about him and will never love him. Stefano, who isn't his father and yet loved him a little, sold us for love of another woman and a more genuine son. What will happen to this child. Now Rinuccio knows that when I go into another room he won't lose me, I am still there. He maneuvers with objects and fantasies of objects, the outside and the inside. He knows how to eat with a fork and spoon. He handles things and forms them, transforms them. From words he has moved on to sentences. In Italian. He no longer says "he," he says "I." He recognizes the letters of the alphabet. He puts them together so as to write his name. He loves colors. He's happy. But all this rage. He has seen me insulted and beaten. He's seen me break things and shout insults. In dialect. I can't stay here any longer.

114.

Lila came cautiously out of the room only when Stefano wasn't there, when Ada wasn't. She made something to eat for Rinuccio, she ate something herself. She knew that the neighborhood gossiped, that rumors were spreading. One late afternoon in November the telephone rang.

"I'll be there in ten minutes."

She recognized him and without much surprise she answered, "All right." Then: "Enzo."

"Yes."

"You're not obliged."

"I know."

"The Solaras are involved."

"I don't give a fuck about the Solaras."

He arrived exactly ten minutes later. He came up, she had put her things and the child's in two suitcases and had left on the night table in the bedroom all her jewelry, including her engagement ring and her wedding ring.

"It's the second time I've left," she said, "but this time I'm not coming back."

Enzo looked around, he had never been in that house. She pulled him by the arm. "Stefano might arrive suddenly, sometimes he does that."

"Where's the problem?" he answered.

He touched objects that looked expensive to him, a vase for flowers, an ashtray, the sparkling silver. He leafed through a pad where Lila had written down what she needed for the baby and for the house. Then he gave her an inquiring glance, asked her if she was sure of her choice. He said he had found work in a factory in San Giovanni a Teduccio and had taken an apartment there, three rooms, the kitchen was a little dark. "But the things Stefano gave you," he added, "you won't have anymore: I can't give you those."

He said to her: "Maybe you're afraid, because you're not completely sure."

"I'm sure," she said, picking up Rinuccio with a gesture of impatience, "and I'm not afraid of anything. Let's go."

He still delayed. He tore a piece of paper off the shopping list and wrote something. He left the piece of paper on the table.

"What did you write?"

"The address in San Giovanni."

"Why?"

"We're not playing hide-and-seek."

Finally he picked up the suitcases and started down the stairs. Lila locked the door, left the key in the lock.

115.

I knew nothing about San Giovanni a Teduccio. When they told me that Lila had gone to live in that place with Enzo, the only thing that came to mind was the factory owned by the family of Bruno Soccavo, Nino's friend, which produced sausages, and was in that area. The association of ideas annoyed me. I hadn't thought of the summer on Ischia for a long time: and it made me realize that the happy phase of that vacation had faded, while its unpleasant side had expanded. I discovered that every sound from that time, every scent was repugnant to me, but what in memory, surprisingly, seemed most insupportable, and caused me long crying spells, was the night at the Maronti with Donato Sarratore. Only my suffering for what was happening between Lila and Nino could have driven me to consider it pleasurable. At this distance I understood that that first experience of penetration, in the dark, on the cold sand, with that banal man who was the father of the person I loved had been degrading. I was ashamed of it and that shame was added to other shames, of a different nature, that I was experiencing.

I was working night and day on my thesis, I harassed Pietro, reading aloud to him what I had written. He was kind, he shook his head, he fished in his memory of Virgil and other authors for passages that might be useful to me. I noted down every word he uttered, I worked hard, but in a bad mood. I went back and forth between two feelings. I sought help and it humiliated me to ask for it, I was grateful and at the same time hostile, in particular I hated that he did his best not to let his generosity weigh on me. What caused me the greatest anxiety was to find myself—together with him, before him, after him—submitting my research to the assistant professor who was following the progress of both of us, a man of around forty, earnest, attentive, sometimes even sociable. I saw that Pietro was treated as if he already had a professorship, I as a normal brilliant student. Often I decided not to talk to the teacher, out of rage, out of pride, out of fear of having to be aware of my constitutional inferiority. I have to do better than Pietro, I thought, he knows so many more things than I do, but he's gray, he has no imagination. His way of proceeding, the way that he gently tried to suggest to me, was too cautious. So I undid my work, I started again, I pursued an idea that seemed to me original. When I returned to the professor I was listened to, yes, I was praised, but without seriousness, as if my struggle were only a game well played. I soon grasped that Pietro Airota had a future and I didn't.

Then, there was my naiveté. The assistant professor treated me in a friendly way, one day he said, "You're a student of great sensitivity. Do you think you'll teach, after your degree?"

I thought he meant teach at the university and my heart jumped for joy, my cheeks turned red. I said that I loved both teaching and research, I said that I would like to continue to work on the fourth book of the Aeneid. He immediately realized that I had misunderstood and was embarrassed. He strung together some trite phrases on the pleasure of studying for one's whole life and suggested a civil-service exam that would take place in the fall, for a few positions to be won in the teaching institutes.

"We need," he urged me, his tone rising, "excellent professors who will train excellent teachers."

That was it. Shame, shame, shame. This overconfidence that had grown in me, this ambition to be like Pietro. The only thing I had in common with him was the small sexual exchanges in the dark. He panted, he rubbed against me, he asked nothing that I wouldn't give him spontaneously.

I felt blocked. For a while I couldn't work on my thesis, I looked at the pages of the books without seeing the lines of type. I lay in bed staring at the ceiling, I interrogated myself on what to do. Give up right at the end, return to the neighborhood. Get my degree, teach in middle school. Professor. Yes. More than Oliviero. Equal to Galiani. Or maybe not, maybe a little less. Professor Greco. In the neighborhood I would be considered an important person, the daughter of the porter who since she was a child had known everything. I alone, who had been to Pisa, who had met important professors, and Pietro, Mariarosa, their father—I would have understood very clearly that I hadn't gone very far. A great effort, many hopes, wonderful moments. I would miss the time with Franco Mari my whole life. How lovely the months, the years with him had been. At the moment I hadn't understood their importance, and now here I was, growing sad. The rain, the cold, the snow, the scents of spring along the Arno and on the flowering streets of the city, the warmth we gave each other. Choosing a dress, glasses. His pleasure in changing me. And Paris, the exciting trip to a foreign country, the cafés, the politics, the literature, the revolution that would soon arrive, even though the working class was becoming integrated. And him. His room at night. His body. All finished. I tossed nervously in my bed, unable to sleep. I'm lying to myself, I thought. Had it really been so wonderful? I knew very well that at that time, too, there had been shame. And uneasiness, and humiliation, and disgust: accept, submit, force yourself. Is it possible that even happy moments of pleasure never stand up to a rigorous examination? Possible. The blackness of the Maronti quickly extended to Franco's body and then to Pietro's. I escaped from my memories.

At a certain point I began to see Pietro less frequently, with the excuse that I was behind and was in danger of not finishing my thesis in time. One morning I bought a graph-paper notebook and began to write, in the third person, about what had happened to me that night on the beach near Barano. Then, still in the third person, I wrote what had happened to me on Ischia. Then I wrote a little about Naples and the neighborhood. Then I changed names and places and situations. Then I imagined a dark force crouching in the life of the protagonist, an entity that had the capacity to weld the world around her, with the colors of the flame of a blowtorch: a blue-violet dome where everything went well for her, shooting sparks, but that soon came apart, breaking up into meaningless gray fragments. I spent twenty days writing this story, a period during which I saw no one, I went out only to eat. Finally I reread some pages, I didn't like them, and I forgot about it. But I found that I was calmer, as if the shame had passed from me to the notebook. I went back into the world, I quickly finished my thesis, I saw Pietro again.

His kindness, his thoughtfulness moved me. When he graduated the whole family came, along with many Pisan friends of

his parents. I was surprised to find that I no longer felt resentful of what awaited Pietro, of the plan of his life. In fact I was
happy that he had such a good future and was grateful to the
whole family, who invited me to the party afterward. Mariarosa
in particular looked after me. We had a heated discussion of
the fascist coup in Greece.

I graduated in the following session. I avoided telling my
parents, I was afraid that my mother would feel it her duty to
come and celebrate me. I presented myself to the professors in
one of the dresses that Franco had given me, the one that still
seemed acceptable. After such a long time, I really was pleased
with myself. I wasn't yet twenty-three and I had obtained a
degree in literature with the highest grade. My father hadn't
gone beyond fifth grade in elementary school, my mother had
stopped at second, none of my forebears, as far as I knew, had
learned to read and write fluently. It had been an astonishing
effort.

Besides some of my schoolmates, I found that Pietro had
come to congratulate me. I remember that it was very hot.
After the usual student rituals, I went to my room to freshen
up and leave my thesis there. He was waiting for me downstairs, he wanted to take me to dinner. I looked at myself in the
mirror, I had the impression that I was pretty. I took the notebook with the story I had written and put it in my purse.

It was the first time that Pietro had taken me to a restaurant. Franco had often done so, and had taught me everything
about the arrangement of the silverware, the glasses.

He asked me, "Are we engaged?"

I smiled, I said, "I don't know."

He took a package out of his pocket, gave it to me. He murmured, "For this whole year I thought so. But if you have a different opinion consider it a graduation present."

I unwrapped the package, and there was a green case.
Inside was a ring with little diamonds.

"It's beautiful," I said.

I tried it on, the size was right. I thought of the rings that Stefano had given Lila, much more elaborate than that. But it was the first jewel I had received, Franco had given me many gifts but never jewelry, the only jewelry I had was my mother's silver bracelet.

"We're engaged," I said, and, leaning across the table, kissed him on the lips. He turned red, he said, "I have another present."

He gave me an envelope, it was the proofs of his thesis-book. How fast, I thought, with affection and even some joy.

"I also have a little present for you."

"What is it?"

"Something foolish, but I don't know what else to give you that is truly mine."

I took the notebook out, I gave it to him.

"It's a novel," I said, "a one of a kind: only copy, only attempt, only capitulation. I'll never write another one." I added, laughing, "There are even some rather racy parts."

He seemed bewildered. He thanked me, he placed the notebook on the table. I was immediately sorry I had given it to him. I thought: he's a serious student, he has great traditions behind him, he's about to publish an essay on the Bacchic rites that will be the basis of a career; it's my fault, I shouldn't have embarrassed him with a little story that's not even typewritten. And yet even then I didn't feel uneasy, he was he, I was I. I told him that I had applied to enter teachers' training college, I told him that I would return to Naples, I told him, laughing, that our engagement would have a difficult life, I in a city in the south, he in one in the north. But Pietro remained serious, he had everything clear in his mind, he laid out his plan: two years to establish himself at the university and then he would marry me. He even set the date: September, 1969. When we went out he forgot the notebook on the table. I pointed it out in amusement: "My gift?" He was confused, he ran back to get it.

We walked for a long time. We kissed, we embraced on the Lungarno, I asked him, half serious, half joking, if he wanted to sneak into my room. He shook his head, he went back to kissing me passionately. There were entire libraries separating him and Antonio, but they were similar.

116.

My return to Naples was like having a defective umbrella that suddenly closes over your head in a gust of wind. I arrived in the middle of summer. I would have liked to look for a job right away, but my condition as a graduate meant that it was unsuitable for me to go looking for little jobs like the ones I used to have. On the other hand I had no money, and it was humiliating to ask my father and mother, who had already sacrificed enough for me. I became nervous. Everything irritated me, the streets, the ugly façades of the houses, the *stradone*, the gardens, even though at first every stone, every smell had moved me. If Pietro finds someone else, I thought, if I don't get in to the teachers' college, what will I do? It's not possible that I could remain forever a prisoner of this place and these people.

My parents, my siblings were very proud of me, but, I realized, they didn't know why: what use was I, why had I returned, how could they demonstrate to the neighbors that I was the pride of the family? If you thought about it I only complicated their life, further crowding the small apartment, making more arduous the arrangement of beds at night, getting in the way of a daily routine that by now didn't allow for me. Besides, I always had my nose in a book, standing up, sitting in one corner or another, a useless monument to study, a self-important, serious person whom they all made it their duty not to disturb, but about whom they also wondered: What are her intentions?

My mother resisted for a while before questioning me about my fiancé, whose existence she had deduced more from the ring that I wore on my finger than from my confidences. She wanted to know what he did, how much he earned, when he would introduce himself at our house with his parents, where I would live when I was married. At first I gave her some information: he was a professor at the university, for now he earned nothing, he was publishing a book that was considered very important by the other professors, we would get married in a couple of years, his parents were from Genoa, probably I would go to live in that city or anyway wherever he established himself. But from her intent look, from the way she kept asking the same questions, I had the impression that, too much in the grip of her preconceptions, she wasn't listening. I was engaged to someone who hadn't come and wasn't coming to ask for my hand, who lived very far away, who taught but wasn't paid, who was publishing a book but wasn't famous? She became upset as usual, even though she no longer got angry at me. She tried to contain her disapproval, maybe she didn't even feel capable of communicating it to me. Language itself, in fact, had become a mark of alienation. I expressed myself in a way that was too complex for her, although I made an effort to speak in dialect, and when I realized that and simplified the sentences, the simplification made them unnatural and therefore confusing. Besides, the effort I had made to get rid of my Neapolitan accent hadn't convinced the Pisans but was convincing to her, my father, my siblings, the whole neighborhood. On the street, in the stores, on the landing of our building, people treated me with a mixture of respect and mockery. Behind my back they began to call me the Pisan.

In that period I wrote long letters to Pietro, who answered

with even longer ones. At first I expected that he would make at least some reference to my notebook, then I forgot about it myself. We said nothing concrete, I still have those letters: there is not a single useful detail for reconstructing the daily life of the time, what was the price of bread or a ticket to the movies, how much a porter or a professor earned. We focused, let's say, on a book he had read, on an article of interest for our studies, on some reflection of his or mine, on unrest among certain university students, on the neo-avant-garde, which I didn't know anything about but which he was surprisingly well acquainted with, and which amused him to the point of inspiring him to write: "I would like to make a book out of crumpled-up pieces of paper: you start a sentence, it doesn't work, and you throw the page away. I'm collecting a few, I would have the pages printed just as they are, crumpled, so the random pattern of the creases is interwoven with the tentative, broken-off sentences. Maybe this is, in fact, the only literature possible today." That last note struck me. I suspected, I remember, that that was his way of communicating to me that he had read my notebook and that that literary gift of mine seemed to him a product that had arrived too late.

In those weeks of enervating heat I felt as if the weariness of years had poisoned my body, and I had no energy. Here and there I picked up news of Maestra Oliviero's state of health, I hoped that she was well, that I might see her and gain some strength from her satisfaction in my scholastic success. I knew that her sister had come to get her and had taken her back to Potenza. I felt very alone. I even missed Lila, and our turbulent meeting. I felt a desire to find her and measure the distance between us now. But I didn't. I confined myself to an idle, petty investigation into what people in the neighborhood thought of her, into the rumors that were circulating.

In particular I looked for Antonio. He wasn't there, it was said that he had remained in Germany, some claimed that he had married a beautiful German, a fat, blue-eyed platinum blonde, and that he was the father of twins.

So I talked to Alfonso. I went often to the shop on Piazza dei Martiri. He had grown really handsome, he looked like a refined Spanish nobleman, he spoke in a cultivated Italian, with pleasing inserts of dialect. The Solaras' shop, thanks to him, was thriving. His salary was satisfactory, he had rented a house in Ponte di Tappia, and he didn't miss the neighborhood, his siblings, the odor and grease of the grocery stores. "Next year I'll get married," he announced, without too much enthusiasm. The relationship with Marisa had lasted, had become stable, there was only the final step. I went out sometimes with them, they got along well; she had lost her old liveliness, her effusiveness, and now seemed above all careful not to say anything that might annoy him. I never asked her about her father, her mother, her brothers and sister. I didn't even ask about Nino nor did she mention him, as if he were gone forever out of her life, too.

I also saw Pasquale and Carmen: he still worked on construction jobs around Naples and the provinces, she continued to work in the new grocery. But the thing they were eager to tell me was that both had new loves: Pasquale was secretly seeing the oldest, though very young, daughter of the owner of the notions shop; Carmen was engaged to the gas-station man on the *stradone*, a nice man of forty who loved her dearly.

I also went to see Pinuccia, who was almost unrecognizable: slovenly, nervous, extremely thin, resigned to her fate, she bore the marks of the beatings that Rino continued to give her, taking revenge on Stefano, and, in her eyes and in the deep creases around her mouth, even more obvious traces of an unhappiness with no outlet.

Finally I got up my courage and tracked down Ada. I imagined I'd find her more distressed than Pina, humiliated by her situation. Instead she lived in the house that had been Lina's and was beautiful, and apparently serene; she had just given birth to a girl she had named Maria. Even during my pregnancy I didn't stop working, she said proudly. And I saw with my own eyes that she was the real mistress of the two groceries, she hurried from one to the other, she took care of everything.

Each of my childhood friends told me something about Lila, but Ada seemed to be the best informed. And it was she who spoke of her with greater understanding, almost sympathy. Ada was happy, happy with her baby, her comforts, her work, Stefano, and it seemed to me that for all that happiness she was sincerely grateful to Lila.

She exclaimed, admiringly, "I did things like a madwoman, I realize it. But Lina and Enzo behaved in an even crazier way. They were so careless of everything, even of themselves, that they frightened me, Stefano, and even that piece of shit Michele Solara. You know that she took nothing with her? You know that she left me all her jewelry? You know that they wrote on a piece of paper where they were going, the precise address, number, everything, as if to say: come find us, do what you like, who gives a damn?"

I wanted the address, I took it down. While I was writing she said, "If you see her, tell her that I'm not the one keeping Stefano from seeing the child: he has too much to do and although he's sorry, he can't. Also tell her that the Solaras don't forget anything, especially Michele. Tell her not to trust anyone."

117.

Enzo and Lila moved to San Giovanni a Teduccio in a used Fiat 600 that he had just bought. During the whole journey they said nothing, but battled the silence by talking to the child, Lila as if she were addressing an adult, and Enzo with monosyllables like *well, what, yes*. She scarcely knew San

Giovanni. She had gone there once with Stefano, they had stopped in the center for coffee and she had had a good impression. But Pasquale, who often came there for construction work and for political activities had once talked to her about it with great dissatisfaction, both as a worker and as a militant. "It's a filthy place," he had said, "a sewer: the more wealth it produces, the more poverty increases, and we can't change anything, even if we're strong." But Pasquale was always critical of everything and so not very reliable. Lila, as the car traveled along bumpy streets, past crumbling buildings and big, newly constructed apartment houses, preferred to tell herself that she was taking the child to a pretty little town near the sea and thought only of the speech that, to clarify things, out of honesty, she wanted to make to Enzo right away.

But because she was thinking about it she didn't do it. Later, she said to herself. So they arrived at the apartment that Enzo had rented, on the third floor of a new building that was already shabby. The rooms were half-empty, he said he had bought what was indispensable but that starting the next day he would get everything she needed. Lila reassured him, he had already done too much. Only when she saw the double bed she decided that it was time to speak: she said in an affectionate tone: "I've had great respect for you, Enzo, since we were children. You've done a thing I admire: you studied by yourself, you got a diploma, and I know the determination it takes, I've never had it. You're also the most generous person I know, no one would have done what you're doing for Rinuccio and for me. But I can't sleep with you. It's not because we've seen each other alone at most two or three times. And it's not that I don't like you. It's that I have no feelings, I'm like this wall or that table. So if you can live in the same house with me without touching me, good; if you can't I understand and tomorrow morning I'll look for another place. Know that I'll always be grateful for what you've done for me."

Enzo listened without interrupting. At the end he said, pointing to the bed: "You go there, I'll settle on the cot."

"I prefer the cot."

"And Rinuccio?"

"I saw there's another cot."

"He sleeps by himself?"

"Yes."

"You can stay as long as you like."

"You're sure?"

"Very sure."

"I don't want ugly things that could ruin our friendship."

"Don't worry."

"I'm sorry."

"It's fine like this. If by chance feeling returns to you, you know where I am."

118.

Feeling did not return to her; rather, a sense of alienation increased. The heavy air of the rooms. The dirty clothes. The bathroom door that didn't close properly. I imagine that San Giovanni seemed to her an abyss on the edge of our neighborhood. Although she had reached safety, she hadn't been careful where she put her feet down, and had fallen into a deep hole.

Rinuccio immediately worried her. The child, in general serene, began to have tantrums during the day, calling for Stefano, and to wake up crying at night. The attentions of his mother, her way of playing, calmed him, yes, but no longer fascinated him, in fact began to annoy him. Lila invented new games, his eyes lighted up, the child kissed her, he wanted to put his hands on her chest, he shrieked with joy. But then he pushed her away, he played by himself or napped on a blanket on the floor. And on the street he got tired after ten steps, he said his knee hurt, he demanded to be picked up, and if she refused he fell on the ground screaming.

At first Lila resisted, then slowly she began to give in. Since at night he would quiet down only if she let him come into her bed, she let him sleep with her. When they went out to do the shopping she carried him, even though he was a well nourished, heavy child: on one side the bags, on the other him. She returned exhausted.

She rediscovered what life without money was. No books, no journals or newspapers. Rinuccio grew before her eyes, and the things she had brought no longer fit him. She herself had very few clothes. But she pretended it was nothing. Enzo worked all day, he gave her the money she needed, but he didn't earn much, and besides he had to give money to the relatives who were taking care of his siblings. So they barely managed to pay the rent, the electricity, and the gas. But Lila didn't seem worried. The money she had had and had wasted were all one, in her imagination, with the poverty of childhood, it was without substance when it was there and when it wasn't. She was much more worried about the possible undoing of the education she had given her son and she devoted herself to making him energetic, eager, receptive, as he had been until recently. But Rinuccio now seemed to be content only when she left him on the landing to play with the neighbor's child. He fought, got dirty, laughed, ate junk, appeared happy. Lila observed him from the kitchen, from there she could see him and his friend framed by the door to the stairs. He's smart, she thought, he's smarter than the other child, who's a little older: maybe I should accept that I can't coddle him, that I've given him what's necessary but from now on he'll manage by himself, now he needs to hit, take things away from other children, get dirty.

One day, Stefano appeared on the landing. He had left the grocery and decided to come and see his son. Rinuccio greeted him joyfully, Stefano played with him for a while. But Lila saw that her husband was bored, he couldn't wait to leave. In the past it had seemed that he couldn't live without her and the child; instead here he was, looking at his watch, yawning, almost certainly he had come because his mother or even Ada had sent him. As for love, jealousy, it had all passed, he wasn't agitated anymore.

"I'll take the child for a walk."

"Watch out, he always wants to be picked up."

"I'll carry him."

"No, make him walk."

"I'll do as I like."

They went out, he returned half an hour later, he said he had to hurry back to the grocery. He swore that Rinuccio hadn't complained, hadn't asked to be picked up. Before he left he said, "I see that here you're known as Signora Cerullo."

"That's what I am."

"I didn't kill you and I won't kill you only because you're the mother of my son. But you and that shit friend of yours are taking a big risk."

Lila laughed, she provoked him, saying, "You're only tough with people who can't crack your head open, you bastard."

Then she realized that her husband was alluding to Solara and she yelled at him from the landing, as he was going down the stairs: "Tell Michele that if he shows up here I'll spit in his face."

Stefano didn't answer, he disappeared into the street. He returned, I think, at most four or five more times. That last time he met his wife he yelled at her, furiously, "You are the shame of your family. Even your mother doesn't want to see you anymore."

"It's clear that they never understood what a life I had with you."

"I treated you like a queen."

"Better a beggar, then."

"If you have another child you'd better abort it, because you have my surname and I don't want it to be my child."

"I'm not going to have any more children."

"Why? Have you decided not to screw anymore?"

"Fuck off."

"Anyway, I warned you."

"Rinuccio isn't your son, and yet he has your surname."

"Whore, you keep saying it so it must be true. I don't want to see you or him anymore."

He never really believed her. But he pretended, because it was convenient. He preferred a peaceful life that would vanquish the emotional chaos she caused him.

119.

Lila told Enzo in detail about her husband's visits. He listened attentively and almost never made comments. He continued to be restrained in every expression of himself. He didn't even tell her what sort of work he did in the factory and if it suited him or not. He went out at six in the morning and returned at seven in the evening. He ate dinner, he played a little with the boy, he listened to her conversation. As soon as Lila mentioned some urgent need of Rinuccio's, the next day he brought the necessary money. He never told her to ask Stefano to contribute to the maintenance of his child, he didn't tell her to find a job. He simply looked at her as if he lived only to get to those evening hours, to sit with her in the kitchen, listening to her talk. At a certain point he got up, said goodnight, and went into the bedroom.

One afternoon Lila had an encounter that had significant consequences. She went out alone, having left Rinuccio with the neighbor. She heard an insistent horn behind her. It was a fancy car, someone was signaling to her from the window.

"Lina."

She looked closely. She recognized the wolfish face of Bruno Soccavo, Nino's friend.

"What are you doing here?" he asked.

"I live here."

She said almost nothing about herself, since at that time such things were difficult to explain. She didn't mention Nino, nor did he. She asked instead if he had graduated, he said he had decided to stop studying.

"Are you married?"

"Of course not."

"Engaged?"

"One day yes, the next no."

"What do you do?"

"Nothing, there are people who work for me."

It occurred to her to ask him, almost as a joke: "Would you give me a job?"

"You? What do you need a job for?"

"To work."

"You want to make salami and mortadella?"

"Why not."

"And your husband?"

"I don't have a husband anymore. But I have a son."

Bruno looked at her attentively to see if she was joking. He seemed confused, evasive. "It's not a nice job," he said. Then he talked volubly about the problems of couples in general, about his mother, who was always fighting with his father, about a violent passion he himself had had recently for a married woman, but she had left him. Bruno was unusually talkative, he invited her to a café, continuing to tell her about himself. Finally, when Lila said she had to go, he asked, "Did you really leave your husband? You really have a child?"

"Yes."

He frowned, wrote something on a napkin.

"Go to this man, you'll find him in the morning after eight. And show him this."

Lila smiled in embarrassment.

"The napkin?"

"Yes."

"It's enough?"

He nodded yes, suddenly made shy by her teasing tone. He murmured, "That was a wonderful summer."

She said, "For me, too."

120.

All this I found out later. I would have liked to use the address in San Giovanni that Ada had given me right away, but something crucial happened to me as well. One morning I was lazily reading a long letter from Pietro and at the end of the last page I found a few lines in which he told me that he had had his mother read my text (that's what he called it). Adele had found it so good that she had typed it and had sent it to a publisher in Milan for whom she had done translations for years. They had liked it and wanted to publish it.

It was a late autumn morning, I remember a gray light. I sat at the kitchen table, the same one on which my mother was ironing the clothes. The old iron slid over the material with energy, the wood vibrated under my elbows. I looked at those lines for a long time. I said softly, in Italian, only to convince myself that the thing was real: "Mamma, here it says that they are going to publish a novel I wrote." My mother stopped, lifted the iron off the material, set it down upright.

"You wrote a novel?" she asked in dialect.

"I think so."

"Did you write it or not?"

"Yes."

"Will they pay you?"

"I don't know."

I went out, ran to the Bar Solara, where you could make long-distance phone calls in some comfort. After several attempts—Gigliola called from the bar, "Go on, talk"—Pietro answered but he had to work and was in a hurry. He said that he didn't know anything more about the business than he had written me.

"Did you read it?" I asked, in agitation.

"Yes."

"But you never said anything."

He stammered something about lack of time, studying, responsibilities.

"How is it?"

"Good."

"Good and that's all?"

"Good. Talk to my mother, I'm a philologist, not a literary person."

He gave me the number of his parents' house.

"I don't want to telephone, I'm embarrassed."

I sensed some irritation, rare in him who was always so courteous. He said, "You've written a novel, you take responsibility for it."

I scarcely knew Adele Airota, I had seen her four times and we had exchanged only a few formal remarks. In all that time I had been sure she was a wealthy, cultivated wife and mother—the Airotas never said anything about themselves, they acted as if their activities in the world were of scant interest, yet took it for granted that these activities were known to everyone—and only now began to realize that she had a job, that she was able to exercise power. I telephoned anxiously, the maid answered, gave her the phone. I was greeted cordially, but she used the formal *lei* and I did, too. She said that at the publishing house they were all very excited about how good the book was and, as far as she knew, a draft of the contract had already been sent.

"Contract?"

"Of course. Have you dealt with other publishers?"

"No. But I haven't even reread what I wrote."

"You wrote only a single draft, all at once?" she asked, vaguely ironic.

"Yes."

"I assure you that it's ready for publication."

"I still need to work on it."

"Trust yourself: don't touch a comma, there is sincerity, naturalness, and a mystery in the writing that only true books have."

She congratulated me again, although she accentuated the irony. She said that, as I knew, even the Aeneid wasn't polished. She ascribed to me a long apprenticeship as a writer, asked if I had other things, appeared amazed when I confessed that it was the first thing I had written. "Talent and luck," she exclaimed. She told me that there was an unexpected opening in the editorial list and my novel had been considered not only very good but lucky. They thought of bringing it out in the spring.

"So soon?"

"Are you opposed?"

I quickly said no.

Gigliola, who was behind the bar and had listened to the phone call, finally asked me, inquisitively, "What's happening?"

"I don't know," I said and left.

I wandered around the neighborhood overwhelmed by an incredulous joy, my temples pounding. My answer to Gigliola hadn't been a hostile way of cutting her off, I really didn't know. What was that unexpected announcement: a few lines from Pietro, long-distance words, nothing certainly true? And what was a contract, it meant money, it meant rights and duties, was I in danger of getting in some trouble? In a few days I'll find out that they've changed their mind, I thought, the book won't be published. They'll reread the story, those who found it good will find it pointless, those who haven't read it will be angry with those who were eager to publish it, they'll all be angry with Adele Airota, and Adele Airota herself will change her mind, she'll feel humiliated, she'll blame me for disgracing her, she'll persuade her son to leave me. I passed the building where the old neighborhood library was: how long it had been since I'd set foot in it. I went in, it was empty, it smelled of dust and boredom. I moved absentmindedly along the shelves, I touched tattered books without looking at title or author, just to feel them with my fingers. Old paper, curled cotton threads, letters of the alphabet, ink. Volumes, a dizzying word. I looked for *Little Women*, I found it. Was it possible that it was really about to happen? Possible that what Lila and I had planned to do together was happening to me? In a few months there would be printed paper sewn, pasted, all covered with my words, and on the cover the name, Elena Greco, me, breaking the long chain of illiterates, semi-literates, an obscure surname that would be charged with light for eternity. In a few years— three, five, ten, twenty—the book would end up on those shelves, in the library of the neighborhood where I was born, it would be catalogued, people would ask to borrow it to find out what the daughter of the porter had written. I heard the flush of the toilet, I waited for Maestro Ferraro to appear, just as when I was a diligent girl: the same fleshless face, perhaps more wrinkled, the crew-cut hair white but still thick over the low forehead. Here's someone who could appreciate what was happening to me, who would more than justify my burning head, the fierce pounding in my temples. But from the bathroom a stranger emerged, a small rotund man of around forty.

"Do you want to take out books?" he asked. "Do it quickly because I'm about to close."

"I was looking for Maestro Ferraro."

"Ferraro is retired."

Do it quickly, he was about to close.

I left. Just now that I was becoming a writer, there was no one in the entire neighborhood capable of saying: What an extraordinary thing you've done.

121.

I didn't imagine that I would earn money. But I received the draft of the contract and discovered that, surely thanks to Adele's support, the publisher was giving me an advance of two hundred thousand lire, a hundred on signing and a hundred on delivery. My mother was speechless, she couldn't believe it. My father said, "It takes months for me to earn that much money." They both began to brag in the neighborhood and outside: our daughter has become rich, she's a writer, she's marrying a university professor. I flourished again, I stopped studying for the teachers' college exam. As soon as the money arrived I bought a dress, some makeup, went for the first time in my life to the hairdresser, and left for Milan, a city unknown to me.

At the station I had trouble orienting myself. Finally I found the right metro, and arrived nervously at the door of the publishing house. I gave a thousand explanations to the porter, who hadn't asked me anything, and who in fact, while I spoke, continued to read the newspaper. I went up in the elevator, I knocked, I went in. I was struck by how neat and tidy it was. My head was crowded with all that I had studied and I wanted to display it, to demonstrate that even if I was a woman, even if you could see my origins, I was a person who at twenty-three, had won the right to publish that book, and now, nothing nothing nothing about me could be called into question.

I was greeted politely, led from office to office. I talked with the editor who was working on my manuscript, an old man, bald, with a very pleasant face. We talked for a couple of hours, he praised me, he cited Adele Airota often, with great respect, he showed me some revisions that he suggested, he left me a copy of the text and his notes. As he was saying goodbye he added, in a serious voice, "The story is good, a contemporary story very well expressed, the writing is always surprising; but that's not the point. It's the third time I've read the book and on every page there is something powerful whose origin I can't figure out." I turned red, thanked him. Ah, how much I had been able to do, and how rapid it all was, how well liked I was and how likable I had become, I could speak about my studies, where I had done them, about my thesis on the fourth book of the Aeneid: I replied with courteous precision to courteous observations, mimicking perfectly the tones of Professor Galiani, of her children, of Mariarosa. A pretty, amiable woman named Gina asked if I needed a hotel and, at my nod of assent, found me one on Via Garibaldi. To my great amazement I discovered that everything was charged to the publisher, everything that I spent on food, the train tickets. Gina told me to present a record of expenses, I would be reimbursed, and she asked me to say hello to Adele for her. "She called me," she said. "She's very fond of you."

The next day I left for Pisa, I wanted to embrace Pietro. On the train I considered one by one the editor's notes and, satisfied, I saw my book with the eyes of one who praised it and was working to make it even better. I arrived very pleased with myself. My fiancé found me a place to sleep at the house of an old assistant professor of Greek literature whom I also knew. In the evening he took me to dinner and to my surprise showed me my manuscript. He, too, had a copy and had made some notes, we looked at them together one by one. They bore the imprint of his usual rigor and had to do mostly with the vocabulary.

"I'll take care of them," I said thanking him.

After dinner we walked to an isolated meadow. After we had held and touched each other for a long time in the cold, obstructed by coats and woolen sweaters, he asked me to revise and polish with care the pages where the protagonist loses her virginity on the beach. I said, bewildered, "It's an important moment."

"You yourself said that that part is a bit risqué."

"At the publisher no one objected."

"They'll talk to you about it later."

I became irritated, I told him that I would think about it and the next day I left for Naples in a bad mood. If that episode upset Pietro, who was a young man of wide reading, and had written a book on Bacchic rites, what would my mother and father say, my siblings, the neighborhood, if they read it? On the train I worked on the manuscript, keeping in mind the observations of the editor, and Pietro's, and what I could eliminate I did. I wanted the book to be good, I didn't want anyone to dislike it. I doubted that I would ever write another.

122.

As soon as I got home I had some bad news. My mother, convinced that it was her right to look at my mail when I was absent, had opened a package that came from Potenza. In the package she had found a number of my notebooks from elementary school and a note from Maestra Oliviero's sister. The teacher, the note said, had died peacefully, twenty days earlier. She had often remembered me, in recent times, and had asked that some notebooks from elementary school that she had saved be returned to me. I was distressed, even more than my sister Elisa, who wept inconsolably for hours. This bothered my mother, who first yelled at her younger daughter and then, so that I, her older daughter, could hear it clearly, commented aloud: "That imbecile always thought she was more of a mother than I am."

All day I thought of Maestra Oliviero and of how she would have been proud to know about my degree, about the book I was going to publish. When everyone went to bed I shut myself in the silent kitchen and leafed through the notebooks one after the other. How well she had taught me, the teacher, what beautiful handwriting she had instilled. Too bad that my adult writing had gotten smaller, that speed had simplified the letters. I smiled at the spelling mistakes, marked with furious strokes, at the *goods*, the *excellents*, which she wrote punctiliously in the margin when she found a good expression or the right solution to a difficult problem, at the high marks she always gave me. Had she really been more mother than my mother? For a time I hadn't been sure. But she had imagined for me a road that my mother wasn't able to imagine and had compelled me to take it. For this I was grateful to her.

I was putting aside the package to go to bed when I noticed in the middle of one of the notebooks a small, thin sheaf of paper, ten pages of graph paper fastened with a pin and refolded. I felt a sudden emptiness in my chest: I recognized *The Blue Fairy*, the story that Lila had written so many years before, how many? Thirteen, fourteen. How I had loved the cover colored with pastels, the beautifully drawn letters of the title: at the time I had considered it a real book and had been envious of it. I opened it to the center page. The pin had rusted, leaving brown marks on the paper. I saw, with amazement, that the teacher had written beside a sentence: *beautiful*. So she had read it? So she had liked it? I turned the pages one after the other, they were full of her *wonderfuls, goods, very goods*. I got angry. Old witch, I thought, why didn't you tell us that you liked it, why did you deny Lila that satisfaction? What drove you to fight for my education and not for hers? Is the refusal of the shoemaker to let his daughter take the admission examination enough to justify you? What unhappiness did you have in your head that you unloaded onto her? I began to read *The Blue Fairy* from the beginning, racing over the pale ink, the handwriting so similar to mine of that time. But already at the first page I began to feel sick to my stomach and soon I was covered with sweat. Only at the end, however, did I admit what I had understood after a few lines. Lila's childish pages were the secret heart of my book. Anyone who wanted to know what gave it warmth and what the origin was of the strong but invisible thread that joined the sentences would have had to go back to that child's packet, ten notebook pages, the rusty pin, the brightly colored cover, the title, and not even a signature.

123.

I didn't sleep all night, I waited until it was day. The long hostility toward Lila dissolved, suddenly what I had taken from her seemed to me much more than what she had ever been able to take from me. I decided to go right away to San Giovanni a Teduccio. I wanted to give her back *The Blue Fairy*, show her my notebooks, page through them together, enjoy the teacher's comments. But most of all I felt the need to have her sit beside me, to tell her, you see how connected we are, one in two, two in one, and prove to her with the rigor that it seemed to me I had learned in the Normale, with the philological persistence I had learned from Pietro, how her child's book had put down deep roots in my mind and had, in the course of the years, produced another book, different, adult, mine, and yet inseparable from hers, from the fantasies that we had elaborated together in the courtyard of our games, she and I continuously formed, deformed, reformed. I wanted to embrace her, kiss her, and tell her, Lila, from now on, whatever happens to me or you, we mustn't lose each other anymore.

But it was a hard morning, it seemed to me that the city did everything possible to get between me and her. I took a crowded bus that went toward the Marina, I was unbearably squashed by miserable bodies. I got on another, even more crowded bus, I went in the wrong direction. I got out, upset, disheveled, I waited for a long time, angrily, to make up for the mistake. That small journey through Naples exhausted me. What was the use of years of middle school, high school, university, in that city? To arrive at San Giovanni I had forcibly to regress, as if Lila had gone to live not in a street, or a square, but in a ripple of time past, before we went to school, a black time without rules and without respect. I resorted to the most violent dialect of the neighborhood, I insulted, I was insulted, I threatened, I was mocked, I responded by mocking, a spiteful art in which I was trained. Naples had been very useful in Pisa, but Pisa was no use in Naples, it was an obstacle. Good manners, cultured voice and appearance, the crush in my head and on my tongue of what I had learned in books were all immediate signs of weakness that made me a secure prey, one of those who don't struggle. On the buses and the streets heading toward San Giovanni I fused the old capacity to stop being meek at the right moment with the pride of my new state: I had a degree, I had had lunch with Professor Airota, I was engaged to his son, I had deposited money in the Post Office, in Milan I had been treated with respect by important people; how could these shitty people dare? I felt a power that no longer knew how to adjust to the *pretend not to notice* with which, in general, it was possible to survive in the neighborhood and outside it. Whenever, in the throng of passengers, I felt male hands on my body, I gave myself the sacrosanct right to fury and reacted with cries of contempt, I said unrepeatable words like the ones my mother and, especially, Lila knew how to say. I was so excessive that when I got off the bus I was sure that someone would jump off behind me and murder me.

It didn't happen, but I walked away angry and scared. I had been much too neat when I left the house, now I felt mangled, outside and in.

I tried to compose myself, I said to myself: calm down, you're almost there. I asked the passersby for directions. I walked along Corso San Giovanni a Teduccio with the cold wind in my face, it seemed a yellowish channel with defaced walls, black doorways, dirt. I wandered, confused by friendly information so crowded with details that it turned out to be useless. Finally I found the street, the building. I went up the dirty stairs, following a strong odor of garlic, the voices of children. A very fat woman in a green sweater looking out of an open door saw me and cried, "Who do you want?" "Carracci," I said. But seeing that she was perplexed I corrected myself immediately: "Scanno." Enzo's surname. And then, afterward, "Cerullo." At that point the woman repeated *Cerullo* and said, raising a large arm, "Farther up." I thanked her, kept going, while she leaned over the banister and, looking up, shouted, "Titì, there's someone looking for Lina, she's coming up."

Lina. Here, in the mouths of strangers, in this place. I realized only then that I had in mind Lila as I had seen her the last time, in the apartment in the new neighborhood, in the orderliness that, however charged with anguish it had been, now seemed the backdrop of her life, the furniture, the refrigerator, the television, the well-cared-for child, she herself with a look certainly worn out but still that of a well-off young woman. I knew nothing, at that moment, of how she lived, what she did. The gossip had stopped at the abandonment of her husband, at the incredible fact that she had left a beautiful house and money and gone away with Enzo Scanno. I didn't know about the encounter with Soccavo. So I had left the neighborhood in the certainty that I would find her in a new house among open books and educational games for her son, or, at most, out momentarily, doing the shopping. And, out of laziness, in order not to feel uneasy, I had mechanically placed those images inside a toponymy, San Giovanni a Teduccio, beyond the Granili, at the end of the Marina. I went up with that expectation. I thought, I've made it, here I am at my destination. So I reached Titina. A young woman with a baby in her arms who was crying quietly, with slight sobs, rivulets of mucous dripping onto her upper lip from cold-reddened nostrils, and two more children attached to her skirts, one on each side.

Titina turned her gaze to the door opposite, closed.

"Lina's not here," she said, in a hostile tone.

"Nor Enzo?"

"No."

"Did she take the child for a walk?"

"Who are you?"

"My name is Elena Greco, I'm a friend."

"And you don't recognize Rinuccio? Rinù, have you ever seen this lady?"

She boxed the ear of one of the children beside her, and only then I recognized him. The child smiled at me, he said in Italian, "Hello, Aunt Lenù. Mamma will be back tonight at eight."

I picked him up, hugged him, praised how cute he was and how well he spoke.

"He's very clever," Titina admitted, "he's a born professor."

At that point, her hostility ceased, she invited me to come in. In the dark corridor I stumbled on something that surely belonged to the children. The kitchen was untidy, everything was sunk in a grayish light. There was a sewing machine with some material still under the needle, and around and on the floor other fabric of various colors. Suddenly ashamed, Titina tried to straighten the room, then she gave up and made coffee, but continuing to hold her daughter in her arms. I sat Rinuccio on my lap, asked him stupid questions that he answered with lively resignation. The woman meanwhile told me about Lila and Enzo.

"She makes salami at Soccavo," she said.

I was surprised, only then did I remember Bruno.

"Soccavo, the sausage people?"

"Soccavo, yes."

"I know him."

"They are not nice people."

"I know the son."

"Grandfather, father, and son, same shit. They made money and forgot they ever went around in rags."

I asked about Enzo. She said he worked at the locomotives, she used that expression, and I soon realized that she thought he and Lila were married, she called Enzo, with liking and respect, "Signor Cerullo."

"When will Lina be back?"

"Tonight."

"And the child?"

"He stays with me, eats, plays, does everything here."

So the journey wasn't over: I approached, Lila moved away. I asked, "How long does it take to walk to the factory?"

"Twenty minutes."

Titina gave me directions, which I wrote down on a piece of paper. Meanwhile Rinuccio asked politely, "May I go play, aunt?" He waited for me to say yes, he ran into the hall with the other child, and immediately I heard him yelling a nasty insult in dialect. The woman gave me an embarrassed look and shouted from the kitchen, in Italian, "Rino, bad words aren't nice, watch out or I'll come and give you a rap on the knuckles."

I smiled at her, remembering my trip on the bus. I also deserve a rap on the knuckles, I thought, I'm in the same condition as Rinuccio. When the quarrel in the hall didn't stop, we ran out. The two boys were hitting each other, throwing things and yelling fiercely.

124.

I arrived at the site of the Soccavo factory by a dirt path, amid trash of every type, a thread of black smoke in the frozen sky. Before I even saw the boundary wall I noticed a sickening odor of animal fat mixed with burned wood. The guard said, derisively, you don't go visiting your girlfriend during working hours. I asked to speak to Bruno Soccavo. He changed his tone, stammered that Bruno almost never came to the factory. Call him at home, I replied. He was embarrassed, he said that he couldn't bother him for no reason. "If you don't call," I said, "I'll go and find a telephone and do it myself." He gave me a nasty look, he didn't know what to do. A man came by on a bicycle, braked, said something obscene to him in dialect. The guard appeared relieved to see him. He began to talk to him as if I no longer existed.

At the center of the courtyard a bonfire was burning. The flame cut the cold air for a few seconds as I passed. I reached a low building of a yellow color, I pushed open a heavy door, I entered. The smell of fat, already strong outside, was unendurable. I met a girl who, obviously angry, was fixing her hair with agitated gestures. I said *Excuse me*, she passed by with her head down, took three or four steps, stopped.

"What is it?" she asked rudely.

"I'm looking for someone called Cerullo."

"Lina?"

"Yes."

"Look in sausage-stuffing."

I asked where it was, she didn't answer, she walked away. I

pushed open another door. I was assailed by a warmth that made the odor of fat even more nauseating. The place was big, there were tubs full of a milky, steaming water in which dark bodies floated, stirred by slow, bent silhouettes, workers immersed up to their hips. I didn't see Lila. I asked a man who, lying on the swampy tile floor, was fixing a pipe: "Do you know where I could find Lina?"

"Cerullo?"

"Cerullo."

"In the mixing department."

"They told me stuffing."

"Then why are you asking me, if you know?"

"Where is mixing?"

"Straight ahead."

"And stuffing?"

"To the right. If you don't find her there, look where they're stripping the meat off the carcasses. Or in the storerooms. They're always moving her."

"Why?"

He had a malicious smile.

"Is she a friend of yours?"

"Yes."

"Forget it."

"Tell me."

"You won't be offended?"

"No."

"She's a pain in the ass."

I followed the directions, no one stopped me. The workers, both men and women, seemed to be enveloped in a bitter indifference; even when they laughed or shouted insults they seemed remote from their very laughter, from their voices, from the swill they handled, from the bad smell. I emerged among women in blue smocks who worked with the meat, caps on their heads: the machines produced a clanking sound and a mush of soft, ground, mixed matter. But Lila wasn't there. And I didn't see her where they were stuffing skins with the rosy pink paste mixed with bits of fat, or where, with sharp knives, they skinned, gutted, cut, using the blades with a dangerous frenzy. I found her in the storerooms. She came out of a refrigerator along with a sort of white breath. With the help of a short man, she was carrying a reddish block of frozen meat on her back. She placed it on a cart, she started to go back into the cold. I immediately saw that one hand was bandaged.

"Lila."

She turned cautiously, stared at me uncertainly. "What are you doing here?" she said. Her eyes were feverish, her cheeks more hollow than usual, and yet she seemed large, tall. She, too, wore a blue smock, but over it a kind of long coat, and on her feet she wore army boots. I wanted to embrace her but I didn't dare: I was afraid, I don't know why, that she would crumble in my arms. It was she, instead, who hugged me for long minutes. I felt the damp material that gave off a smell even more offensive than the smell in the air. "Come," she said, "let's get out of here," and shouted at the man who was working with her: "Two minutes." She drew me into a corner.

"How did you find me?"

"I came in."

"And they let you pass?"

"I said I was looking for you and that I was a friend of Bruno's."

"Good, that way they'll be convinced that I give the son of the owner blow jobs and they'll leave me alone."

"What do you mean?"

"That's how it works."

"Here?"

"Everywhere. Did you get your degree?"

"Yes. But an even more wonderful thing happened, Lila. I wrote a novel and it's being published in April."

Her complexion was gray, she seemed bloodless, and yet she flared up. I saw the red move up along her throat, her cheeks, up to the edge of her eyes, so close that she squeezed them as if fearing that the flame would burn the pupils. Then she took my hand and kissed it, first on the back, then on the palm.

"I'm happy for you," she murmured.

But at the moment I scarcely noticed the affection of the gesture, I was struck by the swelling of her hands and the wounds, cuts old and new, a fresh one on the thumb of her left hand whose edges were inflamed, and I could imagine that under the bandage on her right hand she had an even worse injury.

"What have you done to yourself?"

She immediately withdrew, put her hands in her pockets.

"Nothing. Stripping meat off the bones ruins your fingers."

"You strip the meat?"

"They put me where they like."

"Talk to Bruno."

"Bruno is the worst shit of them all. He shows up only to see who of us he can fuck in the aging room."

"Lila."

"It's the truth."

"Are you ill?"

"I'm very well. Here in the storerooms they give me ten lire more an hour for cold damage."

The man called: "Cerù, the two minutes are up."

"Coming," she said.

I murmured, "Maestra Oliviero died."

She shrugged, said, "She was sick, it was bound to happen."

I added in a hurry, because I saw that the man next to the cart was getting anxious, "She let me have *The Blue Fairy*."

"What's *The Blue Fairy*?"

I looked at her to see if it was true that she didn't remember and she seemed sincere.

"The book you wrote when you were ten."

"Book?"

"That's what we called it."

Lila pressed her lips together, shook her head. She was alarmed, she was afraid of getting in trouble at work, but in my presence she acted the part of someone who does as she likes. I have to go, I thought.

She said, "A long time has passed since then," and shivered.

"Do you have a fever?"

"No."

I looked for the packet in my purse, gave it to her. She took it, recognized it, but showed no emotion.

"I was an arrogant child," she muttered.

I quickly contradicted her.

"The story is still beautiful today," I said. "I read it again and discovered that, without realizing it, I've always had it in my mind. That's where my book comes from."

"From this nonsense?" she laughed loudly, nervously. "Then whoever printed it is crazy."

The man shouted, "I'm waiting for you, Cerullo."

"You're a pain in the ass," she answered.

She put the packet in her pocket and took me under the arm. We went toward the exit. I thought of how I had dressed up for her and how hard it had been to get to that place. I had imagined tears, confidences, talk, a wonderful morning of confessions and reconciliation. Instead here we were, walking arm in arm, she bundled up, dirty, scarred, I disguised as a young lady of good family. I told her that Rinuccio was cute and very intelligent. I praised the neighbor, asked about Enzo. She was glad that I had found the child well, she in turn praised the neighbor. But it was the mention of Enzo that kindled her, she lighted up, became talkative.

"He's kind," she said, "he's good, he's not afraid of anything, he's extremely smart and he studies at night, he knows so many things."

I had never heard her talk about anyone in that way. I asked, "What does he study?"

"Mathematics."

"Enzo?"

"Yes. He read something about electronic calculators or saw an ad, I don't know, and he got excited. He says a calculator isn't like you see in the movies, all colored lights that light up and go out with a *bip*. He said it's a question of languages."

"Languages?"

She had that familiar narrow gaze.

"Not languages for writing novels," she said, and the dismissive tone in which she uttered the word "novels" disturbed me, the laugh that followed disturbed me. "Programming languages. At night, after the baby goes to sleep, Enzo starts studying."

Her lower lip was dry, cracked by the cold, her face marred by fatigue. And yet with what pride she had said: he starts studying. I saw that, in spite of the third person singular, it wasn't only Enzo who was excited about the subject.

"And what do you do?"

"I keep him company: he's tired and if he's by himself he feels like sleeping. But together it's great, one of us says one thing, one another. You know what a flow chart is?"

I shook my head. Her eyes then became very small, she let go of my arm, she began to talk, drawing me into that new passion. In the courtyard, with the odor of the bonfire and the stink of animal fats, flesh, nerves, this Lila, wrapped up in an overcoat but also wearing a blue smock, her hands cut, disheveled, very pale, without a trace of makeup, regained life and energy. She spoke of the reduction of everything to the alternative true-false, she quoted Boolean algebra and many other things I knew nothing about. And yet her words, as usual, fascinated me. As she spoke, I saw the wretched house at night, the child sleeping in the other room; I saw Enzo sitting on the bed, worn out from work on the locomotives in who knows what factory; I saw her, after the day at the cooking tubs or in the gutting room or in the storerooms at twenty below zero, sitting with him on the blanket. I saw them both in the terrible light of sacrificed sleep, I heard their voices: they did exercises with the flow charts, they practiced cleaning the world of the superfluous, they charted the actions of the day according to only two values of truth: zero and one. Obscure words in the miserable room, whispered so as not to wake Rinuccio. I understood that I had arrived there full of pride and realized that—in good faith, certainly, with affection—I had made that whole journey mainly to show her what she had lost and what I had won. But she had known from the moment I appeared, and now, risking tensions with her workmates, and fines, she was explaining to me that I had won nothing, that in the world there is nothing to win, that her life was full of varied and foolish adventures as much as mine, and that time simply slipped away without any meaning, and it was good just to see each other every so often to hear the mad sound of the brain of one echo in the mad sound of the brain of the other.

"Do you like living with him?" I asked.

"Yes."

"Will you have children?"

She had an expression of feigned amusement.

"We're not together."

"No?"

"No, I don't feel like it."

"And he?"

"He's waiting."

"Maybe he's like a brother."

"No, I like him."

"So?"

"I don't know."

We stopped beside the fire, she gestured toward the guard. "Look out for him," she said. "When you go out he's liable to accuse you of stealing a mortadella just so he can search you and put his hands all over you."

We embraced, we kissed each other. I said I would see her again, I didn't want to lose her, and I was sincere. She smiled, she said, "Yes, I don't want to lose you, either." I felt that she, too, was sincere.

I went away in great agitation. Inside was the struggle to leave her, the old conviction that without her nothing truly important would ever happen to me, and yet I felt the need to get away, to free my nostrils of that stink of fat. After a few quick steps I couldn't help it, I turned to wave again. I saw her standing beside the bonfire, without the shape of a woman in that outfit, as she leafed through the pages of the *Blue Fairy*. Suddenly she threw it on the fire.

125.

I hadn't told her what the story of my book was or when it would be in bookstores. I hadn't even told her about Pietro, of the plan to get married in a couple of years. Her life had overwhelmed me and it took days for me to restore clear outlines and depth to mine. What finally restored me to myself—but what myself?—was the proofs of the book: a hundred and thirty-nine pages, thick paper, the words of the notebook, fixed by my handwriting, which had become pleasantly alien thanks to the printed characters.

I spent happy hours reading, rereading, correcting. Outside it was cold, a frigid wind slipped in through the loose window frames. I sat at the kitchen table with Gianni and Elisa, who were studying. My mother was busily working around us, but with surprising care, in order not to disturb me.

Soon I went to Milan again. This time I allowed myself, for the first time in my life, to take a taxi. The bald editor, at the end of a day spent evaluating the final corrections, said to me, "I'll call you a taxi," and I didn't know how to say no. So it happened that when I went from Milan to Pisa, at the station I looked around and thought: why not, let's play the great lady again. And the temptation resurfaced when I returned to Naples, in the chaos of Piazza Garibaldi. I would have liked to arrive in the neighborhood in a taxi, sitting comfortably in the back seat, a driver at my service, who, when we reached the gate, would open the door for me. I took the bus instead, I didn't feel up to it. But something about me must have been different, because when I greeted Ada, who was taking her baby out for a walk, she looked at me distractedly, and walked by. Then she stopped, turned back, said, "How well you look, I didn't recognize you, you're different."

At the moment I was pleased, but soon I became unhappy. What advantage could I have gained from becoming different? I wanted to remain myself, chained to Lila, to the courtyard, to the lost dolls, to Don Achille, to everything. It was the only way to feel intensely what was happening to me. Yet change is hard to oppose: in that period, in spite of myself, I changed more than in the years in Pisa. In the spring the book came out, which, much more than my degree, gave me a new identity. When I showed a copy to my mother, to my father, to my sister and brothers, they passed it around in silence, but without looking through it. They stared at the cover with uncertain smiles, they were like police agents confronted with a fake document. My father said, "It's my surname," but he spoke without satisfaction, as if suddenly, instead of being proud of me, he had discovered that I had stolen money from his pocket.

Days passed, the first reviews came out. I scanned them

anxiously, wounded by even the slightest hint of criticism. I read the best ones aloud to the whole family, my father brightened. Elisa said teasingly, "You should have signed Lenuccia, Elena's disgusting."

In those frenzied days, my mother bought a photograph album and began to paste in it everything good that was written about me. One morning she asked, "What's the name of your fiancé?"

She knew, but she had something in mind and to communicate it she wished to start there.

"Pietro Airota."

"Then you'll be called Airota."

"Yes."

"And if you write another book, on the cover will it say Airota?"

"No."

"Why?"

"Because I like Elena Greco."

"So do I," she said.

But she never read it. My father didn't read it, Peppe, Gianni, Elisa didn't read it, and at first the neighborhood didn't read it. One morning a photographer came and kept me for two hours, first in the gardens, then along the *stradone*, then at the entrance to the tunnel, taking photographs. Later, one of the pictures appeared in *Il Mattino*; I expected passersby would stop me on the street, would read the book out of curiosity. Instead no one, not Alfonso, Ada, Carmen, Gigliola, Michele Solara, who, unlike his brother Marcello, wasn't a complete stranger to the alphabet, ever said to me, as soon as they could: your book is wonderful, or, who knows, your book is terrible. They only greeted me warmly and went on.

I encountered readers for the first time in a bookstore in Milan. The event, I soon discovered, had been urgently planned by Adele Airota, who was following the book's journey at a distance and traveled purposely from Genoa for the occasion. She came to the hotel, kept me company all afternoon, tried tactfully to calm me. I had a tremor in my hands that wouldn't go away, I struggled with words, I had a bitter taste in my mouth. I was angry with Pietro, who had stayed in Pisa, he was busy. Mariarosa, who lived in Milan, made a quick congratulatory visit before the reading, then she had to go.

I went to the bookstore terrified. The room was full, I went in with my eyes down. I thought I would faint with emotion. Adele greeted many of those present, they were friends and acquaintances of hers. She sat in the first row, gave me encouraging looks, turned occasionally to talk to a woman of her age who was sitting behind her. Until that moment I had spoken in public only twice, forced to by Franco, and the audience then was made up of six or seven of his friends who smiled with understanding. The situation was different now. I had before me some forty refined, cultivated strangers who stared at me in silence, with an unfriendly gaze; it was in large part the prestige of the Airotas that compelled them to be there. I wanted to get up and run away.

But the rite began. An old critic, a university professor much esteemed in his time, said as many good things about the book as possible. I couldn't understand his speech, I thought only of what I was to say. I fidgeted in my chair, I had a stomachache. The world had vanished into chaos, and I couldn't find within myself the authority to call it back and put it in order again. Yet I pretended self-assurance. When it was my turn, I spoke without really knowing what I was saying, I talked in order not to be silent, I gesticulated too much, I displayed too much literary knowledge, I made a show of my classical education. Then silence fell.

What were those people in front of me thinking? How was the critic and professor beside me evaluating my remarks? And was Adele, behind her air of cordiality, repenting her support of me? When I looked at her I realized immediately that my eyes were begging her for the comfort of a nod of approval and I was ashamed. Meanwhile the professor touched an arm as if to calm me, asked the audience for questions. Many stared in embarrassment at their knees, the floor. The first to speak was an older man with thick eyeglasses, well known to those present but not to me. At simply hearing his voice, Adele had an expression of annoyance. The man talked for a long time about the decline of publishing, which now looked more for money than for literary quality; then he moved on to the marketing collusion between critics and the cultural pages of the dailies; finally he focused on my book, first ironically, then, when he cited the slightly risqué pages, in an openly hostile tone. I turned red and rather than answer I mumbled some banal comments, off the subject. Until I broke off, exhausted, and stared at the table. The professor-critic encouraged me with a smile, with his gaze, thinking that I wanted to continue. When he realized that I didn't intend to, he asked curtly: "Anyone else?"

At the back a hand was raised.

"Please."

A tall young man, with long, unruly hair and a thick black beard, spoke in a contemptuously polemical way of the preceding speaker, and, a few times, even of the introduction of the nice man who was sitting next to me. He said we lived in a provincial country, where every occasion was an opportunity for complaining, but meanwhile no one rolled up his sleeves and reorganized things, trying to make them function. Then he went on to praise the modernizing force of my novel. I recognized him most of all by his voice, it was Nino Sarratore.

ABOUT THE AUTHOR

Elena Ferrante was born in Naples. She is the author of *The Days of Abandonment* (Europa 2005), *Troubling Love* (Europa 2007), and *The Lost Daughter* (Europa 2009). Her Neapolitan novels include *My Brilliant Friend*, *The Story of a NewName*, *Those Who Leave and Those Who Stay*, and the fourth and final book in the series, *The Story of the Lost Child*.

THE NEAPOLITAN NOVELS
By Elena Ferrante

BOOK 1

"Ferrante's novels are intensely, violently personal, and because of this they seem to dangle bristling key chains of confession before the unsuspecting reader."
—James Wood, *The New Yorker*

978-1-60945-078-6 • September 2012

BOOK 2

"Stunning . . . cinematic in the density of its detail."
—The *Times Literary Supplement*

978-1-60945-134-9 • September 2013

BOOK 3

"Everyone should read anything with Ferrante's name on it."—Eugenia Williamson, *The Boston Globe*

978-1-60945-233-9 • September 2014

BOOK 4

"One of modern fiction's richest portraits of a friendship."—John Powers, *NPR's Fresh Air*

978-1-60945-286-5 • September 2015

"Imagine if Jane Austen got angry and you'll have some idea how explosive these works are."
—John Freeman, critic and author of *How to Read a Novelist*